The Prince of Sikrath

By Jack Conway

Table of Contents

Prologue: The Fall 6

1 A Lesson on Patience 10

2 The Do's and Don'ts of Servitude.......................................26

3 An Unwelcome Surprise..38

4 It's Not Over Yet 54

5 Bystanders Beware 70

6 Tickets Please 80

7 Off to a Bad Start 94

8 It's the End of the Line 106

9 Not So Simple...118

10 Not Quite as it Appears 134

11 Stories Told 148

12 Pieces Found...158

13 A Hero? What Hero?..170

14 Questions Unanswered 184

15 Hey, Watch Where You Swing That.............................198

16 Is That Your Legacy?...206

17 Wake Up Please..218

18 You Want a Deal? I Got a Deal....................................232

19 I'm Not Sure I Understand the Game...........................240

20 The Disappointment's All Mine 254

21 The Choice Is Yours..266

22 Well, You Fooled Me 276

23 Well Don't Just Stand There 288

24 It's About Time 298

25 I Guess My Work Here Is Done 310

26 Back to What I Know 324

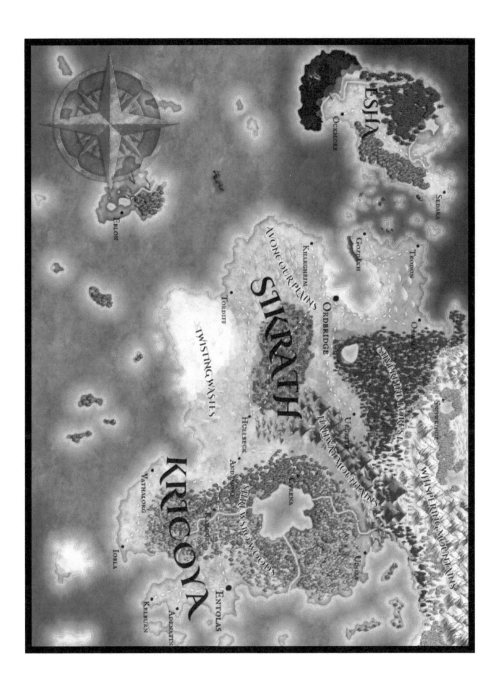

Prologue: The Fall

The sounds of battle raged from outside the tent. It would all be over very soon. This long and bloody campaign had to be worth something; I'd worked too hard to let it slip from my grasp now. My troops may need help with the last bit of resistance, but the city would fall within the next few hours.

I got up from my cot and went to grab my armor and sword, pausing for a moment to admire them. Such a beautiful sword. No one could resist staring at it, motionless, even as it came down on their skull—just the price of being my enemy.

A deafening roar of cheers reached my ears. I rushed outside, pushing past the dark blue tent flaps as I went and looked toward the battlefield. Piles of bodies lay to the side of the fighting, but they were mostly Kricoyan soldiers. My soldiers didn't fall easily. The stench was quite sickening, however. I couldn't wait to be gone from this godforsaken place.

A small elf ran up to me, his face split into a wide grin. "Sire! The walls have been breached! We're forcing our way into the city, even as we speak. I'm confident that it will fall in a matter of minutes," he said.

I smiled and drew my sword. "Excellent." I made my way over to the gates in no particular hurry. I'd waited years for this moment, I could wait a little bit longer.

Soldiers rushed past me, climbing over the broken blocks of stone that had previously stood behind the gate. There they were—the last people of Kricoya—fighting desperately to save their precious city. My sword pulsed, eager to taste more flesh, and I tend to give it what it wants.

As I made my way toward the group, the sounds of battle faded around me and my vision narrowed. Just one more obstacle in my way.

I made short work of the soldiers, not stopping for a second. Most fell to the ground within a few seconds, and the ones that stayed up couldn't seem to do much more than throw themselves at me, swinging their swords wildly, only to be struck down by my weapon. I moved past the outer walls and made my way deeper into the city. The search was almost over. My soldiers poured through the gate and swept through the city like a flood. In a matter of minutes, the screams and clashing of metal on metal dimmed and the city quieted. All that was left was to find what I came for.

Once I found myself at the palace entrance I strode inside, my pace quickening as I neared my destination.

There it was.

The large wooden doors of the throne room flew open, and I walked inside.

"You!" I shouted, pointing toward the defiant King of Kricoya, now on his knees with his hands bound. The room seemed to shrink as I homed in on my target. One look at his face as I pulled him to his feet was all it took for me to know he would never tell me.

Sighing, I asked him the futile question. "Where. Is. It?"

He just laughed and gazed back at me. For a moment I thought that he wasn't going to respond, but then he finally answered. "You have been blinded by your assumed victory. There's always another way."

Suddenly, another soldier rushed into the throne room and headed toward us.

"Sire! Several soldiers have escaped the city on horseback. We stopped some of them, but they jumped our barricades and many of them made it out. Most of our soldiers were in the city."

A chill went down my spine and I turned back to face the king. He glared back at me with a look of pure rage and satisfaction. No. This couldn't happen. I had come so far.

"Send out the riders, immediately," I told the soldier, raising my sword.

"I have already won," I said to the king, my grip tightening against the handle of my sword. "It's only a matter of time." I grabbed his shoulder and pulled him closer to me. "You've lost," I whispered into his ear, as I thrust my blade deep into his stomach.

He let out a small gasp before quickly falling silent. A moment later the body slipped from my grasp and fell to the floor, lifeless. "Go now!" I snarled at the soldier who was still standing next to me. "I want that compass."

1
A Lesson on Patience

Matt

"Just a little farther..." I told myself as I reached a hand towards the top of the stone wall. A slight breeze blew past me as I neared the top, which made it a little harder not to think about falling to the ground far below. My fingers were feeling the strain of the climb as well; the sharp rocky edges of the wall weren't exactly designed for climbing. But that didn't matter! Nothing was going to stop me from getting to the top. Of course, as soon as I thought that I heard a gruff voice calling out to me from below.

"My prince! You need to get down from there immediately! Your father wishes to speak to you."

Groaning, I peered over my shoulder and looked down. A guard with a long, dark coat and a leather cap gazed back at me. Not too surprising.

I sighed and, after a moment, reached downward toward a lower handhold on the wall. "Alright, Harry, I'll come."

After making it back onto solid ground, Harry pointed toward the door to the roof, as if I didn't know the way to the throne room and raised his eyebrows at me.

"Yeah, yeah, I know." I started to move toward the throne room, but stopped to call back behind me, "And you don't have to be so formal, Harry. I've told you a million times to call me Matt."

Harry waved away my comment and turned back to his post, but I noticed he glanced around to make sure no one was listening. People were far too concerned with what my father thought or heard about them. I've certainly been punished by him before, and it's not nearly as bad as you'd think. The worst thing I've had to do is write extra assignments for my tutor about some old war.

I could see why Harry might want to avoid my father, however. He isn't very understanding. He's always going on and on about my duties, but I really just want to go explore. I'd love to go on an actual adventure, like in my fantasy books, but my father will most certainly never let me do that.

Some people just didn't know how to have fun. I was so close to getting to the highest point in the palace. It would have been amazing. Now I had to talk to my father, which wouldn't be nearly as much fun. It was hard enough to entertain myself without him lecturing me about something. There was never anything to do around here.

There hadn't been for a long time.

There weren't a lot of children in the palace, so I spent a lot of time looking at the portraits when I was growing up. If not for them, Joe, and my twin brother, I wouldn't have had much to do every day except train to be the next King of Sikrath.

Now, I know what you're thinking, and yes, my father is the King, but really, it's not as fun as you might think.

The large map hanging on the wall of the main hallway soon came into view, as it had for as long as I could remember. It showed the land under our control and everything else in the known world. Geography wasn't something I was very interested in, but my father told me not to worry about learning about all the other countries. He said that the only ones that I really needed to know about were Sikrath and Kricoya.

Sikrath is our country, one of the best in the world. We controlled over 40% of the known world. Kricoya was once a serious threat, but we pushed them back in the last war. Now they barely survive on the outskirts of our territory.

Passing the portraits and map reminded me of how my brother and I would run around the palace when we were younger, causing all sorts of trouble to keep ourselves amused. But my brother went to study in Hullbeck about a year ago, so it's been a while since we did any of that. When he first left, I wrote to him a couple of times but I never got a response back. My father said that he was too busy with his studies, which was a shame because we were very close a couple of years before. I wished that I could've gone with him. Anything was better than being stuck here in the palace all day.

The large oak doors that led to the throne room came into view. I'd always admired them. A design of small silver triangles was spread across the wood planks, breathing a small bit of life into an otherwise cold and foreboding room. As a child, whenever my father would make me come to the throne room for some formal event or meeting, I knew that at least I'd get a chance to look at the doors.

Past the entrance the room itself was very tall and narrow. The walls stretched far up above us until they joined into a dome at the roof. Antique gold armor and weapons and such were scattered around the room, prominently displayed on their stone pedestals. Most of it was boring, but a few pieces were actually very interesting—the ones from the Kricoyan War, especially. I remembered seeing a shattered sword, used by a former King of Sikrath many centuries ago, in one of the great wars in the far reaches of the empire. It had a light glow to it whenever I looked at it. My father had told me it was infused with some magical properties.

I walked between two of the marble pillars dotted around the room and approached the throne.

My father and my tutor sat in their respective seats, my father's obviously much larger and fancier.

"You wanted to see me, Father?" I asked.

My father had short, white hair; it had been the same for as long as I'd known him. He was almost always wearing a fur cape and drowning in gold jewelry. His striking blue eyes were usually the first thing people noticed about him.

Today he looked angry. Unfortunately, it could have been about any number of things, but I was sure it would be directed at me.

"Matthew," my father responded rather gruffly, "it's about time you showed up. Kings don't dawdle. You must always plan your next moves, so you don't appear weak and foolish."

"Yes, Father." I sighed. "I'll try to remember that next time." I'd learned long ago that there was no point in trying to argue with my father. I could have pointed out that I'd just found out that he wanted to see me, or that if he really wanted to talk to me, he could have gone to find me himself instead of sending a guard, but I didn't.

"So, what did you—" I started to say.

"Matthew, it seems to me that you need another lesson about leadership," he interrupted.

I groaned. "Father, I really—"

"I heard that you are still spending a lot of time with that servant, and I want to make sure that you know my views about it."

I might have laughed if the situation wasn't so infuriating. "Yes, Father, I believe you may have mentioned it a few times," I said dryly.

"So perhaps you can finally listen to me and do what you know is best for the kingdom," he demanded.

"I'm not sure I see what the problem is," I said. "Joe is my friend. Just because he's not royalty doesn't mean I can't be near him."

"He is a servant!" my father practically shouted at me. "Kings can't associate themselves with servants. You'll ruin your reputation and the reputation of the entire Wettin name! You have no idea what you're doing; you're gambling with my legacy here! You need to learn how to rule, or I'll find someone else to run the kingdom."

Sitting next to my father, my tutor Adil glanced back and forth between us, as though unsure of which side to take, or at least pretending to be unsure. Sometimes I could count on him to give me a smidgen more sympathy than my father, but my father was still the king, so in the end it didn't really matter what Adil thought.

"Matthew," Adil finally said. "I'm afraid that your father is correct. The King of Sikrath is one of the most powerful figures in the world. He can't be spending time with a servant. The people will say he doesn't care about power or start to lose faith in his rule. It is simply too dangerous. For your own good, you should listen to your father."

I glanced back and forth between the two of them. My father had an angry, self-assured look on his face, like he knew that whatever I said wouldn't matter and he'd already won. My tutor had a more calculating look, almost as if he was playing a game of chess in his head and he'd just enacted his master plan. This wasn't the first time my father had brought up Joe, but I was always able to turn his attention to something else. This time I wasn't so sure that I'd be able to do that. My father had been much harder on me since my brother went off to study, as if he couldn't sit still and wait for me to discover things for myself. He wanted the future King of Sikrath to be fully prepared for whatever problems arise under his watch.

"Alright, fine," I snapped. "What is it you want me to do, suddenly stop talking to him altogether?"

"Yes, that is exactly what I want you to do," my father said. "If this is how you want to lead your life you are not ready to rule at all. You need to start taking this seriously."

"Adil? Are you gonna let him do this? It's absolutely ridiculous!"

My father sighed. "Matthew, you know I'm just doing this for your own good, right?" His expression softened and he looked at me with sad eyes, like he was afraid that I would never see reason.

Adil shifted in his chair. He leaned forward and looked at me. "Matthew, I'm sure that we can come to a compromise here. Perhaps you could just limit the time—"

BOOM! An enormous explosion rocked the palace. Loud screams sounded in the distance. BOOM! BOOM! More explosions went off, this time much closer than before.

"What's going on?" I shouted, my heart freezing. The door burst open, and several guards rushed in to secure the throne room.

My father jumped up. "Guards, with me!" he shouted as he drew a large sword from a sheath on his belt and ran out of the room with at least fifteen guards at his heels. Adil stared at the walls, his eyes wide as though afraid that they would suddenly come to life and attack him.

I ran over to him. "Come on. We have to get out of here!"

"Yes, that would be good," he muttered.

I led him out of the throne room as another explosion sounded. I turned left and headed down the stairs, but I had to keep checking that Adil was following me. He was moving slowly and glancing behind himself every few seconds.

"Come on!" I said. "We have to get to shelter."

I led him down several flights of stairs, passing only a few other people on our way. Why did the throne room have to be on the fifth floor? Each passing second my panic grew as I thought about the palace collapsing on top of us. I couldn't die before I even had a chance to leave the palace and do something with my life. Then I thought about my father. He had just run out of the throne room, into whatever was waiting outside. I hoped he wasn't in trouble; I would have no idea what to do if he never came back.

Everyone we passed was running away, screaming whenever another explosion went off. We ran down to the ground floor until at last I saw a pair of guards waving at us to follow them.

"My prince, come with us. The safe room is just down here," one of them said as they rushed towards us, their heavy armor clanking as they ran.

I grabbed Adil's arm, and we followed them down another flight of stairs and into a dark stone room. The thick iron door slammed shut behind us. I'd only been there a few times before, but never in an actual emergency. The gray walls loomed over us from all sides, and the mild shaking as the explosions sounded nearby didn't help to reassure me of their strength.

I still couldn't help but feel like I'd never see daylight again. As the guards closed the large door, the room was engulfed in darkness, except for a small, dim, lamp in one corner of the room. The door looked strong enough, but I didn't know if it could hold against a direct hit from an explosion. We would just have to hope that the army could deal with whatever threat was out there before they breached the palace.

Around ten other people stood in the room with us, including several heavily armored guards near the large iron door. It was hard to see their faces from where I was sitting, but I could sense their agitation. A few were shaking as they held their shields up. Several other nobles sat on chairs and stools as they chatted with each other or poured over long documents. I was amazed at the immediate shift in the mood as I looked back and forth between the guards and the nobles.

The voices in the room came to a halt as more explosions sounded; I was unsure if they were getting closer or farther away. As each one sounded a thick layer of dust fell from the ceiling, obscuring my view of the room for a moment and causing me to cough. Adil had stopped trembling, and he paced next to me, muttering to himself.

It was hard to relax, even inside the secure room we were in. I could feel every explosion wash over us. The room continued to shake as more dust or small pieces of rock fell from the ceiling. I tried to breathe slowly, calm my mind, but the constant barrage of explosions made it impossible.

As the battle raged on, I started to process what had happened. There were rumors that there had been some skirmishes near the outskirts of the empire, but it was unthinkable that the trouble would ever reach here. There was no way the city would fall.

Our soldiers were the finest in the world, and our army was strong. Even so, it would have been nice to have a window to reassure myself.

Looking around the room again at the other people with us, I watched them flinch with each new explosion. For a moment I considered going over to talk to a few of them to give them some reassurance that we would win the battle, but how helpful would my words be? How did I know we would be alright? The thoughts popped into my head but there really wasn't any other choice but to believe that we would be alright. I was the future King of Sikrath. A real leader is fearless.

So, I stayed still as I sat on my small wooden chair in the back of the room. We all endured the bombardment for what felt to me like hours. As the long minutes passed, I started to grow tired of sitting in the room. Tired of waiting to hear what was happening to the city. I didn't know how it was possible, but I started to get bored, as though I just couldn't wait to see whether or not I was about to die.

Finally, the sounds of battle seemed to fade. There weren't any more explosions for several minutes, but I thought I could hear something else. Cheering? I was about to suggest to the guards that we should go out and see what was happening when someone hammered on the door. The guards hesitated for a moment before one of them stepped forward and opened a metal slat. After a moment of listening to what the person on the other side of the door had to say, he opened the door.

Another guard rushed in. "The enemy has been pushed back! The city is now safe." He ran off, presumably to tell other rooms.

I hesitated as I looked around the room at the others nearby, almost daring them to leave first. They all glanced around at each other, hoping someone would make a move. Eventually, someone near the front of the room carefully walked out and peeked around the corner. A moment later he disappeared down the hallway.

"Adil?" I said. "Do you know who was out there?"

Adil glared at the door, perhaps he finally was processing what had just happened. He started walking toward the door without answering me, and I followed him. We walked back up the stairs to the throne room. He went over to the throne, and for a second, I thought that he was going to sit down on it, but he sat off to the side at the last second. There was no other chair in the room besides the throne, and I wasn't about to sit there, so I stood beside Adil as we waited. The throne room didn't appear to be damaged at all. The explosions must not have made it too far into the city.

At least not to the palace.

After a few minutes my father burst through the doors, a few guards trailing behind him. He stopped when he saw us and cocked his head to the side.

"Have you two been sitting there this whole time?"

"How did he get so close to the city?" Adil interrupted.

My father paused. "I'm not entirely sure. I thought we had delayed him in Kamoor, but his forces managed to move past the city much quicker than expected."

"You know who it was that attacked the city?" I asked. "Does this have anything to do with the rumors about fighting on our eastern border?"

My father and Adil exchanged glances. They seemed to be arguing silently with each other. Finally, my father turned to me.

"A dangerous leader has been rising in power lately. He has..." he paused for a moment, considering his words carefully, "...expressed a desire to invade us. Our army has it under control, however. He has somehow managed to convince several small villages to join him at our eastern border, but it's nothing to concern yourself with, Matthew. There's nothing you can do about it."

I looked back and forth between my father and Adil. I got the sense that it was a bigger deal than they were letting on. The eastern border was hundreds of miles away from the capital. This dangerous leader must have significant power to be able to launch an attack on Ordbridge.

"I can't help at all? I'm seventeen now. Surely, I can look at the battle plans and maybe learn more about the situation."

My father and Adil exchanged more looks.

"Come on. I can help."

"...No, I think that it will be better for everyone if you stay out of it," my father firmly said.

Adil hesitated for a moment, but he stayed silent. I had held out some hope that my tutor might side with me, though I knew it wouldn't have mattered either way. My father had the final say. He sent me off to my room, or anywhere else really, so that they could plan out their next moves. It was tiresome, but it was something that I was all too familiar with. I was never allowed to know what was happening. I'd barely even left the city before. A few times I went with my father when he had business in a nearby town, but I hadn't been allowed out of the carriage.

How was I supposed to prove myself if he won't give me the chance to? I felt stuck, unsure what I could do to change anything.

I wandered down the long stone hallway, which was illuminated by several electric bulbs. The palace had been outfitted with electric lights in the last few years. The technology was still a bit new, but obviously, we were the first ones to get it. We used to have magic fires along the walls, but it was really a hassle. One would go out every day or so and we would have to call in a wizard from across the city to come fix it. Such a nuisance. There aren't that many new wizards nowadays, anyway. Traditionally, it was the people of Kricoya who became wizards, and it took a long time for that to spread throughout the continent. Wizardry became very popular, and one of the things that Kricoya was known for. It wasn't until after the Kricoyan War that it became harder to find any trained wizards. With their defeat, Kricoya didn't have the resources to train as many as before, and the craft has been dying out ever since. Sikrath has become increasingly reliant on technology to solve our problems. My father has said that within ten years there will only be about 25% of the trained wizards that we have today.

It was about midday, but fewer people were walking around than usual. I guess the threat of invasion and death messed up people's schedules. Though that might turn out to be a good thing, I thought, because that meant that Joe might not be too busy.

Joe did a lot of the cleaning work during the day, but if there were fewer people roaming around, then maybe there would be less to do.

I started walking toward the janitor's closet. Along the way I only passed one other person, a treasury advisor. I nodded hello but he didn't nod back. I'd always thought that people who worked in the treasury were rather cold, though I'd never seen this man before. He was at least a foot taller than me, with long white hair. He was wearing a black robe with a badge featuring a silver chest overflowing with coins, the sign of the treasury. I hurried past him and went down another flight of stairs.

Finally, I made it to the supply closet, and there he was! "Hey, Joe!"

Joe turned. His eyes looked tired, and he seemed wary for a second but managed a grin when he saw me. "Hi, Matt."

He wore the standard cleaning crew uniform: a black robe with a badge featuring a mop. He had short, curly brown hair and hazel eyes, but he wasn't a big fan of them. People in Sikrath, and especially Ordbridge, mostly had blue eyes. Darker eyes were a sign that you're from one of the colonies. Also, his light brown skin would have given you a clue. He and his family were from Esha, a colony of Sikrath. He didn't talk about it, and I didn't know if he really remembered that much anyway, since he moved here when he was very young. I'd known him since we were about six or seven. His father used to be a janitor here as well.

"Are you alright, Joe?" I asked. "Y'know, with the explosions and everything."

"Yes, I made it out alright. I didn't get to see any of the actual fighting, but I could hear it very close by." Joe paused for a moment before shaking his head.

"I don't know how they could have made it so close to the city."

I nodded. It didn't make a lot of sense to me either, but my father wasn't telling me anything.

"So ... you got a lot of work to do?"

"You know I do." Joe looked at me with a frown for a few seconds before sighing. "Okay, what were you thinking?"

I grinned. "I thought you might be interested. So, I have it on good authority that my father won't be bothering us for a while. They're up in the throne room deciding what to do about this dangerous leader who's threatening the city." I paused for a moment to judge his reaction, but he just stared back at me, not giving anything away.

"Anyway, I thought we could hang out for a bit."

"Sure. But I do have a lot of work to do, Matt."

"I can always help you later if you want."

He stopped and frowned at me. "No, you know what happened last time. Your dad doesn't want you cleaning up the palace," he said bitterly. He looked around, perhaps making sure that my father wasn't right behind him, listening.

"Joe, it's fine, I wasn't even punished. It was just a warning."

For a moment Joe's eyes flashed angrily and he shook his head.

"Matt, *I'm* the one who got in trouble. I was almost fired. Your old man definitely doesn't want his precious son doing servant work."

I stepped backward in surprise. I'd never seen Joe this upset before. Usually, he wasn't one to hold a grudge.

He gave a long sigh and started to turn around. "Maybe I do have too much work to do. How about another time?"

"No, wait! It'll be fine. My father won't even know about it. But why didn't you tell me about that? I could have done something. I could have talked to..." My voice faded away as I realized that I really couldn't have done anything. My father never listens to me, and Adil has been siding with my father a lot more lately.

"Well ... maybe you're right." I hung my head and stared at the ground. "It might be too dangerous for us to hang out." I was about to walk back down the hallway, probably to my room, even though I really didn't have anything to do, when a guard walked past us with a huge armful of printed flyers. He stumbled and started to lose his grip on them before tripping over the stone bricks and dropping them all over the floor right in front of us.

"Oh! I'm so sorry, my Prince. I-I didn't mean to drop them. I just..." The poor guard looked terrified. He must be new. He was probably only a few years older than me.

"It's fine," I said. "We'll help you clean them up."

Joe and I bent down and started grouping the flyers into stacks. As I picked them up, a few words flashed by that caught my interest—something about a dangerous quest?

"What are these flyers even for?" I asked.

"I-I'm not sure, my Prince. The king ordered them to be made up as soon as possible."

We finished grouping up the flyers and I took one for myself before the guard picked up the rest.

He thanked us and hurried away, no doubt to distribute the important announcements. I looked down at the one in my hands. It appeared to be an advertisement for some kind of competition. **"The kingdom needs you!"** it read. I started reading aloud.

"The latest attack on our benevolent kingdom was an atrocity! Many soldiers and civilians tragically lost their lives in the defense of the city. The tyrannical rebel, known as Glyndwyr Brice, needs to be stopped! A competition of strength will be held tomorrow to form a group dedicated to stopping this vicious dictator. Their quest will begin shortly after tomorrow's competition and more details will be given to those who sign up at the north barracks by tomorrow morning. The competition will test many things. The best of you will be chosen. Good luck to everyone."

I looked over at Joe. He'd narrowed his eyes and was listening intently, anger flickering across his face.

"The king is sending out his subjects to do his work for him, I see," he muttered.

"Oh, come on," I said. "Can you imagine my father doing his own work? He barely gets up from his throne at all."

Joe gave me a small smile. "Ha, I suppose the quest would fail immediately."

"But anyway," I said. "Don't you see what this means? Since my brother has been gone, my father is even harder on me than before and there isn't much to do around here anyway. This is a perfect opportunity!"

"What do you mean?" he asked cautiously.

"Joe, I can finally prove my worth! My father never includes me in anything. If I go on this quest and succeed, then he will have to listen to me."

"What? Matt, you can't be serious. You've never even left the city!"

"Well, I'll need your help. You know more about traveling than me. Besides, if I'm going to be left out of everything around here, what else am I going to spend my time doing?"

"I could think of many things that would be better than—"

"Look, Joe, I've made up my mind. Tomorrow, I go on a quest!"

2
The Do's and Don'ts of Servitude

Joe

I sighed to myself. How exactly did we come to this? Matt and I were in his room, a place I'd only been a few times, though it hadn't changed much since I'd last seen it. The large mirror in the corner was still there as well as the piles of expensive clothes littering the ground. His dad wouldn't like me being with him, but Matt assured me he wouldn't find out.

"Matt, tell me why you could possibly think that this is a good idea. You've hardly had any training and you'd be walking into an active war zone."

"Joe, come on," Matt said, before standing up and pacing around the room. "I'm fast and quick on my feet, and I do know how to use a sword."

I sighed again and rested my chin on my arm. Why did it fall upon me to save him from killing himself over and over again? He didn't understand how anything worked. He thought that the world was like his adventure books. If he went through with this, he would find out the truth soon enough; I knew I had to put a stop to it.

"You really think your dad, the king, is gonna let his precious son go on a dangerous mission like this?" I asked.

Matt paused and looked over at me, a slight frown set on his lips. "That's the whole point! I have to go so that he will let me go on these things in the future," he said. "Maybe I could talk to him…" He paused and winced. "No, he would never let me go."

He looked down at the ground with a scowl. It was good that he was finally seeing the reality of the situation. I tried to stop myself, but he looked so dejected that I couldn't help but give him some hope.

"I guess you could find some sort of disguise," I mumbled, regretting the words the moment they left my lips.

Matt looked up at me, his eyes widening. "Joe, that might work! It would have to be magic, though, so that I can talk to my father without him realizing it's me."

He started pacing around the room, nodding, and muttering to himself. I shouldn't help him. He was definitely going to die if he went to that competition, but my stomach was starting to stir at the thought of coming up with a plan. I hadn't done anything exciting in a very long time.

"I think I might know a spell that could work," I said, after a slight hesitation. Matt stopped and looked at me in confusion. "You might know a spell? What do you mean?"

I looked away sheepishly. "I may have studied a few spell books. No guarantees, but I might be able to help you."

Matt raised his eyebrows and his mouth fell open. "You're a wizard?! That's amazing! Why didn't you tell me?"

"I'm not a wizard. I may know a few spells, but you know just as well as I do that I couldn't have gotten any formal training."

He wasn't listening, of course. He went right back to his pacing and muttering.

"Okay, if you can disguise me..." he paused, deep in thought. "Yes, this should work. I just need..."

I watched him with apprehension. I might have just sentenced him to his death. The best soldiers in the kingdom would be at the competition tomorrow. But there was no point in trying to change Matt's mind once he'd had one of his ridiculous plans in his head. I didn't know what to think.

"Alright, well, I'll go look for the spell. You should prepare for tomorrow."

As I left I could see him running around his room, gathering supplies that he might need for the competition.

Regret prickled beneath my skin, and I tried to suppress it. It was possible that he would win tomorrow instead of dying, which actually wouldn't be much better.

If he won, that would mean that he would actually go looking for Glyndwyr Brice. But I couldn't let that happen. All Matt knew about adventuring, he had learned from his adventure books. Real adventuring was much more dangerous. With no formal training or experience, he was sure to be seriously injured or die on this trip. There was no good outcome at this point.

I walked down the hallway from Matt's room and turned left. It was a short walk back to the servant quarters. There were a few flights to go down before I came to the side door. Servants weren't allowed through the main one. I turned to the left before I was shoved forward by someone. After stumbling a few feet forward I turned to see what had happened. A short, older man with black robes was on the ground trying to pick up all of his papers that had fallen. He wore the badge of the military on his robes, a pike and a spear crossed behind a shield.

"Well, don't just stand there, boy!" the man shouted. "Help me pick up my papers!"

The commotion drew a guard over to us from his patrol. As he came closer, I could see the deep frown and narrowed eyes on his face. I'd seen it many times before. The expression of someone who thought I was wasting their time.

"What's going on here?" the guard asked. The question was directed at both of us, but he was staring right at me.

"He tripped," I muttered, pointing to the other man. "No need for any intervention here."

"Don't lie, boy! You walked straight into me," the man said.

I stared at him in shock. Even after enduring treatment like this for twelve years, I was still surprised by people sometimes.

"Excuse me?" I asked, standing up a little straighter and preparing for a fight. "That's not what happened."

"You heard me," the man said. "I was just standing here, minding my own business, and you walked into me, spilling all of my papers."

"I think you owe this man an apology, boy," the guard said as he crossed his arms and raised an eyebrow at me.

I glanced back and forth between the two of them in exasperation, unable to respond for a moment. There was no arguing with people once they made up their minds about what happened. For all I knew, the old man had actually convinced himself that this whole situation was indeed my fault. I sighed and gritted my teeth. "I'm sorry for walking into you, sir."

"Fine. I suppose it's alright."

I took that as an invitation to leave. As quickly as I could without sprinting away from them, I stood up and walked down the pathway in the opposite direction that the man had been walking in. It would add some time to my trip, but I didn't want to take any chances of him tripping again. Everyone always blamed the servants.

I got to the servants' quarters without further incident and went up to my room. The building itself was decent if not a bit bland. The walls were made of plain stone and there weren't any decorations. It stretched up four stories and housed every servant employed by the palace and surrounding houses. A few people in the city besides the king could afford to hire servants.

I liked my room well enough. It was a modest 100 square foot area. A shared bathroom down the hall was used by all the servants in this hallway. I had a bed in one corner, and some chests for my things off to the side. Some days I thought that it was enough space, but usually I thought about what it would be like to live in the palace.

Matt's room was about twenty times bigger than mine.

I went to my oldest, most beat-up chest and rifled through it before pulling out a small, leatherbound notebook, where I'd written down the spells I'd found. I'd wanted to become a wizard apprentice for so long, but almost everyone followed their parents' craft, which was why I became a janitor. It was so hard to break that cycle. My dad worked at the palace for nine years, but about two years ago, he died after falling down a flight of stairs while carrying a heavy box of cleaning supplies. Apparently, his head slammed into the stone steps, killing him instantly. For a while it was hard to keep going because he was the one who always motivated me to keep trying even when things were hard. He believed that I could have a better life than he had but his death didn't help that dream much. It was around that time when I also became a janitor.

I still dreamed of learning magic, but I thought that it would never happen. There was no one around here that would support an immigrant wanting to learn magic. "Too much of a liability," they'd say. "What if he lost control and burnt down the city?"

There was a time when it wasn't so hard to learn wizardry if you really wanted to. As magic spread throughout the continent, everyone was looking for more and more people to train as wizards. But ever since the Kricoyan War, wizardry had been dying. Those that were left had much more pressing concerns than training new wizards after the war was over. Now, with so few wizards left, only the rich and powerful had any chance of getting a wizarding apprenticeship. Ever since the war the king had been pushing for more technological advancements instead of training more wizards for his armies. At this rate it wouldn't be long before the old Kricoyan tradition would be extinct.

I'd always loved the idea of learning magic because I'd heard so many amazing stories about wizards, but what I'd come to understand was that magic didn't work like most people thought it did. It was almost impossible to generate enough power to use deadly spells in battle without a lot of rest or a whole team of wizards. Because of this, most of the magic in the Empire was used for smaller things, like the old lights at the palace. So many people got caught up in the idea of magic as a weapon that they forgot about using magic as a tool to better society in general. Another reason that wizarding was being allowed to die off.

I thought that I'd have to learn to live as a janitor until a few months ago, when I found an old, dusty book in the palace library with a few spells. It was some sort of textbook for young wizards. I thought about taking it with me, but I didn't want people to know that I was trying to learn magic. If anyone found out they would find some excuse to take the book away from me, so I hid it in one of the oldest parts of the library, where only scholars or professors went. The next day I came back with a notebook, and I copied down the spells so that I could practice them in my room.

I flipped through the book. By now I knew several of the spells very well (about ten). Soon, I came to a spell that I had never tried before, something that promised a disguise that would fool anyone. It seemed like the best option, but I wasn't sure what exactly to expect.

I also still wasn't sure I wanted Matt to even try to go. It was so dangerous. Even if he somehow survived the competition tomorrow, then he'd set out on a dangerous quest into enemy territory with absolutely no guarantee that he would make it back home.

I tucked the notebook back into the chest and sat down on my bed. There really weren't any other options. I had to help Matt, or he would never shut up about it. He'd been bringing up his adventure books even more lately, always talking about how he's going to go on a quest of his own someday. I suppose at least if he did go, he'd soon realize how different real life was from his books.

I spent the rest of the night going over the spell. It took a few tries, but eventually I had it down relatively well. Hopefully it would work on Matt. I went to bed and tried to prepare myself for whatever the competition would be the next day.

The next morning, I woke up, gathered my stuff, and headed down to the kitchens. I could smell the food before I even made it out of my doorway. Servants got meals if we wanted, but it came out of our paychecks. That day was soup day, so there were a few options, but I chose a simple chicken broth with some cornbread. I wasn't a fan of a lot of the fancier soups—not that the other choices were any better. No one spent very much time planning the servant meals.

As I sat on one of the benches near the kitchens, drinking my broth, I saw someone slip through the door and look around. He was tall with shoulder-length blonde hair and blue eyes. He wore dress pants and a silk shirt which caused him to stick out quite a bit among the poorly dressed servants and knowing that it was his attempt to blend in made it all the worse.

He saw me and walked over. I glanced around, making sure no one was watching, but everyone around us seemed too absorbed in their meals or company to pay us any attention.

"Hey, Joe," Ben said, as he sat down across from me.

"Ben. What a surprise," I said pointedly.

"Calm down," he responded. "My mother doesn't know I'm here."

I glanced around the room again, making sure I hadn't missed anyone staring at us. Charles at the table in the far-right corner was having a heated debate with his roommate about something. I could only imagine it was the same thing they had been discussing all week: the proper way to skin a deer.

"No! No! It's a counterclockwise motion. Everyone knows that," I heard him say.

I turned back to Ben, stood up, and motioned for him to follow me. Ben and I sat down as far as we could from everyone else.

"So, what are you doing here," I asked; my voice strained as I looked past him at everyone enjoying their breakfasts behind us.

"I just thought that we haven't talked in a while," Ben said. He slid his hand across the table until it was resting on top of mine. "What's up?" he asked.

I barely resisted the urge to look around again to make sure that no one was listening. Instead, I took a deep breath and tried to relax.

"It's good to see you, but we should really go somewhere else," I said. "You never know who could be listening."

Ben nodded as he glanced around the room a few times, almost as if he expected his mother to jump out from behind one of the nearby doors and attack us.

I stood up and led him outside. We wandered down the street past the servants' quarters and the barracks. As we passed, almost all of the soldiers were running around with supplies or weapons in their arms, loading up dozens of wagons, no doubt bound for places all over the city. I still had yet to see the true extent of the damage that had been done to Ordbridge from the attack yesterday, but if the soldiers' haste was any indication, there was still a lot to repair or reinforce.

We were on the main street in the city—not someplace I typically enjoyed. It was crowded, even for nine o'clock in the morning. I had to resist the urge to grab Ben's hand and pull him away from the claustrophobic throngs. It was also the loudest place in the city. Wagons rumbled by, bells rang, and there was a constant drone of conversation. The competition was at 10:00 a.m., so we had about an hour to ourselves since everyone had been given the day off to observe.

We walked beside each other for a few minutes, mostly just watching everything that was going on around us and talking a little about what had happened since we'd last seen each other. Ben stopped for a moment outside a bakery before walking inside and motioning for me to follow. The outside was decorated with posters advertising the baked goods inside. A couple jumped out at me: pistachio brownies and plum cobbler. I'd never had pistachios before, but I loved plums.

The shop had a homely feel. Large log pillars stretched from the ground to the ceiling. The walls were also made of wood but almost every available spot was decorated with either a piece of art, a plant, posters for various events around the city, or any random knick-knack you could imagine. We walked over the chiseled stone floor up to the counter and peered into the two display cases set in front of the counter.

"Anything look good?" Ben asked. "My treat, since I interrupted your breakfast."

I smiled at him. "Thanks, Ben."

We ended up getting a couple of brownies which the shop owner was more than happy to grab for us. Apparently, they were a family recipe, and he was very excited at how well they were selling in the shop. The man was content to ramble on for several minutes before we were able to stop him and pay for the brownies. Sharing a grin and an eye roll, we walked towards the fire and took a seat at an empty table.

There was hardly anyone else inside, so it wasn't hard to find a place with some privacy.

"I'm glad you came to see me," I said. "We haven't been able to talk much lately."

"Yeah, sorry about that. My mother has been even more strict than usual recently. I haven't been able to do anything except study all week."

"You didn't tell her you were here, right?" I said, glancing around.

"Joe, of course not. You know she wouldn't approve of this. I just told her I was meeting a friend."

"Right. Obviously."

"So, what have you been up to?"

Ben and I talked for a while, enjoying the time to ourselves before it was time to head to the competition. I told Ben I had to see Matt before it started, and he offered to walk with me.

The competition was being held in a large stadium near the palace. It was usually used for different fights and performances that the king put on, but no one knew exactly what the competition would involve. Many rumors were flying around but I had no idea what was true. The king could've been planning anything.

We walked down the street toward the stadium, continuing our conversation about the upcoming Firestalkers game. I wasn't a huge sports fan, but Ben enjoyed the games, so I tried to find something of interest there. It wasn't a long walk to the stadium and soon we were next to the main entrance.

"Okay, I'll see you later," Ben said.

"Alright. Hopefully, soon."

Ben turned to leave, but then quickly turned back around and leaned in to give me a quick kiss.

For just a moment, I stopped worrying if anyone was watching and leaned into it. I could almost imagine myself belonging to a wealthy, powerful family who weren't servants at the palace—people that Ben's mother could respect and accept and perhaps even want Ben to be involved with. Sadly, all fantasies have to come to an end.

I pulled away from him and gave him a smile, which he returned before turning around again and walking off toward the stadium, waving back at me as he went. My smile slowly fell as I watched him leave. I wished that we had more time to be together.

I turned around in search of Matt. We'd said that we would meet near the stadium, so that I could cast the spell on him, but we didn't have a lot of time. I didn't know exactly how long it would take to work, or if I could even get it right on the first try, so I had to hurry. It wasn't until I'd spun around a few times, searching the nearby crowds for signs of Matt, that I was able to spot him. He stood about ten feet away, staring at me with a look of surprise.

3
An Unwelcome Surprise

Matt

I woke up early, but no matter how hard I tried to fall back asleep I couldn't. I was too excited to sleep. Hopefully, Joe had found a spell that would work for my disguise, but if not, I was planning on wearing a large helmet. I didn't think that it would work for very long, though, especially if I won the competition. Then I'd probably have to meet with my father. I guessed I would have to cross that bridge when I came to it. I had to actually get through the competition first, of course.

The walls of my room were covered in intricate hand painted designs of exotic animals. A giant bat, a panther, a dire wolf. I knew what they were, though I'd never seen any of them in person. I'd certainly read enough stories and seen enough pictures to recognize them and what they were known for, though. A beautiful maroon and black rug adorned the floor with a series of circles interlocking with each other. It was one of my favorite rugs in the palace. It used to be in the office of the captain of the guard, but one day when I mentioned to my father that I liked the rug, it was moved to my room that very night. My father said that the captain of the guard was happy to give it up to please the prince.

Before I could get ready, though, I had to wait for the cleaning service to get to my room. They were scheduled early today because of the competition so I knew that I wouldn't have to wait long. My father would be expecting me to be with him in his booth at the stadium to watch the competition, but I was going to be a little busy. Not long after, I heard a small knock on my door, and I rushed forward to open it.

"Hi," I said to the small elven man now standing in the hallway. "Um, I'm kind of sick so you can just skip this room for now, alright?" I cleared my throat and coughed a couple of times for good measure. "In fact, can you let my father know that I won't be able to make it to the competition today? Great, thanks!" I quickly closed the door before the confused elf could say much more than a word of protest and waited for him to leave.

As I heard his footsteps retreating down the hallway I lurched into action, pulling on whatever clothes I saw lying on the ground and rushed around my room, gathering everything that I'd need for the day. I had my sword, a leather chest-plate, and a helmet. Hopefully I wouldn't need much more armor than that. It was all kept in the barracks next to the palace, and there was no hope of sneaking past the guards without raising suspicion. They'd report anything I took directly to my father. Glancing into the mirror I tried to imagine looking back at a reflection of someone different from me. Someone without short blonde hair, blue eyes, and a relatively thin frame. Usually, fashion is the least of my concerns, quite honestly, and I couldn't remember anyone ever mentioning a problem with how I looked, so I figured I must be doing something right.

I grabbed everything that I had and left my room, walking down the many flights of stairs to the ground floor of the palace. I hardly passed anyone on my walk, which I was thankful for since I didn't have an excuse for why I was wandering around with armor and weapons if anyone recognized me. I walked through the servants' door so that the guards wouldn't see me leave.

As I left, I got a great view of the barracks that I'd been thinking about sneaking into the night before. It was a large, stone building that branched off to the side of the palace. It mimicked the design of the main building with tall marble pillars stretching up for about 80 feet on all sides, except for the side that was connected to the palace. The roof was a deep black, made from Darkwood. Inside the building was a large collection of weapons and armor and war supplies so, of course, it was constantly guarded. Even as I walked by, I could see the guards on their patrols, circling the building to ensure that no thieves could sneak inside.

I wandered down a side street on the way to the stadium, which gave me a momentary break from the huge crowds that were walking through the main streets. The street was one of the nicer ones in Ordbridge since it had just been repaved not too long ago, so there was a fresh layer of stone that hadn't been covered in layers of dirt and mud yet. I turned back onto a main street, leading me back into the crowds. To my left were dozens of crowded shops lined up next to each other, ranging from a blacksmith to a bakery and everything in between. I followed the crowds, knowing we were all headed to the same place—the stadium.

The buildings themselves were mostly made out of a pale wood that I thought I recognized as Copperwood, but I couldn't be sure. Copperwood was fairly commonly used around here, but it could also have been just a simple silverpine.

As I neared the stadium the crowds grew even more packed together until I was forced to shove my way through to get to where I was supposed to meet Joe. I couldn't help overhearing many interesting theories about what the competition would involve.

"I'm telling you!" a large, red-haired man practically shouted to his companion. "They're gonna go through an obstacle course to prove who would be able to handle going on the quest most!"

His companion, a shorter, black-haired man wearing a dark crimson robe scoffed at him. "Oh, please. As if they would base everything on an obstacle course!"

Their conversation faded into the background as I pushed past them further into the crowd.

"So, it has to be a fight to the death!" I heard an excited voice exclaim. "That's the only thing that makes sense."

Finally spotting Joe past the crowd, I ignored the speculations that were being thrown around and pushed through the throng to get to him. He was walking with somebody, but I couldn't get a good look at him from the angle I was at. I'd just passed through the crowd when I saw the guy lean in and kiss Joe. I paused and took a step back, staring at the two of them, open mouthed. As I watched, he turned to walk away, giving me a clear view of Benjamin Holverk, the son of one of the most powerful people in the kingdom. Suddenly Joe turned, saw me, and froze.

"Hey, Joe..." I hesitated for a moment, rubbing my neck as I walked up next to him. "Um, was that Benjamin Holverk?" I asked cautiously.

"Oh..." Joe replied, eyebrows raised. "Well." He glanced around as if looking for a way to escape. "Yes, that was him, actually." He quietly cleared his throat.

"Do you...know him?".

"Well, yeah, of course I know him. I've met him a few times. His mother and my father work together a lot."

Joe looked around awkwardly, then stared at the ground as if searching for something that would end this conversation.

"Wait, you didn't tell him anything about our plan, did you?" I asked.

Joe flashed me a glare. "No, I didn't tell him anything about it, Matt. Let's just get on with this, okay?"

"Okay, that's good," I said. "So, you found a spell that would work?"

"Yes, I think so. At least I hope it will."

"Okay, well c'mon, the competition is about to start. I need the disguise now." I led Joe over to a nearby alley across from the front stadium entrance and stood watch while he rummaged around in his bag, occasionally pulling out some crumpled piece of paper and muttering to himself before stuffing it back into his bag. As I waited, the delicious smell of cinnamon bread wafted across the street from the nearby food carts that were set up in front of the stadium. It brought back fond memories of my brother and I going to see different performances here. My favorite was always the circus that would come every few years. My brother's favorite was the magic show. We always got cinnamon bread. It was a tradition. I hadn't thought about that in a while; we hadn't gone to one of those shows in over a year now.

Joe finally found the right paper in his bag and pulled it out. He read through it again and prepared himself.

"Okay, this lasts one hour, so make sure to keep track of the time. We don't know how long the competition will last but it could take a while. So, are you ready?"

"Yeah, do it, I'm ready," I said. I closed my eyes and waited for something to happen. I could hear Joe mumbling something under his breath, and after a few seconds, my skin started to sting and tingle, and I got a weird feeling that it was somehow moving itself across my body. After a few more seconds, I opened my eyes and looked down at my hands. They now were a dark brown color, darker than Joe. I touched my hair and realized that it fell down past my eyes, which I was not used to. My hair was always short. I looked up to see Joe gaping back at me. He blinked a few times before looking me up and down.

"Wow," he said. "That actually worked."

I stumbled out of the alley to the closest shop window and hesitated for a moment before looking at my reflection. A stranger gazed back at me. My face was now completely different. I was half expecting to still recognize myself at least a little bit, but I didn't at all. I'd known my own face for my whole life and suddenly it had completely changed. This new person moved whenever I did and turned whenever I turned, but I couldn't help but feel like it was someone else just standing near me, blocking my reflection from showing up in the window.

"You okay, Matt?" Joe asked.

"Yeah…" I paused, still looking at my reflection. "I'm fine. I just have to get used to this," I said. "No one will recognize me now, that's for sure." Even my voice had changed, getting deeper with a slight accent.

"Alright, well, see you after the competition." I said.

Joe waved and started making his way over to the main entrance for the stadium. I had to go over to the back with the rest of the contestants so that I could register, which hopefully wouldn't be too stressful.

I was still marveling at the change to my appearance when I accidentally walked into a guy in front of me, knocking him over.

"Hey, watch where you're going, boy!" he hissed.

"Oh, I'm sorry, I didn't mean to run into you," I said.

"Yeah, sure, buddy, whatever. Just beat it!"

I ran off, knees shaking, careful not to hit anyone else. No one ever talked to me like that. I was used to everyone at least treating me with respect, but that man almost looked disgusted.

I was almost at the door when I spotted my father and Adil walking toward me. I froze. They wouldn't recognize me, right?

"Ah! There you are. We were looking all over," my father called out.

I stared at him in shock. How did he know it was me? Did he know all about my plan to enter the competition? Was it all over? I was about to respond when I heard a voice behind me. "Yes, I wouldn't miss an important event such as this."

I spun around to see some guy standing behind me. I almost sighed with relief. He looked very familiar, but I couldn't quite place him. He was wearing a blue and white cloak draped over dark brown robes.

He leaned down to pick up a long wooden staff and suddenly I remembered who he was. Rowan Decker, the greatest Sorcerer in the city! He was well known for his amazing work during the last war. Rumor had it that he'd single handedly wiped-out hundreds of enemies in one day. I'd always wanted to meet him.

I almost wanted to speak to him right then, but I stopped myself. My father and Adil were right there, and I needed to get to the gate before the competition started.

"So, Mr. Decker, I assume you're on your way to registration?" I heard my father say.

I turned back around quickly. He was competing? I wouldn't stand a chance against him.

Rowan looked startled. "Oh, no, actually I wasn't planning on it. I was just headed for the stands. I certainly wouldn't want to miss the event."

"Really?" Adil replied. "We need the best of the best, and really, there wouldn't be a better person to lead the quest than you."

Rowan's eyes widened and he looked back and forth between my father and Adil in panic as he started shifting backwards. "No, no, really. I'm sure I wouldn't be able to lead very well. And I have to protect the city after all. With me gone, who knows what would happen."

"Oh, I see the problem. You think you'll win the competition too easily, right?" my father asked. "Well, not to worry. It's going to be a real challenge for everyone."

This didn't appear to reassure Rowan in the slightest, and he opened and closed his mouth a few times searching for something to say. "I-I suppose you're insisting I participate?"

My father and Adil exchanged looks and then leaned in closer.

"Well, Mr. Decker," my father said. "You've been so loyal to us in the past that I suppose we could overlook it. After all, we remember everything you did in the war."

Rowan paled and gripped his wooden staff tighter.

"You know what? I think I will join after all," Rowan said. "I wouldn't dream of ignoring my king's wishes."

"Excellent! We'll look forward to seeing you in there."

I watched my father and Adil walk off for a few seconds before remembering that I needed to go register for the competition.

I hurried off to the side gate, glancing over my shoulder at Rowan as I went. There was hardly time to think, but it was finally starting to sink in. I was about to compete against Rowan Decker! I was half excited to finally meet him, and half terrified that he was about to wipe out all of the other contestants—myself included.

Two guards stood at the side gate with a clipboard, and I assumed they were there for registration. I walked over to them and told them I wanted to sign up for the competition.

"You sure, kid?" one guard asked. "It's pretty dangerous."

"Yeah, I'm sure. I'll be fine," I replied.

He shrugged and handed me the clipboard to write down some details about myself. I realized that I hadn't thought of a fake name for myself yet, so I just wrote down the first thing that I thought of and handed the clipboard back to the guard.

"Alright, you're all set..." The guard paused and looked down at the clipboard. "Nathaniel Valdez. Just go up the stairs and wait at the first room you get to. There's some equipment if you need it as well."

I walked through the doors and up a flight of stairs. I was starting to get a little nervous as I heard the crowd above me talking and shuffling around, getting to their seats. My stomach flipped over as it dawned on me that I'd be out there in just a few minutes doing some sort of performance, and I still didn't even know what it would be. A fight? A debate? Maybe some sort of elaborate game of capture the flag? Well, I would find out soon enough.

I came to another door, which was unguarded and considerably smaller than the last one. After a slight hesitation, I pushed it open and stepped into a large room. It was long and narrow, and I could see a large door at the very end, presumably the door that led out to the stadium. Several long benches lined each wall and were filled with people. Everyone was wearing some sort of armor and carrying at least one weapon, though quite a few had many. It was very dark, with only a few torches giving off light, illuminating the benches and several small metal lockers along the far wall. I looked around hoping to find some helpful instructions about where to go, or at least maybe a sign saying, "This way, Matthew! Everything's gonna be fine!"

Unfortunately, I didn't see anything like that, so I glanced around and caught the attention of one of the guards. He was sitting in a chair that looked much too small for him, but he still seemed to be very relaxed in it. He glanced around, perhaps hoping that someone else would help me, but seeing that wasn't going to happen, he sighed and made an exaggerated effort of standing up and walking over.

He pointed to a row of weapons on the wall. "Weapons are over there. Take what you need and sit down on one of the benches. It's about to start so don't take too long. You can also put anything you don't want with you in the lockers." He walked off again, returning to his small chair.

About twenty other people filled the room, putting on armor or testing weapons. Some people seemed at ease, as if they did this sort of thing all the time, and others looked even more nervous than me, no doubt pondering what they'd have to do in a few minutes.

I walked over to the nearest open spot on the bench and sat down. I did have my sword and helmet with me, but I thought having some other gear might be nice. Along the wall there were several small shelves filled with an assortment of weapons and armor, but I couldn't quite see what was there, so I got up and walked over.

It was not a large selection. Only two swords were left, a few spears, some bows and quivers, and a little bit of light armor. Of course, most of it had dents everywhere or was bent at a weird angle, but as I turned back to the bench, I saw an interesting shield propped up against the bottom of the wall. It looked much different from the others, older almost. I picked it up curiously and examined it.

It was made of a strange type of wood, something that I didn't recognize. It was darker than most wood around the capital. A silver metal cover encased it that had been carved to form different scenes. On one, there was a figure cowering behind a shield while dragon fire rained down upon him. On another, soldiers wearing masks marched through a marsh while gas clouds billowed around them. One soldier seemed to lead the rest, brandishing a shield in front of his face. On another, huge ships were thrown around as waves crashed around them. Some of the ships were pushed together and the sailors were boarding each other, trying to take control of the enemy vessel. On one ship, a figure who appeared to be wearing a crown fought to retake his craft. He attacked with an axe in one hand and blocked attacks with a round shield in the other.

Many other scenes were depicted, mostly involving battle, but there was also some blank space still on the cover, which struck me as weird. Why would someone stop decorating a shield halfway through? Whatever the reason, I thought it might be nice to have a shield out there, so I took it and walked back to the bench where I'd left my helmet.

As I sat back down, I looked around for it, but it wasn't on the bench anymore. I looked on the floor near me.

Nothing.

My heart started to pound a little harder. The helmet was an expensive and beautiful one, and my father might notice if it was gone. I asked the guy who was sitting near me if he'd seen it.

He looked positively menacing with his dark clothes and spiked armor, but when I asked him, he wouldn't look at me. "No, I seen no helmet," he muttered in a thick accent. I couldn't quite place where he was from.

"Are you sure?" I asked. "It was right here when I left to look at the weapons, and now it's gone."

He waved me away. "No! I tell you I not seen it! Go away."

I hesitated. I got the feeling that he knew what had happened to it, but I didn't Think I'd have any chance against him in a fight. He looked very strong.

Then, another guy came up and put his hand on the other guy's shoulder. "Just give him back the helmet, Bernard," he said.

Bernard backed up against the locker and started waving his hands around. "No. No. Really. I not have it!"

The other guy gave him a look and eventually Bernard reached down into his bag with a sigh and pulled out my helmet. I reached out and took it from him before he could change his mind and put it on, so no one else got any ideas.

"That usually works, kid," the man said, turning and walking back to his seat.

I sat there for a second, thinking about what just happened. For a moment, I thought I wasn't going to get the helmet back. Usually, I have at least a few guards with me if I leave the palace, and they would've helped me. It was a weird feeling being left to defend your stuff by yourself.

I got up and went to find another seat. There was no way that I was sitting next to Bernard anymore. I found one on the other side of the room and sat down. The competition was about to begin anyway, so it probably didn't much matter.

Almost immediately, the door flew open. It wasn't the door to the stadium, though. It was the door I'd walked through just a minute earlier. I looked over and saw Rowan Decker strutting in very confidently. Everyone started whispering and pointing at him. "Is that Rowan Decker!? There's no way. How are we supposed to win now?"

Rowan gave a jaunty wave to everyone and then sat down on one of the benches. With everything that happened, I'd almost forgotten about the conversation I'd overheard with him and my father. It was amazing to see him in real life, but I had to agree with everyone else. There was no way I was going to win against him in the competition.

Just then I heard a loud alarm go off and the door to the stadium swung open. It was much brighter outside than in the room, so I could barely see anything at first. The guards stood up and ushered all of us through the door. I tried to stay somewhere in the middle, but I was pushed right up to the front of the group.

I walked through the doorway, and immediately the dull roar of the crowd slammed into me. My eyes slowly adjusted to the light as the others walked through. I'd been to the stadium before with my father, of course, but I'd never seen it from this angle. Across the stadium, I could see my father's booth in the front row of the stands. I remembered the many times I'd sat next to him during a fight or a show. Now, here I was, in the stadium myself. I tried not to think about what would happen if the disguise suddenly wore off in the middle of the competition. Or worse: if it never wore off at all. I pushed those feelings down as much as I could. I would just have to trust Joe's abilities to cast the spell well enough. I had enough to worry about as it was without worrying about the spell. As I walked, I began to realize just how ridiculous this plan was. There was a chance that I wouldn't make it out of the stadium alive; all for a chance at adventure. But I knew that I would never forgive myself if I stopped now.

The main floor was covered with sand and four pillars scattered around the arena that appeared to be for decoration as they weren't connected to anything. No pillars were necessary for the construction as it was an open-air stadium. Rows of stands were filled with screaming spectators along the edge and 30 feet above the arena floor, rising at least another 50 feet at their highest point. Several large rocks offered some form of cover, though some were only a few feet wide. There was also a very large iron door under my father's booth with no designs on it, just a blank wall of metal.

The stands were packed; I couldn't see a single empty seat. I tried to stick around next to a few people, but everyone immediately tried to spread out. It was smart, I thought, because we really didn't know what the competition was even going to be. We could be competitors or teammates for all we knew. I wandered over to one of the nearest pillars and waited.

An airship hovered above the stadium, and as I watched, purple sparks started moving across both sides of it. Slowly, they started to form into the silhouette of a person before growing more and more detailed until a perfect image was displayed which looked exceptionally lifelike. A name was shown below the picture. The image faded, only to be replaced by another. Then another, and another. Soon I realized it was showing close ups of the contestants in the stadium. People standing next to me appeared on the ship. Another face flashed up, and at first, I didn't recognize myself, or the name that accompanied it. It was hard to get used to looking completely different.

Finally, after all of that was done, my father stood up from inside his private booth and raised his hands for silence. The cheers from the crows quieted down, but only by a notch.

"WELCOME, HONORED COMBATANTS!" he yelled over the screams of the crowd. "THE RULES ARE SIMPLE. I WILL RELEASE THE MONSTER AND ANY OF YOU WHO ARE LEFT STANDING WHEN IT IS DEFEATED SHALL GO ON THE QUEST!"

My stomach dropped at the mention of a monster, but I also had some hope. We would be working together. I wouldn't have to fight Rowan Decker. I glanced around at the other combatants, and most of them looked ready to fight, like they could handle anything that came at us. They gripped their weapons and glared toward the large metal door. I was kind of hoping to find some people like me, who weren't really that sure what they had gotten themselves into, but unfortunately for me everyone was at least pretending to be brave.

I saw my father and Adil arguing about something in their booth, but finally my father went over to another guy sitting near them and seemed to be explaining something to him. He was wearing a long robe and was holding a staff. It appeared that he was a wizard, but I didn't recognize him and had never seen him in the wizard quarters before.

He stood up and raised his staff. Dark crimson energy flowed out of it before seeping down to the stadium floor like honey pouring out of a bottle. Everyone watched, transfixed, as it reached the floor and sunk through, not stopping for a second. After about a minute of this, the energy stopped, and he sat back down. Nothing was visibly different, but I got the feeling that something horrific was about to happen.

Suddenly, the door at the end of the stadium lurched into motion. I could see large metal spikes sticking out of the bottom of the door as it was pulled up from the ground and soon it was gone, moving up into the wall, rising far too quickly for my taste. Why couldn't we sit here a bit longer? Maybe come up with some strategies, do some brainstorming? We hadn't even elected a leader for our little group yet.

A loud thud echoed through the stadium when the door finished opening and for a few seconds there was complete silence in the stadium. Then, a deafening thump sounded from behind the doorway. Then, another. And another. THUMP! THUMP! THUMP! Whatever it was, it was getting closer with each step it took.

I could almost make out a shape in the darkness, but then it stepped through, and I finally got a good look at it. My heart fell to my stomach. A huge hulking beast made of stone lumbered through the doorway and stopped. It was at least 15 feet tall and vaguely humanoid but incredibly misshapen. The legs were short and the arms long, like a lumpy gorilla made out of different rocks that had been shoved together. Its eyes glowed crimson and it stared at us hungrily, waiting to attack. A gong sounded and the golem lurched forward.

"WHOEVER CAN KILL THIS GOLEM AND SURVIVE, WINS!"

4
It's Not Over Yet

Matt

Immediately, everyone leapt into action. Some shot at the golem with bows, others attacked it head on with swords and shields, and a few, like me, cautiously stood back a bit, waiting to see what it would do. The arrows seemed to have no effect, bouncing off of the golem like twigs, but the few archers in our group kept shooting, perhaps hoping to find a weak spot in the stone.

The golem ripped through the people that had attacked it head on. For such a slow moving beast it managed to attack lightning-fast. It struck before several of them had even gotten into range to use their weapons. The first few were thrown across the stadium after a wide, sweeping blow from the golem's large arm. I could faintly hear their screams, muffled from the loud roars of the crowd as they landed on the sand.

The golem then turned its attention to its next wave of prey. They stabbed at the golem's hardened skin in desperation, but to no avail. It threw several more people across the stadium. I saw it punch one of my companions in the stomach, and he stumbled around for a few steps before collapsing to the ground with a large hole in his abdomen. Dozens of screams filled the air and within a minute, half of us were on the ground, and judging from the amount of blood, not too many were still alive. The ones who did manage to hit the golem didn't seem to inflict any damage on it at all. I was quite tempted to just drop my weapon and run away after what I'd just witnessed, but somehow, I managed to stand firm. I half-heartedly held up my sword and shield, hoping for an answer to come to me, but I had no idea what to do.

Everyone who was left retreated back after realizing that they weren't really doing any damage to the monster. There were only a little more than ten of us left and we formed a loose semi-circle a few yards away from the golem. The one advantage that we had was that it was very slow, and we could outrun it fairly easily, but it was gradually making its way toward our group, one slow step at a time.

I stared into its lifeless eyes as it approached us, steadily closing the gap with each passing second. It didn't look as though it cared at all about the people it had just ruthlessly killed, and it continuously walked closer and closer with no one volunteering any ideas or solutions. Eventually, I just gave up and inched backwards. Everyone else did the same, turning the battle into a race for survival.

The cheering from the crowd had started to die down, as the death they'd been promised turned into a sprint across the stadium as we tried to avoid the golem, almost as if we were playing a deadly game of tag. Of the survivors, there were several small groups that had formed, one of which was arguing about something as we ran.

One woman, presumably the self-appointed leader, explained something to the rest of them until they all cheered in agreement.

"ENCIRCLE IT!" the leader yelled. The whole group held up their weapons and ran at the golem, screaming as loud as they could. More people seemed to rally to them as they cheered and soon almost everyone who was still alive was running at the golem again.

I paused for a moment to gape at them. We'd all just tried that exact thing earlier and it didn't work at all. Why would it suddenly work now? They were all just running to their deaths.

They all approached the golem, encircling it as best they could, and started to hack into the stone with their swords and daggers. The golem didn't seem to mind at all that it was being poked with dozens of sharp pieces of metal. First it went for the small group of fighters in front of it, who were all brandishing spears toward it.

All anyone could do was watch as the golem picked off the petrified warriors, one by one. It flattened them, threw them, or simply punched them all into oblivion.

Several of their bodies hit the wall of the stadium near us, some screaming, others deathly quiet the whole way down to the ground.

Well, so much for encircling it, I thought. With all of the spearmen gone, the golem turned on the rest of us, pushing us toward the wall. Luckily, it was a circular stadium, so most of us were able to slip away before it grabbed at us with its huge stone arms. I did not want to be cornered by that thing. For a moment, it stared directly at me and I looked right into its emotionless eyes. Somehow, I managed to find the strength to run just a little bit faster. The archers were absolutely no help at all. The few that were left were still desperately shooting at the golem, but nothing was even sticking into it. The ground was littered with hundreds of broken arrows now, but they just kept shooting.

By this point, I was wondering how long this would go on for. Most of us were either dead or incapacitated. I mean, my father wouldn't really let this golem kill all of us, would he?

I glanced around at our little group of survivors, and I saw Rowan. I'd completely forgotten about him after everything that had happened, and he hadn't done anything to draw attention to himself, which wasn't what I was expecting, considering what he was known for.

"Does anyone have a plan?" I asked the group, though I was mostly looking at Rowan. Surely, he would know what to do, wouldn't he? He had been in the war, after all. We all continued to glance back at the golem as we talked, to make sure that it didn't sneak up on us as we planned out our next move.

"I don't know, kid," one of the archers said. "I've never fought anything like this before."

I paused for a beat before looking over to Rowan. "You're Rowan Decker, right?" I asked, pointing in his direction.

He glanced at me, and for a moment, his expression betrayed his true feelings. His eyes were wide and panicked, his brow slick with sweat, and his jaw clenched. Rowan was utterly terrified. I barely had time to register my surprise, however, before his fear was gone, replaced with a look of cool determination. "That's right."

"Well, can you do some spell or something?" I asked.

Rowan pondered this for a quick second before quickly shaking his head. "No, golems are usually magic resistant. I fought a few in the last war."

I took a moment to glance back at the golem in question, who was still staring right at us, slowly making its way in our direction.

I looked around at everyone else who was watching Rowan with a look of awe. Was no one gonna step up and form a plan? I couldn't be the only one who actually wanted to live.

The golem was getting very close to us, so we sprinted around it again to the other side of the stadium. It would take the golem quite a while to walk all the way across.

"So..." I paused, giving Rowan some time to elaborate, which he chose to ignore. "How did you stop the golems you fought in the war?" I asked him.

He looked taken aback, as if he wouldn't have expected that someone might be interested in his knowledge about fighting the thing that was currently trying to kill us.

"Well, there are a few different forms. Some are made of iron, some clay, and others from actual flesh. I'd assume that this is a stone variant, which unfortunately, I've only encountered a few times before. In the war, clay, and flesh golems were the most common, as those were easy materials to acquire. You can usually burn flesh golems, and I've seen clay ones defeated by large groups of warriors swarming around it, stabbing it repeatedly." He paused, glancing over to look at the golem again. "Well, clearly that won't work. Stone golems are a little bit harder to take down. With some sort of distraction, we might be able to stay near it long enough to make an impact with our weapons. Usually, stone golems are trapped under something heavy so that warriors can come up and attack it without fear of retaliation. But since we don't have that at the moment … if we could make a small distraction, we might be able to deflect the golems attention for a moment and give us enough time to make a difference." Rowan said, glancing around at the rest of us for a moment. "Does anyone have any ideas?"

The golem was too close now to stay still. We had to run back around the stadium toward our earlier spot.

"Um … I'm not so sure that's a good idea. It seems like it's really resistant to blades. Maybe we should think of something else," I said.

"We don't have time for anything else, boy," Rowan responded. "That golem is gonna catch up to us eventually, and this way at least I can say that I did something about it."

"But what about the distraction?" I stammered. "We don't have anything to distract it with."

Rowan hesitated for a moment, his mouth opening. Before he could say anything, a guy behind him interrupted. "How about a magical distraction? I mean, you're Rowan Decker. Surely you could create something that would distract the beast."

Rowan turned to face him. He again hesitated for a moment, though he managed to speak this time. "Well I ... of course I could ... create something," he said. "But I'm not sure ..."

The group cheered loudly, drowning out the rest of Rowan's words.

"Excellent!" the guy who spoke before said. "Then it's a plan. You make the distraction, and we'll follow up with an attack."

As the golem neared us we began to form a loose semi-circle around it, tightening the line as it grew nearer. Right before it got within range a bright flash erupted from above us, showering shimmering sparks down upon the golem. I raised my shield to cover my face as the sparks fell, though the initial blast was enough to blind me for a few seconds. I stumbled backwards before my vision returned.

As I opened my eyes I got a clear view of Rowan, standing at the edge of the stadium, gazing down at his hands. His mouth was open, and his eyes were wide as though he had absolutely no idea what he'd just done. I didn't have time to think about it or thank him for actually helping us; I had more pressing concerns.

Just as the sparks landed on the golem it reared back and shrieked, as though stung. For a moment we all watched, transfixed, as the golem roared in agony.

"CHARGE!" A yell rose up from the opposite side of the golem, shaking us out of our stupor. We all lurched forward and attacked. I hit my sword into its side over and over but I didn't even notice a dent form in the thick stone hide.

It wasted no time throwing several of my companions toward the side of the stadium like earlier, and also quite similar to earlier, they slammed into the wall and fell to the ground, motionless. It then turned to the people on its left side and made short work of them. One woman was hacking into the golem's leg one moment, and the next she had been crushed so far into the ground her body was barely recognizable through the blood and sand. Her loud scream was quickly cut short.

I didn't know what else to do, so I just kept hitting it, but I knew that this was the end. I thought about what led me to this moment and I realized that I wouldn't change anything. I would've gone crazy if my whole life was spent locked up in the palace. At least I tried to do something else, even if it was going to kill me.

The golem worked its way around the small group, picking off the desperate attackers one by one until it finally turned to me, arm raised, preparing to bring down a few tons of rock onto my face. At the last second, I half-heartedly raised my shield, willing the small piece of wood to protect me.

The golem's arm slammed down onto the shield and a bright, blinding light flashed. A deafening crack shook the ground beneath me, and I was thrown about 30 feet backwards, my shield flung a few feet away from me. The impact was softer than I'd expected, but for several moments I just laid on the ground, trying to process what had happened.

The crowd was silent as well, perhaps wondering why we were all doing so badly, when they had been promised entertainment.

Slowly, I sat up. And then I realized.

I was still alive.

The golem had tried its best to kill me and I was still here, albeit very battered and bruised. I looked down at myself, searching for injuries, but I found none. Amazed, I stood up and went to pick up my shield. It was also still intact, somehow, which was even more astonishing. As I reached my hand out though I realized that the color in my fingers was starting to fade. The disguise was beginning to wear off! We would have to act fast.

I looked around the stadium and saw Rowan running toward me. No one else was still standing. It was just the two of us.

"How are you still alive, boy?" he asked as he ran up next to me.

"I-I'm not really sure."

He stared at me, eyes narrowed, as if he was trying to find something wrong with me.

"How is that possible?" Rowan muttered to himself. "Ah, whatever. We don't have time to discuss it; we need to kill that beast. Any ideas?"

"M-me?"

"You see anyone else here?"

By now the golem had given up beating the dead bodies of our former allies to a pulp and was lumbering over to us. The reality of the situation began to fully set in and it was all I could do not to run away screaming. This golem didn't appear to be even remotely injured after taking out our entire heavily armed and well-trained team. How exactly were the two of us, a young prince and a former war hero, who was content to let others do his work for him, supposed to beat this unstoppable monster?

I had just survived a near fatal encounter with the golem and now it was back and lumbering toward us. I tried to think of something to do, but I was still stuck on the fact that Rowan Decker was now asking me for advice. Me. I looked around the stadium, looking for something that we could use, but nothing seemed useful. Some rocks, a few pillars, the iron door, sand.

Wait.

I turned back to look at the iron door in the front of the stadium. It was still raised from when it opened to let the golem out at the beginning of the battle, and I happened to notice large metal spikes sticking out at the bottom. Would it be possible to lower that door? Say, on top of the golem?

"Can you move that door with a spell?" I asked Rowan.

He glanced over at the large iron door, his eyes narrowing into a glare. "Yeah, I don't know, boy...it might be a little too heavy."

"Oh. Well, maybe there's some sort of mechanism over there to lower it."

"And if there is? You think we could hide behind it? Y'know, that might actually work!" he said, his eyes widening.

"No, I was thinking we could close the door on top of the golem and crush it. I doubt even it could get out from under a few dozen tons of iron."

Rowan looked over at me in surprise. "Okay, boy. We may have a plan. You distract it and I'll go look at the door," Rowan said, already running away.

"Um..." I started to say, but he was already gone. "Okay, then."

The crowd had greatly quieted down ever since our last encounter with the golem, and now they were beginning to scream and cheer again as the golem got closer and closer to us. A few people had been throwing food at it occasionally, and now almost everyone was joining in. Dozens of churros, sausages, and bags of popcorn rained down upon the golem, though none of it seemed to upset it at all and it just walked through the growing piles of debris.

I picked up a small rock that was on the ground and threw it at the golem. It didn't appear to hurt it, of course, but it froze and hesitated for a second. Rowan ran past it now, close to the wall, and the golem glanced back and forth between us. At the last second, it lurched forward in my direction. I was almost hoping that it would just decide to follow Rowan, but of course it wanted me, even if I was farther away. The crowd held their breath as the golem neared closer with each passing second.

As soon as the golem got within striking distance, I ran around it in circles, switching directions constantly. I hoped that if I was fast enough it wouldn't be able to hit me, or if it tried I could jump out of the way. At first the plan seemed to be working. The golem swung around, confusedly, and I was able to dodge any attack that actually went near me. The cheers from the crowd rose again as I went on. I was shocked that I managed to survive; I didn't think that I'd ever been able to jump around so quickly and efficiently before, but then again, I definitely hadn't tried to run around a golem and poke it with a sword before.

I was just beginning to grow more confident as I continued to casually avoid the golem's fatal attacks again and again. Not a big deal. But soon, the golem got a little smarter and it decided to trick me. It pulled back its arm, acting like it was going to punch to the left, and when I jumped to the right, it grazed me with its other arm. I hit the ground, but quickly got to my feet before it could strike again. My arm was bleeding a little, but if I'd stayed put, then I really would have been in trouble. I started running to the iron door. I'd pushed my luck far too much already.

Hopefully, Rowan had found something. The golem started following me, but since it was so much slower, when I reached the door, it was still near the middle of the stadium. The crowd had become more subdued again, as they realized that there wouldn't be any more action for a little while. I could almost hear the disappointment in their voices.

"Rowan. Please tell me you found something," I said as I made it to the door.

"Hmm? Oh, yeah, sure. It's over there," Rowan replied, pointing to a small metal lever on the wall.

"You think that controls the door?"

"Well, it's the only lever or button here, so..." he paused for a moment and shrugged, "maybe."

The lever was on the wall inside of the stadium, so one of us would have to lure the golem through the doorway and then the other would flip the lever, hopefully slamming the iron door on top of the golem.

It sounded dangerous, stupid, and very reliant on luck, but it was the only plan that we had.

"Alright. This might work," Rowan said. "You did so well with the golem the first time, I suppose I'll volunteer to pull the lever. Really, I think it's best to stick to our strengths, here."

"Uh ... you ...I..." I stammered, pointing toward the lever and the golem. "I'm the one..."

"It's coming! Hurry, distract it!" Rowan yelled, running away.

I sighed. Well, all I had to do was lead it through the doorway without it realizing what we were planning before Rowan could pull the lever. Easy, right? The golem was indeed coming toward us, so I waved at it and ran forward, holding my sword and shield. I started running around it again at first, just to get it mad. I wanted to make sure that it would keep following me when I went through the doorway.

Slowly, I led it through the doorway. It walked toward me, getting closer and closer to the right spot. It was just a few feet away and showed no sign of stopping. Its dark crimson eyes were fixed upon me, its stony face giving no hint of remorse. A little bit more. Just a little more ... and ... NOW!

"Rowan, flip the lever!" I yelled. I waited with bated breath to see if the plan would work. The seconds dragged on and my chest quivered as I began to wonder whether the lever controlled something else.

"Rowan?!" I screamed.

"I'm ... trying!" I heard from outside, in between grunts of effort.

I backed away from the golem in horror. By now it was much too late, and the golem was all the way inside the tunnel, advancing toward me menacingly. There was no time to freak out; I knew there was only one thing left to do. I had to somehow get past it so that we could try again.

I prepared to start running, but I was very hesitant to try; the tunnel that we were in was only about ten-feet wide, and the golem took up most of that space. My heart was beating so loudly, I thought that the golem must have heard it. It was too late to change the plan now. All I could do was hold my shield up and charge.

I dodged a few swings from the golem as I ducked under its arms, running for the door. I'd almost made it past him when I turned to dodge another swing coming toward me. Too late, I realized that I was practically jumping into range of an attack from the other side. There was no time to switch directions. I held my shield up to try and block as much of the attack as possible and hoped that I would be as lucky as I was last time.

Its arm slammed into my shield, and I saw another bright flash and heard another loud crack. I felt my feet leave the ground and I was thrown through the doorway. I landed about 30 feet away, but this time I managed to hold onto my shield.

I looked over to the doorway and saw the golem about to walk back outside. Rowan was still desperately trying to pull the lever, but it obviously wasn't designed to be operated by a single person because he was making no progress. I stared at the scene unfolding in front of me as utter horror ran through my veins. In a few seconds the golem would be out of the doorway, and we would be back to where we were before.

In desperation, as a last-ditch effort, I threw my shield like a frisbee toward the lever, hoping it would somehow slam into it and activate it. My throw was very far off, though. At first, it seemed like it might get close, but it veered off suddenly toward one of the large pillars standing nearby. I had just given up hope, when the shield hit the pillar and I heard a loud cracking sound.

The shield had somehow buried itself halfway through the solid stone and the pillar was wobbling and starting to fall. I watched in disbelief as the pillar fell directly toward the lever, knocking it down and activating the door as Rowan leapt out of the way.

The iron door dropped down at the last second on top of the golem. At first, I was worried that it might not be able to hold it, but the golem collapsed and appeared to be stuck under the door. It clawed frantically at the sand, trying to dig its way out, but its claws had no effect. It let out a deafening screech and its movement started to slow. Eventually, it stopped and lay still on the sand, trapped under the door.

I heard a soft sound, like water trickling over stones or rocks, and slowly the dark crimson energy in the golem's eyes drained away and pooled onto the ground. The rocks fell away next, and soon there was nothing left of the monster but a large pile of inanimate stones.

Cheers roared from the crowd as everyone realized what had happened. Rowan had gotten up and apparently decided that it would be extremely appropriate to take a bow at that moment. Which he did. The airship now displayed, "VICTORY!" in large letters, and shot off fireworks into the air. I let out a breath that I didn't know I was holding in. It was over. I could barely believe it. There were more moments during that fight that I thought I was about to die than the rest of my life combined. But I had actually done it.

After a moment I realized that my disguise may have let me be able to do this in the first place but now no one would know that it was me who had just done it, which made the victory a little less sweet. Well, I would tell my father about everything when I got back from the quest, so it didn't matter.

I went over to my shield and pulled it out of the rubble. Remarkably it was still perfectly fine. There weren't any marks on it. And there was something else. I noticed a new image carved into the metal. It appeared to be a small figure holding a shield to his face, while a large hulking beast was attacking. The beast looked very similar to the golem that I had just killed. And I swore that I had looked over the whole shield before and hadn't seen this image. It was almost like someone had carved it into the metal in the last few minutes.

"WELL DONE! YOU TWO HAVE DEFEATED THE MONSTER!" my father shouted.

"GO BACK TO THE BARRACKS AND WE WILL BRIEF YOU ON YOUR NEW QUEST."

Rowan and I headed back to the door that we first came through as it swung back open for the first time since we started the fight. The same guards who'd ushered us onto the battlefield were still there, apparently having not seen the event at all. They looked bored and didn't congratulate us or ask how it went. They just opened the door and sat back down which, to be honest, sounded very nice to me at that moment. I didn't want to fight anything else for years, if ever again.

We went and sat down on one of the benches.

"Ha! Not bad, boy. You did some good work out there," Rowan said. "Someday you might be as successful as me!"

I just nodded. I really had nothing to say to him now, even though I'd wanted to meet him for so long. I had imagined what it would be like to talk to him about his great deeds for years. I had looked up to him as a strong and powerful adventurer, but I guess that's why they say that you should never meet your heroes. They'll never live up to your expectations.

We'd been waiting for about ten minutes by the time my father and Adil arrived to talk to us. I could feel my disguise sliding off as the seconds ticked by. My whole hands were almost back to normal now and I could only hope that my face was still different. If I didn't get out of there soon everyone was gonna find out it was me. Hopefully, this would be a quick conversation.

"Well done, you two! Rowan Decker, of course. How could we not expect that?" My father gave a tight smile to Rowan. "But who are you?" my father said, pointing at me.

"N-Nathaniel Valdez, sire," I stammered, looking down at the floor.

"Well, good job, Valdez. Especially for someone from the colonies!"

I stared back at him for a moment and opened my mouth a few times, unable to find a response. He'd already moved on, however. He wasn't waiting for me. At the very least, I knew that my disguise was still working.

"Alright. I'm sure that you two have heard of Glyndwr Brice," my father began. "He has caused so much destruction to our lands. But we will finally stop him now. You two will be joined by our best knight, Olwyn Brewer, and a servant of your choice to help with your supplies. You will set off tomorrow morning toward Brice's territory and eventually, using stealth or force, your choice, you will break into his camp."

"Then," Adil said with a wide grin upon his face, "you'll kill him."

5

Bystanders Beware

Joe

I watched Matt leave the alley in his disguise and make his way toward the stadium. No one seemed to give him any more than a passing glance as he walked past them, so the spell must have been working. Hopefully, it would last as long as he would need it. I still wasn't sure about helping Matt with this ridiculous plan, but he wouldn't understand if I didn't. He really didn't know anything about the world outside the palace.

I swallowed hard, trying to push away all thoughts of Matt getting hurt. I'd known him for so many years, and he was the best friend I'd ever had. My *only* friend, but still the best one I had. I was on good terms with everyone who worked at the palace, but I never really knew any of them as more than just coworkers. I had Ben too, but there was only so much I could count on him for. Matt was always great company—when he wasn't acting like an ignorant spoiled rich kid.

When we were younger, I really didn't know any better. I'd never thought about how Matt had everything, and I had nothing until I got older. My dad tried his best, but there really weren't any better jobs available. He worked as a janitor for years just so that we could survive.

I remember walking through the city with him on his days off, watching the construction of all the new buildings. All the materials were carted in and arranged around the area. There was always so much noise. From hammering to chopping the site was always buzzing with activity. My dad had always wanted to be an architect, but it wasn't something that anybody could just become. There was a long process that we couldn't afford to go through. Not to mention that not many people would accept someone like him, from the colonies, in such an important field.

After he died, I came to realize that dreams like that were pointless for people like us.

I walked out of the alley and looked around. Everyone was walking toward the stadium, talking excitedly about what they were about to see, or buying food from one of the vendors near the entrance. The smell of cinnamon bread filled the air, taking me back to the days when I'd go to this stadium with Matt and his brother, Wyatt, to watch the fights. We hadn't done that in a while. Not since Wyatt left for Hullbeck over a year ago.

As I walked up to the entrance of the stadium, I noticed several guards watching everyone as they moved through the doorway. "No weapons of any kind are allowed inside the stadium!" An officer standing behind the table by the entrance shouted out to the crowd. "Be ready to be searched for any contraband!"

As I waited, the line picked up speed until soon, I was at the front. A guard waved me forward. She wore a bored look on her face as she motioned for me to stand in front of her before reaching forward and patting me down.

"I'll need to look in your bag as well," she said, her hand outstretched in front of her.

I hesitated for a moment, but I couldn't think of any reasonable way to protest this, so I handed it over. My spell book was still in the bag, which wouldn't be apparent at a glance, but I didn't know how in-depth the search was going to be. She rifled through the bag for a few tense seconds, though her expression didn't change at all throughout the entire process. Finally, after what felt like several minutes, but I knew must have only been mere seconds, she handed it back and waved me through the checkpoint.

Breathing a sigh of relief, I strode forward into the main entrance hallway of the stadium. Though it was made entirely out of stone, it was very well lit. There were torches mounted to either side of the wall all along the passage. After a moment of walking, I made it to a large staircase that I knew led to the stands up above us. As I got to the top of the staircase, I was finally able to get a good look at the stadium. It was the first time that I had seen it since I had been there with Matt and Wyatt a year earlier. The stands were extremely crowded. As I looked to my left and right, I could only see a couple of seats still available anywhere around the stadium. I was glad that I had hurried to get inside.

Looking into the stadium, I could see a large group of warriors running out through the large doors on the opposite wall. I tried to spot Matt among the other warriors, but they were too far away to recognize.

"WELCOME, HONORED COMBATANTS!" The king yelled from his booth, which was slightly to my left and at the very front of the crowd. "THE RULES ARE SIMPLE. I WILL RELEASE THE MONSTER AND ANY OF YOU WHO ARE LEFT STANDING WHEN IT IS DEFEATED SHALL GO ON THE QUEST!"

The battle slowly dragged on as I watched with dread, each death making my anxiety grow worse. How would Matt ever survive? He would need some sort of miracle. Or magic.

The small group of survivors prepared to make their final attack. As they charged, I just couldn't help myself anymore. I had to act. Running through the short list of spells that I knew in my head, I quickly realized that there wasn't a whole lot that I could actually do. The best spell that I could have a hope of casting without everyone around me almost instantly realizing what I was doing was a small distraction spell. But it was better than nothing.

Closing my eyes, I began to whisper the words of the spell under my breath, careful not to let my neighbors know what I was attempting. I had a feeling that most of the spectators wouldn't feel too kindly to someone trying to cheat the competition. My concentration waned slightly as the crowd began to cheer violently again, their excitement no doubt at an all-time high as they prepared to watch more brutal deaths, but I slowly began to cut out the sound around me and focus only on the spell. One step at a time, the magic wove itself together, until finally with a small popping noise it shot through the air, almost invisible in the bright light of the day, and made its way down to the stadium below.

The bright flash and shower of sparks told me that it had been successful. The golem roared and stumbled backward, no doubt trying to distance itself from the light as best it could. I watched the rest of the battle with bated breath, each turn or jump from Matt almost pulling a gasp of surprise or worry from me. Once I saw the golem, crushed beneath the metal door, unmoving, I could finally relax.

Once I got out of the stadium I wandered around for a few minutes, looking for Matt, but soon I realized that he could be talking to the king for a while. I knew that he would come find me when he was done, so I went back to my room and waited for him to show up.

Luckily, I didn't have to wait long. After no more than ten minutes, there was a knock on my door and I went to open it. Matt immediately ran in and started excitedly reliving moments from the competition. The disguise had seemed to have worn off, and from what I could tell from a quick glance, he seemed relatively unharmed. Maybe just a few scratches. I breathed a sigh of relief.

"Wasn't it so cool how I was totally dodging all of the golem's attacks for a while there!? It couldn't do anything to me," Matt said. "Oh! And I met Rowan Decker, who was actually a bit of a disappointment. He was kind of rude."

"Yes, I saw how the golem almost killed you dozens of times …" I said slowly, eyebrows raised.

"I know!" Matt's smile didn't waver whatsoever. "It was amazing!"

Matt then told me the whole story of how he went to the locker room and waited for the competition to start and everything that had happened after that. I had to admit that I was shocked as well as relieved, that Matt was one of only two survivors. He wasn't exactly one of the best fighters out there.

"Also, my father told Rowan and I that we leave tomorrow to go hunt down Glyndwyr Brice! The best knight in the kingdom is coming as well. I don't know much about her, but I guess she's the best knight for a reason. They also said that we should bring a servant to help with our equipment and stuff, so I was thinking … maybe you would want to come with us."

He raised his eyebrows expectantly. I stared back at him. He was going to kill Glyndwyr Brice? And he wanted me to go with him? My immediate response was to laugh and say no. What ridiculousness was he spouting? I had work to do at the palace; I couldn't just walk away from my responsibilities on a whim.

However, after a moment of thought, I realized that it was a great opportunity. Matt was always talking about wanting to explore the world and see what life was like outside of Ordbridge, and here was an opportunity to do just that. He could finally realize that life wasn't like those adventure books that he loves, and that not everyone can afford to indulge in fantasies like him. But I didn't want him to actually get hurt. If I was there with him, I could make sure that he wasn't in serious danger. I thought back to the many years that I had run around the palace with Matt. We always managed to find some new way to get into trouble. I couldn't imagine my life here without him.

"Well…" I hesitated, looking at Matt's excited expression. "Okay. I'll go with you," I eventually blurted out, wondering if there was a way to stuff the words back into my mouth. Was I going to regret this?

"Really? That's great! We can finally go on an adventure together! I've been dreaming about this for years."

It suddenly occurred to me that I might be risking a lot to go on this quest. There were no guarantees that I'd have my job back once the king found out that Matt was gone. But strangely, I didn't feel upset at that thought. For the first time in a long time, I was excited to do something. I'd stayed here only because it was all that I knew. My dad died a while ago now; maybe it was finally time to move on.

Now there was also Ben to think about. I might be gone for a long time. Just thinking about it made me miss him already. Did I really want to leave him for months? But although I knew I would miss him a lot, I began to feel like I had to go through with this. If I didn't leave Ordbridge now, then I wasn't sure that I would ever leave. I knew Ben would understand why I had to do this.

"Okay, we're supposed to meet at 8:00 tomorrow morning near the East gate. I'm sure you'll see us if you head down there," Matt said. "But you'll need to cast the illusion spell on me again before we leave, in case my father is there, so how about I just meet you here at 7:30 and we go to the gate together?"

"Alright, sure. See you at 7:30, I suppose," I replied.

Matt walked back through my door and out of sight. I sat down on my bed and thought about what would happen tomorrow. Surely the king couldn't expect this mission to succeed? How could four people, one of which was there purely to carry supplies, assassinate Glyndwyr Brice? It didn't make a lot of sense. But who was I to argue about it? It was then I realized that I had forgotten to tell Matt about my role in the competition. Surely, he had noticed the magic spell appearing out of nowhere, right?

I took a moment to think about what might happen on this quest. There would be danger; did I have what it took to protect myself and Matt from whatever would be coming at us? If my life was in danger, would I be able to kill someone to stop them from killing us? I didn't know. Maybe it wouldn't come down to that, but in my heart, I knew that I would have to decide the answer to that question soon enough.

I looked around my simple room, making a mental note of everything that I would need for tomorrow. There wasn't much to look over. The cramped room could only fit my tiny bed and a couple chests that stored my few possessions. It wouldn't take long to pack almost everything that I owned for the trip. I could just pack it all up later so I would be completely ready tomorrow. Since I was essentially ready to go, I decided to go visit Ben.

Most Tuesdays we'd meet by the fountain in the center of the town square, but I knew that he wouldn't be waiting for me today since we'd already seen each other today, so I'd have to sneak into his room. Sneaking in was always a big risk, but I had to see him again before I left.

I walked down the road until I eventually came to a small alley. A metal ladder on the side of one of the buildings led up to the roof. From there, I just had to walk over to the other side and jump down a couple feet and I was on Ben's balcony. It was a great way to see each other, but risky, so we tried not to use it very much. All it would take was someone to see me climbing on the roof and start asking questions for us to be discovered. My stomach flipped as I got close to his room. What if he didn't understand why I was leaving? Maybe this whole thing was a mistake.

He had a small balcony with a nice view of the city. I knocked on the door that led directly into his room and waited for a few seconds. At last, the door slid open, and Ben came outside.

"Joe! What are you doing here? I just saw you a few hours ago," Ben said.

I took a deep breath as I searched for the right words. In the end I just blurted it all out, forcing myself to look him in the eyes, and bracing myself for the pain to arrive in them. "Well, I'm leaving tomorrow so I thought I should see you before I go. I might be gone for a while."

"What? What do you mean you're leaving?" Ben asked, his eyes widening as he took a seat in one of the nearby chairs and motioned for me to take the other chair next to him.

I took a seat and looked out at the view. I could see all the way to the harbor from here—over the restaurants, stables, armory, the airship base, and hundreds of houses. It must've been nice to live in a place like this.

"Well, you know about the competition today?" I asked.

"Sure, something about Glyndwyr Brice? Wait, you weren't in that today, were you?! I thought you were just meeting Matthew there."

"No, no, I wasn't in the competition, but ..." I paused for a moment, looking out at the view again. "Matt was."

Ben looked relieved for a second, but his expression quickly shifted to confusion.

"The king let him compete? That's very surprising. Wasn't it quite violent?" Ben asked.

"Well ..." I hesitated for a second, wondering if I should tell him everything. "Yes, that would have been surprising," I said slowly. "Which is why I may have disguised him a little bit."

"What?! You tricked the king? What disguise would even work? It would have to be some sort of magic."

"Well ..." I paused for a second to consider my words. I hadn't told Ben about my new magical abilities yet. He might have thought I was crazy, but I suppose I'd have to tell him eventually. Why not now? "Well, it might have been a spell, actually."

"You ... cast a spell. Uh ..." Ben paused, staring at me. "Has this been going on for a while?"

"No, I just looked at a book in the library. It really isn't that big of a deal."

"Fine, fine. It seems like kind of a big deal to me, but whatever you say," Ben muttered, holding up his hands in surrender. "So, you're going with Matt, then? To hunt down Glyndwyr Brice?"

I nodded. "Yes, and I might be gone for a while." I'd let Ben think that I was some sort of master wizard. In reality, I only knew a few minor spells from the book I had found. I knew the disguise spell, some telekinesis, and small "attacks" if they could even be called that. The worst thing was some confusion or blindness. It was nice to think of myself as a wizard, despite knowing how different an official wizardry education was than practicing a few spells out of a book.

Ben paled. "Are you sure about this Joe? This quest sounds really dangerous."

"No, no, no, don't worry, okay?" I said. "I don't know what the king is thinking, but there's no way that we can actually kill Glyndwyr Brice. We just don't have the strength to do it with four people. The king will have to send reinforcements if he wants Brice dead, and in the meantime, I'll make sure Matt stays out of harm's way."

Ben nodded slowly. "I suppose you're right. Well, let's just enjoy the time we have left, okay?"

I leaned over and rested my shoulder on his. Ben and I talked for a few hours, enjoying each other's company. Ben told me about his mother's latest scheme to consolidate even more power for herself using her connections with the king. Just a usual thing for someone like Ben's mother. Her company managed most of the security for the palace and the city, so she was constantly trying to impress the king and everyone else important here to expand her business. She was essentially raising Ben to be some sort of prince, as if she thought that somehow, she could weasel her way into actually ruling over the city someday. Neither Ben nor I were huge fans of hers.

Eventually, the conversation faded away and we fell silent, looking out at the sunset.

6
Tickets Please

Matt

I was beginning to think that this day would never come. I'd thought about it and dreamed about it for years. It'd always been just a fantasy to me, but not anymore. Today I was actually leaving Ordbridge to go on a quest. I felt so relieved to finally leave my boring life in the palace behind. I knew that Joe thought it was stupid to believe all the stories I'd heard and read about life outside the capital, and he probably had a point. I mean, of course some of the stories were embellished to a certain degree, but there must be some truth to them. And I knew that wherever we were going might be dangerous but if I could survive that golem in the stadium then I could survive anything.

Well, Joe was coming with us, so at least he would get to see for himself what was true and what wasn't.

I wasn't sure exactly what the plan was for getting into enemy territory, but I thought I remembered some talk about a train. I knew that I wouldn't have to wait long to find out, though, because I was supposed to meet up with Joe soon, and we'd both head to the gate together.

I left a short note for my father on my desk: "Dear Father, by the time you see this I'll be gone. It was me you saw yesterday in the stadium, fighting that golem and I'm leaving to track down Glyndwyr Brice. I know you don't believe I'm worthy of being involved in any of your plans, but I hope you'll think differently of me when I return after a successful quest. -Matt"

I hoped he wouldn't see it before at least a few hours had passed.

Looking around my room, I suddenly felt a little bittersweet about leaving. On one hand, I had always wanted to go on an adventure, and here was a real life opportunity to do just that. On the other hand, I had almost never left the city before and I didn't really know what would happen. There was still a chance, however small I thought, that I would get injured.

In the end, it was an easy decision. I had gone so far already, and I'd never have forgiven myself if I'd just stayed home. This city was all that I knew but I didn't want to keep it that way for my whole life. It was time that I took my life into my own hands. For a moment I thought about what Wyatt was up to in Hullbeck. I hadn't talked to him in so long; I missed seeing him around the palace every day. We used to run around, pretending we were off on some adventure. We always said we'd go explore the world together someday. But then father sent him off to a fancy school far away when I began my training to be the king and I began to think that would never happen. Until now.

I took a last look around the room, making sure that I hadn't forgotten anything. I'd packed the night before, trying to bring only the essentials. Unfortunately, I didn't have a lot of survival equipment laying around my room, and I couldn't take it from somewhere in the palace without anyone noticing.

So, I packed some clothes, a sleeping bag, and my sword and shield. I had also managed to find some rope outside by the barracks that no one was watching.

With all of my supplies ready, I set the note down on my desk and left the room. As I walked, I began to grow restless at the idea of someone walking up to me and questioning where I might be going with a large backpack full of supplies and weapons strapped to my sides, but luckily the palace was surprisingly empty. I didn't run into anyone except a few servants who I quickly walked past, keeping my gaze to the ground. I knew that they probably wouldn't say anything, anyway.

I walked out the servants' entrance and breathed in the fresh air. It felt completely different from yesterday, as if I was already out of the city on my quest. The sun felt warm on my neck and there wasn't a single cloud in the sky as I walked down the street, completely carefree.

Almost immediately I spotted a couple of guards walking toward me and I had to practically throw myself into a nearby alleyway. I didn't dare peek around the corner or move a muscle for several long moments until I heard the familiar sound of jangling keys and boots hitting the ground. I hoped that they would move on quickly, but their footsteps seemed to slow as they approached the alley, and to my horror, I saw them stop almost directly in front of the alley's entrance.

"Did you see that Firestalkers game last night?" one of them asked.

The other one groaned and turned to the other. "No, I had to work, man. Was it a good game?"

The other guard laughed. "Ah, you gotta stop taking such late shifts! You'll miss all of the games this season, otherwise."

I held my breath, considering what to do if they walked into the alley. Should I run? Just act like I was supposed to be there? I crouched down behind a nearby dumpster and hoped that they wouldn't turn around.

The guards stood there for a few moments before the first guard spoke again.

"Come on, I'll show you the ball I got last night," he said, motioning for the other guard to follow.

"What!? You actually got a ball?"

Their voices slowly faded out of range, and I could finally breathe a sigh of relief. There was no time to waste. I had to get to Joe's place and get that disguise as soon as possible. I peeked around the corner and glanced back and forth down the street. The guards were gone, but a lot of other people were walking around. I kept my head down and moved forward as quickly as I could without drawing any more attention to myself.

Finally, I got to Joe's building. I hadn't been there many times before; usually I'd just see Joe at the palace. It was a simple three-story building, painted a dark gray with several windows along the walls. It was very drab, but a few small trees framed the front entrance. I went inside and, trying to keep my head down, walked up the stairs to the third floor.

Joes' room was right by the staircase. I quietly knocked on his door and he answered almost right away. He was wearing long, dark pants, a thick sweater, and large heavy boots. I stared at him for a moment and tried not to laugh.

"Are you sure you're gonna be warm enough, Joe?" I asked, holding back a smile.

"I hope so," Joe responded. "We're probably gonna be camping for a large part of the journey. We can't stay in fancy hotels the whole way, you know."

I looked down at my own clothes: An average shirt and a simple pair of pants with thin leather shoes. The clothes were made with a very nice, imported cloth from the colony of Eblon. Very breathable and comfortable. "Um … Yeah, I think I'll take my chances," I said, smiling.

Joe just rolled his eyes and walked over to his chest in the corner. He pulled out an old sword and sheath and put it on his belt. "Okay, so should I cast the disguise now or right before we get to the gate? Also, you didn't tell me the plan for revealing that you're actually you. Are we gonna have guards with us or not? I doubt that most guards wouldn't have a problem with this," Joe said.

"Well, first of all, there aren't gonna be any guards with us after we leave the city. I think that we're taking a public train to Andamore. That's the closest that we can get to enemy territory. It will just be us, Rowan Decker, and some knight," I said.

"Some knight? That sounds like it might be a problem," Joe said, pausing to look up at me, eyebrows raised.

"Well, yeah, it could be, but hopefully if you do the disguise for long enough, then it will be too late to turn back," I said.

"For long enough?" Joe asked slowly, a frown forming on his face. "Matt, you do realize that it lasts for one hour, right? I can't be casting this disguise dozens of times."

"Alright, fine, I'll tell the knight that the King sent me on a special mission. She would be crazy to go against the King, right? She'd have to let me keep going on the mission."

"I don't know about this, Matt. It seems like a flimsy excuse to me. But if you're sure—"

"It'll work, I promise."

Joe just sighed, shaking his head and turned around to grab the rest of his things. I saw him put in a few books, some dried food, and cooking equipment.

"Alright, so should we go then?" Joe asked, looking at his watch. "We have to be there in about fifteen minutes."

My stomach filled with butterflies. "Sure, let's go."

We walked down the stairs and out onto the street. I half expected to be stopped by some random person, or worse, a guard, but everyone we passed was just going about their day as usual.

Soon, we made it to the east gate. It looked like there was a temporary outpost set up there. I saw a small, covered area with a few tables set up underneath. Several crates lay around on the ground and on the tables, and a group of guards were talking with someone who was very clearly upset about something because they were practically shouting in their faces. Joe and I ducked into a nearby alley and started the spell.

I again felt the uncomfortable feeling of my skin shifting around, changing into new colors and shapes, creating a completely new person. It only took thirty seconds or so until it was over. It wasn't as bad as it was before; maybe I was getting used to this magic thing.

I glanced at my reflection in a nearby window and shuffled to a halt.

"Wait, Joe, I look different," I said, quickly realizing something was wrong.

Joe frowned. "Well … yes. That's kind of the point, Matt."

"No, Joe! I look different from the last disguise. This is a totally new person!" I said, my voice rising as panic started to set in.

Joe pulled out his spell book and flipped through a few pages before stopping on one. He stared at it for a long time, while I paced back and forth, watching.

"Okay, got it. I see the problem," Joe said, finally looking up from his book.

"Great! Now turn me back," I said.

"Right, well, it turns out that this is actually designed as a one-time use spell." Joe grimaced, a flicker of guilt crossing his face. "So…you either stay as you are now or go back to regular Matt."

"What?! Joe, that's not gonna work!" I complained. I could sense the annoyance start to creep into my voice as I talked. "Surely you have some spell that you can use to change me back to how I was last time."

Joe shook his head. "Sorry," he said matter of factly. "We're gonna need to come up with a new plan."

I stood there for a few moments, thinking about what we could do to help us out of the situation, but I knew that nothing I could think of would work. I'd have to talk to someone eventually and I looked very different from how I looked yesterday.

Joe watched me pace around with an almost amused expression. "Are you sure you're even going to see anyone from yesterday?" he asked. "I doubt your father will be there."

"Well, Rowan will be there for sure. I mean, I'm pretty sure that he would recognize the difference," I said.

Joe checked his watch and looked around the corner at the gate. "It's really our only option. We were supposed to be there a couple of minutes ago," he said.

He was right, but I was in no way happy about it. I definitely didn't want to go back home when we hadn't even left yet. We had to get on that train somehow. Our only chance was avoiding Rowan as much as possible and hoping that no one else I saw yesterday was there. I took a deep breath and walked out.

Joe looked taken aback that I was still going through with the plan, but he quickly followed and walked up in front of me. Soon, one of the guards noticed us and turned around along with the person who'd been yelling at them before.

Now I could clearly see who the knight was. She was only a couple inches taller than me but seemed to tower above us as she scowled down in our direction. She wore a few pieces of metal armor: a silver chest-plate with matching arm and leg attachments, along with a pair of black boots. Her blonde hair was even shorter than mine, brushed to one side haphazardly as if she couldn't be bothered to keep track of it. Her expression told me that she knew exactly how late we were. As she scowled at us, I got the feeling that she was not used to slowing down for anything and that we would be jumping right into the mission. The schedule would most definitely not include any downtime.

Her arms were crossed, and she looked at me with interest as I approached, perhaps wondering why I'd even bothered showing up at all if I was going to be this late.

"Hello. I'm—" I began.

"Late," she said. "Yes, I realized that." She turned to the guard next to her and pointed at a crate nearby on the ground. "Show them the equipment."

"I'll be over there," she said to us, pointing at the gate, "when you decide you're finally ready to go."

I opened my mouth to say something, but she immediately turned around and walked away. I glanced over at Joe, and he seemed to be just as speechless as I was. What had we got ourselves into?

The guard in question dragged a large crate over to us and opened it up. It was filled with weapons and gadgets. He started pulling things out and setting them down on a nearby table. "Okay, you two can pick whatever you want to help with the mission. Just tell me before you take anything. Also, these are mandatory," he told us, handing a small purple amethyst rock to each of us. "They're enchanted. You can talk to people from far away, as if they're sitting right in the room with you. Very handy."

I stared at the gem in amazement. I'd heard of some magical items being able to do something like this but I never imagined they would be so readily available to the average soldier. I looked through the rest of the equipment after looking over the stone for a while. There were the usual swords, spears, and knives, but I also saw what looked to be some sort of miniature bomb. The guard said that most soldiers just called them "rockets". It was essentially a single-use hand-held bomb. I thought it might be useful, so I took one. As I carried it around, I felt like a real soldier. I really wanted to see it in action, but I also kind of didn't.

Most of the other things weren't that exciting. There was some armor and shields and really just all the usual equipment. I still had my shield from the competition, so I didn't need any of those. I still found it strange how I had just found it lying in the barracks.

Joe took a small dagger, but he didn't seem interested in much else. After a couple of minutes, we went to the guard and told him what we chose. He just nodded and wrote something down in a small, leather notebook.

"Be careful with that rocket. Usually there's a safety course before you're allowed to handle one of those. I've seen a couple of guys lose hands trying to throw it…" he paused, gazing off into the distance, no doubt thinking about all of the injuries he had witnessed due to what I was now holding in my hand. "But we don't really have time for that. Just try not to be too rough with it."

"Ummm…okay," I said, more than slightly concerned that I could die at any moment.

"Oh yeah, I almost forgot. I just have to double-check you're the right guys," the guard said as he stepped over to a nearby table with a large crate full of files and rifled through them for a few moments before pulling one out and opening it. I looked inside the crate for a second and saw hundreds, maybe thousands, of files inside. "Okay, so, you're Joseph Farberos?"

Joe seemed taken aback for a second. "Uh. Well, yeah. That's me."

He glanced at me for a second and I didn't immediately understand what he was concerned about. "Can I ask how you knew my name?" Joe said.

The guard looked up from his paper. "Oh, the king just sent over a list of who was going along. I was told to confirm. You're good, though. You match the picture."

I glanced to the side for a moment, looking down the street that we had come from earlier at the perfect moment to see Rowan Decker finally arriving. He strolled over to the group, offering no apologies for his lateness. He didn't even look at me or Joe, either. "Are we going to go soon?" he asked.

Joe and I exchanged glances, waiting for the inevitable carnage. The knight walked over to us slowly, with a look of pure disgust on her face. "So that's how it's going to be, huh?" she said. "I'm going to have to deal with this the entire trip?"

Rowan patted me on the shoulder and smiled at her. "Well, I had to look after these two, didn't I? It wasn't easy, let me tell you."

At this point I was thoroughly tired of Rowan and couldn't believe that I'd ever wanted to meet him in the first place. "How about we just leave now?" I asked.

The guard cleared his throat and pointed at me. "I still need to check you in, actually." He went back to the enormous crate and started flipping through the files again. He spent a few moments on each one before moving on, so I knew we didn't have much time. It had only taken the guard a few seconds to locate Joe's folder, but it would take him considerably more time to find mine, considering that "Nathanial Valdez" didn't actually exist. I glanced around, hoping for some sort of miracle, or else this mission would end much sooner than expected.

I nudged Joe and whispered to him, "Do you have some sort of confusion spell?"

Joe looked startled and stared at me for a few seconds before finally leaning in. "I do, actually. But people will notice if I cast something. There's no way I can do it without everyone else freaking out!"

"Just leave it to me. Wait for them all to be distracted and then cast it on Rowan and the guard," I said, before casually strolling over to the weapons crate. I went through the weapons again, trying to make it seem like I was considering bringing something else. The guard was now clearly having problems finding a file. He kept flipping back and forth through the V's, I assumed. Finally, he seemed to just give up and started taking out random files.

At that moment, I grabbed one of the leftover rockets. "AH! It's gonna blow!" I yelled, throwing it away from me and diving backward. Chaos immediately erupted and everyone scrambled out of the way, tripping over equipment, and running as far away as they could in their haste to flee the now deadly scene.

I glanced over at Joe and saw him whispering something and waving his hands in the direction of Rowan and the guard who had been going through the files. I tried my best to create as much confusion as I could by tripping over another crate and falling into a nearby guard, but after a few moments everyone realized that they were not actually in any danger. They all looked at me accusingly, until one guard broke the silence with a laugh. "First time using rockets, son?" he asked. "Don't worry, you'll get it eventually."

And with that, people seemed to accept that the strange event was over and went back to whatever they had been doing before. The guard who'd been helping us wandered back over to the table and looked over several files that were laying open. He had a strange look on his face as he did it, as though he was doing something that he hadn't done in a while and wasn't quite sure what to do anymore.

"Uh, I think that's my file right there," I said, pointing to one of the files he was holding. The guard looked up at me in confusion and then down at the list of names on the table.

"So, you are ... Nathaniel Valdez, correct?"

"Yep. That's me," I said, holding my breath, waiting to see his reaction.

He looked at the picture and frowned. "Hmmm. Wasn't—didn't I just...Oh, well, never mind. I must be imagining things," he said, looking up at me. "You both seem to be in order. Good luck."

Rowan, Joe, and I started walking over to the gate. Rowan looked over at us, his expression more relaxed than before. "You know, you look different from yesterday," Rowan said. "Hmm… did you do something with your hair?"

I breathed a sigh of relief. "Yeah, you're right. I got a haircut."

Rowan just nodded and turned to look at something else. I was honestly shocked that the "plan", if one could even call it that, had worked. As soon as the adrenaline wore off, I realized how insane it was to try. So many things could have gone wrong. We were starting off the mission very strong, that was for sure.

The knight came over to us again and motioned for us to follow her. She led us over the gate and then stopped for a moment, tilting her head to the side and frowning. We waited for a few seconds before she let out a heavy sigh and opened the gate. "My name's Olwyn, by the way," she said, sounding almost disappointed that we had to know her name. "I'm sure you'll need to know it sooner or later."

We walked through the gate, past several soldiers who were guarding the exit, and down a stone pathway. There were train tracks off to the right of the path as we walked. I listened for a train, but I didn't hear anything. We were either too early or our lateness had made us miss our ride. I hoped for the former, but as we walked for another twenty minutes or so, I realized that we weren't even remotely close enough to the station to hear a train earlier.

Soon, we came to a small wooden building with a few people standing around beside it, in silence, either looking off into the distance in search of a train that might never arrive or looking over their fellow passengers with a look of concern and annoyance at their new companions for the trip. There was a shocking amount of the latter, but then again, I wasn't too thrilled with my present company either.

The station itself was very small. On the sides of the tiny building were dozens of posters, advertising different places all over the continent that you could visit. "Come Visit the Mines of Udora! So much fun, you won't even think for a second about 'coaling' home!"

That was about all that the station had to offer. It obviously wasn't a very popular stop, which I assumed had something to do with the twenty-minute walk from Ordbridge. There was a nice platform to wait for the train on, but other than that and the ticket office, there wasn't much else.

Olwyn pulled out several tickets from her bag and handed one to each of us. "Our tickets are already paid for. Please, try to get on the train before it leaves," she told us. "I'd so hate for any of you to be left behind." She hurried away from us toward the ticket window, as if trying to find any excuse to get away.

I looked at the ticket, which informed me that the train would be here in approximately seven minutes and that I'd be sitting in compartment 3B. None of us seemed too interested in talking, so we just stood in silence, waiting for the train to arrive. It gave me plenty of time to think about the adventure that we were about to start.

The train came in after a few minutes, slowly coming to a stop in front of us. It was painted a dark maroon with gold trim. It must have been new because I didn't see a single scratch or sign of age on it. In fact, it looked elegant, much more so than any train that I'd seen before.

Everyone on the platform walked toward the entrance and we followed near the back of the group. I still didn't fully believe that I was actually about to leave Ordbridge, but I just kept walking, and before I knew it, I was on board. We got to our seats without incident and sat down. The inside of the train was beautiful. Intricately carved wood panels divided the compartments, a rug decorated the floor with mesmerizing swirls of color, and plenty of room for each of us to relax and get comfortable.

A lot of people were already on the train, most of whom I assumed were from Ordbridge. I looked out the window of our compartment at the station and parts of Ordbridge that were still visible in the distance, mostly just the tallest buildings and the palace. Soon, the train lurched forward, and we slowly picked up speed until we were flying past the station. I watched the palace fade from view behind the rolling hills of the countryside until there was nothing left to see.

I exhaled a long breath. Finally, I was leaving the city where I had lived my whole life. Who knew what we would find on our adventure? Would we have to fight off some Kobolds or sneak our way through an Ogre stronghold? Maybe we would even see a dragon? There were so many creatures and places that I had never seen before, just waiting to cross my path. As the train continued forward, traveling down the weaving tracks, I sat back and relaxed, waiting for adventure to strike.

7
Off to a Bad Start

Joe

I sat directly across from Matt, looking out the window at the disappearing landscape as the train hurtled forward. The rolling hills of the grasslands flew by, the enormous, wild Yak herds roaming beneath us. A bridge had to be built over their lands after so many trains had either been greatly delayed or run off the tracks by the sheer number of herds wandering across the plains. It was truly a revolutionary project, but I knew that it was not all good for the people of Sikrath. It had been built with slave labor, thousands of workers that were shipped over from Sikrath's many colonies. If I had been alive then I no doubt would have been pulled into it as well.

Matt was staring in wonder at the Yaks, having never seen anything like them before in the city. I, myself, hadn't seen them for many years as they don't live anywhere near most large cities.

It had been a long time since I was this far away from the capital. Living as a child in the island colony of Esha would have been the last time, and I hardly remembered it at this point. I left when I was six and I haven't been back since. For years I had fond memories of Esha, and I wondered why we'd left. But once, after a particularly horrible day at work for my father, I asked why we even left Esha in the first place. He told me what it was really like there; oppression was rampant, everyone was forced to work in the gigantic factories that were built everywhere because there were no other jobs. There were a few good people managing the workers, he said, but mostly everyone only cared about power and money.

He said that many people tried to leave, to find work in the capital or anywhere else, but that was much easier said than done. You needed permission from the local government to leave, and that was given to very few. The entire government was fully controlled by Sikrath, caring only about their needs and not for the people of Esha.

Only the wealthy or politically connected got to leave legally. So, as you might imagine, there was a large smuggling business in operation, usually goods and supplies, but it soon became a way for people to leave the island. It was extremely expensive, but technically affordable. The smugglers knew that not many people could pay very much. So my mother and father decided that they had to leave as soon as possible. As much as they loved their homeland, it had changed so much in the last few years. Thirty years earlier, the only Sikrathian presence on Esha were a few small military outposts and some trading ports. But suddenly more and more soldiers started arriving every day and slowly they took more and more control over the island. We tried to resolve the issues peacefully until it finally became too much, and people tried to fight back. By then, however, it was much too late. Many people pressured the government to push back, and for a short while, things appeared to get better. But then came the election.

Aditya Cope ran against our incumbent president. My parents didn't vote for him. They didn't know anyone in their neighborhood who had voted for him. Everyone knew that he'd be much too friendly to the invaders. But somehow, he won by a landslide. It wasn't even close at all. Many people thought that it must be a mistake.

How could he have won by that much? The old president, while not doing much to stop Sikrath, was at least better than Aditya Cope. Almost immediately after he won, Sikrath moved in and took control of everything. New laws were put in place to limit what we could do and where we could go. We couldn't say whatever we wanted anymore. If someone thought that it was treasonous, then you could say hello to a prison cell.

Extra taxes were hefted upon everyone as well, just to ensure that no one had enough money to get by. People speculated about the election, saying that it was rigged by Sikrath. My father didn't explicitly say what he thought, but I could tell he knew.

Sikrath wanted more power, and they didn't care how they got it.

My mother and father put up with the new rules for years, but after a while it became too much for anyone to bear. They packed up everything that they could carry and went to find the smugglers. I had no idea what was happening, being six years old. Initially, I was excited about the trip, but it would turn out to be much harder than I had imagined.

We had to leave in the middle of the night to meet the smugglers. At first the journey wasn't too bad; we didn't run into any guards or police, but we found out once we got there that we couldn't afford to fully pay them. The price had been changed. The only thing that we had with us was my mother's necklace. It had been passed down for at least ten generations but, after a slight hesitation, my mother handed it over.

My father told me later that he was sure of the price that they had told him earlier and they must have purposely raised it at the last second to try and get a little more money out of us. That necklace was worth much more than the difference, but we had no time to sell it. Some people just tried to make more money however they could.

The trip over to the capital was very long. We were crammed into a tiny ship and hidden under the deck with five or so other families. I remember my father telling me stories about what we would have once we got to the capital. Anything that I wanted and worked hard for, I could get.

It took over a week to get to Ordbridge because we had to avoid checkpoints along the normal route. We found out about halfway through that some of the other families were sick, coughing and sneezing everywhere in the confined space. We tried to stay away from them as much as possible, but my mother also fell ill near the end of the trip. None of us expected that she wouldn't make it. How could you imagine going so far to find a better life, just to die from sickness hours away from your destination?

"Are you ok, Joe?" Matt asked.

I turned away from the window and looked at him. He was staring at me with a concerned frown.

"Yes," I said, clearing my throat. "I'm fine. Just thinking about what happens next."

Matt nodded. "Yeah, I've been thinking about that too. After we get off this train, I don't know what the plan is at all."

"Well, I'm sure Olwyn would love to tell us all about it sooner or later," I said.

Matt gave me a half skeptical, half amused look and went back to staring out the window. Olwyn had left our compartment near the beginning of the trip and hadn't returned since. I suppose she was trying to spend as little time with us as possible. Rowan had fallen asleep next to Matt almost as soon as we left, and he hadn't moved since.

After a while, I too decided that I needed a break from everyone. A short walk around the train would do me some good. I felt a pang of sadness as I thought of Ben, all alone back in Ordbridge. How long would he have to wait for my return?

I remembered seeing a map of the train near the front entrance, so I decided to go check it out. I hadn't gotten a chance to look at it when we first got on board. I wandered through several cars, eventually getting to the car with the map of the train that I had seen before. I passed a few people on my way there, but almost no one was out of their compartments. There wasn't much to see in the room besides the map.

This was the first time I'd been on a train, so I thought I might as well enjoy it as much as I could. The interior matched the exterior in color, but it was even fancier with elaborate designs painted all over the walls. It was quite a sight to see for someone like me, who was definitely not used to having nice things. I started looking over the map, which was a simple diagram showing how many cars there were on the train, and what was commonly stored on each, but I saw a sign next to it that said, "Push for 3D model." I stared at it for a few seconds, glanced around to see if anyone was watching, and determining that I was in fact alone, I pressed the button.

Immediately, a flash of green light jumped out the map, blinding me for a moment. It was so startling that I backed away, tripping over my feet and fell over onto the ground. I quickly got back up and glanced around again, thankfully not seeing anyone who'd witnessed what just happened.

I walked back over to the map and inspected it again. It now showed a three dimensional model of the train in bright green light. I stared at it in wonder for a few seconds. I'd never seen anything like it before. It showed everything that it had before, but now I could see what it actually looked like, just on a smaller scale. It must have taken a lot of magic to get that amount of detail.

On closer examination the model exactly matched everything that I had seen of the train so far. According to my best guess, that map was completely accurate. I decided to marvel over it later and instead searched for a good place to walk around.

Soon I made my way up a flight of stairs and outside, onto the balcony. I glanced around at the view, happy to have some time to myself. The porch extended up and out from the back of one of the train cars. A metal railing surrounded it on all sides so that no one could fall off, and a roof was held up by four poles.

At first, I thought that I was alone, but when I looked around, I saw Olwyn staring off into the distance on the far side of the porch. I stood for a few moments, contemplating what exactly I should do when Olwyn turned her head "You have something to say? Just say it. I came up here to avoid awkward silences."

I walked over and stood next to her, staring in the same direction. There was an excellent view of the Haliway Mountain range from this angle.

"Well," I said. "I didn't know that you were up here. I wanted to get away from everyone for a while too."

She looked over at me, an eyebrow raised, with a look of complete disinterest on her face. "Did you need something?"

"Now that you mention it, I did have some questions about the trip. What exactly is the plan here?" I asked. "It seems to me that we have a very hard job ahead of us." She continued to look absolutely uninterested in what I was saying. "Look, I really don't have to tell you anything, okay?" she said. "But, since I'm such a nice person, I'll give you the basic outline. First, we'll get into enemy territory, then do some reconnaissance—find a way into the headquarters or whatever they're using. Finally, we try to find a way to eliminate Glyndwyr Brice. But if we don't have the equipment to do it, we can just turn back. The King had to show people that he was doing something. That doesn't mean that it actually has to work."

I turned to look over the railing again, thinking about what she'd said. Her explanation certainly left a few things unanswered and made me realize how naive I had been about this whole situation. Why had I assumed that I would be able to protect Matt throughout this process? I didn't even know where we were going. I could feel my fear seeping deep into myself, something I hadn't felt to this degree since my father's death. It was the feeling of having no control whatsoever about what happens to you or the people you care about. I knew that I had to know more about the plan if I wanted to have any hope of protecting Matt, but I was afraid to ask any more questions. Before I could decide either way, Olwyn turned around and walked away, back down the stairs and out of sight.

I stood there for a few more minutes, trying to enjoy the fresh air after the unpleasant encounter. I could smell the sage wafting up to the train from the valley below and hear the constant dull roar of the wheels sliding over the metal tracks, steadily making its way to our destination.

Soon, I made my way back into the train and down the stairs. I passed a few empty compartments as I went back through the corridor toward our compartment. "Okay, it's almost time," I heard a deep, husky, voice say. "Are you ready?" The voice sounded like it was coming from the next compartment.

I was about to keep walking and not pay any attention to them, but then I heard: "And you're sure the weapons are in that crate?"

Immediately, I stopped walking, glanced around, and decided to creep a little bit closer to their compartment. "Yes, I'm sure! Stop asking. The information is good," another voice said.

"Just a few more minutes and then the guard should be gone."

I waited for a while in silence. *What should I do?* Soon, I heard someone stand up and I jumped away from the door as fast as I could. As the door opened, I pretended to walk past, down the corridor. I wandered away for a few feet, attempting to look as inconspicuous as possible, and listened for footsteps behind me. I walked for a few more steps forward before chancing a look behind me, which gave me a view of two people walking away from me down the corridor.

After a moment's hesitation, I followed, keeping at least twenty feet between us. They were both wearing average, unremarkable clothes, but they were also wearing black masks, so I couldn't see either of their faces. No one wore a mask like that without committing a crime. I had to keep following them. They walked through several cars, eventually stopping at a closed door. I quickly ducked into a nearby open compartment and waited, slowly peeking out the doorway to see what they would do. One of them bent down to look at the lock, and after a minute or so, I heard a click and the door swung open. They both went through the door, and I crept closer.

I heard a shout and then some sort of struggle on the other side of the door. I inched my way out of the compartment that I was in and towards the door that they'd just disappeared inside. Very cautiously I peeked around the side of the doorway and watched the scene unfold. Inside a train guard wrestled with one of the people I'd been following. The other one stood off to the side, calmly watching the two of them struggle. I considered rushing in to help the guard, but I wasn't armed, and I still didn't know what these two were planning.

Before I could decide what to do, the guard finally stopped struggling and collapsed to the floor. "You could have helped," the one who had done the fighting said.

The other shrugged. "You looked like you had it covered."

The first one grunted. "Just get the door, would you?"

Instantly, I whipped my head back from the open door and slowly crept my way back to the compartment I'd just been in. Just as I turned into the doorway, I heard the sound of a door closing nearby.

After taking a moment to catch my breath I crept back out of the compartment and went to the now-closed door. I could hear them both walking around inside the compartment and something that sounded like a large crate or box being moved.

Against my better judgment, I decided that I had to see what these two were up to. I grasped the doorknob and steadily pushed it open, no more than a few inches every couple seconds. I was ready to bolt away as soon as I heard either of them notice the door opening, but as I continued neither one of them said anything.

Finally, the door was at least a foot open, and I thought I might be able to squeeze through the crack. I paused to think about whether I should go through with this or not. Our adventure had clearly already begun, and with it came a lot more danger. I saw a flash of my companions finding my body later if these bandits caught me and Matt having to tell Ben about what had happened. But I knew I had to find out what these two were up to, no matter the risk. I took a deep breath, exhaled, and pushed my way through before I could change my mind.

I inched my way into the compartment, toward a small chair that sat a few feet past the doorway. With any luck I would still be able to run if either of them spotted me. I had to close the door behind me, however, as I didn't want them to come over to investigate. Both of them had their backs turned to me and were busy searching through the stacks of large wooden crates housed at the back of the compartment.

There was also a desk with some papers and folders left open on it near the doorway. It must have been a storage car, I realized. I'd seen several of them earlier on the map. One of them went over to the desk and startled rifling through the papers. After a moment searching, he pulled out a piece of paper from the thick stack on the desk.

"Aha! Here it is," he said, and walked over to his companion and showed him the paper. "Perfect. Okay, so the weapons should be in … crates J7 through…K4," he said. They both started searching all around the compartment looking for the right crates. I watched for a few minutes until they stopped and opened several bags that they had brought with them. "Okay, you take those crates over there and I'll do these ones," I heard.

I watched them open up the crates and put a small device inside each one.

"Alright. That should do it."

It was at this point that I realized how bad of a situation I was really in. I didn't know what these people were capable of, but I knew that it was nothing good. As slowly as I could, I inched backwards, keeping my eyes on them. Steady. Just a little bit at a time. Thump! I had backed into a small table against the wall. I froze, praying that they hadn't heard. A few seconds went by, and it seemed like I was in the clear, before a very loud shattering sound came from directly behind me. I spun around, only to discover broken glass all over the floor from the vase that had fallen off of the table.

"Hey! Who's there?" one of them shouted.

I immediately took off running as fast as I could, out of the compartment and down the corridor. I heard footsteps chasing me, and before I could even make it into the next car, one of them had tackled me and knocked me to the ground. He grabbed my neck with both of his hands and started choking me. I pulled at his hands, but his grip was too strong; I couldn't get away from him. I started gasping for breath, thinking that it was all over. In desperation, I slammed my elbow down into my attacker and I heard a cry of pain. His hold loosened, and I was able to struggle free.

As soon as I stood up, however, the other man tackled me, carried me back into the storage compartment, and threw me on the ground. "What the hell were you thinking!?" one said to me. "Who are you?"

"No one," I said. "I just wandered in by accident. I was looking for my compartment!"

They glanced at each other and then walked a little way away from me to discuss. They whispered, so I couldn't hear much of what they were saying. I tried to stay calm, but it was difficult. I still didn't know what they were capable of, but it certainly seemed like they were up to no good. They probably weren't happy having a witness to their crime. How far would they go to stop me from telling someone?

Finally, after several minutes, they walked back over to me, frowning. "Look, it's a shame that you happened to see this, but we really can't let you go anymore now, so I think we're just going to stuff you into one of these crates and be done with it."

My stomach lurched as I eyed one of the boxes nearby. "You won't get away with this! Whatever you're doing in here, you'll be stopped. Just you wait!"

My heart was beating so fast I felt like I was about to explode. Stuff me into one of the crates? That didn't sound very good to me. It sounded quite dangerous, in fact. How long could I survive in there before I ran out of oxygen? Not very long, probably.

All I could do was wait and see what happened. I was powerless to stop anything now, but they didn't seem interested in doing anything just yet. Perhaps they hadn't quite made up their minds about what to do with me. They stood near the doorway, making sure no one was coming and one of them kept checking his watch.

I had to do something. I wasn't armed and they were guarding the doorway, but I couldn't just sit there while they did whatever it was that they were plotting. At least they hadn't tied me up. I suppose they weren't expecting to need any rope.

I jumped up, grabbed the chair that I was sitting on, and charged them. One of them barely jumped out of the way, but the other fell to the ground, dazed, as I hit him with the piece of furniture and made a break for the door.

I almost made it. I was so close. "Almost" really doesn't help in this situation, however. The other man tripped me, and I fell flat on my face. I rolled over to see one of them standing over me holding the chair. "I really didn't want to have to do this," he said, "but you leave me no choice." He slammed the chair down on my head, and my vision went black.

8
It's the End of the Line

Matt

The trip was very pleasant at first. After spending my whole life in the capital, it was exciting to see all the new sights. I recognized many things from my adventure stories, like the enormous yaks that grazed outside the train window. The heroes I read about might ride them valiantly into battle, and I could see why; they looked strong enough to carry ten people.

The wild Avoncour Plains stretched out below us with a mixture of sprawling hills and deep, murky bogs. Before these tracks were built, everyone had to travel on foot, because most animals didn't want to set foot in the treacherous landscape. My great grandfather created the vast rail system that now spans across the continent, connecting the empire as it had never been previously. He was truly a great man.

I glanced over at Rowan, who was asleep next to me. I had read about his great deeds in the war, casting massive spells that wiped out thousands of soldiers and leading the charge into Kricoya. In reality, though, he just didn't live up to the stories.

Maybe no one could.

The door to our compartment rattled open, and I turned, expecting to see Joe. He had been gone for about twenty minutes now, and I was starting to think that he just didn't want to talk to me. I was starting to get nervous that the disguise would wear off soon. I knew that Joe couldn't keep casting the spell forever, but I hoped that he would at least be able to cast it one more time. Olwyn stepped inside, glanced around quickly, and then took a seat across from Rowan, without acknowledging my presence at all. I waited for a few seconds to see if she was going to start a conversation, but she started to pull a book out of her bag, so I had to take the initiative.

"So, how's the trip been for you so far?" I asked.

She looked up from her book and stared at me with a mixture of confusion and annoyance on her face, like she couldn't quite understand why someone would be speaking to her right then, but she knew she didn't like it.

"Fine," she said. "I assume you're going to ask the same thing your friend did?"

I hesitated for a second, unsure for a moment what she was talking about. Had she and Joe been talking?

She looked at me, obviously waiting for something. It took me a few seconds to realize it was my cue to ask my question.

"So ... is there a plan after this?" I asked. "How are we going to get through enemy territory without giving ourselves away? I mean, we're gonna have to sneak past the enemy lines, right?"

Olwyn just rolled her eyes and sighed. "Yes, we're going to sneak past the enemy lines. I'll tell you about it later. Look, this is mostly just a reconnaissance mission, okay? It's probably going to be too difficult to actually kill Glyndwyr Brice, but we'll do some investigating and find out."

I felt a frown fall across my face as my head spun in confusion. . "Why would my f- uh I- mean *the king* have made such a big deal about how we were going to go and kill him, then? It doesn't really make sense…" I said, slowly trailing off at Olwyn's expression. She stared at me blankly, her obvious impatience at my questions growing greater the more I spoke.

"The king wanted to appease people, alright? That's all I'll say," she said, lifting her book back up, ending the conversation.

I looked back out the window for a while, thinking about what she'd said. Maybe it would be hard for the four of us to kill Glyndwyr Brice, but if all we were doing was reconnaissance, it certainly made the adventure a little less exciting. How was I supposed to prove myself if the quest was over before it had even begun? My father wouldn't be impressed by a train ride and a little reconnaissance.

Soon after that, I grew bored of looking out the window and watching Olwyn read her book (Something about military history? The title "Top Ten Greatest Weapon Advancements in the Last Century" was barely visible on the front cover). I decided that the only thing left to do was to go and find Joe, who had been gone for quite a while now, so that he could cast the spell again and I could tell him what Olwyn had said about our mission.

I got up, without so much as a glance, my way from Olwyn and opened the compartment door. I made my way down the hall, still admiring the amazing designs as I went. Joe had said that he was going to get some air, so I wandered down to the main car in search of some balcony or open area.

I walked down the corridor, glancing into the different compartments as I passed. Most of them seemed very full. No one was out walking around like me, going to some balcony on a train. They probably just opened their windows. Soon, I made it past the compartments, up a short flight of stairs, and onto the balcony. I had to admit, the view was very nice. I could see all across the plains in every direction.

I glanced around, but no one else was there. Maybe Joe had gone back to the compartment while I'd been looking for him. I stayed for a few more minutes, enjoying the view, but eventually I headed back down the stairs toward the others. Aside from the sound of the train on the tracks, the corridor was silent.

A loud bump right next to me from behind a closed door made me jump and turn around. The door in question was made of a light gray metal as opposed to the wood doors from our compartments.

No doubt it wasn't a passenger area. I moved closer, almost walking into a large display case, showing off several plaques that read: "Winner of the Annual Sikrathian Rail Awards" inside.

As I approached the door, I listened for any other sounds, but I couldn't hear anything else. I began to think I'd just imagined the noise, but then I heard another. Loud thumps thudded from behind the door, and I heard the clatter of many objects falling to the ground.

I kneeled down and looked through the keyhole of the door. At first, I couldn't make anything out, but after shifting to the side I found the right angle and I could see three figures wrestling with each other. One of them was much smaller than the other two, and just as I thought it, he went down. One of the others slammed a chair onto his head and he went still. I froze, waiting, straining my ears to hear what they were saying.

"You should've been more careful," one of them said. "I guess you weren't even paying attention at all."

"Oh, come on," the other replied. "Like it's all my fault. You didn't see anyone following us either, did you!?"

"Just get the crates ready, alright? I've had enough distractions for today."

One of them went over to a large pile of wooden crates on the far side of the room and started closing them. I watched the scene in confusion, struggling to understand what exactly I was witnessing.

I stared at the figure on the ground, trying to make out any discernible features. The room was quite dark, so I had some trouble distinguishing anything about the figure. It also didn't help that I was peering through a small keyhole.

One of the men came over to the figure and nudged him. "You didn't kill him, did you?" he asked, kneeling down to inspect the person on the ground. He lifted him up and placed him down on a nearby chair. He rustled around for a little bit before finally stepping back and taking a quick glance at his handiwork. The figure was now sitting on the chair, somewhat precariously, and after observing for several seconds, the man apparently decided that the figure was probably not going to tumble back onto the floor.

"He's fine," the man said. He wandered back over to his friend, and for the first time I could clearly see the figure's face. Wait...was that...Joe?! What was Joe doing there? He had somehow gotten himself knocked unconscious by a pair of bandits while riding on a train. My heart pounded as I thought about what they had done to him. I couldn't tell if he was okay or not from where I was. A creeping feeling of guilt slowly spread through me; Joe wouldn't even be here if I hadn't asked him to come along.

I knew I had to save him, but how? The door that I was looking through was the only entrance from what I could tell. I'd have to just wait for the right moment.

I watched the two of them seal up the rest of the crates and stand guard for what felt like a very long time, probably because the keyhole was just high enough that I couldn't kneel on the ground and just low enough that I couldn't stand up, leaving me in a very uncomfortable squat like position. Surely, they would move eventually, right? All my legs and I could do was hope.

They were both pacing and checking their watches repeatedly. Hopefully whatever they were waiting for would happen soon so that I could do something to help Joe.

I watched for another couple of minutes, until finally, one of them noticed something in the corner of the room. He wandered over and then started laughing.

"Hey, Jerry, you gotta see this," he said. "There are the mice that I was telling you about before. I've always loved mice; they're just so cute."

Jerry slowly walked over to get a good look at the mice, giving me a perfect opportunity. As quickly as I could, while still being relatively quiet, I opened the door, crouched down and slowly made my way over to Joe. Almost there...just a few more feet...

"Whatever, just pay attention. We don't want anyone else coming in here," Jerry said.

I froze and watched Jerry start to turn around. Time seemed to slow down as I frantically glanced left and right for a hiding spot, but I couldn't move. He would see me any second now. Where could I go? At the last moment, I dove under the desk right behind Joe. I sat there, as still as possible, listening for the sound of boots stomping over in my direction. But they never came. His footsteps moved away from me in no real hurry.

I let out a sigh of relief. I was sure that I was about to be discovered there. Unfortunately, I may have been in a worse situation than I was in before. I was now trapped under a desk in a room with two bandits, who had just knocked Joe out, or worse. I had to get to Joe soon if he needed medical attention. It was at that point that I started to question my plan.

Well, I was already in the room. I had to finish it. I looked around from under the desk for anything that I could use against them. There was a broken chair, some papers scattered around the room, what I thought was a radio of some kind sitting next to Jerry, and some other furniture and office supplies. I couldn't see much of the room, though, because Joe was sitting right in front of my hiding place.

I briefly considered grabbing the trashcan and using it as a club against the bandits, but I quickly came to the conclusion that would not end well for me. Evidently from the smashed chair on the ground, Joe had already tried something similar.

Jerry picked up the radio next to him and motioned for his companion to come closer.

"It's almost time. We might as well get out of here. The remote is all ready."

"Alright, but what do we do about him?" the other one asked, pointing at Joe.

Jerry just shook his head and pointed to one of the crates. "Hey, he brought it on himself. Just silence him, permanently, and throw him in one of those," he pointed toward the creates they were going through. "We won't have to deal with him after that."

The other man started walking over to Joe and me. It was now or never. As he lifted Joe up, I charged out from under the desk, grabbing the trash can on my way.

Before either of them could do much more than open their mouths in surprise, I slammed Jerry in the head with the trash can. He immediately fell to the ground and the remote flew out of his hand, but he didn't even look dazed, merely stunned at the appearance of yet another adversary. To my horror he almost immediately jumped back to his feet and stepped toward me. I backed up, now realizing just how much danger I was in. All I could think to do was to grab the remote now lying at my feet and retreat as far back as I could. "Stop! I have...this...thing! Don't come any closer," I yelled.

Jerry and his partner exchanged worried looks and slowly put their hands up. "Don't do anything rash, boy," Jerry said. "Do you even know what it is you're holding?"

I looked down at the remote and examined it while still keeping an eye on the two of them. It was all black and there was one red button and a small antenna on it. I was almost tempted to just press the button, but it was my only bargaining chip at the moment, so I stopped myself. "Let Joe go and go stand against the wall," I said.

Jerry slowly stood and stepped a few feet back. "Don't push that button, boy," he said. "We will all die if you push that button."

The other person had put Joe down on the ground and had backed up to the wall like I instructed. "He's right, kid," he said. His voice was a mix of fear and pity, like he was scared of what I might do but also felt sorry for me because he thought that I really just had no idea what I was doing. "Take your friend, put the remote down, and leave. Okay?"

I considered it, but I knew that as soon as I'd put the remote down, they would both rush at me. Probably if I tried to carry Joe out, they would also try to take the remote from me. There was only one thing left to do.

I walked right up next to Joe. "Okay, you can have it," I said, throwing the remote toward the back of the room. As soon as I threw it, I grabbed Joe and dragged him as fast as I could toward the door. I heard Jerry and his accomplice scrambling to get the remote back behind us.

We had just gotten through the door when I heard a loud beep. "NO!" Jerry screamed. All of us froze for a moment before Jerry and his partner both sprinted for the door. As fast as I could, I closed the door and then pushed against the display case sitting nearby as hard as I could. It slammed down onto the ground, covering the bottom half of the door completely, just as I heard Jerry slam into it, trying to get it open.

My heart was racing as I dragged Joe toward our compartment as fast as I could.

"Help us! Please!" I heard from behind me as I dragged Joe away from the compartment. I continued pulling him down the corridor and we made it into the next car before I heard it.

BOOM! A massive explosion rocked the train, and I was thrown off my feet. I heard screaming all around me and the sound of groaning metal, as the train leaned more and more to the side, threatening to come off the tracks completely. I backed up opposite the wall and grabbed a metal handle welded to the side of the train.

Joe was just starting to wake up and I tried to get him to hold on to the bar as well, but I wasn't sure if he really understood what was happening yet. The train had now turned almost 45 degrees above the track. All I could do was hang on to the handle as hard as I could with one hand as I grabbed hold of Joe with the other. After what felt like forever, but must have only been a few seconds, the train groaned again and tipped even more to the side.

Suddenly, we were falling. The train had come completely off the tracks and was dropping into the bog far below. I braced for impact, waiting for the inevitable collision into the cold depths of the marsh.

THOOM! The train smashed into the water below, the windows shattering instantly and water quickly rushing inside.

After the train settled, the silence was deafening. Only the sound of rushing water came to my ears. I couldn't hear anyone else. Maybe we were the only survivors.

Then I heard the sound of glass breaking. All the way down the car, the windows that hadn't already broken were cracking and letting in even more water from the bog outside. We were nowhere near out of this nightmare yet.

My strength was spent. I let go of the handle and dropped down into the quickly rising water. "Joe!" I said. "Joe! Are you ok?"

Joe just groaned and sat up. "What happened?"

I grabbed Joe's hand and pulled him up. "I could ask the same of you, Joe, but now is really not the time. We have to get out of here!"

I waded through the rising water over to the door nearest to us. The train was completely on its side, so I had to lean down and reach under the water to get to the handle. Just a little more … there! I turned the handle and pushed as hard as I could, but almost immediately, the door hit something solid and stopped moving. I tried closing it again, and slamming it open, but whatever was blocking the way was not budging one bit. "Come on!" I yelled. The train groaned again as hundreds of gallons of water poured inside.

We waded through the now waist-high water toward the door at the far end of the car. All we could do was hope that it would open. If it didn't ... well, we were running out of options. The water level was rising so fast now that it was hard to push forward.

"We'll have to swim, Matt!" Joe said.

The door was now over halfway submerged, but we swam the rest of the way fairly easily.

I reached the door and stood up again. The water level was at my neck now. We had no time to lose. I tried the door and…nothing. It wouldn't even open a little bit. I started to panic at that point. How would we get out? The windows would be our only hope but the ones below us were blocked by the mud and dirt at the bottom of the bog and we wouldn't be able to climb out of the ones above when water was flooding inside through them. Not to mention the shards of glass still covering almost all of the windows

At that moment, the lights in the car flickered once, twice, and then shut off completely. How would we find the windows now? The water was so murky that I could barely see a few inches in front of me.

"Matt! Are you there?" Joe yelled at me. "Come on, we have to find a window. You look on this side and I'll take the far end."

I heard Joe dive underwater again and it was enough to restore my motivation.

No. It wasn't over yet. I squinted in front of me to try and make out any windows near us, but I couldn't see anything from where I was, so I reached upward to try and feel my way to an open window. The water was now almost at the ceiling, which at least meant it would be easier to find a window.

After a few moments, Joe resurfaced and looked around for me.

"Anything?" I asked.

"No. You?"

I shook my head. He swam back toward his side and kept looking and I did the same. The water crept higher and higher until I was pressed against the ceiling. I took one last breath and the water finally rose to the top of the room, submerging us.

When underwater, sound reaches you in strange ways. You might call out to someone a few feet away and they won't understand. You might be drowning, and you could never tell them. You might sink below the murky water, and they wouldn't know anything was wrong until you never came back up.

I never did like swimming very much.

9
Not So Simple

Matt

I swam through the murky water in circles, searching through the same area over and over again in desperation. I looked over in the direction that Joe had disappeared, and I knew that I had to try to make it over to him. I didn't want to die with no one by my side. I swam through the water, farther and farther, reaching out for him, until I felt it.

An opening! I could see just a hint of light from the surface shining down through it. The glass was completely gone, leaving a large square with plenty of room for us to slip outside; it was exactly what we needed.

"JOE! OVER HERE!" I shouted, but the water muffled my voice, transforming it into an unrecognizable yell.

I shouted again and again with the last of my breath. It couldn't end like this, could it? Maybe I should have stayed home, listened to my father, and learned how to rule the kingdom. Surely, anything was better than an ending like this.

I sunk down even farther, the last of my energy and oxygen spent. I stared up at the opening above me, questioning if I still had the strength to at least save myself—and if I would even want to if it would mean Joe's death. I had almost lost all hope when I felt Joe's hand on my arm. I would have cried out with relief, but I had no more oxygen left in my lungs.

Joe had to pull me through the window and toward the light up above. I was too weak to move anymore; my vision turned more and more fuzzy with each passing moment. We finally reached the surface after what felt like an eternity and both gasped for breath. With the last of our strength, we clambered onto shore, next to the wreckage of the train that was still on land, and laid there for a few moments, trying to process what just happened.

Should I have done something differently? Maybe the train wouldn't have fallen if I had gotten help instead of going in alone.

But the train was gone, sinking into the bog, and nothing was going to change that. I sat up and finally took in the destruction. The windows had all been shattered from the fall and I could see where the train had been blown apart by the explosion. Several of the compartments had been crumpled, torn up, and blown aside. The compartment that we'd been in just minutes before was now completely cut in half, severing the connection between the front and back halves of the train, which would explain why the submerged frontal part of the train hadn't dragged the rest of the cars underwater. In general, though, the train was in surprisingly good shape considering that it had just fallen off the track from the 80-foot-tall bridge above us into a swamp.

My heart lifted and relief tugged at my muscles when I saw people clambering out of the open windows and helping others get to safety. I knew that it was pointless to blame myself for what had happened, but I couldn't help feeling some guilt about how things had turned out. I tried to push down my worry for Olwyn and Rowan. Maybe there was no one left to wait for us to come back.

Joe frowned and hesitated, but eventually he got up with me and we started walking down the length of the train, toward where we thought our compartment was.

As we walked, we passed more and more people who had made it out and were looking around for supplies and other survivors. We also had to walk past many bodies lying on the ground or inside a destroyed compartment. I could feel nausea build up inside me as we passed them. Some of them were almost unrecognizable but others looked too real, as if they had just paused for a quick nap in their compartments and would soon spring back up with energy. Soon after we started, I had to look away as we passed. I could feel their eyes on me as we walked but I couldn't force myself to look back.

I glanced up above us at the bridge that we had been on not long ago; it looked as though a huge chunk of it had been blown completely off.

"Help me!" I heard from under a huge sheet of metal beside us.

"Someone help me!"

Joe hesitated for a moment before stumbling over the nearby rubble toward the voice. I carefully stepped over the debris and helped Joe lift up the large piece of the train wall. We raised the metal up and there was a short scream as the rest of the debris shifted around. Slowly, we managed to lift the wall off of a small, bald man who pushed the leftover debris away and scrambled past us before collapsing back onto the ground. Joe leaned down and placed a hand on his shoulder, but the man pushed him away, leapt to his feet, and limped off before either of us could say anything.

Joe and I shared a quick look of concern before we set off again. I looked around for Olwyn or Rowan but I couldn't recognize anybody. I didn't see anyone stepping up to lead us out of this, either. Maybe the engineer didn't make it out. He probably would've been near the front of the train that was now fully submerged in the deep swamp water.

After a few more steps I realized Joe had stopped in his tracks behind me. "Matt!" His voice was strained as he lifted his hand to point to my face. "Your disguise! It wore off."

My eyes widened and I rushed over to the bank of the swamp. Sure enough I could see the face of the Prince of Sikrath staring back at me as I looked into the water. The face I had known for my entire life.

"What are we going to do?" I asked Joe quietly. I didn't think I even had the energy to argue if Olwyn decided to send me back to Ordbridge, let alone come up with a reasonable way to convince her to let me stay.

Joe just shook his head and sighed. "I'm not sure anymore. Do you even want to keep going?"

"But ... Joe, I have to stay!" I said, my voice rising. "If I just give up on the first challenge then there was no point in even leaving at all! I'm not sure what I can tell Olwyn, but I have to at least say something for my benefit. Even if it's just the truth. Is there any way you could cast the spell again?"

Joe shook his head again. "I'm not sure that I have the energy to do that, Matt. I need to rest before I can cast anything again."

I sighed and nodded as Joe patted my shoulder once before we started off again on our search. Finally, I spotted Olwyn and Rowan standing right next to what I thought used to be our car. Joe and I carefully made our way over to them. Soon, Olwyn looked up and noticed us. At first all she did was glance our way and nod but then she took a closer look. She raised her eyebrows and her mouth fell open.

"Who is this?" she asked, glancing back and forth between us. "Where is Nathaniel?"

"Well?" she asked after neither Joe nor I had said anything. "You look suspiciously like the king's son," she said, pointing at me. "What exactly are you doing here?"

I opened my mouth to say that I was on a special mission for the King, like I had planned, but as soon as I started talking, I knew that I just didn't have the energy to lie to her right then. So, I told her the whole story about how I disguised myself and won the competition and made it onto the train. I tried to cut it down as much as possible and make it sound like it was sort of a casual thing and that Joe and I hadn't thought out this extremely elaborate plan to leave Ordbridge.

At the end, I paused and waited for her response. She appeared to be thinking things over. Her eyes were pointed toward the ground and her head was tilted to the side.

"Well, there's not much we can do about it right now, I suppose," Olwyn said. "The train is not going to be operational for some time and no other trains can come this way until that track is repaired. The safest course of action is to continue our journey toward the front lines and then, perhaps we can send you back to the capital."

She looked quite satisfied with her solution and I didn't question it. At the very least I wasn't leaving anytime soon.

"Well, great," I said. "Were you able to salvage any of our stuff?"

She simply picked up two bags from the ground and threw one to each of us. I looked it over and confirmed that it was, in fact, my bag. Nothing seemed to be missing, either.

"Do you two know what happened to the train? Everything was fine and the next thing we knew the train had come off the rails." Olwyn asked.

Joe and I exchanged looks.

"Maybe the engine overheated or something," Rowan muttered.

"Well, actually, there were some bandits in one of the storage cars. They took Joe prisoner and then a bomb they had with them detonated as we were getting away," I said.

Rowan's eyes widened. "Bandits?" he said, scrunching up his face in thought. "What happened to them? Are they still here?"

I looked over at Joe. "Um no, probably not," I said. "They were in the car when it exploded so I doubt they survived."

Rowan relaxed at this news, though he still seemed to be on edge.

"It looked like they were trying to rob the storage car," I said.

"Well, that didn't go too well for them, did it?" Rowan said with a laugh.

"I wouldn't say it went too well for us, either". Olwyn muttered from a few feet away.

"Come on. We have to get out of here before everyone gathers up and starts forming a plan. We don't need any extra questions, especially now," Olwyn said, pointedly, looking in my direction. She banged on the side of the car a few times. "Let's move!"

Rowan was carrying several bags. I couldn't tell exactly how many, but certainly more than I would've thought possible. He glanced over at me and frowned. "You're really the prince, huh? Well, try to keep up with us." He started walking away before I could respond.

Olwyn glanced around to see if anyone was watching, and then, apparently satisfied that everyone was occupied with other things, most likely the train crash, she led us underneath the bridge and off to the left of the railroad tracks. I almost asked where exactly we were going, but I thought better of it. I was just happy to still be there. And we were making our way out of the bog and onto dry land, so I was more than happy to follow Olwyn. I slowly noticed a difference as the ground became firmer and firmer and I stopped sinking down a few inches with every step.

I looked over at Joe, trying to judge how he was doing after our near-death experience. He seemed perfectly fine to me, although I wasn't the best at telling what people were feeling. I watched him look at the new flowers that we kept passing with a slight smile on his face. Hopefully, he was doing alright. The plants that we passed were pretty amazing, though. The capital didn't have too much variety, but out here we must have passed a new plant every couple of feet.

I thought about what had happened back on the train. I realized that Joe might have been right about this trip being more than I could handle. But I couldn't give up now. If anything, this had proved to me how much I needed to continue this trip so that I could have something worthwhile that I had done to show my father. He knew what this adventure would be like. He would have to be even more impressed with me than I had thought when I came back successfully.

A short way into our trek, we walked over a large, steep hill. I was starting to get a little tired and I had slowed down considerably. Luckily, Rowan also seemed to be having some troubles, so Joe and Olwyn waited for us at the top. After a few quick breaks and a lot of heavy breathing, we made it to the top and I stopped to rest. I looked out into the distance, taking in the scene. The hill offered an incredible view of what must have been dozens of miles in every direction. I could see the train down in the bog from where we came from. The tracks above it stretched out into the distance, leading all the way back to the capital, though I couldn't actually see the city. I could see a dense forest back past the train in the direction that we came in.

Luckily, we didn't need to go through there. I was sure I would've gotten lost somehow.
It made sense that Olwyn wanted us to get out of there as quick as possible to avoid questions; Our exact mission was still secret even if everyone in the Kingdom knew about the competition. I certainly wouldn't have minded a short break, though.

I looked over the other side of the hill, toward where we were going—or at least the direction that we'd been walking in. I still didn't actually know where we were going. The bog stretched out for miles behind us, but in the distance I could see sprawling plains covering the landscape, and were there some buildings out there too? Maybe a village of some sort?

"Hey, it looks like there's a town or something over there," I told Olwyn, pointing in the direction of the buildings I had seen.

She nodded. "Yes, we'll need to stop there to resupply."

After our very short rest we continued down the hill. It was definitely a fast pace, but going downhill helped a lot. Plus, I got to look out at the excellent view the whole way down.

By the time we made it to the bottom of the hill, it was well past midday. Olwyn apparently thought that meant we had to pick up the pace even more, so we practically jogged down the path toward the plains ahead. No one said a word as we marched through the rest of the day. We must have been walking for at least three hours by the time we made it into the plains.

I dug around in my pack, looking for some food, but, of course, I didn't think to put any in. I assumed that we would be getting food on the train or when we got off but obviously, that wasn't happening anymore.

"Does anyone have any food?" I asked, glancing around at the others. Olwyn didn't even bother to turn around, so I assumed that it was a no from her, and Rowan and Joe just shook their heads.

Finally, after many hard hours of marching, we made it within sight of the village. There were around fifty houses in all, and they all seemed to have about the same simple design, made primarily out of wood. I did see a much larger building past most of the houses, which I assumed was some sort of bar or inn, but we would have to get closer to be sure. There weren't a lot of people out on the streets as we passed, though it was around dinner time.

Olwyn glared at anyone who walked too close, and she quickly led us to the large building without incident. We passed several houses with broken windows and doors that had been hastily repaired as well as houses that had fully collapsed. In fact, almost every house that we passed had serious damage, as though they'd been built a long time ago and no one cared about them enough to fix them. The people we saw all looked about as dirty as we did, which was surprising, considering that we'd just survived a train bombing. On the way into town, we passed several large fields of crops. A lot of people were probably just getting out of the fields and walking home.

Olwyn stopped us at the back of the inn. "Alright, stay here," she said. "I'll be right back." And she walked around the side and disappeared from sight.

We all leaned against the side of the inn, but it couldn't have been more than a minute before Olwyn returned.

"Come on. I got us dinner," she said, leading us around the building to a side door and knocking once.

After a few seconds, the door opened slowly, and a very short man stood in front of us. He must have been shorter than four feet tall and looked to be at least sixty years old. He had long, gray hair that went down to his shoulders, and wore a relatively clean black tunic. He didn't look happy to see us, but he wasn't exactly hostile. His features formed sort of an *alright, fine. Let's just get this over with* look.

"Follow me," he said and disappeared into the inn.

Olwyn immediately followed, and after a moment's hesitation, Joe, Rowan, and I went in as well. The door led to what must have been the kitchens for the inn. The walls were lined with a rather small selection of pots, pans, and other cooking instruments. I could almost imagine people rushing around, preparing food for their customers, but something about the room was unsettling. Perhaps it was the lack of light, or maybe the fact that there wasn't a single piece of food anywhere in sight, but it felt like the room had been abandoned for a long time. I took a deep breath, expecting to experience the familiar smell of the kitchens at the palace that I was so used to, only to find that the room smelled nothing like them. I smelled only dust and stale air.

We followed the man through the kitchen, down a long, dark, hallway with blank walls, and finally into what appeared to be an office of sorts. A desk stood in the corner with paperwork scattered across it, and large stacks of papers were piled into small baskets on the ground. A table had been laid out for four, and the man gestured for us to take our seats.

Olwyn pulled out the chair right next to the wall and sat down. Joe, Rowan, and I glanced at each other briefly before doing the same until the little table was far too crowded. The short man excused himself and left the room. We all just sat there, silently waiting for some unknown event.

Olwyn seemed perfectly comfortable, leaning back in her chair. I assumed we were about to eat something, but it didn't seem usual that we'd have our own private table in what appeared to be the manager's office. Had Olwyn talked to him about our mission for the king and he offered to help us? It would be nice to have someone loyal to the crown here with us as we gathered our strength and supplies for the next part of our journey.

As I fidgeted in my still-damp clothes, I wondered why it was decided to eat before going up to our rooms. But then I realized that Olwyn and Rowan hadn't fallen in the water. Olwyn must just have been very oblivious to other people's needs, but I swore I saw her glancing at me a few times with a smirk on her face.

After only a few minutes, the man came back through the door carrying a tray of food. We each got the same thing: A small bowl of brown soup (I had no idea what kind it was), a piece of hard, seedy bread, and a mug of ale. The man tried for a smile as he set the tray down on the table but failed miserably, leaving his features in a sort of pained grimace before rushing out of the room.

I looked closer at the soup, trying to determine what exactly was in it, and glanced around at the others to see if they'd already tried it. Joe and Olwyn were eating the soup normally without much hesitation, but I couldn't tell if they actually liked it. Rowan was attempting to choke his portion down bite after bite. I was not heartened by this, but I figured it might be the only food we would have for the rest of the night and I was starving.

I took a hesitant bite, scrunching up my face, trying to prepare myself for the worst, but it was actually not horrible. It really wasn't very good either, though.

We all ate mostly in silence. It had been hours since any of us had eaten and we'd just walked for miles, and the group was also not made up of many talkers.

I finished the soup rather quickly and started looking around the office to pass the time. Rowan, though very determined to eat, was perhaps the slowest eater ever. There really wasn't much to see in the office. A few picture frames hung from the wall, featuring people that I assumed were the man's family. Interestingly, none of them were anywhere near as short as he was.

On the desk in the corner, next to the stack of papers, were several pens and pencils scattered around and what appeared to be some sort of measuring scale. It seemed slightly out of place among all the other office supplies and papers, but I suppose a lot of things seemed odd on this trip.

Finally, after another ten minutes or so, everyone else was done with the soup. Olwyn stood, walked over to the door, and opened it. The man who'd brought us our food was standing a few feet away and he turned when he heard the door open. "Are you done?" he asked.

Olwyn nodded.

"Great. Well, I actually have some bad news, I'm afraid. It turns out that there aren't any rooms available at the moment. I hope you understand."

He looked very nervous, but he stayed relatively still, except for a slight shift from foot to foot.

Olwyn sighed and walked a little closer to him. "Look, I thought you realized who I was. Who I work for," she said.

The man took a step back but looked determined not to run away. "I do understand," he said. "And I'm sorry, but there just isn't room."

Olwyn looked almost sad that this was happening, but she led the man down the hallway in the direction that we had come inside from. "Look," she said, quietly. "For your sake, I would rather you just give us the rooms, alright? Do you really want the King's attention on this place? Maybe have some soldiers show up and do some inspections?"

The man paled and glanced around nervously. "Alright, alright. I suppose I could manage a few rooms. We'll see."

Joe, Rowan, and I were all standing in the doorway to the office, watching this exchange anxiously. I didn't know what I would do if we couldn't get a room; I'd been waiting to lie down all day after our harrowing experience on the train. Just as I was pondering this, I felt a tap on my shoulder. I looked over to see a girl who must have been about my age standing beside me. I looked at her in surprise; she was the most beautiful person that I had ever seen. She had long, thick, curly brown hair that stretched down past her shoulders and two emerald-green eyes that seemed to glitter in the pale light of the hallway lamps as she stared at me. I opened my mouth to say something but no words came out; I couldn't take my eyes off of her.

"Excuse me," she finally said, "I must clear the table now."

I blinked a few times, trying to register what exactly she had just said to me. I was too busy staring at her to even attempt to understand her words.

"Excuse me," she said again, trying to push past me.

"Um, oh," I muttered, finally understanding what it was that she wanted. "Y-yeah, of course, go ahead," I said, moving to the side to let her get into the office.

I continued to stare at her as she packed everything up and carried it out of the room. I almost called out to her to wait just for a second, but for the life of me I couldn't think of a single reason to stop her. We watched her disappear down the hallway, tray in hand.

Joe looked at me curiously. "You okay, Matt?" he asked, an eyebrow raised.

I looked over at him to see a slight smirk on his face. My face burned; I had just made a fool out of myself, hadn't I? And in front of her, no less.

"I-it's nothing, Joe," I stammered. "I just thought that I recognized her is all. But I don't, so there's nothing to be concerned about."

Joe continued to grin. He started walking down the hallway, nudging my shoulder slightly as he went. "You should have asked for her name," he whispered to me, so Rowan and the others wouldn't hear. I could feel myself getting red again as I ran after him down the hallway.

"Come on," I said. "Let's go look around a bit." We walked down the hallway in the opposite direction that we had come from. I wanted to see more of the inn and I was sure that Olwyn could sort out the problem with the rooms. Besides, I needed a distraction after that embarrassing encounter. We'd walked for only a short distance before we came to a large wooden door. I hesitated for just a moment before pushing it open.

I walked through the doorway and looked around. In front of us was a large open room, filled with tables and chairs, stools sitting next to the bar in the corner, and over a dozen people. Large windows in the front showed a view out into the street, though they were so filthy that we could barely see anything out of them.

The few people there were talking amongst themselves and having dinner, but I could sense a sort of dull misery about them, as though they'd lost the motivation to keep going but were still trying to go about their normal routine.

As soon as Joe and I walked through the door, everyone stopped whatever they were doing and looked up at us. We froze. I considered just slowly backing away through the doorway, but after a few seconds, people started talking again and turned away from us. Some of them still gave us some odd looks, but I felt comfortable enough to stroll around and take in the rustic, small-town feel.

There wasn't much to see in the bar. It all looked a bit run down. A few of the chairs set up around the room were completely broken and couldn't be used. The bar was the nicest part of it. A few working stools were scattered around, and a dozen or so bottles were stacked up on shelves. A chandelier hung from the ceiling, and it might have helped brighten up the room and make it look a little cleaner and fancier, but more than half of the candles weren't lit, making it look even gloomier and creepier than it most likely was.

The locals seemed curious about the strange new visitors, but some glared at us through hostile eyes. I walked up to the bar and ordered an ale. Maybe it would stop them from thinking we weren't bringing anything good to the village. The barkeep leaned down and pulled out a bottle from under the counter.

"That'll be four copper," he said.

I dug around in my pockets for some copper pieces, but I couldn't find exact change. All I had was a pouch with some gold coins. "Um, do you have change for a gold?" I asked, pulling out a handful from my pouch. The man just stared at me, mouth open. I realized that the bar had gone deathly silent, and I looked around hesitantly.

Everyone was staring at me, some with wonder, some with concern, others looking ready to snatch the pouch from me as soon as I walked within 20 feet of them. "…Okay," I said, sliding a gold coin to the barkeep. "Um…just keep the change." I grabbed my ale and glanced around again. Everyone was still staring at us and some had stood up and walked a little closer. Joe tapped my shoulder and pulled me toward the door.

We took a few steps back but now at least ten people stood near us. About half of the people surrounding us glared at me and stared hungrily at my pouch; they looked like they were just about to lurch forward and snatch it out of my hands. The other half also peered at it in the same manner, but they didn't seem to even notice who was holding it; all they cared about was the money.

Most of them seemed almost half-dead. They wore ragged clothes and their eyes drooped, like they hadn't slept in days. I got the feeling that most of them had completely given up hope and would truly do anything to get their hands on some money. They were so much more frightening than the others.

"Perhaps I should just make a run for it," I thought to myself. I inched closer to the doorway. But then the door flew open, and Olwyn rushed into the room.

"What the hell is going on in here?!" she yelled. "Get away from them!" She ran at the group of people surrounding us, and they scattered, running for the front doors. Olwyn grabbed us by the shoulders and pushed us, practically shoving us to the ground and then through the back door. We stayed silent as she led us upstairs and down a hallway until we stopped in front of two doors on opposite sides of the hall.

"Don't go near the villagers!" she almost screamed at us, though it really felt like she was talking more to me. "Did you show them you had money? Never do that! Okay? Can you handle that simple task?!"

I just nodded and looked down at the floor. Olwyn looked genuinely worried for the first time since we had met—even more than when the train had come off the rails. She glared at us for another few seconds before sighing and gesturing for us to go into our rooms.

I opened the door and stepped inside. The room was pretty small but cozy. I thought it had a nice log-cabin feel to it, even though I'd never actually been inside one before. I glanced out into the hallway one last time to watch Olwyn walk away. She was muttering something to herself and shaking her head.

She stopped, quickly wiped her eyes a few times, and turned into the nearest room. I got a glimpse of her face and her eyes looked redder than usual. I shook my head in puzzlement as I leaned back into my room, closed the door, and locked it.

10
Not Quite as it Appears

Joe

I woke up feeling unrested after our encounter with the villagers the night before. Eager to continue our journey, I quickly packed my clothes and other belongings into my bag. I made sure that my spell book was safely inside before walking out of the room. There was no sign of Matt or Olwyn in the hallway, so I decided to go look in the back room where we ate last night. If they weren't there, then I didn't know what I'd do; I wasn't exactly ready to go back into the front room. For a moment I thought about Ben all alone back in Ordbridge; I already missed him, and I was afraid I wouldn't be able to see him for a long time. I'd have given a lot to be back on his balcony with him instead of here in this old inn.

I got up and after an unnerving walk, I made it down the stairs and through the hallway that we'd walked down before. Fortunately, I saw Rowan a moment later. He was leaning against the wall, right next to the room where we'd eaten dinner the previous night.

I nodded to him and leaned against the opposite wall. "Are we going to leave soon?"

He nodded and continued to stare at the ground. I considered leaving him alone and going to find Olwyn, but she probably wouldn't have much to say to me either.

"I get the feeling that you aren't a big fan of the crown, boy," Rowan said, breaking his silence.

"What makes you say that?" I asked after giving a cautious look around.

Rowan studied my face. "Let's just say that as a fellow critic, I can tell who agrees with me."

We stood there for a moment as my mind raced. Why would Rowan say this? What did he expect me to say to him? Those were probably more words than he'd ever uttered to me on the whole trip. Perhaps I should take a risk and see where it led. I didn't see Rowan trying to trick me at that moment. If anything, this felt like the most honesty that I'd ever seen from him.

"Okay," I said. "Maybe you're right."

Rowan stayed silent for several moments before finally speaking. "Alright, I think that I can trust you," he said. "I get the feeling that you may have a similar problem to mine." He hesitated again and then sighed. "I suppose I'll start from the beginning. I'm sure you heard about my exploits during the Kricoyan War. I got to be quite famous from it."

I rolled my eyes. Yes, everyone had heard of Rowan Decker, famous for killing hundreds of soldiers a day. He was a hero for Sikrath, and many people looked up to him, including Matt. At least, Matt used to look up to him. I simply nodded and motioned for him to continue.

Rowan cleared his throat. "Well, anyway, some of those stories may have been, um, slightly embellished. I mean, most of them, I suppose. Um," Rowan paused, looking at the ground and rubbing the back of his neck. "Okay, fine, I've gone this far. They're all made up. I'm not really a wizard and I can barely do any magic. I just took credit for great wizards' accomplishments during the war." Rowan wouldn't look up at me after saying this, and for a second, I genuinely believed that he might feel some shame about his actions, but he quickly recovered and looked back up with a large smirk on his face.

"It worked perfectly," Rowan said. "Well, almost. But I suppose I'm getting ahead of myself. I should start from the beginning. There's quite a lot to tell. So, it all started—" Rowan's eyes widened, and he closed his mouth quickly.

I was about to ask what the problem was when I heard Olwyn's voice to my right. "Well? Don't you want to get out of here too? Stop talking and carry these supplies out to the back," Olwyn said, swinging a large bag over her shoulder and walking past us toward the door.

I inhaled sharply. It didn't seem like Olwyn had heard what we were talking about. Even if she had, it was mostly a problem for Rowan. It wasn't my fault that Rowan was a fraud. I had nothing to do with whatever scheme he was concocting.

Rowan walked over to the pile of bags and grabbed one. Normally, he might make some complaint or say that he wasn't here to provide manual labor, but he merely took the bag and headed for the door.

"Just think about what I said, alright?" he whispered to me as he left.

What the hell was that supposed to mean? He hadn't said anything at all. He'd just started his story when Olwyn stopped us. Still, I had learned some very interesting news.

Rowan had faked all of his famous accomplishments.

I could imagine the look on Matt's face if I told him. He was obsessed with the great Rowan Decker before he'd met him. He wouldn't shut up about all the great things that Rowan had done. I couldn't tell Matt about it, however, because it almost sounded like Rowan was suggesting that we team up to…what? Overthrow the kingdom?

No, I must have misunderstood. It couldn't be anything like that. I'd have to just wait until Rowan and I were alone again. Maybe once we stopped for camp we would have an opportunity to talk.

I grabbed another sack from the ground and walked out the door. I couldn't see Olwyn anymore, but Rowan was walking past the side of the inn and as I watched, he turned to the right toward the back of the building and went out of sight. I quickly followed. Olwyn was right to want to leave as soon as possible after what happened last night.

I made it around the building and deposited my bag on the ground next to Rowan's. Olwyn was busy loading several other bags onto the back of a small mule. I raised my eyebrows. Where were all of these supplies and rooms and food coming from, exactly? As soon as I had the thought, I relaxed. We were working for the king, after all. He could probably afford to buy anything. Or just take it.

I considered offering to help Olwyn get everything ready, but it seemed to me that she didn't actually want any help. I would probably do something wrong and she would only have to redo it.

After a short wait, however, everything was ready. We had all of the new supplies loaded up, including all the food we were going to eat during the journey. Everything was done, and we were ready to leave.

Except for one thing.

Matt finally came scrambling down the stairs ten minutes later. I was shocked that we'd waited; Olwyn looked like she wanted to rush upstairs and drag him out of bed, but she somehow managed to resist. Although he was late and hadn't helped us load our gear, Matt seemed to be in good spirits.

"So, what's for breakfast?" he asked.

Olwyn sighed deeply before rummaging around in one of the bags. Soon, she pulled out an orange and tossed it over to him. "There you go. Feel free to savor it as long as you want."

Matt's face fell and he looked around at all of us in confusion, like this was some huge prank and Olwyn was about to announce that we were going to go get waffles. Not receiving any sympathetic looks, Matt seemed to accept the truth and pocketed the orange.

"Did you two grab the rest of the bags?" Olwyn asked Rowan and I after a small pause. "I only see three of the bags here but there were five sitting on the floor inside."

Rowan and I exchanged glances, unsure of how to respond. We'd quite obviously forgotten to bring the other bags but what, if anything, could be said to stop Olwyn from killing us right where we stood?

I cleared my throat. "I think we may have only brought three of the bags," I said.   Olwyn just sighed again and threw her arms up in the air. "Alright, fine," she said, her voice strained. "Would you just get them now?"

The three of us quickly rushed off back to the inn to grab the two remaining bags and bring them back to Olwyn as quickly as possible. Luckily, the bags were sitting right where we had left them. There also happened to be something else standing nearby. Someone else. The girl from last night who Matt had taken such a liking to stood next to our remaining supplies, looking unsure of what to do. We all stopped when we saw her.

"You're back," she said, looking relieved. "You need to take your supplies as soon as possible. There are too many people here that are more than willing to take them."

She spoke with a slight accent that I wasn't sure that I had ever heard before.

"Um, yeah," Matt mumbled. "We were just getting them now. Thanks for guarding them."

She just nodded and turned away to leave.

"Wait!" Matt said, walking up to her. "I, uh, just wanted to talk to you a little bit because…um…I was just curious about the village. Why was everyone acting so strangely last night?"

I watched this interaction with amusement before grabbing one of the remaining bags and motioning for Rowan to take the other. I could try and get Olwyn to wait for a few minutes. The least we could do was give Matt a chance to get to know the girl a little.

"I wouldn't expect you to understand," I heard her voice angrily exclaiming behind me. "You come in here from the capital, waving around your money like you think that you should own the entire town. You will never understand what it is like for us here, barely surviving every day, with nothing to do but tend to the farms! You'll just go back to your city and forget about us, just like everyone else." She turned away and walked down the hallway, not pausing to look back once.

"Wait!" Matt half-heartedly called out to her. "It isn't like that. I don't…I haven't…"

She walked around the corner and disappeared from sight. Matt stood still for a few moments in silence, staring down the hallway.

I walked up next to him. "Are you okay?"

He looked over at me sadly. "I don't understand why she thought that about me. I'm not like that."

I resisted the urge to laugh. As much as Matt might not want to believe it, that was exactly what he was like. He was literally the prince of the Sikrathian Empire, and this small village was a part of it, poverty included.

"Matt, I think that she has a point," I said, matter of factly. "You grew up in the palace of Ordbridge and have never experienced any sort of financial troubles your entire life. You have to understand that a lot of people are not anywhere near that lucky."

He looked hurt for a moment before sighing and turning back around to go out the door. "Yeah, maybe," he mumbled.

I sighed. He'd need time to process what had happened. He reached down and grabbed the last bag before we finally headed back to Olwyn, who was waiting impatiently with our things.

We finally headed out of the village and my spirits lifted as we left. The supply stop was necessary, but we were such outsiders that we really couldn't relax anywhere we went. Especially after Matt had practically thrown dozens of gold coins all over the place at the bar. Obviously, they didn't get many visitors.

At the very least, the walk was pleasant. We quickly made it into a dense forest that stretched far past our line of sight. The tall trees reached up fifty feet into the air to form the thick canopy above, which blocked most of the sunlight, but I didn't have any trouble seeing in front of me. In fact, the forest seemed very bright and illuminated.

We followed a small path through the forest, but it wasn't well maintained. The forest had grown over it in many places; sometimes entire trees stood directly in our way. I got the feeling that there weren't a lot of people traveling around the area.

We walked for a long time and, like last time, no one made any effort to start a conversation. It was fine with me; I didn't feel like talking right then. I was still thinking about Rowan and what he'd done during the war. Matt used to talk about him all the time but I never paid much attention to the details. It wasn't as if I could ask him at that moment, either. Rowan was standing about ten feet away from us and Matt would know something was up. So, I walked in silence.

After several hours of walking, we came to a large hill. It didn't seem that unusual, since we'd gone up a few hills on our way there, but it was the largest that we'd seen so far. We started making our way up the side of it, and at the top, I thought I saw some sort of sculpture. A huge piece of stone seemed to have been carved into some odd shape, but I could only see the top of it from where I was.

When we made it to the top, I was able to get a better view of what I'd seen from down below. It was, in fact, a sculpture, but it was so incredibly lifelike that I had thought it was real for a second. It appeared to be a huge troll or giant. It must have been almost ten feet tall and at least five feet wide. I'd never seen anything like it before. Its face was carved into a permanent frown, and I thought that I saw a hint of panic in its eyes, as if it was scared and confused to be surrounded by strangers.

Matt immediately ran up to it. "A troll!" he said. "It must have been caught in the sunlight and turned to stone!" Excitement shone on his face. "I've always wanted to see one."

"Wait," I said. "That thing was alive a moment ago?" I took a few steps back.

Matt laughed. "Don't worry, there's nothing to worry about. It's solid stone now. It's not coming back."

I stared at the now stone troll with apprehension. I would not have been surprised if it suddenly came alive and attacked us, but for now it continued to stand there innocently.

"Hey, look!" Matt said. "There's another one over here." He walked past the first troll and pointed to something about twenty feet away that was partially covered in branches and debris. We all crowded around it, and sure enough, it was another stone troll. It almost perfectly resembled the first one, but his hand was raised in front of his face and he brandished a large stone club. It looked as if he'd been in the middle of a battle as he was turned to stone.

"Why would there be two of them?" I asked.

Matt looked around, most likely searching for more trolls. "Oh, they usually live in a small pack of two or three. They can only go out at night, so it's useful for them to have help gathering resources."

We all wandered around for a few minutes looking at the trolls and glancing around at the surrounding trees for anyone trying to sneak up on us. At least, I did.

Eventually, to everyone's surprise, Olwyn suggested that we stop here for an hour or so to eat and rest. I'd assumed that we wouldn't be stopping until night, so I was happy to rest, but I was still uneasy about stopping right next to the trolls. No one else seemed to mind, so I tried to accept it and pulled up a log to sit on.

Olwyn passed around some food from the supply bags. There was a little bread and some dried fruit. Almost like a plum but slightly sourer. Either way, I liked it and happily ate several pieces.

After a while, I started to get the feeling that someone was watching us. Matt, Rowan, and Olwyn didn't seem to be alarmed at all, so I tried to shrug off the feeling.

We sat in a rough circle eating our food and I glanced around; yet again, looking for someone hiding in the trees. Something seemed to move behind Matt, but I wasn't completely sure.

I got up and walked over to the trees. A strong wind blew past, so I couldn't hear any footsteps. All I heard was the rustling of leaves in the wind and pleasant sounds of the tree branches bending.

As I approached the trees, I still didn't see anything wrong. I was about to accept that I was going crazy when a small shape suddenly burst out of some nearby bushes, brandishing a blade. My blood turned to ice, and I couldn't move for a moment. By the time I was ready to run, the cold metal of a knife brushed against my throat.

"Not another move, boy," someone growled behind me. It wasn't whatever had jumped out of the bushes, though, as I could still see him in front of me.

Olwyn, Matt, and Rowan instantly jumped to their feet (Matt, a little bit slower) and drew weapons.

Whatever was holding me laughed and said, "It would be a real shame if I would have to kill your friend, here. I'm sure we can reach a peaceful understanding if everyone would just lower their weapons." He spoke in a high pitched, nasally voice that somehow sounded intimidating.

I finally got a good look at his accomplice, and I was sure he was some sort of goblin. Maybe a kobold or gremlin, but he certainly had the goblin-like way of moving around, shifting from side to side, like if you dropped your guard for one second, he would pounce and take everything you owned. They were trying to rob us, I assumed, so I suppose that made sense.

Olwyn, Matt, and Rowan seemed hesitant to attack as I was being held hostage, but they also didn't want to drop their weapons, so we all just stood in tense silence for a few moments.

The goblin holding me cleared his throat. "Alright, perhaps you need some more convincing," he said, motioning toward the trees opposite of where I was standing. Three more goblins jumped into view, all holding knives.

It was not looking good.

We were outnumbered and I was already incapacitated. Our only hope was some big distraction that we could hopefully use to subdue several of them. I didn't know how good at fighting the goblins were exactly, and I'd never actually seen Olwyn in action, but I was counting on her being able to overpower them. They were about half her height, so it looked promising.

I tried to remember one of the spells that I'd written down. Some sort of shield or invulnerability? I wished I'd memorized all of them. From what I remembered, it was a difficult spell. I had only tried it a few times and it never seemed to actually work as described, but it was my only choice.

"Well?" the lead goblin asked. "Do you choose death for your friend and later yourselves, or do you choose to lose a couple of valuables? Really, the choice is clear, I would say."

I wracked my brain for the right incantation. I closed my eyes and started repeating the words quietly to myself, over and over. Saying them out loud wasn't actually necessary, but sometimes it was easier for me. Invulnerability. Invulnerability. Come on, I could do it. I could hear the goblins advancing closer and closer to Matt, Rowan, and Olwyn. I had to act soon.

Suddenly, I felt an odd sensation all over my body, as if I was covered in some sticky substance that I couldn't wipe off. It almost felt like someone had poured a bucket of honey right over my head. I opened my eyes and looked down at myself, my stomach lurching. Sure enough, I could see a slight glow coming off of my skin. The spell had worked.

As quickly as I could, I shoved my neck into the blade of the knife. The goblin was so surprised that he dropped me and the knife on the ground. "W-wha—" the goblin began before I jumped up holding the knife, and I stabbed it deep into his side.

He howled with pain and stumbled backward onto the ground a few feet away. Everyone froze for a moment, staring at the two of us with wide eyes. No one moved except the lead goblin as he crawled across the ground toward the trees, bleeding everywhere.

"Attack!" yelled the first goblin, and all four of them charged into the group. All I could do was watch as the goblins came closer and closer in what seemed like slow motion, and I found that my feet were rooted in place. There was nothing I could do, except to watch the carnage unfold.

Olwyn jumped over the outstretched arm of one of the advancing goblins. Axes raised, she slashed into him over and over, flinging pieces of flesh all over the battlefield. The goblin could barely raise his knife in a half-hearted effort to put on some sort of defense. Then, with a final swing, she lodged one of her axes deep into his neck. The goblin wavered on his feet for a second or two and then fell over backward, dead.

I could barely take in the amount of brutality as I watched with wide eyes. Another goblin had also rushed toward Olwyn and she was now attempting to fight him off with one axe, as her first was still stuck in the corpse of the other goblin. Matt and Rowan each were fighting off their own enemies, Rowan brandishing his staff, and Matt his sword and shield.

I assumed Rowan wouldn't be very quick on his feet or useful in a fight, another rich and powerful type that didn't do anything himself, but he was holding his own, for now at least. The goblin he was facing kept dashing around him, trying to stab or slash him with his knife, but Rowan wasn't giving him any opportunities. He expertly swung his staff around over his head and slammed it down onto the goblin.

I thought he would go down there, but no, the goblin lurched forward, trying desperately to inflict any damage to his opponent. Rowan easily dodged the attack and, producing a dagger of his own from some unknown location, stabbed the goblin through the heart. He pulled the dagger out and the goblin's body fell lifelessly to the ground.

Meanwhile, Matt was still locked in a vicious battle with his own goblin which may have been the most skilled of our attackers because, as I watched, he deflected Matt's attack with his knife and flicked his blade in such a way that Matt's sword, a blade at least twice the length of the goblin's knife, was thrown from his hand.

I cried out to Matt and stumbled in his direction, somehow hoping to get there quick enough to stop what was going to happen, but it was hopeless. I saw the knife as it was thrusted toward Matt, closer and closer. I closed my eyes.

I heard the sound of contact, but it wasn't metal on flesh. Was that wood? I looked again and saw the blade sticking into Matt's shield. Before anyone could move, however, I heard a deafening crack, like a whip, and saw a flash of light. The goblin was thrown at least thirty feet away from Matt and landed with a sickening crunch on the hard ground.

My heart climbed further up my throat as I stared at Matt. He had fallen to the ground still holding his shield, but he appeared to be perfectly fine. I opened my mouth, tried to speak, and promptly closed it again. What had I just witnessed?

The goblin slowly got to his feet, clutching his left arm close to his body. He had lost his knife somewhere during the trip over there and he now looked harmless. As he watched, Olwyn finished off the other goblin with a quick strike to the face with the blunt side of her axe, and he immediately turned and ran away as fast as he could.

"Hey!" Matt shouted. "Get back here!" He started running after him and Olwyn followed, disappearing into the trees ahead.

I finally started to take in what had just happened. Had I just killed someone? I felt a sinking feeling in my stomach that wouldn't go away.

I looked around the battlefield, but I couldn't see the goblin. Luckily, there was a very handy trail of blood that led into the forest. I started following it and sure enough, I heard some grunts and whimpering a short while later. He couldn't have gotten far as the battle had only lasted a few minutes.

I was scared to look, but I kept going until I could see a figure on the ground, leaning against a tree. The goblin screamed as I came into view. "No! I surrender! Don't hurt me," he wailed. I kneeled down next to him and looked at his wound.

"I won't," I said quietly. "Just rest."

I looked at the gash on his side and barely resisted gasping at the sight of it. I had stabbed him very high up, close to his heart. I was no expert, but it was going to be very hard to recover from a wound like that.

He took a few shaky breaths and stared up at me. "I-I d-don't want t-to die," he stammered weakly. All I could do was stare in horror as the breaths became fainter and fainter and his large, dark green eyes slowly lost their life. He reached out his shaking hand toward me one final time before collapsing to the ground.

He was gone.

His eyes stared at me unblinkingly and he went still.

I hadn't witnessed a death as personally as this since my own mother had died. But this was different. Never before had I willfully taken someone else's life.

11
Stories Told

Joe

I sat on the ground, staring at the body in shock. This was so different from anything that I had experienced before. I barely remembered my mother. Her death had never been like this. So...permanent. Obviously, I missed her but I'd still been young when she died. Sometimes I felt like I didn't remember her well enough to really miss her, and instead I missed the idea of her. You might say that I didn't know the goblin, either, but that didn't stop me from crying.

I felt a hand on my shoulder, and I looked up. Rowan pulled me up with a grunt.

"I know what you're going through," he said quietly. "My first wasn't easy either." He led me back out of the forest toward the clearing and sat me down on one of the logs.

"Look, maybe now we can continue our conversation from earlier. It might help to keep your mind off of..." he paused and looked over at the dead goblins lying on the ground, "everything."

I nodded and he cleared his throat.

"So, I believe all that I told you was how I was a fraud, and I don't know any magic? Well, the story is much more complicated than that. It might help you to understand a little bit more about what the king is doing and why there's a rebellion going on right now." He glanced around, mostly in the direction that Matt and Olwyn had run off in.

"Get ready. I haven't told this story to a single soul, and believe me, I've wanted to quite a few times over the years," he began. "It all started a few years before the Kricoyan War. At least my part in the story starts there. The real plot started thousands of years ago, with the creation of the four artifacts. I don't suppose you've heard of them?"

I shook my head.

"No, I didn't think you had. You see, these artifacts are very powerful and very ancient. Anyone who possesses one has the chance to become all powerful." He paused for dramatic effect.

I almost laughed. It sounded like some sort of fairy tale that you would tell a child, but I was also intrigued.

"Only four were ever made: the sword, the compass, the helm, and the shield. Each one gives its owner a unique power. The compass allows its wearer to become extremely knowledgeable about strategy. You can look at someone and know exactly what they are going to do next. It is almost impossible to outsmart anyone who wields it."

Rowan paused for a moment to glance at me, perhaps ready to answer any questions, but when I said nothing, he continued the story.

"The helm grants its wearer complete invisibility. Anyone who wears it can gain access to even the most secure places as easily as just walking in. The sword gives its user unbeatable skill in combat. No one has ever been beaten in a fight while using the sword. And finally, the shield. The shield is the least talked about artifact, perhaps because it is so rarely seen, but it allows its user to deflect any strike made against them. No substance can pierce the shield." Rowan stopped for a few seconds to let it all sink in.

I had never heard of these "artifacts" before, but Rowan had talked about them without a hint of a smile. He was far from trustworthy, but something about his words rang true.

"The artifacts were created by master sorcerers after the invasion in 1239 from the island of Grumus. Our ancestors couldn't stop the invading orcs and kobolds as they were so vastly outnumbered. The invaders rapidly occupied the continent and we were losing more land by the day. But one sorcerer had an idea. It was possible, with enough power, to create very strong magical artifacts. No one wanted to try it because there was a large chance of something going wrong, and when you're working with that much concentrated magic…" Rowan paused, shaking his head. "Well, most of them thought that they wouldn't survive it. They thought that they wouldn't survive either way, however, the sorcerers agreed to try it. By this time, just about everyone who was left had retreated to a small village named Ordbridge."

I looked up at him. "So, it became the capital," I said. "I take it they succeeded, then?"

Rowan nodded, looking grave. "Yes, they succeeded. Partly, at least. You see, magic is an unstable energy, which is why we use so little of it most of the time. Lights, small spells, teleportation—" he paused, looking off into the distance, "—is truly just scratching the surface. When those sorcerers combined that much magic together, there was no telling what would happen. They got lucky. They managed to create the artifacts with only several of the weaker sorcerers perishing in the process."

What Rowan had said so far seemed bad enough, but I got the feeling that there was much more to come. Why would these ancient artifacts matter to us today?

"At first, our ancestors thought that everything had been solved and they started to use the artifacts against the invaders. The amount of power that someone could wield with one of these artifacts…well, there was nothing that the enemy could do. They were obliterated, quite literally in some cases, in days. For a short while, it did appear to be over, but quickly, it was discovered that the artifacts had other powers. To have that amount of power over others was…" Rowan paused again and sighed, "quite desirable.

"Several soldiers were caught trying to steal a few of them. At first this was dismissed as an unfortunate incident;

tighter security was put in place and the artifacts were brought out as little as possible. However…" he looked up at me dejectedly, "it didn't work. Again, and again people tried to steal the artifacts, and it became too hard to protect them. The war had been won by that point with the help of the artifacts and many people began to question why they were still being used. Items of that much power should surely be locked away somewhere, they argued."

"They just locked them away? Couldn't they have been used for good if the right person got them? They could've helped to balance the power here instead of consolidating it all in Ordbridge." I interjected.

Rowan stopped and shook his head, staring at me with sadness in his eyes. "That is where the problem began. Many people didn't want to get rid of these artifacts that could wield so much power. But some people were afraid of keeping the artifacts around when there was no war or anything that they needed them for, so they tried to take them away. The artifacts had been entrusted to four generals in the remaining army, and let's just say that they didn't exactly hand them over when asked. One thing led to another, and a fight broke out. No one knows who attacked first, but suddenly there was war again. This time, it was over the artifacts. The empire was split into dozens of factions, all warring over who got to control the artifacts. The groups that controlled them ended up inflicting massacres against their enemies, until eventually they collapsed as different members of the group turned on one another for control.

"Several hundred years passed like this with no end in sight. No one survived long enough to control even two of the artifacts at a time. Finally, after years and years of conflict, a new group was formed, determined to put a stop to the destruction. They vowed to seal away the artifacts if they were ever to find them, so that they couldn't be used for evil again."

I swallowed hard, my mind spinning.

"You see, magical items of that amount of power can only be destroyed by something of equal power. But if they were to keep one of the artifacts long enough to acquire a second, then the risk of losing control and turning into exactly what they were trying to stop would be much too high. The only option was to lock them away and hope that people would start to forget about their power.

"At first, they had almost no success at finding any of the artifacts, so they spent most of their time training new recruits to resist the tempting nature of these artifacts, in case they were ever to find one. They reasoned that the first step toward peace would be to train their members in the ways of discipline instead of warfare. And those people, undergoing now ancient traditions, became the first ever Knights of the Kingdom of Sikrath.

"They waited for the right moment to strike against their enemies, in the meantime gathering larger and larger forces and spreading their beliefs and practices across the continent. Eventually, the time came to claim the first artifact. The helm. It was in the possession of a notorious bandit who used it to steal riches beyond measure. No one could stop him while he was wearing it because combined with his experience as a thief the helm gave him the power to practically never be seen again if he so chose."

Rowan was getting more into the story as he talked, becoming much more animated with each sentence, and I found myself also being pulled into this fascinating tale about our history. I even began to forget that Rowan had a point with this whole story and that I was expected to help him in some way after this.

"Knights had been sent out to find the locations of all four artifacts, but it was much easier said than done. Many of the warlords or self-proclaimed 'kings' were extremely paranoid and they didn't exactly broadcast their whereabouts, especially considering that everyone was basically at war.

Dozens of groups fought for control over the continent, even if no official war was declared. It was odd that the helm was the first artifact to be found, considering its invisibility, but perhaps the bandit finally became a little too arrogant, thinking that nobody could even see him, let alone stop him."

Rowan got up and began pacing around the small clearing. "This is the real history of Sikrath, Joe. The first step to becoming the largest empire the world would ever see."

Rowan paused for a second, letting his final words hang around a bit longer, pushing their way into my brain. Obviously, he was getting to the important part very soon, although the whole story seemed to be important. Magical artifacts capable of destroying vast armies and retaking the entire continent in days? That seemed like something that might be important to know about.

Rowan glanced around. "Okay, I won't bore you with the details. The others could be back at any time and I still haven't told you how I fit into this whole mess. Essentially, an ambush was put together to trap the bandit and get the helm away from him. I don't know exactly what happened myself, but they succeeded. From then on, they were one of the most powerful factions in the conflict.

"Now, they ended up containing the helm as well as they could in a temple of sorts with all kinds of traps and whatnot, but there were plenty of people who wanted to use its power to help them get other artifacts. It was discovered that some people had a higher tolerance to the artifact's manipulation, and momentarily they were able to resist the temptation of the artifact, which was an historic turning point because never before had such a large group been able to resist them. It was a decision that would ultimately win them the war and control over the continent. It is possible that they could have controlled the power…but it's so unlikely. Almost no one can resist for a long period of time. Eventually, everyone fails. The more powerful you become, the less power you truly have over yourself.

"The next several years were spent getting more and more powerful—militarily powerful, as well as improving the order of their society. If they were ever going to advance past that horrible point of division in their history, they were going to need something to pull everyone together. And they had just the thing.

"Our ancestors realized that there was something that was missing from so many power-hungry groups and it was something that so many people wanted. A sense of purpose. A feeling that you were a part of something that was doing the right thing. Because of that, knighthood became a sort of religion. More and more people were recruited into it and taught how they should think and act. People were so tired of living in constant fear that they easily bought into it.

That sounded all too familiar to me. Sikrath would come in and take over a community in the guise of helping everyone to find a better purpose, but they always just took whatever they wanted and didn't care who was hurt in the process.

"With the support of the people, Sikrath increased their efforts to find the remaining artifacts. After years of searching, they managed to find both the sword and the shield and put them safely into sealed vaults, underground. The last artifact, however, was very elusive. Nobody claimed to have it or seen someone with it. The compass remained lost, and gradually, people began to forget all about it. Hundreds of years went by and the artifacts began to pass down into myth. Many began to question if they had ever existed at all. Still, the compass remained, waiting for the right moment.

"Finally, we have come to the present day. At least, almost the present. The Kricoyan War. Just saying the name brings shivers down many people's spines. Kricoya and Sikrath had emerged from the destruction of the artifacts, both competing world powers, trying to make up for the disorder by bringing unity to everyone. If you didn't want unity, well, it wasn't really your choice. If you lived here, you were a part of Kricoya or Sikrath.

"It started out like that, but before long, Kricoya began to change, mostly for the better. They became almost entirely peaceful, though they still kept an army for defense, and restricted their influence to this continent. Almost no one knew at the time, but king Balder of Kricoya was in possession of the compass. We don't know exactly how he was affected by it, but it is very curious that under his rule, the kingdom grew more peaceful. Almost always the artifacts make people more aggressive, violent, and power-hungry, but perhaps in this case the compass enlightened him to the greater good.

"The artifacts were safe over the years as the knowledge of their locations had long since been lost. They were supposedly locked up, so that it was almost impossible for anybody to get to them. But as you can probably guess, that didn't really work out too well.

I couldn't help but feel a desire to hold one of these artifacts in my hands as Rowan told his story, but I quickly realized that their power was already influencing me. If just hearing about these artifacts was all it took to want their power, they truly were incredibly dangerous things.

"A young prince stumbled upon the containment vault while he was out in the woods. Perhaps the metal had eroded over time, but somehow, he was able to lift the lid open just enough to get inside and retrieve the sword kept there. At first, he didn't know anything about what the sword was capable of. He hadn't even heard of the artifacts before, but gradually he began to notice odd things about it: He suddenly had incredible skill in a fight and even the best soldiers couldn't match him.

"He grew angrier as he got older, with one task in his mind. He had seen Sikrath's decline in recent years, now that Kricoya was emerging as a trade empire rivaling even Sikrath in power and influence. He wanted to make Sikrath more powerful than it had ever been before. He called in experts of all sorts of different fields, from weaponry, to magic, to railroads. Finally, he heard a story that he had never heard before—one about four magical artifacts of extreme power. You see, not everyone had forgotten about the artifacts, and one only had to find the right people to learn the truth.

"It became his quest to find all four of the artifacts and combine their power to make himself and Sikrath invincible. There was a legend that many people didn't even believe back in ancient times, that if you combined all four artifacts, their powers would turn you into the most powerful being in the world. And he wanted that more than anything.

"He hired thousands of spies to go to every corner of the world to find any news of the artifacts, and not long after, he received word that the compass was in Kricoya. It was all the excuse he needed. He had never had much love for Kricoya in the first place as they were still Sikrath's main trade competitor. This was the perfect opportunity to not only get one of the artifacts, but also to seize control of trade throughout the entire continent. He declared war on Kricoya and invaded. That is the true history of the Kricoyan War," Rowan paused and looked me straight in the eye, "and as I am sure you have realized, that man is the King of Sikrath."

12
Pieces Found

Matt

The goblin was very fast. I almost lost him in the trees but, luckily, he left a small trail of blood on the ground. I ran through the tall trees, peering down at the blood-speckled pine needles and fallen branches every once in a while, to make sure that I was still on his path. The forest was the perfect place to disappear into, but I was confident that the goblin wouldn't be moving very quickly for long after that injury he took.

What had happened back there? All I saw was a flash of light and a loud crack sounded, and the next thing I knew, the goblin was on the ground 30 feet away. I didn't understand it, but I could think about it later. I had a goblin to catch.

I paused for a moment to listen until I heard the rustle of leaves and sticks breaking. I crouched down and slowly crept toward the sound as I scanned the nearby foliage. Finally, I spotted the goblin through the trees. He was in a small clearing with a huge stone wall towering in front of him. He was pounding on the wall, wailing about something in his language. I had no knowledge of the goblin tongue.

I stared at him for a moment, unsure what to do. Had he gone crazy? Maybe he lost too much blood from the fight. I felt a hand on my shoulder, and I whipped around to discover Olwyn standing right beside me. She held a finger to her lips and nodded toward the goblin.

We both crouched down behind a large bush, watching the goblin for another minute or so until, finally, Olwyn had enough, and she stepped out to approach him. I jumped up too, just to give Olwyn some backup, though she probably didn't need any.

If a fight broke out, the goblin would be dead before I'd even have time to pull out my weapon.

"Hey!" Olwyn shouted at the goblin. "What are you doing?"

The goblin jumped back and glanced left and right, looking for any possible escape route. "N-n-nothing," he stammered in his high-pitched voice. "You don't need to hurt Blaadiart. I-I just go. Yes! I go now." He stumbled a few steps away from us, but Olwyn went around to block him.

"Hold it," Olwyn said. "You have some explaining to do. Are we special or do you just go around robbing travelers going through these woods?"

Blaadiart shook his head a few times. "Rob you? No, no, no, it was simple misunderstanding, no harm done. I go now?" He tried to take a few steps around Olwyn, but again, Olwyn stopped him.

"No, I'm afraid not. Do you know who I work for?" Olwyn asked. "The king. Do you really want to go against him?"

Blaadiart just laughed. "King? No. I think not."

"Really?" Olwyn asked, as yet again, Blaadiart tried to walk around her. She stopped him and sighed, glancing over at me with a questioning look. I stared at her in a mix of surprise and confusion. Was she actually asking me for advice about the situation? After a moment, I opened my mouth to say something, but before I could, I heard the sound of a blade being drawn and Blaadiart stepped back from Olwyn, one of her knives clutched in his good hand.

He laughed. "Now I go." He turned to walk away, but before he could make it more than a few steps, Olwyn had her axe out and was swinging it toward his head. I looked away at the last second and heard a sickening thunk, followed by a thud of something heavy hitting the ground.

I looked up again to see Blaadiart lying on the ground, obviously dead, with a large gash on his head. Olwyn sighed again, retrieved her knife, and started cleaning off her axe.

Well, it really was Blaadiart's own fault for trying to run away, I told myself. All we wanted him to do was answer some questions! He didn't have to die; If he'd just listened to us, it wouldn't have happened. I went over to go look at the stone wall that he'd been scrambling against. I found it weird that he'd decided to go there when he was wounded instead of trying to just run away. There must be some secret to the wall.

I walked over and started moving my hands over the stone. I wasn't sure exactly what I was trying to find, but that was what Blaadiart had been doing earlier. I kept at it for a few minutes to no avail. Maybe he was just in shock, and he threw himself into the wall for no reason? That probably made more sense than a hidden cave.

Finally, I reached a little higher and I heard a soft click. I stepped back and looked around, searching for the source of the noise. It was very hard to see, but after a moment or two, I saw what looked like a very small seam in the stone directly in front of me, almost like there was a doorway there. It was right below where I'd seemingly found the button to activate it, but I hadn't seen any sign of it before then. It had just appeared as soon as I hit the button.

I stepped forward and ran my hands over it, trying to pry it open. I spent a few more moments doing that before realizing that lower down there was another crack in the stone that looked suspiciously like a handle. I pulled on it and slowly a huge chunk of stone in the shape of a door swung away from the wall.

I stared at it in amazement. I'd never imagined finding a secret room built into the side of a hill. This was some serious adventure book stuff. I called Olwyn over, maybe partially to make sure that I wasn't just seeing things.

She wandered over and looked at the door through wide eyes. "Hmmm. Interesting," she said. "It looks like it leads farther inside." She glanced at me once before stepping into the doorway and advancing down the tunnel, as if daring me to follow.

I hesitated for a second but quickly went in after her.

The tunnel ran for about 30 feet or so, but there was plenty of room to stand and walk around. I couldn't believe that the goblins were capable of making something like this. First of all, most goblins are only about four feet tall, so they don't usually build large tunnels. Secondly, they aren't exactly well known for their construction skills.

The tunnel stretched down sharply and to the left, forming a winding path. The walls were made of what I thought was limestone, but as the light from the doorway faded, the walls began to glow more and more until the only light in the tunnel was from the small twinkling sources on the walls. As the light dimmed, I grew more and more disoriented. I just stared at Olwyn and took one step at a time. Without her I might've forgotten which way I was supposed to walk. I stumbled forward, hoping that we would find the end soon. Finally, after several minutes of walking, I could see a brighter light in front of us.

We emerged from the tunnel to discover ourselves in an enormous cavern. It looked natural in some places but most of the walls had an artificial look to them, as if someone had spent a long time carving the place out. The walls and ceiling were made up of many different types of rocks and minerals. I was amazed at the variety that I could see in the room. Andesite, granite, basalt, and many others that I would have no hope of identifying. I had only a passing knowledge of rocks and minerals, but even I could tell how incredible the room was.

After wobbling around for a moment or two from the disorienting tunnel (I did, at least), we took a closer look around the room. It appeared to be empty but not abandoned. There were signs that someone had been there very recently, from the fresh footsteps in the mud to the assortment of dust-free equipment scattered around the area. I assumed that this must have been the hideout of the goblins we'd just encountered, but I still didn't think that they had actually made the room or tunnel.

Across the cavern we could see several large tunnels that cut into the stone and wove deeper into the area, no doubt leading to another room.

"What is this place?" I asked Olwyn. She was looking around the room with some suspicion on her face but mostly awe. It felt nice to not be the only one impressed with what I was seeing for once.

"This must have been the cave of those trolls that we saw turned to stone back there. Only an earth troll could have cleared out this room and that tunnel. It would have taken a hundred goblins years to complete this," she said.

Suddenly, I admired the room all the more. An actual Earth Troll cave. I had always imagined seeing an Earth Troll in person, but they were so rare, not to mention dangerous, that I hadn't thought I would actually get to see anything like this in real life. This was exactly why I had decided to come on this adventure; there was too much to see to spend my life sitting in the palace in Ordbridge.

We wandered around the cave, taking it all in. There was so much to look at that I wasn't sure which way to go. Now that we were closer, I could see that the tunnels led much deeper into the cave. Olwyn and I chose the path to the far left and started walking down it. This one was very well lit, compared to the entry tunnel, with small, illuminated lanterns hanging from the ceiling, giving off a bright glimmering light.

We finally emerged from the second tunnel and stepped out into yet another huge room. Dozens of chests and bookshelves lined the walls, overflowing with books and gold.

Luckily, the books were human sized, which wasn't surprising because Earth Trolls could shrink or grow to practically any size they wanted to be, and human-sized books were most likely a lot easier to find.

I ran over to the books and started examining them. Olwyn went to look at the chests. The shelves looked ancient and were covered in layers of dust. I ran my hand down the spine of one leather-bound work only to find my fingers caked in grime. I tried to blow as much dust away as I could, but I couldn't help myself from examining the books. I was too excited to find out what secrets they held. One had been shoved lazily on top of the others, as though the last reader just couldn't bring themselves to put it back in its proper place. I looked at it for a moment before picking it up. A thick layer of dust coated the entire thing. The large book had a fancy dark red leather cover that seemed to invite a certain amount of mystery to what I might find hidden in its pages. I slowly opened it, careful not to damage or rip the old, cracked, yellow paper.

I was pleased to discover that I could still make out the words, which were luckily written in a language that I could understand. *Magic, Artifacts, and the Unknown* was proudly displayed on the title page. Intrigued, I flipped forward, intent on discovering what the book had to offer.

I don't know how long I stood there reading the story, but I couldn't turn away. The book told a fascinating tale about an ancient war between different factions that would one day become Sikrath. I had never heard anything like it before. I had learned about our history, of course, but nothing about this. It described magical artifacts that were created to stop an invasion from the island of Grumus. I wondered if this was a fictional story because I had never heard a single thing about any artifacts.

I read about how one war ended only for another, this time a civil war, to start up, over the artifacts that had just been their saviors. The artifacts caused hundreds of years of chaos before they were eventually locked up.

The book went on to say that they managed to lock up three of the artifacts, although there were doubts that they could truly be contained well enough to keep others from finding them. There were also concerns that the Shield of Protection couldn't actually be stored because it had a unique ability; it couldn't sit still very long before the magic embedded in it began to become unstable. Once every several hundred years or so it was possible for the Shield to teleport itself to someone in need of its protection.

The book said that the shield may be one of the most sought after magical artifacts that has ever been created, and certainly the most powerful one that almost no one knows about. A picture was included of the shield, and it was in fact quite average to look at. It showed a medium-sized, round shield, with a metal covering on the front. I never would have known that it was magical just from looking at it. It probably looked like half of the shields in use today.

In fact, it looked just like my shield.

I glanced over at Olwyn, who was still searching through all of the treasure chests. Mostly, it appeared to be dishes, jewelry, and other objects made of gold, but I saw that there were also quite a few jewels to be found. After I was done with the book, I tucked it into my bag; there was no point in letting it sit there on the shelf, collecting more dust.

I went over next to Olwyn and looked at the overflowing chests. Olwyn had searched through a few of them while I was reading the book, but quickly grew tired of it and started looking around the room for other things that we'd missed. I was surprised that she didn't seem to care at all about the treasure. I didn't even see her take any of it.

Yes, I went for the books first, but eventually, I made my way over to the gold. Who just leaves money on the floor?

I picked up a few jewels and put them into my bag, but as I reached for more, I heard the sounds of something clattering as it fell onto the stone floor. Olwyn quickly drew her axes and crouched down. She moved to the far wall, where another tunnel led deeper into the cave and motioned for me to get down. I tried to crouch down without making a sound, but somehow, I managed to drop just about half of my items onto the floor. I flinched as my equipment and supplies clunked onto the ground, making a few small clanging sounds as they went. I held my breath, unsure if it was loud enough to alert anyone who was in the next room to our presence. One second passed with no visible reaction. Two seconds. Three. I finally allowed myself to breathe a sigh of relief that I hadn't caused us to be discovered. Not yet at least. As quickly as I could without making any sound, I stuffed my things back into my bag and made sure to secure the latch properly.

Olwyn had already moved farther into the new tunnel, and I followed her from about twenty feet behind. We hadn't heard any other sounds from the room as we moved forward.

The new tunnel was much shorter than the last two. After a few moments we made it to another small room, which appeared to be a workshop of sorts. There was large smithing equipment everywhere, as well as piles of metal ore and wood logs. A quick glance around didn't immediately show anyone present, but we couldn't deny that we'd heard a loud noise coming from the room. We crouched down in the corner, behind a crate full of tools.

Finally, a small shape emerged from the shadows, clutching a large box of machinery parts. I saw a few gears and some metal wheels and other various things inside. The figure set the box down on a nearby table, revealing his face.

Another goblin! I was very sick of goblins now, and maybe Olwyn was too, because she immediately jumped out from our hiding spot, brandishing her axes.

"Who are you!?" she asked. "Why are there so many goblins here?"

The goblin jumped back in shock, toppling over several crates that were sitting behind him and sending him to the floor. He slowly got back up to his feet and looked us over. He was more than a foot shorter than me and wore a brown leather tunic with many burn marks dotted across its surface. He wore an expression of surprise and annoyance on his face, as though we had just barged in to interrupt his time off when we clearly should have known better.

"What are you two doing here?" he asked. "How did you get past the others?"

"They're dead," Olwyn said bluntly. "Now tell us why you're here."

If the goblin felt any sadness at the news that all of his companions had been killed, he didn't show it. Instead, he put his hands up and gestured to us in a calming motion. "Alright, alright, I got it," he said. "You don't have to intimidate me or anything. I'll tell you. Even if there's nothing to tell."

I leaned against the far wall and listened to what he had to say. I was in the mood for a good story.

"So, I met those other guys on the road. I'm what you might call a blacksmith; I make weapons and armor and other tools. Perhaps you've heard of me? I'm decently famous, actually. The name's Hezdek," he said, pausing to see our reactions. "Hezdek, the Master of Smithery?"

Olwyn just stared back at him with a bored "get on with it" expression and I looked at him blankly, not so much on purpose, but because I actually had never heard the name Hezdek before.

Hezdek rolled his eyes. "Fine, fine, whatever. Anyway, they were in need of some weapons to do some sort of bandit job or something. I never really knew what they were up to, but they promised to pay me well and I would get some free food and shelter out of it. So, I took it. Who wouldn't have taken it in my position? I mean, come on, it was a good offer," he said with a shrug. "So, I followed them here where they had set up this base out of an old troll cave. I have to say, it's pretty nice. There's plenty of materials here and a lot of tools as well. Pretty much my dream workshop."

Olwyn glanced around the cave. "So, that's it? You're really just an overrated weaponsmith working for those thugs?"

Hezdek cleared his throat. "Well, I don't know if I would say—"

"Whatever," Olwyn said. "Let's get out of here before we find even more goblins." She motioned for me to follow her.

"Wait!" Hezdek called out. "Maybe I could possibly..." he hesitated and gave us a small smile, "join you kind people wherever you're headed? If my employers are truly dead, then there really isn't much point in my staying here, now is there?"

"No way," Olwyn replied, motioning again for me to follow. "Come on, let's go."

"Wait! Surely you're in need of something. New weapons perhaps? Maybe you have always wanted to try something new. Well, if I join you, I can make anything that you desire..." he paused for a moment and considered. "With the proper tools, obviously," he conceded.

Olwyn opened her mouth to say no again, but I jumped in. If he could really make anything, then he could be a real asset when we got to the front lines.

"Olwyn, maybe we should let him come with us," I said. "We might need his help later on, and if we're behind enemy lines, then we most likely won't be able to get aid anywhere else."

Olwyn just sighed and shook her head. "Fine. You can walk with us for a while if it'll get you to shut up, but the second we make it to some scrap of civilization, you're out. Alright?"

Hezdek smiled. "Perfect. I wouldn't ask for anything else. But you never know how you'll feel later. I can be quite charismatic," he said. Olwyn just glared at him.

"Okay, okay. Just give me one second to grab my tools." Hezdek went into a back room, and we heard some clanks and thuds.

Finally, he emerged with an enormous bag that I was honestly shocked he could carry by himself and nodded to us.

As Olwyn hurried us out of the tunnel, I almost wanted to ask if we could explore a bit more, but I was also scared we'd find another group of killer goblins if we went in any deeper, so I walked briskly behind Olwyn and Hezdek down the tunnel and back into the sunlight.

13

A Hero? What Hero?

Joe

How was it possible that I'd never heard the story before? Four incredibly powerful artifacts that shaped our world and are still in use today and I had no idea. It seemed impossible, and yet...I had no doubt that Rowan was telling the truth. Whatever he was afraid of, it was a very real threat.

"Alright, there are dangerous magical artifacts lying around the world and that does seem like a problem, but where do you fit in?" I asked Rowan.

He sighed and gazed off into the trees. "Well, it's a long story, but you do need to hear it. It's about time I told someone. So, it all began, well..." he paused for a moment, considering. "I suppose it began at my birth. My family was not wealthy at all. In fact, we were quite poor and living in a very small cottage on the edge of Ordbridge, trying to get by as best we could. As a child, my parents struggled to give me anything that I wanted. I think they wanted me to live in the illusion of a satisfied life as long as possible, but I began to realize something was wrong when I was around ten years old.

"My parents would always get home late, and they were exhausted. I realized that a lot of my classmates lived in much nicer houses and had much nicer things. There really wasn't much I could do about it at that time, though, so I tried to accept it as well as I could, but it was hard. By the time war came to Sikrath, I was nineteen and was working at a small farm near our house. Looking back," Rowan paused and shook his head sadly, "I realize that it was a great job. But I wanted more. I wanted to see the world and bring glory to my family.

"So, when the posters went up, advertising a way to do just that, I was very interested. That 'way' was enlisting. Fight for the king and gain treasure and glory. It sounded amazing, and I joined up. It sounded amazing to a lot of other young people too, apparently, because the army doubled overnight. Thousands of people from the colonies were shipped over as well. They didn't exactly have much of a choice.

"I was barely given any training before I was sent off to the front lines. At that point, I was still excited to start fighting. I thought that I would go out and earn a lot of respect from everyone and then head home after a month or so."

Rowan sighed and looked at me with remorse. "I wish I could talk to that naive boy now and tell him what a mistake he was making but—" he hesitated for a moment, looking off into the distance, "—it's far too late."

Rowan's tale already reminded me of my own upbringing back on Esha. Maybe the two of us had more in common than I had thought. I often thought about what I would say to my younger self, but I knew I could never say enough to prepare myself for what was coming.

"At first, there wasn't a lot of action and I barely got to even use my weapons, but I would be using them soon enough. We started pushing forward, deep into Kricoyan territory. We walked at least ten miles a day as the Kricoyan army retreated farther and farther into their country. The farms and villages that we passed were usually abandoned and burning so that their supplies wouldn't fall into enemy hands, but we were forced to take any other supplies that we could find from the civilians.

"Soon, I got my first taste of combat when a group of cavalry charged us a few days after I got to the front lines. It was nothing like what we were told it would be. I was frozen with fear, barely able to lift my sword. Somehow, I survived the first wave and threw myself behind a nearby tree. I told myself that I had to stand up and help the other soldiers, but I just couldn't do it. I couldn't make myself approach the fighting or even look at the carnage that was being inflicted on my fellow soldiers.

"The battle lasted for over an hour and the entire time I sat there behind that tree, with my eyes shut as hard as possible. I clutched my sword to my chest, praying that I would get away soon. It was all I could do."

"It was at that point that I realized what a mistake I'd made. I had a good job and a comfortable life and I gave it all up for a chance at glory. Well, I decided that I had to get back to Ordbridge as quickly as possible."

Rowan looked at me ruefully.

"This was easier said than done, however. You didn't just pack up and head home. There were three ways of getting out, but none of them were exactly promising.

"If I was injured during battle, then I could be sent back home, but I would only be sent back if the injury was bad enough, and I didn't love the idea of getting a serious injury.

"Another option was to become famous for doing something amazing and courageous or saving a bunch of people. They might send me home and use me for some sort of propaganda campaign. If I was lucky." Rowan stayed silent for a moment, tapping his foot nervously. I waited, unsure for a second if he was going to continue.

"This left one more option," he said after another moment. "Deserting. I was not happy about this option for several reasons. For one, if I was caught, then I would be killed. Another thing was that it wasn't exactly easy to desert. Suddenly, I would be running from two different armies instead of one, and if I returned to Ordbridge I would be endangering my entire family with my presence.

"It was my best option, however, so I started preparing everything for when I would leave. I gathered extra food and supplies, tried to remain as anonymous as possible, so that no one would miss me, and tried to mentally prepare myself for the journey that I was about to start.

"I think it all would've worked if I had just left one night earlier..." Rowan paused and sighed as he stared off into the distance and relived his story.

My plan was about to fall into place. One more night and I would be out of the camp. But the king just happened to visit our battalion that night. And, of course, I seemed to make a certain impression on him.

I was emptying the latrines, as I'd been told to do. I saw three large shapes creep out of the shadows, moving quickly forward. Immediately, I jumped back and pulled out my sword. I didn't feel the same fear I felt before. I knew in that moment I had to fight or die.

One of the figures swung a sword forward but I barely jumped out of the way and his swing went wide. Taking advantage of his temporary vulnerability, I swung my sword down hard onto his arm and he fell to the ground, screaming and holding his now bleeding forearm. Then, I kicked him backward, to the ground.

The other two were smarter about it and they attacked me at the same time. At the last second, I dodged out of the way, barely missing one of their blades. Without thinking, I attacked while they were still bringing their swords back up to defend themselves. I threw my blade into one of them, barely managing to stay standing as he cried out and fell to the ground. His companion swung at me, but I lurched to the side with my blade, pulling the soldier I had just killed in front of me to block his swing.

He swung at me wildly in desperation, realizing that his advantage against me had greatly diminished, but I deflected it and swung back at him. We went back and forth for a few moments until he lost his grip on his sword. With one final swing, I twisted it out of his hands, and it fell to the ground.

We both froze for a moment before he turned and sprinted away from me as fast as he could. Before I could start after him, an arrow whizzed right by my shoulder and slammed into him, throwing him to the ground. I spun around quickly to see what new enemy I would have to face, but discovered a small group of Sikrathian soldiers standing about twenty feet away from me, watching.

I stood there, trying to catch my breath, and looking around to make sure that no one else was coming. The sound of slow clapping came to my ears, and I looked back at the group of soldiers. On closer examination there was a man in the middle of the group with his arms outstretched, clapping slowly, and nodding at me.

Wait. Was that man…no. Surely, he couldn't be—

"Great performance, soldier! You've made your king proud," the man said.

I kneeled. "Um…yes. Thank you, sire."

He looked at me thoughtfully for a second. Finally, he nodded. "I've decided that you're perfect material for the King's Guard. What do you think of that?"

I looked around at the now large crowd, watching the king, and I realized that there was no way that I could refuse him. My plan had just been ruined because I had done the exact opposite of not getting noticed.

"Thank you, sire. It would be an honor," I replied reluctantly.

"Excellent," he said. "Report to my tent tomorrow morning for your new orders. Now, somebody sweep the area! There better not be any more of these gnats sneaking up on us tonight."

He then walked off, followed by most of the crowd. I knew that I was going to have to stay a soldier for a while longer.

I went to bed knowing that I wouldn't be able to leave, so I slept until morning, dreading my new duties as a king's guard. I woke up the next morning and went to find the king's tent. I found it very easily as it was the only tent that was four times the size of all the others and had its own contingent of guards surrounding it.

The king looked up as I walked through the tent flaps. He was pouring over some maps or papers that had been placed on a large desk in the corner of the room and there was no one else with him. Although there were thirty guards outside, I was surprised to find myself alone in the tent with the King. Was he not concerned about his safety with me at all? He had just watched me fight off three attackers the night before. There was a large sword on the table next to him, though I had never seen him in combat. He was putting a lot of trust in the fact that I wouldn't attack him.

I was very intrigued with his sword as I had never seen anything quite like it before. It must have been at least three feet long and was made from the darkest metal that I had ever seen. The blade was practically black. There were also engravings all along the length of the blade in a language that I couldn't understand.

"Ah. Finally decided to show up, I see?" the king asked. "If you want to join my elite guards, you're going to have to do better than that."

I almost blurted out that I didn't, in any way, want to join his stupid elite team, but I held myself back. A comment like that would have sent me to the execution block so fast that I wouldn't have been surprised if the king just pulled out his sword and impaled me right then and there.

"My apologies, sire," I said. "I will make sure to do better next time."

He looked me over again and raised an eyebrow. "I liked what I saw yesterday. Don't make me regret it."

He handed me a new uniform and told me to go report to the man in front of the tent. I went outside and was shown to my new post right outside of the tent, watching for any hint of trouble.

My dreams of leaving the army soon diminished and I started to wonder if I would ever make it home. It certainly didn't seem like I could leave then, and the longer I stayed working for the king, the harder it would be to leave later.

Though the new job had many disadvantages I had to admit there were a few perks. I had to stand in place for hours with nothing happening, though I almost never had to fight in battles. Against any actual enemies, that is. Part of our guard duties included hours of sparring with each other to improve our skills. We had to be the best of the best if we wanted to protect the king. We were also first in line for meals, as we were so much more important than the common soldier. To some people, at least.

My new routine was drastically interrupted one night when I was on guard duty. A few wizards came to see the king in his tent. I was on duty for the front entrance, so it was my job to let them in. I had seen them before as they were a key part in the king's war efforts and had to discuss things every once and a while. There weren't any problems with their identification, so I let them in.

A lot of times I didn't hear anything that was very interesting or valuable on my guard duty, but occasionally I would hear some piece of gossip that I might or might not pass on to the other guards. That night I heard some very dangerous information.

"We know they have it," one voice faintly said. "If we could just get to the city, it would be ours."

"With two of them no one would be able to do anything to us!" another voice declared.

They were talking about the artifacts. I had never heard anything about them before, and at first, I thought that they must have been talking about some sort of story, but it became clear that, at the very least, they themselves completely believed in their existence.

So, I decided, perhaps against my better judgement, that I had to search the king's tent for information about them. I was curious and nothing can stop me when I want to figure something out.

After being a guard for a month or two, I knew the king's schedule very well. And, unfortunately, the only time that he left the tent for very long, besides during a battle, was during dinner. He liked to wander around the tables, occasionally rallying the soldiers or picking on them for his own amusement. It all depended on his mood.

The longest that he was gone at one time was around ten minutes. It was in no way ideal, but I felt that I had to know. One night when I was sure that he was gone, I snuck in and searched the entire tent. I went through the papers all over his desk, but those turned out to not be very interesting at all. I searched his desk more and after a minute or two, I found a very old book that talked about the artifacts. It went into quite a bit of detail, but I didn't have time to read much of it. Eventually, years later, I was able to finish that volume, but at the time, I had a bare understanding of the artifacts. I had learned enough, though, to be extremely concerned about the king finding any of them.

I stayed as long as I dared and then quickly put everything back and headed for the exit. As soon as I was a foot away from it, the flap flung open and the king strolled inside. We both froze, staring at each other for several long seconds. Finally, the king spluttered at me: "What the hell are you doing here!?"

I just stood there, my mouth opening and closing for several seconds.

"Well, spit it out!" the king cried.

"I-I...I'm sorry, sire" I mumbled. "I just wanted...um...to ask you something."

The king looked at me quizzically. My mind was racing and I thought everything was over. He would know that I had listened to his meetings; There was no way that I was getting out of the tent alive, so I just said that first thing that came to mind.

"I could do better than your generals! If that's the kind of leadership that we have, I'm surprised that we even made it this far in the war!" I said.

The king stood there, speechless, probably for the first time in his life. Finally, I heard a small chuckle, and then a laugh, and eventually, the king was roaring with laughter in front of me.

"You could do better, eh?" he said.

I held my breath. This was where I died.

"Fine." the king said. "Come join us tomorrow for a meeting. Let's see just how much better you can do. Now, get out of here!"

I was momentarily shocked, but I wasted no time in rushing for the exit. "Oh, and one more thing," I heard right as I was about to leave. "If you turn out to not be better..." he paused and smirked at me, "Well, I'm sure we can find another use for you elsewhere."

I left the tent with a feeling of worry, amazement, and fear. The king's threat left no doubt in my mind that I had to put everything into my job now. My life depended on it.

But by the time I had made it back to my own tent, I had decided that I just couldn't let a man like the king have access to those artifacts. The amount of destruction that he would cause...well, I wouldn't exactly consider myself a good person, but I wasn't willing to let him destroy the entire world.

The next day I reported to the king, determined to prove that I was better than all of his generals. You see, I had the soldier's perspective, which could be very valuable when trying to find the right strategy. His generals were assembled in the tent, all watching as I walked in. I could see the scorn on their faces as they looked at me. I doubted they would have accepted anyone that wasn't high born.

"Ah, there you are, soldier," the king said as I walked through the tent flaps. "We've been waiting for you."

The generals were extremely hesitant to listen to me, but the king made them. It shows a lot about him that he was willing to risk losing the war, just to see if he got to execute me.

"Well," I began, my hands shaking slightly as I looked around the room at the eyes on me. "For one thing we need better synchronization between our units. We'll be in a battle, and it'll take an hour for reinforcements to get to a certain area if they're needed. And we need to improve troop morale. If we don't think of ourselves as one force, how can we be united against our enemies?"

The general's glares seemed to deepen the more I talked. By the time I was done I tried to ignore them and instead looked at the king. He sat on his throne and nodded once to me. His eyes scanned me with interest, before nodding again.

"Alright. You may have been right after all. It remains to be seen," he said with a small wave of his hand toward the entrance to the tent. I saluted and turned to walk out.

I didn't know what to think of his reaction, but I soon saw the changes I had suggested all over the camp. I waited for the king to come back and tell me how I had led him astray, but instead we started winning. Every single battle. We won over and over and over. I hadn't realized at the time, but we had almost stopped our advancement before I came along. With my strategies, however, we were back to advancing miles every day. Soon, I was one of the king's most trusted advisors. Still, there was always a gap between us, since I was from a poor family, and he was royalty.

Before long, he grew even more cocky, if you can believe it, and started his most ambitious plan yet. The next meeting, he couldn't help himself from grinning as he told us about it, sure that it would be the key to ending the war. He laid out the plan which involved an entire circle of sorcerers to harness the power of his 'magical relic' as he put it with a quick glance at me. The power from the artifacts would generate enough energy to wipe out an entire army. We all agreed to the plan, though it was unlikely that the king would listen to any of us if we had disagreed anyway.

For the entire war, I hadn't been considering why all of this was happening. We invaded Kricoya. What had they done to deserve this? It was so easy to detach yourself from reality and simply think of them as enemies to be stopped. But did they deserve what was about to happen?

I couldn't let him do that to them. I just couldn't let that happen. For all of Kricoya to be sacrificed to satisfy the king's desire for more power was something that was just too hard to swallow.

The spell started the next day when we came to the outskirts of Kricoya's main camp that housed almost the entirety of what was left of their army. The circle assembled on a tall hill overlooking the camp so that there was a clear view of our target.

I still hadn't made up my mind about what I would do as I watched the king walk up the hill to observe the set up. He wore a smirk on his face; one of pure pride and contempt. He was sure that he couldn't be stopped by anything anymore. In his eyes, he had already won. At that moment I knew what I had to do. If for nothing else but to wipe that stupid smirk off his face, I knew that I had to somehow stop the circle.

When the time came to start the spell, most of the viewing audience, which consisted of the king and a few other members of royalty, moved away from the circle to another part of the hill that overlooked the enemy camp, so that they wouldn't be hit with any stray magic that leapt out from the artifact.

When the sorcerers got into position, I waited close by, concealed in a small bush, ready to act at the right moment. The entire circle began their chant, the string of words foreign to me, though I could surmise what it was that they were talking about. The king's sword had been placed in the center of the circle, and as I watched, small, blue, magic particles were slowly pulled away from it into the sorcerers. All of them had their eyes closed and were fully concentrating on their task. It was my chance.

I readied myself as I felt the hum of magic slowly grow louder and louder until it was a dull roar. I leapt out from my hiding spot and ran into the circle of magic, which flowed over me with warmth, though not any kind of warmth that I was used to. The heat seemed to flow up from inside myself, as though I was using my own lifeforce to provide heat; if I had stayed in the circle for very long, no doubt I would have been fully consumed by the magic.

I looked around the circle at the assembled sorcerers. As I watched, all of the magic that they had been collecting was beginning to feed into one sorcerer at the front of the circle. If I could stop him, then maybe the spell would be broken. I ran at him and fully tackled him to the ground as quickly as I could. He had no idea that I was coming and he fell to the floor easily. By then, the magic had distorted the air so much that I could hardly see what was happening ten feet in front of me.

At first I thought that I had succeeded. I had the sorcerer on the ground. He lay there unmoving, but the magic wasn't retreating. It kept flowing through both of us now, growing stronger and stronger as each second passed.

For a moment it stopped growing before it started to pour out from me. I tried to stop it but I had absolutely no idea what I was doing; I had no wizard training. The magic pulsed through me, and I was stuck, frozen in place, forced to watch as the energy fell to the ground and lit up the world in a bright pink light. After what felt like days, the other sorcerers pulled me to my feet, and I got a good look at the sorcerer that I had tackled. He was dead. Since I had knocked him unconscious, he couldn't protect himself from the powerful magic. I looked around at the now broken circle. Out of the original group of 15 sorcerers, 11 had died from the strain of trying to shape and contain the gigantic amount of energy. I myself could barely stand as they hauled me to my feet.

"I saw him collapse," I spluttered as I gestured toward the wizard on the ground that I had tackled. "I ran in to try and help him…but he was already gone when I got here."

The surrounding sorcerers patted me on the back and led me over to a small group of logs lying beside us and sat down.

"No one without potent magical abilities could have survived that amount of magic," one of them said, his eyes wide as he looked at me. "You must be a wizard."

I was too stunned to even think of another response. I had just killed hundreds of people in only a few seconds. What else was there to think about? I had just done exactly what I was trying to stop.

The rumor quickly spread like wildfire through the ranks, and soon I was known as the wizard who had saved the day and destroyed our enemies. I turned into a hero, just like I had always wanted so long ago.

The king suspected that I had tried to stop the spell, though. I could see it on his face. He no longer trusted me when we talked, and he began to have guards with him whenever I was around. Maybe he wanted to kill me, but I was a hero now. It would have been so stupidly complicated, even for him.

So, he let me go. I got to be a hero. It was all so strange. I had always wanted to be known for doing something amazing, but...just not that. I was finally able to get home months later, only to discover that in my absence...my entire family had died in a raid. They were common, but never so close to the capital. I knew exactly who had done it.

I could see Rowan's eyes come back into focus and he looked back down at me. "I went to the king again and told him what I had heard that day in his tent. That I knew what he was searching for. That I knew exactly what he wanted most and that he would never get it. I should have known that I wouldn't last long after that." Rowan finally turned to me. "And that, Joe, is why I need your help."

14

Questions Unanswered

Matt

We finally made it out of the cave after what felt like hours. The dead goblin still lay on the ground near the stone wall, covered in blood. We started walking back toward camp with Hezdek trailing behind us. So far, he hadn't said much, but I got the feeling that would change the more we got to know him. He certainly didn't hesitate to tell us his story back in the cave, after all. The three of us walked through the dense forest, going back over the path that Olwyn and I had made trying to find the other goblin. Luckily, there didn't appear to be any other bandits trying to kill us—at least, not at the moment.

After tromping through the thick foliage on the forest floor, we finally got back to our temporary camp. I assumed that Joe and Rowan would have just packed up all the stuff and stood next to each other awkwardly until we got back, but no. They were sitting down on some logs and talking. I frowned, confused. I didn't think that Joe liked Rowan at all.

"Um, hey," I said. "You ready to go?"

Joe jumped as if startled and he shifted away from Rowan. "Yes! Definitely ready," he said, and stood up to grab his pack.

"Yes, I suppose we should leave," Rowan said, standing up alongside Joe.

I looked back and forth between Rowan and Joe. Rowan wouldn't meet my eyes, and Joe's brow was furrowed.

"You okay?" I asked him, once Rowan had wandered off.

"Yeah," he said in a higher-pitched voice than usual. "Why wouldn't I be?"

"Um...okay. Well, what were you and Rowan talking about?"

"Oh, nothing really. We were just..." Joe paused for a moment and glanced over at Rowan. "Thinking about the future. Y'know, the future of the mission. Some serious strategy talk," Joe said, staring at the ground.

I blinked. What would Joe tell Rowan and not me? I couldn't think of anything that they might even have in common, let alone want to talk about. Well, maybe I was just imagining it. It wasn't like Joe and Rowan were constantly talking. It was probably nothing to worry about.

"Um..." Joe said, taking a step backward. "Who's that?" he asked, pointing to Hezdek.

"Oh, that's Hezdek," I responded. "We found a secret goblin hideout and he was there. He said he could make us new weapons and stuff and that he never really agreed with the bandits robbing people, so he's going to come with us."

Joe frowned and hesitated before nodding slowly to Hezdek. I could understand a little apprehension but no doubt they would be great friends after a while. We all grabbed the rest of our stuff and continued the same way that we'd been marching for hours. I opened my mouth to complain about the constant walking, but I stopped myself; Olwyn probably wouldn't appreciate hearing my thoughts on the matter. We were in the middle of a forest, traveling toward the nearest civilization. There wasn't much else that could be done.

After a couple of hours of marching, I was ready to stop, but none of the others seemed to feel the same way. Even Rowan, who'd had trouble before, seemed determined to keep up with the others, almost like he was trying to prove something. So, we kept on.

Eventually, we stopped for a small break in a clearing with a few logs arranged in a manner that suggested they had once been used as seats, surrounding a fire or small camp.

There was enough room for at least ten people on them, so we all set our stuff down and took a seat.

Olwyn handed out a few apples and some sort of dried meat.

"Um…" I said, frowning and glancing around at the others. "Is there anything else?"

Olwyn raised an eyebrow. "Such as?"

"Oh, never mind," I said, reluctantly biting into my apple. They just couldn't understand what this was like for me. I was used to having any food that I could possibly imagine at my disposal. And it would be ready in minutes. To go from that to this, was just…hard to swallow.

"We're getting close to the frontlines now," Olwyn said. "We should get there in a few hours."

I nodded. After the train crash Olwyn told me that once we got to the front lines, that would be the end of our adventure. For me, at least. Perhaps she had forgotten? It didn't seem likely.

"Look, you two haven't been to war," Olwyn said, looking at Joe and me. "You might not know what to expect and—" she looked off into the distance, frowning and shaking her head. "Well, I just wish that when I first became a knight that I had someone who could tell me what had to be done, how to do it, and…what to expect." She fidgeted slightly as she spoke and wouldn't meet our eyes.

"I grew up on a huge farm near Ordbridge; life was good. And then my parents decided that I was getting a little too close with our servants and shipped me off to Ordbridge to train as a knight. They said I needed a lesson on loyalty."

"I just thought that…maybe…I could teach you a few things that I've learned since then. Because it wasn't really that great for me. I mean, just so that you're not a danger to us, of course."

I stared at her in amazement. Was Olwyn actually offering to mentor and teach us the knowledge that she'd gathered over her years as a soldier? For a second I thought that it must have been a joke. Olwyn had been saying how annoyed she was with us for the entire trip.

"Sure, Olwyn, that'd be nice," I said. She nodded back, still averting her eyes.

We all finished our food before packing up our supplies again. Before we left, I took one final look at the clearing. It could be the last time I'd be sitting around with the others on this quest. The thought saddened me, and a flicker of anger flared up inside my chest. Who were they to tell me that I couldn't go with them? My father would be angry if something happened to me, yes. But it should still be my decision.

Once we left the clearing, I was able to walk with Joe a little way behind the others for a while. After a few moments of silence, I glanced over at him questioningly. I would try to move past what had happened earlier with Rowan.

"So, what happened with you and that girl at the village?" Joe asked with a smirk on his face. "It looked like you were trying to get to know her a little bit better for a second there."

I sighed. "Yeah, I did try to, though I failed miserably," I said with a frown. "I still have no idea what she was talking about."

Joe's smile slowly faded as he turned to look over at me. "Matt. You are a literal prince. You haven't had to worry about money in your entire life and you can't understand the people who have. That girl and her family back there have probably been barely managing to stay afloat their whole lives, working in that tiny village." He paused for a moment and looked down at the ground, deep in thought. "I don't blame her at all for what she said," he said quietly.

I let his words sink in. No doubt there was some truth to them, but I couldn't help but feel the girl overreacted earlier. I'm sure she had a hard life, but there was no reason to take it out on me. I mean, what had I ever done to her?

"So, what's going on with you and Benjamin?" I asked, partly to change the subject and partly because I was actually curious about it.

Joe stayed quiet for a while, staring straight ahead at the path, but I waited for his response; I could tell that he was simply thinking about how to respond, not just ignoring me.

Joe sighed. "Well, it's actually going pretty well, if you must know," he said with a small smile on his face.

I couldn't help but grin as I saw his shy, embarrassed smile. "Well, I can't say that I understand how exactly you came to meet Benjamin Holverk, but as long as you're happy, I guess it's good."

"I'll tell you about that another time. It's quite a story actually. I'm sure you'll enjoy all the twists and turns," Joe said, amused.

We fell silent for a few moments, continuing down the path. "You know you could have told me earlier, right?" I asked gently. "I don't have a problem with a janitor dating a nobleman. Well, as long as he treats you alright, I suppose."

"I know, Matt," Joe said, a slight smile on his lips.

The rest of the journey passed by very quickly for me. One moment we were walking through the forest, and the next, the trees started to get smaller and more spread out and I could hear people in the distance. Eventually, we could actually see a few soldiers wandering around, carrying weapons or supplies, or just leaning against some barricade, laughing and talking amongst themselves.

A few of them looked at us strangely, but most of them paid us no mind as we passed. On the surface, the army looked to be in high spirits and quite prepared for what was coming, but if you looked closer, you could see the fear and exhaustion on everyone's faces. They didn't think that they would live through the next battle.

I was so absorbed with taking in all of the different aspects of the camp that I wasn't even paying attention to where Olwyn was leading us. There was just so much to look at that I didn't know where to start.

Soldiers were digging out some small trenches toward the front of the camp for the incoming threat. Others were moving large crates full of weapons and supplies forward. There were even several soldiers playing a few instruments near the center of camp.

Olwyn led us directly through the camp and toward a large tent near the middle. When we got there, she told us to wait outside and then she disappeared behind the flaps. I assumed that she was talking to the commander or someone in charge of the troops, so that we could get safe passage across the front lines. At least, on our side.

A few soldiers passed us, but most were busy with whatever task that they'd been assigned. Everyone we saw was coated in mud. The entire camp, in fact, was covered with it. After a short wait, Olwyn emerged with a uniformed soldier beside her.

"Yes, yes, just go south for around three miles and you should come to a spot that you can cross," she said.

Olwyn nodded and thanked her and motioned for us to follow her again. "Okay, I just spoke with the commander and she said that the enemy is very close to the north and east, but if we traveled south for a while, we might be able to cut east, through their lines," she said. "Their trench line goes for about a mile one to the east, so we should have good cover for some of the trip."

I didn't love the idea of walking through a trench for a mile, but it also meant that I'd get to continue the adventure for a while. I pictured myself boarding the train again and arriving back in Ordbridge. My father would probably restrict everything I could do even further. I would be stuck in my room forever. And I knew this would just prove him right; he would never involve me in anything.

The road that we would most likely have taken back to the capital was directly to the east of where we were, which was in enemy hands. I was just lucky that Olwyn didn't seem to care that much about me getting home. She seemed much more focused on the mission, which was exactly what I wanted. As long as I didn't bring it up, maybe I could stay with the others. We headed for the first opening in the trench line, which was a couple hundred feet away. It was so interesting being a part of an army camp. Everything from the smell of fresh stew cooking to the sounds of soldiers chatting to one another as they carried supplies or shored up defenses was a new experience for me. As we finally made it to the trench, I thought I saw some dust rising in the distance to the east, but I couldn't really make out anything; it was much too far away to see anything.

The trench itself was disgusting. There was mud everywhere and none of us could take a step without stepping in it. It was deep in some spots too.

"Come on," Olwyn said. "Just a few miles this way."

The entrance to the trench was wide enough to easily fit all of us, even if we wanted to walk side by side, but as we got further into the trench it got very tight.

There was barely enough room for us to move forward when soldiers were going by in the opposite direction. The number of troops we passed varied considerably. At some points, there were as many as twenty or thirty soldiers right next to us, struggling to get by, and at other times, I couldn't see a single person even walking toward us. The worst part was the smell. It was overpowering. The second we walked into the trench it hit me. It smelled like hundreds of animals had died and they decided to just bury them right below the mud. I knew it probably wasn't animals that they had buried but I didn't want to think too much about what that implied for us and everyone around us.

Death quite literally hung in the air as we walked.

Soon, I noticed that Hezdek was looking a little nervous. He'd been almost silent the entire time that we had walked through the camp, which made me think that he must have had some bad experience with soldiers. I was about to ask him about it when Joe interjected.

"Do you guys hear that rumbling sound?"

I paused for a second and listened. It was very faint, but now that Joe brought it up, there definitely was a vague rumbling off in the distance. It sounded like it was getting closer. I looked around us as if I thought that whatever was big enough to make the rumbling sound would also fit inside the trench.

Olwyn's eyes widened and she opened her mouth. Before she could say anything, though, a very loud alarm bell started to ring and there were several shouts from all over the camp.

"ARCHERS! GET INTO POSITION!" we heard the commander Olwyn had spoken to earlier shout from behind us. "Fire the artillery now! Hit them with everything we have! Fire at will!"

BOOM! BOOM! BOOM!

The cannons above us fired again and again, shooting at whatever unseen enemy we were about to face.

I was momentarily frozen. All the sounds around me evaporated and I stood there in silence, watching Olwyn yelling something at us. What was she saying? All I could do was try to read her lips.

We...dangerous...charge. We have to go?

Suddenly my hearing flooded back to me, and everything was returned to normal. Well, as normal as it could be at the moment.

"Hurry!" Olwyn shouted to us. "The enemy is coming! We have to get away from the front lines as fast as possible!" She started running down the trench line at a decent pace, though almost immediately she had to wait for all of us to catch up.

Soldiers around us scrambled around frantically, reaching for their weapons and grouping together along sections of the trench line.

Why was the enemy attacking right then? Couldn't they have waited just a few hours until we had left? I was dimly aware that I was most likely about to be in combat, but I was in no way ready for it. I had absolutely no idea how I had survived the last battle we were in. Somehow the goblin was thrown back after he jumped at me, but I still wasn't sure what had actually happened.

I could hear the squelch of the mud underneath my feet, threatening to burst through my expensive leather loafers. As we ran down the trench line soldiers rushed past us or jumped down from the camp to fortify different places. The rumbling had gotten much louder by then. I almost wanted to peek over the top of the trench wall, but I was afraid of what exactly I would see if I did. I hesitated, but at that moment, an arrow whizzed through the air and pierced the far wall, right next to me. Then, another, and another, and suddenly arrows were raining from the sky, dropping everywhere.

"TAKE COVER!" Olwyn shouted.

I dropped down into the mud and curled up into as tight a ball as I could, but I could still feel the arrows thudding into the ground, some just inches away from me.

The barrage must have lasted at least a full minute, but eventually it came to an end, and we could finally stand up again. Luckily, none of us were hit, but I could see that the ground was covered in arrows. There must have been hundreds and hundreds of them just in the small section of the trenches that we were in. I turned to look at the others.

Joe looked about as scared as I felt, which is to say terrified. Hezdek and Rowan were both wide-eyed and pale, and Olwyn had her usual calm expression, but I could see a hint of panic on her features.

The rumbling was now deafening and getting louder every second. Olwyn took off running again with the rest of us trailing behind her as close as possible. I risked a quick look over the side of the trench, and what I saw took my breath away.

Hundreds, no, maybe thousands of soldiers were charging directly at us, swords raised with looks of murderous rage across their faces. Arrows and cannonballs flew through the air toward them, but they hardly seemed to make a dent in the vast hordes that were coming toward us. I ducked back down and ran to catch up to the others.

Unfortunately, the bottom of the trench was extremely uneven, making it very hard to run, and the mud didn't make it any easier, but I tried my best to sprint forward as fast as possible without twisting an ankle on one of the dips in the ground.

To my left, the rumbling was getting louder and louder, and I started to hear the shouts and yells of the soldiers as they neared our position. We kept running, but I knew it was a losing battle. I was breathing hard, which was only partly due to the running. It finally occurred to me that I might not get out of there alive. I looked over at Joe; I had to make sure we both made it out of here. I could find another time to be heroic. All I cared about then was getting away from this battle.

The rumbling was right next to us, and suddenly they were upon us; we had no more time. One more step forward. Two more steps. Three—

"AHHH!" The enemy soldiers at the front of the pack jumped, rolled, or slid into the trench, splattering mud everywhere, and started hacking into the defenders around us.

Instantly I saw five soldiers right next to me impaled or cut down by the enemy; their lifeless bodies fell, immediately sinking down several inches into the thick mud that covered the ground, as though they had never existed in the first place. I glanced back and forth around me, unable to decide what to do. What could I do with the sheer amount of chaos all around?

If not for Olwyn, we all would've instantly died. She pulled us all together and herded us down the trench line. At first, we were completely surrounded by enemies, but Olwyn pushed forward, knocking down soldiers left and right. After killing at least a dozen enemies around us, we were able to keep running forward without much to stop us, besides the few soldiers that bothered to try to intercept us as we ran. We quickly managed to find a relatively empty stretch of trench line after that. We all stuck to the left hand wall and brandished our weapons to the right as we ran, trying to knock back anyone foolish enough to come at us so that we could still travel through the trench line as quickly as possible.

I could hear the sounds of battle growing around us the farther we went down the trench line. We pressed on until we finally turned a corner, and there it was! We came upon a central hub for the trench line; it opened up into a much larger area in front of us, with at least half a dozen paths leading in different directions. There were at least a hundred soldiers packed in next to each other, trying desperately to kill their opponents.

Olwyn charged into the conflict without hesitation, motioning for us to follow. I looked over at Joe, fear in my eyes, only to see the exact same expression mirrored on his face. But beneath the fear on Joe's face, I saw determination. I could tell that Joe wasn't about to just cower in a corner. He was going to fight his way out or die trying.

I tried to look inspiring but the most I could manage was a weak smile. Joe and I took deep breaths and ran after

Olwyn. We could barely see her anymore, as she'd advanced so far into the sea of enemies and was so covered with blood and guts, that she was hard to tell apart from anyone else. I managed to spot her, and I pulled Joe along with me as I tried to cut through the path Olwyn had made. Almost immediately, a sword swung right at me. I barely was able to raise my own sword to counter and the blow of the collision nearly knocked me to the ground. I shook my head and pulled at all of the courage that I had left in me.

CLANG! My sword slammed into my opponent's, and for a moment, we both stood there staring at each other, pushing with all of our strength into the other. I could feel my blade slipping ever so slowly downward, inch by inch. I held on with all of my strength, but I was losing.

Finally, my sword was pushed aside, and it was all I could do just to keep it in my hand as it fell. The man raised his sword, preparing to bring it down on me. Suddenly he cried out in pain and fell to the ground. I looked up and saw Joe standing over him, holding a sword that was covered in blood. He looked down at the soldier he had just killed with a frown and for a moment his shoulders slumped forward. I rushed up to him and pulled him toward me. I didn't have time to analyze his face; we were still in the middle of a battle.

My heart slowed slightly now that the immediate peril was dealt with, but it was in no way still. I looked around for Olwyn, but I couldn't see her anywhere. Rowan and Hezdek were right beside us, each fighting their own enemies. I tried to motion to them to push forward in the direction that I thought Olwyn had disappeared in, but I couldn't tell if they saw me. The most I could do was grab Joe and run as far as we could get, which turned out to be no more than ten feet.

Yet another sword swung right toward my face, but at least this time I was ready. I ducked and readied my sword for a counterattack, though I barely moved out of the way in time. I could feel the blade of the sword slicing away a few hairs from the top of my head as I rose to strike my attacker. I could vaguely sense Joe next to me, battling someone else, but I needed all of my concentration to win my own fight.

I jabbed my sword up as hard as I could into the side of the enemy soldier. He cried out in pain and lurched away from me. I was shocked that I'd actually managed to inflict some harm, which left me unprepared for him to come back with another attack. His sword slashed toward me in a jab, but I narrowly deflected it to the side with my own blade. The tip must have grazed my ribs, though, because I felt a searing pain in my side right after his sword withdrew. I almost collapsed on the spot as I reached down to grab my side and saw blood covering my fingers. My breathing grew even heavier, but I pushed down my feelings of panic as much as I could.

I blinked over and over. I had to stay conscious. To pass out then would have guaranteed my death. I wobbled but composed myself as much as I could, and struck back against my attacker. My blade found its mark and I heard an accompanying yelp of pain as the soldier fell to the ground. I didn't even have time to congratulate myself before a third soldier ran over to me, axe in hand.

By then, I was starting to get used to the battle. I had just faced two people. Surely, I could take out another one, right? I quickly realized that the other two soldiers who I had just fought were complete amateurs compared to my new foe. He moved so quickly I could barely keep up with him and I could tell my movements were slowing with each passing second.

It was all I could do to stay standing as blow after blow came at me, pushing me farther and farther back the way I'd fought so hard to pass through. In desperation, I swung my sword around wildly, hoping to somehow score a hit against him. As my panic grew, my attacks became even wilder and wilder until finally my attacker deflected one of my feeble attacks and used the momentum to swing my sword out of my hands and to the ground.

I stared at it in horror, laying at his feet, taunting me.

It was over.

I was defenseless and my weapon was practically in the hands of my enemy. I looked down in despair as the sword sunk deeper and deeper into the thick, almost black, mud that covered everything around us. As he swung his axe down, all I could do was stumble backward to the ground as quickly as possible. I could hear the blade whip through the air as it passed directly in front of me, raising an audible THUNK as it embedded itself into the soft ground. He raised the axe again and this time, I was out of options. He was going to bring it down right on top of me and I was out of room to crawl away.

I desperately raised my shield at the last second, hoping that somehow it could protect me like it had with the goblin. I braced for impact as the axe collided with the wood. I heard an ear-splitting crack, and my vision went white.

15
Hey, Watch Where You Swing That

Joe

I heard a thunderous crack and saw a blinding light before I was thrown into the mud-splattered ground where I felt many people beside me. For a few seconds, the sounds of battle faded as everyone close to the blast turned to look at what had happened. I saw Matt lying frozen on the ground, holding his shield, with a look of shock on his face.

This was our chance to escape.

As everyone began to recover, I somehow found the strength to jump up, pull Matt to his feet and start running the way that we had seen Olwyn go. I could hear the soldiers slowly resume their fight around us, and soon the battle seemed to be back in full swing, but the momentary distraction created a gap in the soldiers that Matt and I were able to squeeze through.

Where was Olwyn? I glanced around wildly, in hopes of catching a glimpse of her, but I could hardly see anything past the soldiers immediately in front of me. I squinted through the crowd to see two figures clashing viciously. As I watched, one of the figures raised a large axe and brought it down onto the other. Then again with another axe in their second hand.

"Come on! I saw Olwyn over there!" I yelled at Matt, pulling him along with me as I pushed through the crowd. Block. Block. Attack. Duck. It was all I could do to just keep moving and stay alive as Matt and I ran past people who were either dying before our eyes or trying to kill us.

"Olwyn!" I shouted. "We have to get out of here."

She nodded, breathing hard, and motioned for us to follow her. She looked very different from when we had last seen her before the charge; now her short hair was tousled and she was covered in blood, which I assumed wasn't hers.

I noticed Hezdek and Rowan beside her, so, at last, we could try to get away from the battle. Our group came together and started pushing east, down the trench line. For a moment we had a brief respite from the fighting, though that soon ended as a few enemies trickled down toward us. Having Olwyn with us was a huge help, luckily, and she struck them down quickly, letting their bodies fall into the mud below us. I paused for a moment to watch them sink, before Matt bumped into me, and we were moving forward once again.

Finally, we broke through and ran down the path away from the battle. Surprisingly, we didn't see anyone for at least a couple of minutes. Every soldier in the area must have been in that central hub. We all collapsed for a short rest after several minutes of running.

"Is everyone alright?" Olwyn asked.

I glanced up at her. She actually looked concerned for us, which was somewhat shocking, but I decided not to mention it, as it would most likely be revoked afterwards.

"Yeah, I'm fine," I said. Everyone else nodded their agreement.

"Okay, well, we need to get moving again," Olwyn said. "We still have miles more to go and I'm sure that there will be more soldiers to deal with before we get there."

She wasn't sitting down to rest like the rest of us, so she simply started walking away, leaving us to scramble to our feet and run after her.

We had a few minutes of quiet after that. My heart was still hammering, though, so it didn't exactly feel like a break. I couldn't help but wonder whether or not we would actually be able to escape the trenches. If there were soldiers ahead of us, as well as behind, then it looked like we were surrounded.

I also questioned how long our march was going to take. Apparently, we still had miles left to walk, and we'd already encountered a lot of trouble.

Eventually, we heard some voices ahead, and Olwyn motioned for us to stop and crouch down. We slowly advanced and the voices got louder and louder. It was hard to tell which side they were on, however.

"Do you think that was the last of them?" one voice asked. "It seems like they just keep coming back."

"Yeah, I think so. This area looks clear to me."

"Alright, let's move out. I'm sure we'll find more of those Sikrathian bugs soon enough."

The voices started getting closer and closer, and it sounded like there were more than just two people walking over. Olwyn held up three fingers and then lowered one. Then, the next. I barely had time to understand what she was saying before she lowered the last one, leapt up, and charged around the bend in the trench. We all followed after a second or two, charging right into a group of surprised soldiers.

Olwyn took down two before any of them could react, but there were still plenty more to deal with. Olwyn fought a couple of them and each of us took one. I readied myself for another fight. I still wasn't used to fighting people myself instead of watching Olwyn handle whatever threat we encountered. The soldier I was facing held a sword in one hand and a shield in the other and was wearing something of a uniform, though it was hard to distinguish from normal clothes. It looked like someone had tried to make the right uniform using whatever they had lying around and hadn't been very successful.

Uniform or not, the guy was still trying to kill me. He started out strong with a hard swipe downward with his sword, which I easily dodged, even though I was unprepared. I countered with a jab from my own blade, which he blocked with his shield. His sword narrowly missed me a few more times, and I began to realize I was outmatched. It was only a matter of time until I couldn't dodge one of his attacks and that would be the end of it. He was relying heavily on his shield to block me, and so far it was working very well. I had to get creative.

His next attack I tried to block with my sword instead of dodging, so that I could try and swing his weapon out of his hand, or at the very least, unbalance him. I swung my sword and managed to tip him to the side a bit, but he recovered quite quickly. The next time, though, I was able to slide his sword slightly out of his grasp, and when he started to fumble it, I went in for the kill. Using my sword, I jabbed right under his shield and pulled up, which gave way easily as his focus was on stabilizing his grip on the sword in his other hand. Then, another quick jab to the chest and he fell to the ground.

I stood over the fallen soldier for a moment, catching my breath. I tore my eyes away from his lifeless body before I had time to think too hard about what I'd just done and saw that most of the others were still fighting their enemies. Olwyn was down to her last one and Rowan, Matt, and Hezdek were all still fighting. I was about to go help Matt when suddenly his opponent dropped his weapon and fell to the floor with a scream. Matt held his sword out, forcing him against the wall, but it became clear that he was no longer a threat. His weapon was on the ground a few feet away and he was sitting there, holding his bleeding arm against his chest.

I waited for Matt to lower his weapon, but he quickly held his sword up to the man, before raising it and bringing it down directly on top of him, killing him instantly. I flinched and took a step backward.

"Matt," I stammered. "W-why…" I glanced at the now-dead soldier on the ground. "He was surrendering…t-there was no need to…"

He turned to look at me, a frown on his face. "It needed to be done, Joe. We can't exactly take prisoners with us."

"I-I suppose not..." I said.

Matt went over to help one of the others finish off their opponents, leaving me to stare after him in shock. He did have a point, I thought. We really weren't in a position to take prisoners. But it still just didn't feel quite right.

Olwyn finished off the last soldier a short while after that. We all took a quick inventory, making sure we were all in one piece, and then headed out again. I was sure that we were getting close to the end of the trench, as we'd been walking for what felt like a very long time. Luckily, however, it seemed like we'd finally passed almost all of the soldiers. I couldn't hear any sounds of battle in the distance or voices or footsteps coming closer.

It was another hour before we actually made it to the end of the trench. By that time, I was more than ready to be gone from the whole area forever, but we couldn't exactly jump out and run away. There was still the possibility of running into enemy patrols, so we needed to slowly make our way out of the trench and into the nearby trees for better cover.

Olwyn climbed out first and glanced around before motioning for the rest of us to follow her. There was only a small wooden ladder leaning against the wall for us to use, so we had to go up one at a time.

The whole time I was just waiting for a group of soldiers to wander over and see us and that would be the end of it. We had been incredibly lucky up to that point, and I was not used to my luck lasting very long.

Despite my lingering fears, however, we all made it out of the trench and started heading for the tree line. We walked, crouching down to hide ourselves in the tall grass and trees for a couple hundred yards before we came to a stretch of empty field. The trees were just visible on the other side, calling to us to go hide in their depths, but that was much easier said than done. We would be very easy to spot as there was no cover whatsoever to hide behind. We were stuck in a small clump of dense trees and shrubbery that stretched out along the length of the long, open field.

I sat down, contemplating what to do. As we paused to rest my thoughts shifted to Ben; I wondered what he was up to back in Ordbridge. Probably something much less dangerous than what we just went through. Hopefully I'd get to see him again soon.

We could wait until nightfall to cross, but there was no guarantee that we wouldn't be found before then. If the rebels won the battle, then they would probably take control of the entire trench line and go search around the area for remaining soldiers. We could also crawl or run across the field toward the trees, but that would take a long time, and I wasn't sure whether it would be better to be very visible for a short period of time or partly visible for a long time.

I had to leave it up to Olwyn, anyway, so it didn't really matter what I thought. She also sat in the grass, reviewing the options. We had to decide soon.

"Look, I appreciate you fellows letting me come with you," Hezdek eventually said, breaking the silence, "even though we all just about died back there. I may have a solution to this problem." He started rifling through his bag and a moment later, he pulled out an assortment of tools and different colored fabrics. "I not only know how to make armor and weapons, but I can also make a very accurate camouflage when necessary."

We all stared at him in surprise for a moment until Olwyn finally asked, "You can really make camouflage for all of us to get across that field?"

Hezdek nodded. "I just need a few things, but I can get started while the rest of you gather them."

We all stared back at him, but readily agreed to get whatever he needed to work. He asked for some leaves, sticks, and small plants from around the area, as well as each of our cloaks, so that he would have something to put the camouflage onto. We all complied and spread out a bit to gather as many things as we could. I crouched down and moved quickly through the nearby area, trying to spot any leaves, sticks, or plants that would help Hezdek. The entire time, I pictured rebel soldiers coming up behind me as I picked up random plants from the ground. Luckily, I didn't see anyone on my short journey. It was hard to find very many useful plants or items because the area of trees we were in was so small, but after a while of searching I managed to scrounge up quite a few usable things.

Hezdek was already working when I finished gathering my items. He took the cloaks, most of which were already a dull green color, and started attaching the leaves and other bits to them. I was very skeptical that they would turn into something that we could actually use, but Hezdek seemed to know what he was doing, so I decided to wait and see how they would turn out.

Slowly, the cloaks started to take shape and they began to resemble the green, plant-covered ground of the field. It almost appeared to be some sort of sorcery, but I didn't see Hezdek use any magic, just his own two hands. After only about half an hour, he had five complete cloaks for us to try on. We all put them on and glanced around at each other. They were very close to the green foliage covering the ground of the nearby field. With the leaves and sticks and other stuff, it really looked like we were just wearing a regular stretch of the ground on our backs. All of my skepticism washed away and based on the expressions of the others as they tried on their cloaks, they all felt the same.

Deciding not to waste any more time, Olwyn crouched down and started crawling across the field. We waited for a few seconds to see what would happen, and when she didn't seem to be in any danger, I followed her.

The field was long, but we made good time. In no more than ten minutes, we were almost across to the other side. I was just thinking that we had finally made it out of that death trap when someone whispered loudly, "Someone's coming!"

Immediately, I laid flat on the ground, and curled up underneath the camouflage. I heard the rustling of several other bodies moving around for a moment before there was complete silence. I waited for something to happen, but there was no movement or sound at all. I was just considering peeking out from underneath my cloak when I heard several sets of footsteps getting closer and closer.

"I haven't seen anyone for the entire patrol," one voice said. "I swear, this is such a waste of time. If there's no one in this area either, I'm just heading back."

The footsteps came even closer until I thought for sure that they were standing within ten feet of my hiding spot. I held my breath, wondering if the camouflage would hold up. There was silence for what felt like hours. A cold wind blew at the edge of the cloak, and I tried to shift around as little as possible while I firmly held it down.

Finally, I heard: "Alright, fine. Let's just get out of here," followed by the sounds of receding footsteps.

I waited at least another minute before I dared to move, and even then, I questioned if I should or not. I decided to wait another couple of seconds and try to listen for anyone nearby, but I hadn't heard any voices or footsteps in a while. I decided that if anyone was still there, then surely, we could handle them. We'd just gotten through that trench battle and at that point, I was ready to just be done with the whole event, no matter what happened. As I raised my cloak and sat up, however, I found myself staring directly into the eyes of Matt's brother, Wyatt.

16
Is That Your Legacy?

Matt

"Wyatt!?" I heard Joe say.

Immediately, I pushed aside my cloak and sat up. Surely, it was a different Wyatt that Joe saw. It couldn't really be...

"Wyatt?" I asked in disbelief. "What are you doing here?"

My brother looked very different from when I last saw him. He'd grown several inches and was now wearing baggy, drab clothes, compared to the usual palace attire. His short, curly, brownish blonde hair was slightly longer, just barely covering his green eyes which had a certain life to them that I hadn't seen in a long time.

"Matt? Joe? What's going on? Why are you so far from Ordbridge?" Wyatt asked.

Joe and I exchanged a glance. "Well," I began, "we're on a mission for Father. To stop Glyndwyr Brice."

Wyatt raised his eyebrows and looked back and forth between us. "Father sent you out here? To the front lines? I can't really picture him doing that."

I cleared my throat nervously and glanced at the ground. "Well, he might not have actually known that it was me when he sent me out here."

Wyatt opened and closed his mouth a few times. "Let me get this straight. You somehow disguised yourself, and convinced Father to send you out on some top-secret mission and he has no idea that you're here now?"

"Well, I'm sure that he knows now. I left him a note and I've been gone for a while."

Wyatt blinked. "I suppose that's easier to believe than Father actually sending you on a mission. So, what exactly are you here to do? Assassinate Glyndwyr Brice?"

"Who the hell is this?" Olwyn finally growled from beside me.

"Don't worry," I said. "It's okay. He's my brother."

Olwyn's eyes grew wide. "I…really? What the hell is he doing out here?"

I opened my mouth to respond when I realized that I, in fact, did not know the answer. "Uh, yeah, what are you doing out here, Wyatt?" I asked, turning back to him.

Wyatt glanced around nervously. "Look, what has Father told you about me?"

"Um. Just that you went off to study in Hullbeck a while ago. Wait, did Father send you on a secret mission too?"

Wyatt hesitated. "Okay, Matt, I have to tell you something." He paused and bit his lip. "This isn't going to be easy to hear but you need to know this." He reached over and grabbed my shoulder as he stared at me. "Our father is not the kind of person you think he is. I found out what he did in the war and…it's horrifying."

I blinked at him. Horrifying? What was Wyatt talking about?

"He massacred the people of Kricoya, took their land and possessions, all to get his hands on some stupid magical artifacts. All he cares about is getting these artifacts and controlling everything. You can't trust him."

I stared at Wyatt in disbelief. What was he talking about? I wasn't particularly fond of my father, but surely, he wasn't an evil person. He just wanted what was best for us, right? During war, you have to do some things that you don't want to do. He couldn't have actually enjoyed doing any of those things, could he?

"Wyatt, you must be exaggerating. Sure, Father can be harsh, and he isn't the best person in the world, but he wouldn't just cause wanton chaos, would he?"

Wyatt sighed. "Matt, I'm sure you wouldn't be able to accept it unless you saw for yourself what he was capable of doing, like I did. But you have to believe me. At the very least, don't report back to him at the palace. Let me take you back to the rebel camp and show you what they're trying to do here."

"Wait, you're working with the rebels?" I spluttered.

Wyatt paused for a second. "Well, yes, Matt. I am. But just hold on, it's not what it seems like."

I stared at him in shock. How could he side with the enemies of the crown? With the enemies of the entire country? It went against everything that we had learned growing up. I wanted to just walk away from him, but I couldn't make myself do it. My brother had been practically my only friend for years. If not for him, I don't know how I would have made it through all the years of boring schoolwork and lessons from Father.

"Just let me show you that I'm telling the truth about Father," Wyatt pleaded with me. "What the rebels are doing is amazing, and you'll think so too after you hear their story."

How could he say these things? I found myself surprised, not only at what Wyatt had said, but also at my anger because of it. I hadn't thought that I had much love for my father, but perhaps there was still some left. "Alright, fine, I'll come with you."

Wyatt looked relieved and I got the sense that he thought I was going to just walk away from him. Hopefully, it wouldn't take long to see whatever Wyatt wanted to show us. But surely we would be safe with him, right? This couldn't be a trap, could it?

"Now wait just a second," Olwyn interjected. "I don't care if you're his brother or Not. You're the enemy. We are working for your father; I can't trust anything you do or tell us. How exactly were you expecting to get us into the camp anyway? And why would you want us there?"

Wyatt glanced at her, seemingly noticing for the first time that there were several other people with us. "Look, I can't say I really want you at the camp; not all of you, at least. But I need to show Matt what I've seen at the camp. Once you see it," he turned to me, "you'll understand everything that I'm talking about. Maybe…just Matt could come with me and the rest of you could stay here or camp nearby? It'll be quick. There's nothing to worry about. I can get him in and out."

Olwyn shook her head. "No, I don't think so. You aren't just going to walk off with the Prince of Sikrath. You aren't taking him anywhere."

I hesitated as I watched Wyatt's reaction. He seemed unsure of how to argue his case, but I could tell that this was important to him. Whatever it was that he was talking about, he wanted me to see it very badly.

"Olwyn, please let me go," I said, turning to face her. "I trust him. It'll be fine."

Olwyn stared at me for several long moments, concern written across her face, before she finally nodded once, sighed, and shook her head. "Fine, I suppose you can go, but not without the rest of us." She turned to Wyatt. "You can either take all of us to the camp or none of us."

Wyatt raised an eyebrow and glanced around at the small group assembled next to him. "You're all working for my father. Why should I let you inside the rebel camp?"

Olwyn shrugged. "You can do whatever you want, but you can't take Matt without us."

Wyatt glanced back and forth between me and Olwyn, a deep frown on his face. I could see the confusion and worry written across his features. He desperately wanted me to come with him, but we were all enemies to the rebels. Enemies to him.

Wyatt sighed. "Alright, fine. You can all come, but you better do exactly what I say, and you'll leave as soon as I prove to Matt what I know about our father."

We all nodded in agreement before he turned and motioned for us to follow him. He led us through the field and into the forest that we had tried so hard to get to earlier.

Rowan and Hezdek followed us without complaint, as did Joe, though he looked at Wyatt cautiously, as though he was unsure of how to act around him.

I glanced at Olwyn before fixing my eyes straight ahead as she turned her gaze toward me. It was odd to see her care so much about my well-being after how she acted when we first met. I assumed that it had something to do with finding out that I was the prince, but I still liked it. It kind of felt like having a mother again.

Wyatt led us into the forest for a few miles before I started to wonder just how far away we were being led. Surely, we would get there by nightfall, right? I would just have to hope so, because I didn't have much food and we had left our supply horses at the military camp. Of course, it did give me some time to admire the nearby trees, which I hadn't been able to do in a long time.

The trees in question were mostly made up of Rosecork and a few Copperwoods. I had always admired the Rosecork tree, and many people thought it was very valuable because of its durability and fire resistance, so it was often used in building. Personally, though, I thought that the amazing red and gold color of its leaves paired with the rich dark brown of the bark beautifully. There were a few Rosecorks growing back at Ordbridge, but I had never seen an entire forest made up of them before. I suppose that I had never even seen a forest at all before this trip.

After an hour or so, we finally emerged from the trees, and came to a large clearing that was filled with activity. There were hundreds of tents scattered as far as I could see, with soldiers ducking in and out, carrying their weapons and supplies out for use or cleaning. I was shocked at just how big of an operation the rebels had. From what my father had told me, the rebellion was just a minor issue that would be resolved shortly, but it looked to me like they were almost an actual army.

Surprisingly, there weren't really any guards that I could see patrolling around the camp, though I had no idea what their system was. We walked further into the small village of tents, and luckily, no one gave us any odd looks or seemed to pay any attention to us at all. I was half-relieved, half-insulted.

As we passed a few tents, I tried to get a better look inside, to see what exactly the conditions were like, but I wasn't able to see much. Unsurprisingly, though, the camp didn't appear to be in great condition. A lot of the tents had rips in them and were covered in mud. No one had a uniform, which I suppose I couldn't really hold against them. Everyone we passed looked disheveled and unkempt, and I didn't see a lot of excess supplies laying around the camp.

I saw a large tent in the center of the clearing that was much bigger than the rest. This tent was the only one I saw that looked well cared for. The fabric was crisp and clean, which was a sharp change from the small dirty tents beside it. I almost wanted to run in and see if Glyndwyr Brice was there so I could finally see him for myself, but I knew that I couldn't betray Wyatt's trust like that. He had brought us to the camp to try and prove something about Father to me. I didn't believe for a second that he was leading us into a trap unless his time with the rebels had drastically changed him. Besides, according to Olwyn, we were supposed to gather information about the rebels before we attacked, and this seemed like the perfect opportunity to do just that.

We came to an open, central area of the tents after a couple minutes of wandering through the apparent maze all around us. A large black canopy covered tables which were overflowing with pots and pans and other cooking equipment. Ingredients were piled up on tables and people were throwing various things into several large pots, but I was surprised to see so little food for the whole camp. Maybe this was just part of the food they would be serving?

As I got a feel for the camp, I came to realize that the rebels were somehow simultaneously very organized and disorganized. On one hand, they seemed to have a large, almost city-esque arrangement of tents all around the clearing and everyone appeared to have a job, even if some of the soldiers were looking a little worse for wear. But I could sense the fear in almost everyone I looked at. My brain told me that something wasn't right, but my heart said to just keep on hating them for everything that they had done to Sikrath. Maybe I hadn't heard much about them before this adventure, but just that battle back in the trench was enough to convince me that they were no good.

Wyatt quickly led us past the kitchen area, with a few suspicious glances left and right, toward the main group of tents on the far side of where we had emerged from the forest. I got a glimpse of a large open field as we passed that had several racks of various weapons and a huge assortment of training dummies. There was something of an obstacle course set up and I could see a few soldiers running through it as we went by.

Finally, Wyatt led us to a small tent right in the middle of the camp. There didn't seem to be anything interesting or unique about it to me. It was made from a simple black fabric that was covered in mud and debris, though something about it made me pause; the grass immediately next to it had turned a much deeper green than what I had seen in other parts of the camp.

Wyatt stopped us short and turned to face us. "Okay, look, inside the tent is one of their elders. His name is Master Shankar, and he is very old and very wise, so please show some respect. I'm going to ask him to tell you a story about these people and I realize that you might not like what he says, but it would be great if you could just listen. I'll say that you're new recruits and you just want to hear about your people's past, okay? So, no need to worry."

Wyatt led us inside the tent. After stepping through, it took me a moment to notice the small man sitting on the ground on the far side of the entrance. I was caught up in the beautiful patterns of wool covering the walls of the tent. They were made up of several different colors, ranging from a dark red to a light yellow, and they depicted many scenes, some involving battle or conflict and others a peaceful ceremony or the gentle sowing of crops into massive fields. I was struck by how the intricate designs were somehow expressed so well through nothing but woven wool. I had never seen anything quite like it.

"Hello, hello," the man said. "What can I do for you, today?"

Wyatt stepped forward and did a short bow. "Hello, Master Shannkar. These are new recruits and I wanted them to hear the inspiring story that you told me about our past."

Master Shannkar nodded. "Of course, of course. Please, gather around. Take a seat anywhere you like," he said, gesturing to the cushions arranged on the floor in front of him.

We all sat down, some of us more reluctantly than others, and waited for the story to start.

Master Shannkar took a deep breath and closed his eyes. "This part of our story began several years ago, on a day similar to this one at our former capital city of Entolas."

He spoke very gently and slowly, and I got the feeling that he had said those words many, many times before. As he said them, I felt a cool breeze on my back and heard the sound of a wind chime near my ear. It almost felt like we were slowly moving up and away. Just as I thought that, my vision started to change. I could see the city laid out in front of me. But I could also still see the inside of the tent as well. It was as if I had two sets of eyes sending two different images to my brain at once. At first it was very disorienting, but I slowly grew used to it.

I glanced over at the others to see how they were handling it. Joe and Hezdek seemed to be perfectly fine, Rowan looked to be struggling a bit, but Olwyn was having a lot of trouble. She was waving her hands around and lurching to the side.

"What witchcraft is this?!" she exclaimed. "How can I see two things at once?"

Master Shannkar calmly stood up, took her arm, and led her back to her seat. "Try to relax and experience your history."

Olwyn squirmed, but she allowed herself to be sat back down at her spot without much complaint.

"Now, on this particular day, the city was under siege."

My vision of the city suddenly shifted down toward the ground to the front gate where there were hundreds of tents laid out, almost like the tent that we were in now, except they were made from a rich red fabric and were clearly a different design.

"The city had been under siege for several weeks at this point," Master Shankar said. "By the forces of Sikrath."

I realized that we were watching the Kricoyan War unfold right before our eyes. This was the siege that I had learned about in school, though we hadn't focused much on it. In fact, I was taught very little about the war. I could see the Sikrathian soldiers running at the city, trying to breach it with a ram or explosives. I couldn't help feeling some pride about our victory. We had beaten back our enemy and taken a lot of new land and resources. The Kricoyan War was a great example of the might of Sikrath.

"As you will see, the gate will be breached very soon." Indeed, as he said the words, the scene that he had laid started to play out in front of us. "The soldiers showed no mercy toward the Krikoryan defenders, and they slaughtered nearly all of them as they took the city. Now, the main reason for this conquest was the search for a powerful magical artifact in the possession of the King of Kricoya at the time. A compass. A compass of immense power. The king knew that the city's time was limited, so he devised a clever plan to thwart the invaders." The scene continued to play out as he talked, showing how the soldiers ran through the city, killing anyone that they encountered.

Suddenly someone burst into the tent, interrupting the story. "Wyatt!" the man cried. "Commander Brice is looking for you! He said it's urgent."

Wyatt looked over in surprise before glancing at us, worriedly. He hesitated for a moment before answering. "Okay, tell him I'll be there in a minute." The soldier left the tent again and Wyatt turned to us. "Alright, I'll try to be back soon. Just…" he hesitated again, as he met my eyes. "Listen to the story and try not to get into any trouble. I'll meet you back here soon." He walked out of the tent and Master Shankar continued his story.

"As soon as word came that the invaders had breached the gate, the king ordered several riders to set out with the magical compass."

I watched the king talk to the riders and hand one of them a small glittering object. He looked very young to be a soldier and it was hard to tell, but I thought I saw tears in his eyes as he rode away from the city.

"The king then returned to the throne room to await his fate. He knew that he wouldn't be able to make it out, but it was his hope that the small group could rally the support of the citizens left alive and perhaps, one day, Kricoya could rise again.

"Indeed, it was soon after that the Sikrathian soldiers stormed into the room. The soldiers didn't kill him immediately, however. They tied him up and waited for their leader to arrive."

I watched the soldiers tie up the king and then stand around waiting for a few minutes for someone to get there. In the meantime, they ransacked the throne room, taking anything of value that they could find. There were a few other people in the room, most likely the staff or perhaps other members of the royal family, but they were all killed.

Finally, a figure emerged from the shadows and strolled into the room. There wasn't anything particularly scary about him, but by the way he carried himself, I could tell he was used to getting his way. He wore a metal helmet that completely covered his face, so it wasn't clear who it was.

"The rival King of Sikrath entered the throne room and tried to coax the information from our king to no avail. After that, in his eyes, there was no use for him anymore."

I watched the man reach up to take his helmet off and I saw the face of my father. I suppose I should have seen that coming, but he had never told me much about the war, so I didn't recognize this scene. He started talking to the king, but he clearly wasn't happy with his responses, and he soon drew his sword and calmly, without showing any concern, impaled the king.

17
Wake Up Please

Joe

As we left the tent, I felt even more confused than I had before. Well, I think I knew what I had to do, but I really didn't want to do it. Instead, I focused on the small details that I noticed around the rebel camp, such as the soldier sitting on a small stump, polishing his sword, or the woman peeling a pile of some sort of root vegetable and throwing them into a pot next to her. It was just easier than thinking about what I should have been thinking about right then. I felt a shiver work its way up my spine.

Wyatt still hadn't returned from whatever meeting he had gone off to, so the five of us just sat next to the tent in silence. We all seemed to have a lot on our minds. I glanced over at Matt, but I couldn't tell what he was thinking. He didn't look very concerned about watching his father massacre an entire city but maybe he was still processing.

After several minutes of staring at the people who'd walked past us, which was considerably more fun than you might expect, Wyatt arrived back at the tent. He wore a frown on his face and he stared off into the distance as though he was deep in thought, but I saw his eyes light up with excitement after a moment.

"Hey, guys. Sorry that took so long," he said.

I shrugged. "It wasn't that long."

He just nodded and glanced over at Matt. I got the sense that he was searching for some sign of what Matt was thinking, but from his raised eyebrow, I gathered that he was unsuccessful. "So, uh, what did you think about the story?" he asked Matt.

Matt looked up at his brother. "Well, it was interesting to see what the war was like. Father never really talks about it."

Wyatt frowned and shook his head, as though he couldn't believe that Matt wasn't getting something, but also didn't want to keep explaining it.

"Look, Matt, didn't you see what Father did in the war? All to get more power? He really wants these magical artifacts and he's willing to completely destroy what's left of Kricoya to get them."

Matt didn't appear to be very moved by this, but he did start to look a little uncomfortable under Wyatt's gaze. "Well, I don't know, Wyatt. I think that you're exaggerating a little bit here."

At these words, Wyatt took a step backward and glanced back and forth as though looking for anyone listening in. "Please don't make me regret bringing you here, Matt. I took a big risk to get you all here."

Matt flushed and shook his head fast. "Well, Wyatt, I mean…" he frowned. "Do I have to agree with everything you say? Why can't we just disagree on this?"

Wyatt sighed and shook his head. "I'm sorry, Matt, but this is not something that we can have differing opinions on if I'm going to continue to have you at this camp. Father has done some terrible things, and he is doing terrible things now. We can't support him."

"Can I at least think about it for a little bit?" Matt asked.

Wyatt hesitated for a moment before slowly nodding. "Alright, I'll give you some time to think about it. For now, though, you guys need to leave as soon as possible. I am already stretching my luck by bringing you guys in here in the first place, not to mention my personal morals, so you need to get out of here. I'll lead you out of the camp and from there you can do whatever you need to do, alright?"

As Wyatt started to lead us back through the winding paths of the rebel camp, we heard a shout from behind us. "Hey, Wyatt! Are you ready to get going? Commander Brice wanted us to leave immediately."

Wyatt whipped around, searching for the source of this disturbance. "Oh! Yes, Sarah, I'm just about ready. I just have to, uh," he paused for a moment as he looked back at us, eyes wide in alarm, "find these new recruits some lodging."

Sarah glanced over at us with a look of mild interest. "Oh, well, I'm sure you could find someone to do that for you." She leaned in closer to Wyatt with a quick look around for any possible eavesdroppers. "Commander Brice told us that this artifact they found on the front lines wouldn't stay there forever. We have to act quickly."

Wyatt's eyebrows shot up in alarm. "Y-yes, um, well, t-that's true. I suppose you have a point. Um, we might want to stay a bit more discreet about this, though." he said with an exaggerated glance around us in all directions. "You, uh, never know who could be listening, right?"

"Ah, sorry," Sarah said with a sheepish smile. "You're probably right. Anyway, come on, let's go. We can get anyone to show these guys to some lodgings. Like that guy for instance!" she said, pointing to a middled-aged man who was wandering by us as they spoke. He was wearing a plain black tunic and pants with leather boots. There didn't appear to be anything unusual or unique about him; he looked like the classic soldier. Though, he did have a very long, curly, beard that stretched down almost to his stomach.

"Can I help you folks?" he asked with a deep accent that I couldn't quite place. It sounded like he was from somewhere east, maybe around Vathalorg or Iobla. Either way, I hadn't heard anyone like him in a long time.

"Yes, can you please show these new recruits to some lodgings? We have important work for Commander Brice to attend to," Sarah asked, grabbing Wyatt's arm and pulling him away from our small group.

"Yes, Ma'am, I sure can do that."

The last I saw of Wyatt was his panicked expression as he was dragged away, arm firmly held in Sarah's grasp.

"Well, a'right then," the man who Sarah had recruited called out to us. "I can show you folks to some accommodations 'round here now if you'd like."

We all nodded our agreement. "Well," he continued, "just follow me, then. I can get y'all situated." He wandered off in the opposite direction that Wyatt had gone.

As we followed, he led us past a huge tent that was unlike anything else that I had seen in the camp so far. It must've been thirty times the size of a normal tent and of far better quality. We watched a few very well-dressed people walking in and out, and a few soldiers trailed after them, carrying bags and maps and other important papers.

"Ah, yes," he said, pointing over to the tent. "That's for the generals and such. Commander Brice lives in there as well, 'course."

We followed him for a couple of minutes before he finally stopped in front of a row of three tents. "Alright, these three are available for use. You can decide amongst yourselves, of course, how you want to split 'em up. Just let me know if you need anything else," he said, before walking off.

All five of us paused for a moment, unsure how exactly to proceed after what had just happened. We were loose in the rebel camp, free to explore the area and collect information on everything we saw.

Finally, Olwyn addressed the rest of us. "Well, I think that this is an excellent opportunity. For now, we can learn as much as we can about their routine and security, and then if we see an opening later to go for Glyndwyr Brice, then we take it. For now, we have to simply blend in as well as possible and observe, so I expect none of you to draw any unwanted attention to us, alright?" She looked each of us in the eye individually as she said this, gathering our agreements with nods or grunts of understanding.

We then turned our attention to the tents that we had been led to. Of the three tents in question, two of them appeared to be the same. Two people could comfortably fit inside at one time. Not counting the tent itself, all that was provided were two small cots that were set on the ground. I didn't mind, though; I had certainly been in smaller places before. The third tent, however, was much nicer than the others. There were still two cots inside and everything else that was in the other two, but there was much more room to move around; you could actually stand up, unlike the other two, and there was even a light attached to the inside of the roof.

We stood around for a few moments, considering what to do, when Olwyn walked over to the nicer tent and looked over at us, smirking. "I think we all know who's going to get this. You four can arrange yourselves any way you want in the other two." she said, waving in the direction of the other tents before ducking down and entering hers.

The four of us looked at each other, but no one seemed very mad about it (except maybe Matt). Clearly, Olwyn had done a lot of work on this journey. She had saved us countless times and she definitely deserved the tent. We stood there for a few more moments and then split off to go inside the other tents. No words had been uttered, but there seemed to be a silent agreement that Matt and I would take one tent and Rowan and Hezdek would take the other.

Inside, it was just as nice as it had seemed from the outside. The cots were fairly worse for wear, but Matt showed only a hint of disgust as we each took a seat on our respective sides.

It was starting to get late, and we didn't know our way around the camp, so we decided to stay put for a couple of hours. I pulled out a book from my bag (a thrilling murder mystery aboard a train which was about to become even more exciting now that I had actually traveled on one myself) and laid down on my cot.

After a little while of this, however, Matt looked up at me and hesitated before saying: "I think that we should follow Wyatt tonight."

I raised my eyebrows and Matt let his statement sink in for a few moments before continuing. "Look, I know what the artifacts that that girl was talking about are. There was this book in the cave where we found Hezdek," Matt said, pulling a small book out of his bag. "Apparently, these artifacts are extremely powerful and dangerous. They caused a massive amount of destruction in the past, and people have been searching for them for hundreds of years now. The amount of power one could wield is just…unreal." He paused and looked down at the ground before carrying on.

"I…well, I don't want Wyatt to be in danger even if we don't agree about Father. And, of course, I want to see one of them in person. They sound…incredible." He stopped and waited for my response.

I stared at him. So, he knew about the artifacts? And he wanted to go find one? Something about that made me uncomfortable, but I couldn't quite decide why. If there was trouble on Wyatt's mission, then I did want to go help him. He may be a part of the rebels, but I wasn't such a big fan of the king either. Maybe the rebels were the solution to all the horrible poverty and oppression plaguing Sikrath. But even so, Wyatt could surely handle himself in a fight and, honestly, I didn't feel like leaving the tent after everything that we had gone through that day. I didn't think that I would live through that battle before in the trenches, and now all I wanted to do was just to go to sleep. I realized, however, that Matt was prone to doing stupid things, and I could easily see him wandering off by himself and getting killed. I sighed.

"Can't we just stay here?" I begged. "Just for once, let's not rush off on some extremely dangerous journey."

Somehow, Matt didn't appear to feel at all guilty for interrupting my proposed rest. "Joe, trust me. These artifacts are very important. We can't just sit back and let other people decide how to handle them. We have to see for ourselves what they're like, so we can know how worried we should be."

I sighed again. Matt seemed to be straying off of the whole "we have to protect Wyatt" argument in favor of just getting a glimpse of one of the artifacts. "I don't like the way you talk about those artifacts. Maybe it's best if you aren't around them at all. You know about their influence on people, right?" I asked, frowning. "You already seem to be losing yourself without their help." I muttered.

"What?" Matt asked as he stared at me.

"You killed that soldier back in the trench when he had already surrendered! Is that really who you want to be?"

"I had to do that Joe. We were in the middle of a battle; What was I supposed to have done?" He stood up and started gathering his gear. "I'm going, with or without you."

I jumped up. "Wait Matt!" I sighed and shook my head. "Fine. I'll go with you. But we're not getting anywhere near that artifact."

Matt smiled and nodded. "You won't regret it." Though something in his expression made me think that was exactly what I would be doing very soon.

We gathered our things together. We didn't really have much to carry and we were used to taking all our stuff with us, so there was nothing left in the tent by the time we walked out into the night. We hadn't taken two steps before we were interrupted by the sound of someone clearing their throat.

I glanced around wildly before my eyes registered the shape of a man standing to the right of our tent. Upon closer examination, I realized that the man was Rowan.

"And where exactly are you two going?" he asked casually.

I looked over at Matt. He was staring at Rowan with wide eyes. I thought that this might be a good excuse for us to just return to our tents and pretend like it never happened, but apparently, no one else wanted to do that.

"You better not think that you can go see that artifact without us," Rowan said after a long period of silence.

Hezdek quickly threw the tent flap to the side and went to stand next to Rowan.

"That's right. You aren't going anywhere without me and the old man," Hezdek said, nodding in the direction of Rowan with a smirk across his face.

Rowan just snorted and rolled his eyes before looking at the two of us expectantly.

Matt and I exchanged looks. I was fine with them joining, but a bit startled. Matt frowned and hesitated, but he finally nodded and waved them over. We set out, making sure not to cause any more noise and alert Olwyn. She would most certainly put a stop to our little outing.

The night was still relatively young, so we passed several people on the path out of camp. Every time I would instinctively duck my head and try to shield my face to look as inconspicuous as possible, though all this did was make me look far more suspicious. Luckily, we managed to find our way out of the camp without anything other than a couple odd looks.

The cool breeze blew downward toward us, causing a slight shiver to run down my spine. I really wasn't sure about this plan; I had a feeling that something bad was about to happen. Nevertheless, I walked through the tall grass with my three companions, on our way to the vault.

The trip was surprisingly quick and easy. Wyatt hadn't told us exactly where he was going, but he had said the front lines, which, though it was a lot of land to cover, felt like it had narrowed it down quite a bit. For one thing, the front lines weren't actually as long as you might imagine. To the north, the Shrewsbo Woods cut off any hope of movement of heavy equipment or supplies, so almost no one went through there, and to the south, the coast was only about five miles away. That might sound like a long way, and it was, but we were confident that we could find it.

"Matt, I might have an idea for finding Wyatt once we get to the general area," I said.

He looked at me questioningly.

"I have a spell that sounds useful. Essentially, when I cast it, if the person that I am trying to find is within one thousand feet of me, it shows me the way to them."

Everyone looked at me with surprise.

"Wow. Yeah, that actually sounds perfect," Matt said.

Rowan and Hezdek agreed that it was indeed a very good time to use that spell.

"Also, we may become separated out there and we definitely don't want to be shouting out in the middle of the battlefield in search of each other," Rowan said. "So, I was thinking that we could finally use those communication gems that they gave us back at Ordbridge. I know you don't have one, Hezdek, but you can stick with me."

I looked over at him in surprise. I had all but forgotten about those stones that we had gotten at the very beginning of our journey. We hadn't had any opportunity to use them until now. I rifled around in my pack for a moment before pulling mine out.

"Yeah, that's a good idea. We should all keep those at the ready," I said. I realized that the rebel camp was very close to the front lines, so luckily we wouldn't have to walk far. And, indeed, it wasn't long before we could see the first signs of the most recent battlefields. We all crouched down behind a clump of bushes to look around for any soldiers, but we hardly saw anyone. I hoped that I wouldn't have to cast the spell too many times because there was a limit to what I could handle without rest.

I pulled out my spell book and flipped to the right page. It was a relatively simple spell. A short incantation and a small amount of magic would do the trick. Mumbling under my breath, I began the incantation, vaguely waving my hands in the air. It was odd to cast spells in front of other people after having practiced by myself for so long, but I managed to get over my nervousness and complete it. Slowly, a small glowing cloud of magical particles flew up into the air, pulsating with energy. For a moment, they stopped, illuminating the darkening sky around us, before vanishing without a trace. We all paused for a moment, looking around for any sign of success.

"Was that supposed to happen?" Matt asked.

"Uh, I think so," I responded, still searching the area around us for any possible clues. "I think that means that we aren't within one thousand feet of Wyatt yet."

We all carefully crept out of the bushes and continued on our way down the length of the front lines. We paused twice more to cast the spell before something finally happened. Instead of the energy dissipating around us, it began to condense into one small object. It slowly molded itself into the right form until it was recognizable as a short arrow. It spun in a complete circle several times before finally slowing down to a stop, pointing directly north. We all glanced at one another excitedly, before creeping forward in the direction that the arrow was pointing. We followed for several long minutes, through bushes, clumps of trees, and even a small creek. There were even a few guards that walked by us as we hid. We couldn't tell if they were Sikrathian or rebels but either way probably wouldn't be good. Finally, the arrow began pointing steadily downward until it was almost straight down. We found ourselves in a small, wooded area, relatively secluded from any rebel or Sikrathian military camps, though we could hear movement in the distance.

"Alright, let's all split up and search around for some sort of entrance," Matt whispered. So far, no one had made a sound, but I could sense the presence of multiple people right next to us, behind a row of trees.

We all split up in search of the vault, crawling so as not to alert anyone. I crept through the area, my eyes scanning the ground for any sign of an entrance. I almost hoped that we couldn't find it at all. Or at the very least that Matt wouldn't find it first. He wouldn't really leave us behind if he found the entrance, would he? I wasn't sure.

For a moment I thought back to my life in Ordbridge. There wasn't as much danger or excitement, that was for sure. Although I wasn't sure if that was a good thing. I thought about Ben. It had been so long since I had seen him. I longed for the days that we had back in Ordbridge, spending time with each other when we could both sneak away. But I knew that those days were over. Even if I survived this adventure, I had the feeling that everything would be different when this was all over.

For several tense minutes, I searched, constantly worrying about being discovered by the soldiers, but finally I caught a glimpse of metal almost completely obscured by leaves and branches. I carefully brushed off as much of the debris as I could, but it still was absolutely caked with mud and dirt. It was a miracle that I had even been able to spot it at all. It was a large hatch made of a very dark metal, almost black, which seemed to suck all of the remaining light in the area into its depths. A chill ran down my spine at the sight of it. Something about the smooth, simple design seemed to radiate power, as though it were easy to make something rough and complicated, but to make something truly simple and polished required a tremendous amount of energy. It felt very old, maybe thousands of years old. I had no way of knowing its true age, but as I touched it, I could feel the many, many years that it had spent, buried, with nobody to notice it. I considered opening it, but I was slightly afraid of what I would find if I did. Also, I thought that I should call the others over to see it first. I took out my stone and, though I felt a bit ridiculous, started quietly talking into it.

"Matt, can you hear me?" I whispered.

There was silence for several long moments until: "Yeah, what's up? Did you find the vault?"

"Yeah, I found it. I'm at the entrance. I'm right by the large Oak tree that we saw when we first split up to search. All of you better get over here quickly." I waited by the hatch for another couple of minutes, until finally, the three of them arrived.

For a moment, we all paused to stare at the massive metal hatch in the ground that, no doubt, contained one of the most powerful objects in the world. We crouched next to it, silently daring each other to open it first, before Matt finally reached out and slowly pulled it open with some difficulty. A strong smell of dust and stale air wafted up to us.

From outside we could see a long stone staircase winding down into the darkness. I saw a faint light glowed from the very, but it was so far away that I almost thought that I was imagining it. Again, we all paused for a moment to consider what exactly we were doing. I almost hoped that we might just turn around and head back now, but Matt took a deep breath and stepped inside. There was nothing we could do but follow.

Very carefully, so as not to upset the ancient stairs, we made our way down to the bottom of the pit. The light began to illuminate more and more off the walls, showing intricate paintings and drawings across almost every surface. I paused for a moment to make out one scene directly beside me. It showed a large battlefield with thousands of casualties piled up into huge stacks beside the attacking soldiers. The scene beside it showed yet another battle, and as I moved on toward the next scene, I began to see the story that they told of war dividing the land and separating everyone. Huge armies clashed on the battlefield, frantically pushing forward toward four shining golden objects, held above everyone in the paintings. In some scenes, thousands of people kneeled before each of the artifacts, praying or calling out to them, as if they were deities. In others, people wielded them against vast hordes of approaching enemies, wiping out all their foes. It was all so startling to see Rowan's story come to life like this—to see the drawings of those who actually experienced those events.

Eventually, after a long, eerily silent walk that gave us plenty of time to take in the horrors of our ancient past, we came to the bottom of the stairs. The silence was deafening and I kept thinking that I'd heard something behind me, only to turn and find nothing there. I felt certain that there was something else down there with us.

I almost collapsed with fear when a hand reached out and covered my mouth.

"Shhh," a voice said from behind me. "Don't make a sound."

I froze. Who was it? I didn't want to turn around, but I forced myself to slowly spin around and see who had just come out of the darkness. I turned to find...Olwyn standing behind us, glaring at me, though relief was clearly painted across her face.

"What the hell are you doing here?" she whispered. "Do you have any idea how dangerous this is? Come on, let's go."

Matt shook his head vehemently. "No! We can't leave now. I'll just look around the corner and then go," he said, walking away before Olwyn could respond.

The rest of us crept down the hallway toward the faint light in the distance. I glanced back at Olwyn who was now following us and she seemed to be genuinely afraid of what we might find if we kept going. As you might imagine, I found that quite alarming and would have been fine turning around right then. But it was too late. There was no stopping Matt. We paused at a turn in the hallway to peek around and see if anything was there. I gradually moved my head along the wall until it inched its way into the light. My eyes started to adjust, and finally, I could see down the long hallway in front of us.

I saw several shapes sitting on the ground, tied up. Upon closer examination, one of those shapes revealed itself to be Matt's brother, Wyatt. Farther down, the room opened up and there appeared to be some sort of throne sitting out in the middle of the area. Unfortunately, it wasn't empty.

I heard a sharp intake of breath from behind me, and instantly the figure in the chair glanced up with an evil grin. "Ah. Welcome! I was wondering when our next guests would arrive," the King of Sikrath called out.

18
You Want a Deal? I Got a Deal

Joe

Everyone froze in place. How could the king be there? I thought this vault was only discovered very recently by the rebels. How would he have had time to travel here all the way from Ordbridge? But I didn't have much time to think about it because immediately, dozens of soldiers rushed down the stairs behind us and down the hallway in front of us until we were completely surrounded.

"Come, come," the king said. "Let's see who we have here."

The soldiers led us down the hallway toward the king and his prisoners. The light that we had barely seen earlier now illuminated the entirety of the room. The walls were made of stone, and unlike the entrance to the vault, there were no decorations or anything unique to distinguish each segment of wall from the other.

Being underground, there were no windows, obviously, but it seemed almost intentional to leave the walls bare, as though the people who built it were determined to keep the room as uninteresting as possible.

We continued walking until we were about twenty feet away from the makeshift throne. The king watched us with a smirk on his face. I thought that this little adventure wouldn't turn out well, but somehow, I was still surprised by how much trouble we were really in. Wyatt, Sarah, and three other rebels were tied up next to each other against the wall to our left. Luckily, none of them seemed too badly hurt, besides a few cuts and bruises.

As we passed, Wyatt looked up at Matt and shook his head vehemently, though I couldn't understand what exactly he was trying to tell him before I was led out of his view. I thought that he might have been trying to point in the direction of the far wall past the throne, but from what I could see, there was only a very large black metal door, made from what looked to be the same material as the hatch. I could see there was something engraved above it, but I couldn't quite make it out without getting closer.

"Well, I'm glad you could all make it," the king said. He turned to Matt. "My son." he said, speaking in a surprisingly gentle tone of voice. "I was worried about you for a while after I found your note. You know that I always have protected you before, so for you to leave without even talking to me…well, it really wasn't the smartest idea, was it?"

Matt looked at the ground and nodded. "Yes, father. I know I shouldn't have gone. It's just that I had been waiting to do something like this my whole life and I've almost never even gotten the chance to even leave Ordbridge before now."

I looked back and forth between the two of them. That was not a usual conversation for them to have. Almost always, the king would just lecture Matt and punish him if he ever disobeyed, and I had never heard him say that he was worried about him. It felt like a show was being put on for the rest of us.

"Come here, my son," the king said, motioning for Matt to come sit next to him.

"I know that you didn't mean anything by it. I'm just glad that you're safe. And most likely, you now realize why it is that I have been forbidding you to do things like this, yes? The world is a very dangerous place, especially for us, who have many enemies.

Now…there will be no punishment for you. I can understand why you left. As for the rest of you…" The king turned to face us, his features shifting from a warm smile to a cold, calculating glare. "Well, I'm afraid nothing can be guaranteed just yet. There is still some...unfinished business to attend to."

The king fixed his eyes on me. "Ah, Joseph, you have done so much to try and take Matthew away from me: getting him out of the city, casting spells on my guards, all the while knowing full well how treasonous your actions were."

I stared at him in shock. Was he really trying to paint me as some sort of rebel that only brought Matt out of the capital to disrupt his rule of Sikrath? Surely, he couldn't get away with that, right? Though even as I thought that I knew full well that he could easily do whatever he wanted. If he wanted me imprisoned, or even dead, it would happen without question. The king smirked at me, and I could see in his eyes that he knew that there was nothing I could do to stop him.

He then turned his attention to Olwyn. "Well, Ms. Brewer, congratulations," he said. "I would say that you have completed your mission to the letter. You have led Mr. Decker here right into my hands. After we wrap up here, we should talk about a promotion I have in mind for you."

Olwyn smiled. "Thank you, my king. I just did what you instructed me to do." She bowed her head slightly and looked at the ground. Her smile shifted slightly downward, and I could see barely contained anger in her eyes. The king paid no more attention to her, however, and didn't notice anything amiss.

I stared at Olwyn in shock, but she wouldn't meet my gaze. After all the time we had spent together, it felt like a punch in the gut to see her betray us so easily, though I knew that I shouldn't be surprised. She was a Knight of Sikrath; who else would she be loyal to?

Olwyn stepped back from our group and leaned against the wall to my right. I began preparing myself to not make it out of the vault alive. My allies were slowly dropping, one by one, and the ones that I had left weren't exactly in a good position to help me.

"Ah, Rowan Decker." The king smirked, turning his attention to Rowan. "It's about time you came back to us. I was worried that something might have happened to you. Especially after I received word that your train had been derailed."

I looked up at him questioningly. Had he blown up the train to try and kill Rowan? I certainly wouldn't put it past him; he would be more than willing to kill off a few of his citizens in exchange for the death of one of his biggest enemies.

The king caught my gaze and rolled his eyes with a scoff. "Please. As much as you might want it to be true, I had nothing to do with that explosion. Not everything is a huge conspiracy."

I stared at him, unsure what to believe. As much as I could see it happening, I believed that he was telling the truth. For once he seemed to be genuine.

I looked over at Matt, who didn't appear to even be following the conversation. He kept his eyes fixed on the ground, apparently deep in thought.

"Well," the king continued, looking at Rowan. "I'm afraid your past has finally caught up to you. You knew when you conspired against me that there would be consequences, and now I'm here to give them to you. Rowan Decker, I am hereby sentencing you to death for treason against the crown."

Rowan gave almost no visible sign that he'd even heard the king speaking to him. He continued to look at him, unblinkingly, like he had for the last few minutes. Though, I thought I saw his jaw clench slightly and his eyes narrow. The silence in the room was deafening after the final words left the king's mouth. No one dared to give a strong reaction, though Olwyn frowned, and Matt turned to his father, with wide eyes.

The king himself appeared to be in quite a good mood considering he'd just sentenced a man to his death.

"You're sentencing him to death, Father?" Matt asked. "Are you sure that's really necessary?" He appeared to be fighting for Rowan's freedom, but I knew as soon as the king opened his mouth he would somehow sway Matt completely to his side. Already, he was only giving it a half-hearted effort.

"I hate to do this," the king began quietly, in his twisted, fake-sincere tone, as he placed a hand on Matt's shoulder. "But Mr. Decker here has done some terrible things. Theft, assaulting an officer of Sikrath, deception. He even went so far as to conspire with the enemy. I wish I could do more, but it needs to happen. Surely you're old enough now to see that, right?"

Matt stayed quiet and turned his attention back to the floor. At least he hadn't agreed with the king, but obviously he wouldn't be of much help either. They wouldn't just kill Rowan right then, would they? Things were looking grim, not just for Rowan, but the rest of us too.

The king stood up from his throne and walked past me. He paused in front of Hezdek, and after squinting at him for a few moments, motioned for the guards to bring him over to Wyatt and the other soldiers. The king followed until he stood right in front of Wyatt, looking down at him.

"My son," he said. "How have you been led so far astray? Can't you come home after all this time? Surely, we can move past all of this disagreement and come to an understanding."

There it was again. The King was acting gracious and concerned for his sons, but I had never seen him care this much for anyone before. It was all a facade. Wyatt had betrayed him and Sikrath, and I couldn't see any way that he would be able to go back. Not that he would want to, either. Could this all just be a show for Matt? To try and convey how amazing the king was and how Matt should finally listen to him about his future? It sounded a bit far-fetched to me, but then again, with Wyatt gone, Matt was the king's only heir. If something were to happen to him, he would need someone to control his empire once he was gone.

Wyatt glared at him and refused to answer. After several moments of silence, the king sighed long and hard and shook his head. Finally, he turned back around and motioned for me to follow him. The room wasn't big, so there weren't that many places he could be taking me. He led me around the throne and toward the far wall where the door was. I'd thought that it was closed before, but as we got closer, I realized that it was slightly ajar. Why hadn't the king just gone in and taken the artifact? Did he already have it? Surely, he would have shown us and boasted about how amazing he was to outsmart us.

"We have had some troubles acquiring the artifact," the king said, lowering his voice and leaning in next to me. "You see, there seems to be some sort of trap set up for those hoping to get to it, and ..." he paused, glancing around the room as if looking for something. "Well, let's just say that we are now short a few soldiers. Now, I've thought about it and come to realize something. The others didn't want it enough. They didn't truly understand its value." The king lowered his voice until he was talking in almost a whisper. "Yes, I made them go try to get it for me. I threatened their jobs, their families, even their lives. But fear alone is not the motivator that I need. Someone who knows what it is that they are risking their life for, someone who desires to feel the power of an ancient magical artifact. Someone who dabbles in magic themselves, perhaps. That person might have a better chance of thinking through those traps." He paused and leaned back slightly, looking right at me. I met his eyes, and for several long moments, neither of us said a word.

"Don't think for a second that you fooled me when you tried to sneak Matthew out of the city, but..." He hesitated, a slight expression of pain on his face, as though he hated to say this but knew that he had to. "You showed promise. I can't deny that with some training, you might be a powerful ally to me."

He paused again and looked behind him at my small group of friends. It was laughable for him to suggest that the king had figured out our plan to sneak out of Ordbridge. If he had known, then how come he hadn't stopped us? I suppose that if you control the entire empire, however, you can shape yourself into whoever you want to be.

"If you do this for me, you will live," he continued. "You will receive any training that you wish from the top scholars and wizards. I will even consider..." he stopped for a moment, shaking his head and biting his lip as if he was about to offer me the deal of a lifetime, "lessening the punishments for your companions."

I was startled by this proposition. A minute ago, he'd just sentenced Rowan to death, and now he was offering me an education? For several moments I was speechless. I will admit that I was extremely tempted to take his offer—a chance to learn magic, freedom for my friends, a way to leave all of this war and death behind. It sounded incredible. I thought of what my life could be like if everything I wanted could come true. I could finally be with Ben without his mom saying I wasn't wealthy or powerful enough for him. I would be a wizard! But...well, there was the obvious thing about the king slaughtering thousands of Kricoyans as he brutally sacked the city of Entolas, all in the search of the artifacts. That wasn't great.

I glanced down at the king's sword, resting in a sheath on his belt. So much pain it had caused. I realized that anyone who wielded an artifact couldn't continue to be a good person. The power they exerted was just too great. No one could be trusted not to become corrupt with power. Who knew if the king was ever good once, but he certainly wasn't now. He wasn't someone who I wanted to align myself with; I couldn't accept his offer.

That being said, I wasn't about to just turn him down. That would have been suicide. Was there a way to agree and somehow make it so that the king never got the artifact? I'd almost accepted that I wasn't making it out alive, so perhaps the only thing I could do was make sure the king never got what he wanted.

I took a deep breath. "I'll do it," I said.

The king's face twisted into some bizarre form of a smile. It wasn't pretty to look at, but I would've looked at it for years if it meant that I didn't have to go into the vault. I knew it was too late, however.

"Excellent," he said, opening the door to the vault wider. "Take as much time as you need, as long as you don't come out empty handed."

I gulped as I made my way into the depths of the vault.

No turning back now.

19

I'm Not Sure I Understand the Game

Joe

At first glance the long, dark tunnel that stretched out from the vault door wasn't unappealing. Sure, there was the occasional cobweb, and it was very cold and damp, but at least there weren't any guards, right? That had to be worth something.

Unfortunately, that thought quickly disappeared from my mind when I remembered that I was surrounded by deadly traps ready to kill me at any moment. The tunnel was suspiciously empty for the first hundred feet or so, but I mentally prepared myself to fall into a trap at any moment.

There were no lights anywhere, but the walls seemed to glow slightly, as though some sort of magic was imbued in them. I crept down the hall, peering into the darkness, straining my eyes for anything that was coming toward me and scanning the walls and floor for any traps.

I found it odd that there weren't any bodies lying around. There was no sign of any others who'd been sent to their death by the king.

I suppose I could have taken the lack of bodies as a sign that there weren't any traps for a little while, but that seemed like a dangerous thing to assume. Perhaps everyone else was smart enough to evade the first trap and I would be the first to die.

As I walked down the dimly lit tunnel, I started to make out the shape of a dark doorway blending into the color of the wall. Slowly, I made my way toward it, careful to check for any traps along the way.

I'd made it about halfway down the tunnel before something made me stop dead in my tracks. At first, I didn't even realize what had made me stop, and for a moment I started to continue walking down the hallway. But then I saw it. A thin wire stretching from wall to wall in front of me. It was almost invisible to the naked eye and I was amazed that I'd even spotted it. I held my breath as I slowly lifted each leg and brought them down past the wire, careful not to accidentally bump into it and set it off. I was curious as to what would happen if I were to activate it, but it would most likely mean my death, and that seemed slightly too high of a price to pay to indulge my curiosity. Instead, I continued on down the tunnel, still watching for any hidden traps.

I was quite calm considering that I had, most likely, almost just died. I thought of it as a learning experience. At least now I actually knew that there were traps.

Before, they were a mere possibility, albeit more of a probability, but now I knew what exactly I had to be on the lookout for. Trying not to panic, I thought about seeing Ben again once I got out of here. All I had to do was get out of this vault and I could see him again. I took a deep breath and kept walking.

I made it the rest of the way to the door without further incident, although I moved even slower than I had before I saw the trip wire. Cautiously, I moved my hand to the doorknob and prepared myself for whatever was on the other side. Monsters? Soldiers? Magic?

I opened the door and stepped through to find myself in a large, circular room, about three times the width of the tunnel that I'd just left. It was also just as dimly lit and appeared to be made of the same stone that I had seen before. From the doorway, I could see the entire room, though there wasn't a lot to see. There was another door across from me but the room itself was empty, except for a large table in the center with two chairs on either side of it. The chair closest to me was vacant but the one on the far side of the table was occupied by a dark figure who was slouched down in their seat and staring at the ground, unmoving. I couldn't see their face. In fact, I couldn't see any part of them, as their long, black robe covered them entirely.

On the table, a game of Skripes had been laid out, ready for someone to begin playing. Seeing the board in front of me brought back memories of watching many of the wealthy, powerful people at the palace play the game, a favorite of the so-called "important people" all over the continent. I'd played a few games myself, almost everyone had, but it had been so long since I had even seen the board. I wasn't completely sure that I even remembered the rules.

"Um, hello," I ventured, my voice shaking. "Are you…" I hesitated for a moment and glanced around the room again in case there was anyone else lurking in the shadows, "…one of the king's soldiers?"

The figure jerked up suddenly and lifted its head to look at me. Two glowing red eyes stared at me unblinkingly as I finally got a good look at my new companion.

Something wasn't quite right. Their skin was a dark gray and their face was badly misshapen, as though someone had sculpted them to resemble what they thought a human face looked like but had never actually seen one in real life. The entire figure pulsed with a dull, red energy.

This was most certainly not one of the king's soldiers.

"Take a seat," the figure announced, in a very slow and clear voice. It seemed to be coming from somewhere deep inside of them. The place where a mouth would have been on their face gave no indication that any words had been uttered. I hesitated before stepping forward toward the chair on my side of the table and sitting down.

The figure motioned to the board in front of us. "To pass through, you must vanquish me in a game of Skripes. If you win, I will let you go through the door behind me, but if you lose you will never leave here alive. I will give you one chance to leave now. If you decide to stay, start the game by taking the first move."

The figure reverted to its original position and said nothing more. For a moment I sat in my chair and thought about what to do. I couldn't go back the way I'd come. I wouldn't exactly receive a warm welcome. But what hope did I have of actually winning the game? I hadn't played Skripes in years!

Unfortunately, there wasn't much that I could do about it. My only option was to try to win, though that didn't mean I couldn't use a little help. I uttered the short incantation and waved my hand slightly in the direction of the board to cast my spell. Slowly, the board began to glow with a white light as the energy poured out of me and flowed into it. As the spell took hold, I remembered more information about the board. I couldn't tell you how exactly it worked, but somehow as more magical energy flowed out of me, more information about the board and its uses drifted into my mind. I sighed with relief. At least now I knew that I had some base knowledge of what we were playing.

I moved my hand over the board, hoping that one of the pieces would call out to me. I knew the moves I could make, but that didn't mean I knew any strategy for actually winning. I noticed a small piece off to the far left that seemed like it should be moved. I hesitated, unsure why I'd decided to move that particular piece. I knew it was a legal move to make but had no idea if it was a smart one. I picked up the piece and thought for a second. Skripes was an unusual board game. The pieces were made up of several different sized circles carved out of stone. The board, however, was what really differentiated Skripes from other games. Part of the board was a square that lay flat on the table, facing upward, like most other board games, but more than half of the board curved up and away from the square section on either side, creating a multi-level board with walls connecting each layer together. Magnetic pieces were built into the spaces so that the circles could be attached to the side without fear of them falling off.

I decided to move the piece two spaces forward. The figure looked up at me again as soon as I let go of the piece. It paused for a second before reaching over and moving a piece of its own that was slightly to its left, three spaces up on the board. With that, it froze again, staring at me, obviously waiting for my next move.

Cautiously, I picked up the piece all the way on the right end of the board and moved it forward two spaces and one to the left. I looked up at my opponent, wondering if it would give any indication of how bad a play I was making. Slowly, I lifted my hand away, but my opponent simply started moving through its next turn as if everything was normal, this time picking up a piece in front of it and moving it one space forward.

And so, it continued for several minutes, me struggling through my turns, unsure how to best use my pieces and the figure accepting my decisions without a second glance as it moved its own set. The longer the game went on, the more aware I became that I could easily lose at any moment, losing the game along with my life. It was all I could do not to shake uncontrollably as I played.

The objective of Skripes was to capture all of your opponent's pieces before they captured yours. After several more turns, I decided to try taking one of the figure's pieces. I slowly placed my piece in its spot and then withdrew my hand, placing the enemy piece off to the side of the board. I held my breath for a moment before the figure continued playing as normal. I let out a small sigh of relief. So far, so good.

We continued to play for several long minutes before I realized my opponent was losing a lot of its pieces. In fact, was I starting to win? How was that possible?

I had no idea how long it had been since we had started playing, but it felt like hours. The game moved slowly and yet I was gradually taking the lead. And with that lead came more confidence in my ability to actually win. Finally, after another dozen or so turns, I was staring at the final enemy piece on the board. I sat there stunned for a moment as I prepared to move my piece toward his final unit. How was it possible that I'd won? I'd never even been that amazing at it to begin with, and here I was, beating this magical Skripes player left here to stop people from moving forward. It was almost as if he had lost…on purpose.

I froze, hand hovering directly above the last piece, and looked up at the figure sitting across from me. It stared back at me, unmoving, calmly awaiting its next turn. Why would the builders make this thing so bad at Skripes? Obviously, I didn't know enough to win against anyone, and yet I was about to claim victory any second.

Why would this figure be here if it would be no challenge to beat him? And yet, it was a challenge, I realized. For so long in the game, I wasn't sure if I was winning or not.

Slowly, I began winning until we got to this point. It was as if the figure I was playing against had lured me along on this path by playing just bad enough to get me to keep going. But, why? Was it designed to be like this? Did it want me to win? I pondered this for several moments, watching the figure in front of me.

If this vault housed one of the most dangerous artifacts in the world, then maybe the tests to get to it would be designed so that someone who they wanted to get through would be able to. But what kind of person did they want to have it? Its power corrupted everyone eventually. Everyone who had the artifact, no matter how good their intentions were at first, in the end used its power for their own gain. The builders would want someone who showed self-control, perhaps. Someone who demonstrated an ability to hold back and think about what they were doing.

My eyes suddenly widened with understanding, and I slowly lowered my hand to set down my piece on the side of the board. I stared at the figure across from me and stood up, praying that I was right.

"I won't do it. I have beaten you enough. I know when it's time to stop. Now let me move forward."

My heart was beating incredibly fast as the figure slowly stood up from its chair. Was I about to be brutally murdered? Should I run? Somehow, I managed to make myself stand my ground. The seconds dragged on as the figure stood before me, unmoving.

"Congratulations, traveler," it finally said. "You have passed the test. Only one who has mastered the ability of self-control would be able to stop themselves from seizing such an obvious victory." It pulled a small key out of its pocket and held it up to me. "Go forward, and take the artifact if you can, worthy one."

As soon as I took the key from its grasp, they sat back down in the chair and looked down at the ground. The pieces on the board slowly slid back to their original places, ready to start a new game of Skripes for the next traveler.

I couldn't believe I'd actually solved the puzzle. I was so close to taking that last piece. As I stared at the figure, I couldn't help but get the feeling that it was about to spring up and strike me down, so I moved over to the door on the far wall and unlocked it as quickly as possible. I hesitated for a moment and glanced back at the figure once more before finally stepping through and pulling the door shut behind me.

Beyond the door, the tunnel continued to stretch forward, with the same level of light glowing from the walls as before. I sighed with relief after finally getting away from that creepy figure. I was not at all sure that I was going to make it out of that room alive. Well, now I could worry about other traps instead. How encouraging.

I continued down the hallway, just as slow as before, so that I could watch out for traps. I wasn't sure how far it was until I'd actually get to the artifact, but I was confident there would be at least one more trap. How could they be satisfied protecting one of the most dangerous artifacts in the world with just two traps?

After several minutes of stumbling down the tunnel, I came to another door. It looked exactly the same as the other door I'd seen, so I assumed it led into yet another puzzle trap. I took a deep breath, opened the door and stepped through. As soon as I'd stepped through the entrance, the door behind me slammed shut. I turned to try the handle, only to discover that it was locked and there was no keyhole on this side of the door.

Oh well. I was trying to get to the artifact anyway, right?

But something about it made me feel uneasy, as if something very bad was about to happen.

I was now in a wide tunnel that felt much larger than the passageway I'd just left, though there was a new feature that might have been to blame. The floor was almost completely gone. Scattered all the way down the tunnel were small platforms attached to the stone wall and looked just big enough to support me. Between each platform there seemed to be nothing but darkness that stretched as far as the eye could see. It could have been ten feet down or 100, but one thing I was sure of: it would not be a good idea to fall.

I was standing on a platform that was bigger than all the others, except for the one at the end of the tunnel where I could see another door. After inching forward, I got a better look at the gap between my platform and the one closest to me, but as soon as I moved I heard a sharp click and a dull rumbling of movement. And, suddenly, the wall behind me started to move closer and closer. Rooted to the spot, I watched the platform start to shrink before I could fully process what was happening. And then my heart started to pound.

The wall moved even closer, and I only had about three feet left before I would be completely pushed off into the abyss. I looked at the platform closest to me along the right side of the tunnel; it seemed like a pretty big jump, but I didn't really have a lot of options. I couldn't just stand there and think it out, I had to act. The wall rumbled along even closer now, only two feet away from completely enveloping my platform.

It was now or never. I shuffled forward to the very edge and prepared to jump. It must have been at least three or four feet. Could I really make it that far? Well, I was about to find out. Three…the wall moved even closer…two…I was now halfway over the edge…One! With as much strength as I could muster, I threw myself off of the ledge toward the awaiting platform several feet away. And…yes! After a moment of struggle, I was able to pull myself safely onto it.

I sighed deeply and my body sagged with relief.

I realized then that the wall had not stopped moving even as it passed the edge of my former platform, and it really sunk in that I'd have to keep jumping across to the different platforms all the way to the other door. And to make matters worse, I only had a couple minutes to do so.

As quickly as I could, I pulled myself up and prepared to jump to the next platform. This one appeared to be about the same length as before, but it was slightly to my right along the opposite tunnel wall. I would have to recover quickly and move on before the wall of stone got there. I jumped, this time with slightly more ease, though I did fall to the ground again. There was no time to delay. I looked ahead to the next platform and readied myself.

As I made my way further down the tunnel, I began to gain some distance from the wall of stone behind me, but I could still hear it rumbling closer and closer. I leapt from platform to platform, never pausing for more than a few seconds on each one.

The distance between the platforms was slowly increasing as well. Before I knew it, I was jumping across even wider gaps. With each increase I grew more anxious. But I made the jumps every time and soon I had finally made it to the second to last platform before the door.

I was almost done.

"Stop!" a voice called out to me before I could continue forward to the next platform. I glanced around wildly, searching for the source of the disturbance. "Up here!"

I looked up to see a small gap in the ceiling through which a hooded figure was peering down at me. I could barely make out any distinguishing features through the hood and the darkened atmosphere of the room, but the figure's voice was fairly deep with a hint of an accent that I couldn't quite place.

"You can't jump to the next platform," they called out to me earnestly. "You have to trust me!"

"Who are you?" I called up to them, perplexed as to how they had even managed to get up there in the first place. "Why shouldn't I move forward?"

"It's too dangerous. You'll fall. Just stay there; I'll help you."

I hesitated, unsure of how to respond. I had no idea who this person was; how could I trust them with my life? I looked over at the next platform, a mere five feet away from me, and to the one after which lay just a few feet away from the door. I was so close to making it out. Why should I stop here?

The wall was now halfway through the room and getting closer by the second. I could only assume that the wall was going to follow me all the way to the door before it stopped its pursuit.

"Why do I need your help?" I asked the figure. "I'm sure I could make the next jump."

"No! You won't make it." The figure shook their head vehemently. "You have to trust me! There's no other way to the other side."

The wall rumbled closer and closer, now only a few platforms away from me. I would have to make a choice soon. I looked back over at the nearby platform; it seemed to be so easily in reach. Why shouldn't I just jump over to it? This stranger above me could just be tricking me, so that I would die and they would get the artifact. That's exactly what has happened for thousands of years. People would do whatever it took to get the artifacts. You just couldn't...trust...anyone.

That was it! This was just another test! The builders wanted someone who could trust others, not just hoard all the power for themselves. They wanted someone who could rely on other people.

The wall rumbled even closer, almost coming to the edge of my platform. I had to decide now. It was so tempting to just jump forward to the next platform, but I knew that I was right. If I could just trust this person above me to get me out of this situation like they promised, I might actually make it past this test.

The wall was now only a few feet away from me, the rumbling growing louder with each passing foot. Just a few more seconds and the platform would be consumed. I looked up anxiously toward the figure above me, but they were no longer in view. Were they coming to help me? Had I completely misjudged the situation?

I closed my eyes, preparing for the worst. Whatever happened, I knew I had tried my best to make it through this vault. Three...I took a small step forward...two...I could feel the wall at my back, pushing me forward...one...THOOM!

I slowly opened my eyes to discover the stone wall behind me had abruptly stopped in its path, just inches away from completely consuming my platform. I had hardly any room to stand, but I was still alive.

The figure I'd seen before reappeared above me, this time without a hood to cover its face. I could clearly see now that it was the same sort of magical creation as the Skripes player earlier. It had been left there on purpose; there was no doubt about it.

Slowly, the figure slid down from a short rope that came from the small gap in the ceiling and reached out a large hand toward me. I hesitated briefly before realizing that I was still inches away from death. As I reached up to grab its hand it slowly pulled me up toward the gap in the ceiling, grasping the smooth stone walls as hand holds. It was a feat no living person could have managed without serious magical assistance. We finally made it through the gap and into a small, dark tunnel. The figure set off down the tunnel, with me right behind it.

The tunnel was no more than 20 or 30 feet long. Once at the end, the figure took my hand again and led me into the light. After a moment I realized that we were now standing at the very end of the room, right next to the doorway.

"T-thank you," I stammered. The figure just stared at me, emotionless, before reaching down to pick up a small stone at its feet and throwing it directly at the platform I had been considering jumping onto just a few minutes earlier. As soon as the stone hit the platform, the entire thing collapsed from the impact, sending what looked to be several tons of rock tumbling into the dark void below.

I stared at the now blank wall in shock. I turned back to the figure, only to discover that it had vanished. I spun around wildly, looking for where they could have gone, but it was no use: they had disappeared. The only thing left to do was to continue forward.

This time, the door didn't lead to another tunnel like the others. There was a room, much smaller than the last, with a single table in the center. The walls were made of the same stone as before, but there didn't appear to be anyone or anything else in the room, which I was thankful for. Sitting on top of the table was a glass cube that looked to be attached to the surface of the table. And inside, a large black helm sat, waiting for someone to rescue it from its prison. It almost seemed too easy, though I'd barely made it through the last few traps alive. Slowly, I made my way closer to the cube. Before I could reach it, however, a blinding blue light exploded out of thin air in front of me, and a large figure emerged from it. After stumbling around for several moments, blinded by the light, I was able to regain my vision to see the huge figure made completely out of light now standing in front of me.

"Who dares to disturb the Vault of Thriesoff?!" he thundered down at me.

I sighed. Here we go again.

20

The Disappointment's All Mine

Matt

It all happened so fast. We walked into the vault, and there my father was—a long way from his throne in Ordbridge. I still didn't exactly get along with him, but I think my journey gave me a little bit more respect for his accomplishments. Wyatt just couldn't understand what he had to go through to run the empire. We were at war and sacrifices had to be made. Surely, if someone was going to get these artifacts, we would want it to be father. Someone had to keep the artifacts safe, right?

I watched Father lead Joe to the large metal door on the far side of the room and talk to him, motioning toward the door several times. I couldn't hear what they were saying from so far away, but after a few moments, Father opened the door and Joe walked through. Father then wandered back over to his throne and took a seat. I glanced back and forth between him and the door, unsure how to react. What exactly had he just sent Joe off to do?

"Um, where is Joe going?" I asked, hesitantly.

Father looked up at me with raised eyebrows, as though he'd almost forgotten there was anyone else in the room with him. "He's going to collect the artifact for us, my son. There's nothing to worry about."

I opened my mouth to respond, but quickly closed it again as Father turned away from me to talk to one of his officers beside him, effectively ending the conversation. What was he thinking? He was just sending Joe in to get the artifact for him? Surely, he realized that the vault was full of dangerous traps, right? Why couldn't he have just sent in a soldier instead?

I bit my lip anxiously, unsure of how to proceed. Joe was clearly in danger in the vault, but what could I do to get him to come back? Father was obviously angry at him for his part in my disappearance at Ordbridge. I wasn't sure that I could convince him to let Joe come back.

After about ten minutes had passed since Joe had gone into the vault, Father started to pace around the room and grow more restless. He shook his head and muttered to himself as he went. I could tell that he wanted the artifact badly and his patience was dwindling. I began to grow more and more restless as well.

With each passing second it felt like Joe had a worse chance of coming back alive. Why hadn't I stood up to Father when he first told me Joe was leaving? He could be dead right now, for all I knew. My stomach began to churn.

Father finally wandered back over to where Wyatt sat on the ground, still restrained. "Perhaps you feel as though I am being unfair to you. Maybe we could arrive at some sort of…compromise."

Wyatt raised his eyebrows in surprise, and I couldn't help but agree with him. Since when did Father compromise?

"Alright, I'm listening," Wyatt responded, cautiously.

"Well, I believe that with some training you could come to understand where exactly you went wrong when you left to join the rebels. I know you don't want to hear this, but it's necessary to hear both sides of an argument before choosing the winner. Don't you agree?" Father said, a small smirk appearing on his face.

Wyatt frowned at Father, clearly not impressed with his offer. "Fine, go ahead. What could you possibly have to say that will explain your actions? You have caused so much suffering, not only for the countless lands you've conquered and people that you've massacred, but even in your own capital city there is so much poverty and unhappiness. Nothing you say can change that."

For a second, Father's face paled, and he furrowed his brow, but his features quickly hardened into a cold and calculating expression.

"Well, I see," he drawled coldly. "If that is how you want to be." He paused for a moment to slowly shake his head in disgust. "Without even bothering to hear me out...then you are truly dead to me. I had held out some small hope that I might be able to convince you to come back to your family, to where you were born and raised, but I see now that you are too far entrenched in this treasonous mindset. You will have to be executed."

I froze. Did he just say executed? Surely, he wasn't serious? Would he really kill his own son? I glanced back and forth between them, frozen in place. How could Father even be considering execution? Wyatt's actions were indeed treasonous, but he could still be brought back to the palace and retaught everything that he once understood. I hesitated, unsure what to do. I couldn't let Father kill Wyatt.

I looked over at Wyatt, trying to catch his eye, but he was glaring defensively at Father. Beneath his anger, I could sense his surprise as well, as if he hadn't really thought Father would punish him so severely. Father let the silence grow for several moments before finally stepping back and walking toward his throne again.

"Perhaps that is too harsh," he said. "We can reevaluate later once I have the artifact."

Wyatt continued to say nothing and glared at him, though I was instantly relieved. I felt myself start to relax; Father was just trying to get Wyatt to agree to talk to him. He wasn't actually going to kill him. Obviously not: doing something like that would just be evidence to support Wyatt's insane claims about him.

But before anyone could say anything else we all heard a loud bang coming from above us, followed by several shouts and the sounds of dozens and dozens of people running down the stairs and down the tunnel toward us.

"Guards, prepare yourselves!" Father shouted, as he ran to the front of the room and drew his sword. I hurried over to try to position myself kind of close to the front but ended up near the middle of the room as all the guards rushed forward. I glanced around at everyone around the room and there was quite a mixture of expressions, ranging from Olwyn, who stood fiercely with her axes raised, ready to kill anything that came into the room, to Rowan, who was slowly backing away from the hallway we had come through, a look of terror on his face.

There was hardly any time to think before a wave of rebel soldiers poured out from the hallway and swept into the guards. With such a compact space for combat, the fighting became increasingly vicious with soldiers falling left and right on both sides. As soon as a new guard stepped up to fill an empty spot, another one would fall.

In the corner of the room, I saw Rowan cutting Hezdek, Wyatt and his companions free from their restraints, but with the present chaos, no one paid them any mind.

"Hold! No surrender!" Father called out as he charged forward, cutting down anyone who stepped in front of him. We pushed forward to meet the enemy, but we were all pushed back very quickly from the sheer number of enemies that we were against. Slowly, our motivation waned until we started to become fully overrun, and our small group of survivors was pushed farther and farther toward the throne until finally, a voice called out.

"Hold!"

The rebel soldiers immediately froze and fell back several steps. A figure emerged from behind them and slowly made their way through the group. They wore an intricately carved face mask of what looked to be a leopard and a shiny silver compass tied to a string around their neck. They wore fine silk robes, something a common soldier would never be able to afford.

"Ah, we finally meet," the figure said, bowing in Father's direction. "I was sure that we would see each other soon enough, but I had no idea that it might be in a place such as this." There was a slight pause before continuing. "Allow me to introduce myself. I am Glyndwyr Brice."

There was a long moment of silence after this declaration that no one but Father would dare break.

"What, exactly, are you doing here, then?" my father asked, stretching out each word for at least half a second longer than usual and pointing his sword at Glyndwyr Brice menacingly.

"Well, it seems to me that there is an important artifact to be claimed here and an excellent opportunity to strike down my enemies."

He drew a sword that was sheathed on his belt and held it up, his silver compass glinting from around his neck. He paused for a few seconds and glanced around the room, taking in the open vault door.

"Still waiting for your faithful minions to return?" he asked with glee. "Could it be that you've sent a few too many to their deaths? You look to be quite outnumbered, I'm afraid." He sauntered back and forth in front of his troops as he spoke.

Father stepped forward with his sword raised. "You forget your place, Brice!" he growled. "Have you forgotten the countless victories I have achieved over your worthless soldiers?! Or the sword that I have used to cut down so many who seek to usurp me?" Father was growing more and more aggressive as he spoke; he was almost spitting out his words as he yelled at Glyndwyr Brice. I clutched my sword a little bit tighter and prepared myself for the inevitable fight.

"You think you have power here, but even you know that no one can beat me while I wield this sword!"

Glyndwyr Brice stared back at my father and raised his sword. "Perhaps someone needs to take it away, then." He raised his hand in front of him into a fist and the soldiers around him lurched into motion, charging right at us.

All I could do was hold up my sword and try to stand my ground as the wave of enemies washed over us. I was behind several guards, but as our line started to crumble, one soldier made it through. He locked eyes with me and rushed forward.

I jabbed my sword toward him, but he easily blocked my attack and countered. I was barely able to dash out of the way of his blade before it came crashing down next to me. My opponent slashed through the air with his sword several more times, each one closer than the last, but I couldn't find an opportunity to block with my shield. All I could do was jump back, away from his swings.

All around me, the fighting was getting more and more brutal, and I could feel soldiers fall to the ground by my side, either cut down by an enemy or trampled by the swarming crowds. We were slowly being pushed back toward the throne.

I didn't have time to look around too much, though, as I still had a soldier to deal with myself. We continued to circle each other, until finally, I saw my chance. He moved his shield slightly too far to the right and I stabbed my sword toward his exposed chest, which he managed to block at the last second. I tried to force my sword through his defenses but ended up overextending myself. He brought his own sword down toward me and I was just able to raise my shield to block.

The sound was deafening. A loud crack flew through the air and a blinding flash lit up the room. I heard screams and saw several people waving their weapons around wildly, blinded by the light. My opponent had been thrown backward at least thirty feet and now lay in a heap on the ground. Many people were looking over in my direction, looking for the source of the loud noise and bright light. In fact, the battle had slowed down considerably as people picked themselves up from the ground, trying to get their vision back and looking around to find out what happened.

Glyndwyr Brice and my father, who had previously been locked in an intense duel, stepped back from each other and moved toward me. Father looked at me with amazement as he tried to process what he had just seen. "What was that?" he asked, now standing right near me. "Where did you get that shield?"

"I, uh…" I glanced around at everyone, most of whom were staring at me. "I just found it a while ago in Ordbridge. I-I don't really know how that light appeared. It must be magic or something."

Father just nodded; his eyes fixed upon the shield still grasped in my hands. "Is it possible?" he murmured to himself. "After all those years of searching, it was right next to me the entire time?" He slowly reached out toward the shield. I saw his eyes fill with longing as his hand came closer and closer.

"I don't think so!" a voice said, and Glyndwyr Brice appeared in front of us, sword in hand and ready to continue the attack. His troops had almost recovered from the blinding light and now he led another attack against us.

His sword swung directly in between us, forcing us to jump apart. Father immediately raised his sword and counterattacked. I thought for sure that Brice wouldn't be able to avoid his swing, but somehow, he pulled his sword back in front of him at the perfect time, fully blocking Father's attack. I had never truly seen Father or his sword in battle before, and it was incredible to watch. He and Brice swung back and forth at each other, barely missing each time. An enemy soldier tried to approach Father from behind as he and Brice fought, but

Father saw him, and in the middle of his duel, he leapt to the side right as the soldier lunged forward, causing him to lose his balance and fall to the ground. After that, it was back to the duel as if nothing had happened.

I could have watched for hours, but soon realized that I was actually still in the middle of a battlefield, surrounded by enemies. And no sooner had I thought that, than another soldier charged over to me and attempted to cut me down. He swung his large axe down from overhead with two hands and I narrowly leapt out of the way. The axe slammed into the stone floors of the cave, creating a large indent. Before I could even move, he pulled the axe from the ground and attempted to swing at me again. It was all I could do to jump out of the way as the massive piece of sharpened metal glided through the air, inches away from me.

The swing staggered him, and I took the opportunity to jab my sword into his side. He howled with pain and stumbled back several feet before falling to his knees; I thought that he was done with the fight, but after a moment, he slowly rose to his feet once again and held up his axe. I stepped back, eyes wide. How had he survived that hit? He should have died, or at the very least, been seriously injured, but all he did was hold his side and grin at me with fierce determination as blood dripped from a large gash on his side. I readied my sword and shield for his next attacks.

I didn't have to wait long. He lurched forward and swung his axe to the side with incredible force. I raised my sword in an attempt to intercept his strike, but I gravely miscalculated his strength. My sword was flung out of my hand and clattered to the ground loudly. My heart raced. With no weapon, there was no way that I would be able to defend myself, even if my opponent was mortally injured. I took a few tentative steps backward only to have him run straight at me, axe raised.

I did the only thing that I had left to do; I raised my shield. Again, a blinding light and a thunderous crack emanated from the shield, and I watched as my attacker was thrown backward, straight into a spear that impaled and killed him instantly. As for everyone else in the room, it was about the same reaction as before. Many people fell to the ground or swung around wildly, hoping to get lucky. I noticed that Glyndwyr Brice didn't seem to be as affected by the light and sound as others did. Perhaps his mask helped him to filter out a lot of the bad effects.

Whatever the case was, it did not help my father in their duel. The light and sound seemed to disorient him just like the other soldiers, and Brice took advantage of this opening. He charged at Father and slashed at his chest with his sword. Father cried out in pain, but before he could counterattack, Brice kicked at his leg, sending him tumbling down to the ground.

I had to help him, but I didn't know if I could make it in time; my sword still lay on the ground at least ten feet away. I lunged for it, careful not to put myself in the middle of any other fighting, which there was plenty of. And…got it! I turned around, sword now in hand, ready to help Father get back onto his feet and strike down Glyndwyr Brice. As I watched, Brice surged forward and swung again and again down at Father, who tried to crawl backward and block the attacks, but I could tell that his strength was failing.

I held up my sword, and before I could convince myself to try something else, I threw it directly at Brice. I wasn't sure what exactly I was expecting but, miraculously, the hilt slammed into him, and he stumbled to the side. This gave Father just enough time to jump up and swing his sword right at Brice, who fell to the ground, his sword flung out of his grasp. Father walked up to him with his sword raised.

"You really thought that you could defeat me?" my father laughed. "You never stood a chance. Your puny rebellion will be put down just like all the others."

He started to bring his sword down, but suddenly a figure leapt in front of Glyndwyr Brice, protecting him from Father's blade.

"NO! You can't kill him!" Wyatt screamed as he jumped forward, his sword out in front of him and Glyndwyr Brice—Father's eyes widened, his sword already swinging down toward his son.

THUNK! The blade sliced through Wyatt's shoulder and sunk deep into his chest.

He stared up at Father, his face pale and his eyes and mouth open in shock.

I looked upon the scene, frozen with horror. I tried to open my mouth to call out to him, but my body wouldn't cooperate. All I could do was stand, unmoving, as I watched the blood gush from Wyatt's chest. Wyatt looked down at himself and cautiously placed a hand on his bleeding chest.

"I-I…" he stammered, glancing back up at Father again, a stunned look upon his face, before collapsing to the ground, motionless.

"Why did you do that, boy?!" Father exclaimed. "Look what you made me do!" He paused for a moment, a frown on his face before kicking Wyatt's body out of the way.

"Enough. It's time to end this," he said, raising his sword again and advancing toward Glyndwyr Brice, who had recovered from my blow and had begun crawling backward toward his weapon.

"What have you done?" I whispered, stumbling over to Wyatt's side. "You killed him! You killed your own son!" I sobbed, clutching Wyatt's hand with both of my own as I kneeled beside his body. My vision blurred and my body felt like it didn't belong to me.

Father hesitated for a moment. "Calm down. He did it to himself. If he hadn't thrown himself into my blade, then he would still be alive." He sighed. "We can discuss this later. Right now, I have business to attend to."

He stepped forward toward Glyndwyr Brice, who'd just managed to grab his sword that had been thrown onto the ground and pointed it at Father while still on the ground.

"He was right," I whispered, as a dull pain rose up in my stomach. "About everything. Wyatt was right."

I grabbed my sword from the ground and slowly rose to face my father as I shook with anger. "Wyatt was right about you. He tried to tell me, but I didn't listen. I didn't believe him."

Father began to bring his sword down on Glyndwyr Brice, but I leapt forward and blocked his swing with my own blade. "Not this time!" I screamed at him. "You won't get away with this!"

I managed to push him backward, away from Brice, most likely because he was so surprised by my intervention.

"Stop this right now." he said, menacingly, sword raised toward me. "I'm willing to forgive this considering what just happened to Wyatt, but you better stop right now."

"AHHH!" I charged at him, slashing the air wildly in front of me.

Father jumped backward, not even bothering to block my feeble attacks.

"I'm warning you," he shouted. "You don't want to do this."

I leapt toward him again. This time my blade successfully slashed through his defenses, leaving a thin cut on his left arm.

He stumbled backward in shock before his expression quickly hardened and shifted to one of anger. He leapt toward me, swinging his sword again and again, each attack more powerful than the last. I stumbled back after each hit, my sword barely withstanding the force of his weapon. "I see it now!" he shouted at me in between swings. "You're just like your worthless brother. I thought I could save you, mold you into something resembling a suitable heir, but I see now that you could never have ruled the empire!"

With a final blow, he pushed me to the ground, my sword and shield thrown from my grasp. My head slammed into the wall, causing my vision to blur for a moment.

"Goodbye, boy," he said, raising his sword up one last time.

Suddenly, his expression froze, and his eyes bulged. He opened his mouth, but no words came out, and as I watched, his expression of anger slowly turned to one of shock and fear, an emotion I couldn't remember ever seeing upon his face. He slowly fell to his knees and reached a listless hand out toward me.

A small circle of blood seeped into the front of his shirt, right where his heart was. As I watched, it grew darker and spread out farther and farther before almost his entire shirt was soaked in it.

"H-help...me," he whispered, his voice barely audible, before finally falling face first onto the ground.

"I've been waiting to do that for twenty years," Rowan said, standing where my father had been just a moment before, a black, metal helm in his hand. "You just never knew when to give up, did you, you old fool," he said, kicking the dead body of the king of Sikrath.

21
The Choice Is Yours

Joe

The apparition hovered a few feet off the ground, glowering down at me. It was hard to make out any specific features because it was so bright, but I could only assume that this was meant to be some sort of guardian of the vault. It appeared to be an older man wearing armor and wielding a sword. I couldn't tell much about him, but I estimated that he would have been around forty years old if he were alive.

"I mean you no harm," I said, raising my hands up in front of me. "If it was up to me, this vault would stay sealed, but I don't really have a choice."

The figure paused for a second and considered me. "Everyone always has a choice," he responded in a slow and deep booming voice. "You merely decided that this was the best option to take. Now, what exactly are you doing here?"

I looked up at him as he stood, or floated, I suppose, looking down at me with his arms crossed. I was out of tricks to play. All I could do was tell him the truth. "I'm here for the artifact," I said.

He frowned and squinted at me. "Hmm…well, at least you're honest. Is there a reason that you seek the helm, or is this merely a fun adventure for you?"

"I don't want it," I said. "But I have to get it. You see, the King of Sikrath is out there in the antechamber, waiting for me to come back with the helm. If I don't come back with it, my friends are going to be killed."

The man stared at me as I explained the whole situation, never reacting any more than a casual nod or tilt of the head.

"You believe that this king is all powerful? Nothing can stop him?" he asked after I had finished telling him what happened.

"Well, it certainly seems like it. At least, I don't see what I could do that would be of any importance."

"And, after you leave here with the helm? Will you hand it over to him and let him wield even more power than he already has?"

I stared at him; what exactly did he want me to say? "Look, you don't get it," I said, starting to get a little annoyed. "You can say I have as many options as you want, but this is the only reasonable one. I have to get that helm."

The man turned to look at the helm behind him for a few moments before turning back to me. "So, you say that you don't really want this artifact, eh?" he said, with a smirk on his face. "You think that you just need it to help solve your problems. Perhaps you would be willing to put that to the test?"

I almost groaned at the word test; I'd had quite enough of tests for a long time. I briefly considered just grabbing the helm and trying to run out, but I got the feeling that the man before me was a lot more powerful than he was letting on.

I frowned. "Alright, what sort of test are you talking about?"

He just smiled. "So, you agree to start?"

"Well, hold on. What exactly is going to—"

Before I could argue any further, my vision began turning fuzzy and I swayed on my feet. I stumbled forward, reaching out to try to grab the man, but he dissolved in my grasp. All I could do was wait as my vision slowly faded completely, only to reappear after a few seconds of darkness. I blinked several times, trying to get my bearings, before I looked around to ask the man what he had just done. As I raised my head to look at the room, I realized with a start that

I was back in the antechamber of the vault, surrounded by all of the guards and the king.

"Ah, you're back." The king nodded at me. "Do you have the artifact?"

I took a few more moments to recover from the rapid scenery change, before looking down to discover that I did indeed have the helm in my hands.

"I-I," I started, spinning around slightly and glancing around the room, trying to understand how I'd just teleported back to the beginning of the vault. "Um, yes, I did get it."

"Excellent." The king stared at the helm hungrily, motioning for me to come closer.

I slowly walked toward the throne and held up the helm to him, but as I did, I heard a small voice emanating from it.

"Are you really going to give me up just like that?" it said.

I paused and looked down at the object in my hands. Was I hearing things? Had it really just spoken? I quickly looked around me but no one else appeared to have heard it.

"Come on," it said. "Do you have any idea how much power you could wield if you kept me? And what do you get out of it, anyway? The possibility that your friends will be okay? The better choice is to use my powers to save your friends."

I hesitated. The helm brought up a good point and I couldn't lie; I had wanted to try it on ever since I had seen it. And really what guarantee did I have that the king would let my friends go, anyway? He had given me his word, but that was coming from a man who had massacred an entire city. Could I trust anything that he says?

"Well?" the king said, frowning slightly, unable to contain his obvious annoyance at my delay. "Are you going to hand it over or not?"

I looked down at the helm in my hand once more and tried to imagine handing it over to him. It seemed like such a bad idea. If I used it myself, I could accomplish whatever I wanted. I could save my friends and come home to Ordbridge in triumph, and no one could stop me from being with Ben. I could do whatever I wanted. I could have anything that I ever dreamed of. It wasn't much of a choice.

And yet...as the man had said, everyone always has a choice. Would the power of the helm really allow me to do all those things? It seemed like a gamble. And I wouldn't only be gambling my own life; I would be gambling the lives of all the hostages. When it came down to it, I realized I just couldn't afford to make that choice.

"Here," I said, handing the helm over to the king.

"Finally," he said, staring right at me, after taking the helm from my grasp, his voice growing deeper and more pronounced with each passing second. "I have found someone who can wield the artifact."

My vision again slowly faded into black, and when it returned, I found myself back in the room I had been in just a few minutes ago with the helm on the table and the man made of light. The man now floated in front of me with a warm smile on his face.

"Well done, traveler," he said, nodding to me. "You are the first one to successfully pass the test. Only someone who can resist the power of the artifact enough to willingly give it away can be trusted not to wield it for evil. I assume, also smart enough not to keep it long enough for that willpower to fade, as it has for so many."

He turned back to the table behind him and waved his hand. Slowly, the glass cube seemed to melt away until the helm was left completely uncovered. The man floated backward and motioned for me to take it. I stepped forward, almost unable to believe that I was actually about to get the helm.

Now that I was standing right next to it, I could see it much more clearly. The helm was made of a black metal that I was unable to identify. It was an extremely simple design with just two eye holes leading down to an opening for the nose and mouth. There wasn't anything fancy about it and I could see how people might underestimate its true power.

I reached out and touched the helm, the dark metal cold against my fingers, before finally picking it up and placing it on my head. I paused, holding my breath, waiting for something to happen, but I looked down to discover that I was still perfectly visible. I looked myself over, trying to find some part of me that was now invisible, but I couldn't find anything.

The man chuckled. "Trust me, you are completely invisible to others, even though you can still see yourself. Let me tell you, it comes in handy to still be able to see what you're doing, that's for sure. Now," he paused looking over at the door that I had come through earlier, "are you going to go back and rescue your friends?"

I smiled at him. "Thank you for helping me. I'm glad that I was able to pass your tests."

The man simply nodded, and I turned back to open the door.

"Ahem," I heard behind me as I was about to slip through to the other room.

"I-I suppose that I should tell you," the man said, pausing for a moment to glance around the room. "When you leave this room with the helm, I will disappear. It's just part of the magic of my illusionary body. We assumed that once the helm had been taken away, there was no need for anyone to stay here." He looked down at the ground and frowned. "Which is true, though I can't say that I'm ready to go, exactly. Still, I know that you must leave. It has been so long since there's been someone worthy of the helm, but you deserve to have it. Please use it cautiously. Farewell, traveler." The man held up his hand to wave goodbye and I did the same.

I stepped through the doorway, and as I turned to close the door, I saw the man slowly fade into oblivion. I hoped he was at peace, even if he didn't think that he was ready.

The stone wall in the previous room had fully returned to its previous position. I strode back through the tunnel that I had taken before climbing back onto the platform beneath me and then jumping back across to the other platforms I had been to before. In only a few minutes I was back at the door at the end of the room.

I went through the next door into the room where I had won at Skripes before, or rather, lost at Skripes. The figure was still there, hunched over the board, waiting for its next opponent that would never come now that I was taking the artifact. I wondered what would happen to it. Maybe the magic in it would fade as it did for the man in the other room. Well, I wasn't sticking around to find out; I was more than ready to get out of this horrible vault as soon as possible.

I quickly walked past the figure, who didn't react to my presence at all, and out the other door. I was now back in the long hallway that was at the beginning of the vault. It wouldn't be long now before I was with the others, and I would have to hand over the artifact. I knew it would be bad to hold onto it myself for too long, but there was no way I was handing it over to the King. He was the last person I could give it to. I would do whatever I could to stop him.

I strode confidently down the hallway, tired of delaying the inevitable conflict in the antechamber. As I made my way down the hallway, however, the sounds of metal on metal and screams reached my ears. Immediately, I quickened my pace and rushed forward for the door.

It was at that moment that I remembered the tripwire that I'd narrowly avoided earlier. I scrambled to stop but it was too late; I had already activated it. The floor under me immediately gave way to a large drop and I fell inside. The ground rushed toward me, closer and closer. I closed my eyes and prepared for impact...but nothing happened. Slowly, I opened my eyes again and found myself hanging into the pit with the tripwire tangled around my leg. Looking around, I discovered that the walls were smooth, with no handholds for me to grip, and the ground below me was covered in large stone spikes, several of which had dark stains on them that looked suspiciously like blood.

Suddenly, I lurched down a few more feet. My weight was slowly pulling the tripwire down with me, so I would have to act fast. I reached up and tried to grab onto the wire, but it slipped from my grasp. As I dropped back down, I could feel the wire drop another few inches. I froze, trying to stay as still as possible as the wire slowly stopped swinging me back and forth. I tried to reach up again as cautiously as I could, but I couldn't reach the wire above me. I tried again and again, each time only to fall back down in the same position. Pausing for a moment, I took a deep breath and lurched upward as quickly as I could and grabbed the wire. Finally, I managed to get a good grip and started pulling myself up. With each pull, I could feel the wire slipping downward, as though it threatened to give way at any moment. I hesitated, unsure if I should continue on; if I pulled too hard, then the wire could fall down and I would be dropped to my death, but if I didn't pull enough, then the wire could collapse from my weight at any moment, also killing me. All I could do was move up slowly and hope that everything would work out alright.

Slowly, one hand at a time, I began to pull myself out of the pit. Each time I got closer to the edge I could feel the wire slipping down and sliding against the rock above me, my chances of survival lessening with each passing second. Soon, I could almost reach the edge. I stretched out my hand, but my fingertips could just barely graze the rock before the wire shifted and I was forced to grab it with both hands or risk losing my balance. My heart lurched as I felt as though I was falling for a moment before the wire caught on the rock again, still barely connected to the wall.

I glanced down again at the sharp spikes below me, before taking a deep breath and lurching upward toward the ledge. My hand slammed into it, and I finally managed to hold on. No more than a second later the wire fell away from the wall, down to the spikes below. It took all of my strength, but I managed to pull myself up before collapsing on the cold stone floor.

For several moments, I laid on the ground, breathing hard, trying to process what had just happened. Meanwhile, the battle still raged out in the antechamber, so I didn't have any time to lose. I pulled myself to my feet and jumped across the gap in the floor, which was only a couple of feet wide, and finally made my way to the door.

I peeked through the doorway to try and see what scene was waiting for me on the other side. What was going on? Someone with a leopard mask was fighting the king and there were also dozens of rebel soldiers. Glyndwyr Brice had brought backup?

Maybe it would be easier than I thought to make sure that the king didn't get the helm. Soldiers on both sides were falling left and right. I could see Rowan, Hezdek, and Wyatt off in the corner trying to get away from the fighting, and Olwyn was near the middle, battling several people at once.

I had to do something, so I put on the helm and stepped through the doorway. I still couldn't tell that anything was different, but I would just have to trust that it was working. I hesitated for a moment, unsure of exactly how to proceed. It seemed dangerous to just dive in when I was invisible. I could be killed by an ally just as easily as by an enemy.

But there was no point in delaying any further. Slowly, I made my way over to Hezdek and Rowan. Hopefully we could all find some relatively safe corner to hide in and await the results of the battle. As I maneuvered through the room, it became increasingly difficult to avoid running into people or swinging blades. I had to be extra vigilant if I was going to be able to dodge everyone.

Luckily, however, I was close to getting to the others. A few more quick jumps to the side and I was there. I reached up and took off the helm, which caused me to suddenly reappear. All three of them jumped up in surprise.

"Joe!" Hezdek yelped. "Where did you come from? I swear you weren't there a second ago." He looked at me suspiciously, as if looking for some dark magic that I had used to turn invisible. Which I suppose wasn't too far from the truth.

"I got the helm," I said, holding it up for them to see. "I don't really know what we should do with it, but as long as it stays away from the king, then we should be alright."

They both looked at me in amazement. "Really?" Rowan asked. "That's the helm of invisibility?"

I nodded. "Yeah, it doesn't really look like much, but trust me, it works just fine. Now, what can we do to help the rebels?"

"I'd love to say that now that we have the helm, all of our problems are over," Hezdek said dryly. "But it seems to me like the best thing you can do is to just keep it away from the king."

Even as he said the words, however, we all heard the king laughing and we turned to see Glyndwyr Brice on the floor, with the king pointing his sword at him menacingly.

"Give me the helm," Rowan asked quietly, jaw clenched as he watched the king push Matt toward the wall. "I'll finish this."

I hesitated for a long moment before slowly reaching up and handing him the helm. I was the guardian of the helm, wasn't I? Shouldn't I be the one to end this fight? But I just…couldn't. I couldn't kill the king. Matt's father. Even though I knew all of the horrible things that he had done, I wasn't sure that I would have the strength to do it. Rowan, fortunately, had no such qualms. He nodded once and disappeared in front of Hezdek and I. We shared a quick glance before looking back at their fight.

Then as we watched, Wyatt jumped in front of the King's blade. And Rowan quickly repaid the favor.

I ran over to Matt, but he collapsed as soon as I made it to his side. I quickly confirmed that he was still alive before sighing in relief. I glanced over at Matt's shield and the king's sword on the ground. I quickly picked them up; I wasn't going to take any more chances with who got these artifacts. Rowan handed me the helm back as well.

And with that, the battle slowly drew to a close. The rest of the king's soldiers had surrendered, including Olwyn, who rushed over to us, relief on her face. It was the closest I'd ever seen to a smile from her on the whole trip. I supposed it meant that she'd abandoned the king to join our side, but I was too tired to even think about it right then. I would have to ask her about it later.

"You're going to have to come with me," I heard from behind me. I turned to find Glyndwyr Brice standing behind me, staring at the dead body of the king laying on the ground and the three artifacts in my hands. "We have much to discuss."

22

Well, You Fooled Me

Joe

The trip back to the camp was quiet. We didn't run into any more Sikrathian soldiers, thankfully, but I was too worried about Matt to really enjoy that. I hoped that when he woke up, he would agree with what Rowan had done to his father, or at the very least, agree that the king had done a lot of horrible things and had to be stopped. Surely the death of his brother would help him to understand that a little better.

At least I could be happy that Rowan, Hezdek, and Olwyn were alright, though I wasn't totally sure that I could trust Olwyn anymore. Was she on our side or not? I wasn't sure what to think.

Once we finally made it back to camp, everyone wanted to celebrate. In their eyes, the mission was nothing but a success: the king was dead, and the artifacts were under their control. Many of them seemed to think that the war was going to end, which I hoped was true, but even with the king gone, the war might go on. Someone would have to take his place.

"You did it, boy!" Rowan said, patting me on the shoulder as he came up behind me, drink in hand. "See, this is why I asked you to help me. I knew you had what it took."

"Me?" I asked in surprise. "You're the one who killed the king. You should be congratulating yourself."

Rowan just smiled and nodded. "True, true, but without the helm that you managed to get, I might not have been able to pull it off."

The rebels pulled out all the stops for the party. It was already late when we got back, but everyone stayed up hours longer, anyway. Barrels of mead and wine were cracked open, rations broken into, several musicians came out of their tents and struck up a tune. The impromptu celebration sparked a need for more food, so several cooks were awakened and soon the smell of sizzling sausages and bacon filled the air.

Dozens of people were now waking up and coming over to the center of camp. For a moment I could just stop and relax after the long night we had all been through. After grabbing some food from the kitchen, I found a relatively empty spot on the ground to sit and enjoy the festivities.

Though it wasn't long before I was forced again to think about everything that had happened. Remembering that Glyndwyr Brice had asked Rowan and I to come by his tent when we got back to camp, I thought that it was probably time to head over there. I reminded Rowan and we started walking through the center of the celebrations toward Brice's tent, leading us directly past the funeral pyres being constructed for the fallen soldiers. I paused for a moment before approaching the row of bodies, intent on finding one in particular. Rowan followed silently, close behind.

I passed more than a dozen faces before finally coming to the one I knew. Wyatt lay on the ground next to his fellow soldiers, looking as though he was just peacefully sleeping, except for the large blood stain across his chest. I sighed. Growing up in the palace, I had of course seen Wyatt many times, though we had never really been close friends. Matt and I were friends, and Wyatt was Matt's brother; an acquaintance that was surprisingly unfamiliar to me considering the amount of time I had spent around him.

Though I didn't know him well, I could still feel the sorrow building up inside myself, mostly for Matt. When he woke up, he might forget for a split second what had happened. Maybe he'd think he still had a brother for a moment, before reality came crashing back down.

For a second, I was quite saddened by this thought before I remembered that Matt had Rowan, Hezdek, and I, and maybe even Olwyn, to keep him company now. If he would just let us in, I'm sure we could all work through Wyatt's death together. All I could do was hope.

After a few more moments, Rowan nodded to me, and we both set out once again. We continued walking toward the large tent near the middle of the camp which I had been told was Glyndwyr Brice's. It loomed over everything else, larger than all the other tents combined. Its size was fairly startling, and I wondered why Glyndwyr Brice would need that much space. Surely some of that material could have been used to make other tents or something else for his soldiers.

The tent itself also appeared to be of excellent quality compared to the other tents around the camp; it looked practically brand new. The entrance closest to us featured a large wooden door, which was surprising, considering that the entire thing was a tent, not an actual building. We walked up to the front entrance which was guarded by two heavily armed soldiers. They wore bulky metal armor that almost completely covered them, except for a few slots to see and talk out of. They looked us over for a few moments before waving us through, into the tent.

We found ourselves in a wide hallway of sorts with wood planks running across the floor and large lanterns lighting our way above us. I was amazed that so much could be done inside a tent.

As we walked down the hallway, we passed several openings in the wall that led to small separate rooms. They almost looked like separate tents inside the larger one with their own walls and tent flaps, many of which were closed. I peeked inside a few that were open as we passed: A kitchen, a zoo with several different colorful animals, a sparring area, an armory, a library, and many others. The camp appeared to be so low on supplies and money. Where had Glyndwyr Brice gotten the funds to build this elaborate setup?

Finally, Wyatt and I walked through an open doorway that led to what I thought must be the throne room. There were huge statues on the sides of the long room all the way down to the other end, each holding a weapon and striking a different pose. There was a red-carpeted walkway that led all the way from the doorway to the end of the room with large tables off to the side. Long purple curtains draped down from the ceiling to the ground in between the statues. They were a dark amethyst color that I thought went well with the gray stone floors. On the far side of the room, I saw an intricately carved wooden throne. Sitting on it was the one and only, Glyndwyr Brice, this time without his mask. He looked to be around fifty years old, and he was wearing long black silk robes. His gray hair was cut short and fell over his forehead, slightly covering his blue eyes. He looked like so many of the king's advisors and politicians back in Ordbridge, which I found slightly unsettling.

He saw us as soon as we walked through the door. "Welcome," he called out to us, standing from his throne and walking closer. "I have been waiting for the two of you to get here so that we can discuss what our next steps are." He pointed at Rowan. "I understand that you are the one responsible for ending that tyrant's rule?"

Rowan nodded. "Yes, that's right."

Brice paused for a moment and stared at him. "Well done. You recovered several artifacts as well, I believe?" he asked me, his demeanor immediately changing. I could sense his eagerness to hear my answer and see the artifacts in front of him. It was not something that I liked.

"Yes," I said cautiously. "I did manage to recover two artifacts in the vault. The helm and the sword. We also discovered the shield as well. But I don't think—"

"Excellent work!" Brice interrupted me. "And you have them here with you, I suppose?" He glanced around hungrily, searching for the artifacts. I was starting to get nervous about showing him these powerful artifacts, but I told myself that I was being ridiculous. He was the leader of the rebel army; surely, he was more trustworthy than the king, right?

"Yes, they're right here." I pulled out a small bag that I'd been using to store the artifacts. I didn't want to risk becoming too attached to them or start to use them any more than I had to. With any luck, out of sight meant out of mind.

Glyndwyr Brice gazed at the bag in my hands, and after a few moments, slowly reached a hand out toward them, but I immediately pulled it away.

"Forgive me, sir, but no one should touch any of these," I said, backing away slightly and putting my hand protectively over the opening of the bag. "They're far too dangerous to be taken lightly."

Glyndwyr Brice looked at me, annoyance flashing across his face for a moment. Perhaps he was shocked that anyone would dare to tell him no, but he quickly recovered and held up his hands in a calming gesture. "Now, hold on just a minute, young man. I know exactly how dangerous they are and what needs to be done for all of our safety."

He retreated a few steps backward and motioned for us to follow him. "This right here," he said, motioning to a man sitting at one of the tables on the side of the room, "is one of my best advisors. We have discussed these artifacts at great length, and we understand the dangers that we face."

I looked at the man in front of us. He, too, was wearing expensive clothes, including a long silk cape, and was clutching an intricately carved wooden cane. He wore a small smile on his face, but his eyes stared at me with an eager light.

"Alright," I said. "Well, what's your plan for these artifacts?"

Brice smiled. "Not to worry. We have a containment center for them right here in the throne room. It's virtually impossible to break into and they will be guarded at all times.

This is really one of the safest places they could be at the moment."

I stared at him in disbelief. "You're saying that you're going to be looking at the artifacts and have them right next to you all day? If you knew anything about them, then you would see how bad of an idea that is." I pulled my bag closer and backed away. "I'll find somewhere that these can be properly taken care of."

Brice froze for a moment before quickly throwing a smile onto his face. "Now, wait just a minute there. I have plenty of experience dealing with these artifacts. I've built up quite a tolerance," he said, touching the compass that lay around his neck. "I hate to do this but…" he paused for a moment and leaned in closer to me. "I'm afraid the choice isn't exactly up to you. I can't just let someone wander off with three of the most dangerous artifacts ever created. There needs to be some sort of containment system put into place immediately, or else someone will certainly use their power again, and become corrupted."

I hesitated; what he said was true, but I had such a bad feeling that he was the wrong person to give it to. Maybe I had just expected him to be more 'for the people' and not have so much wealth displayed around his tent. Either way, I didn't see a good way out of this. He was right when he said it wasn't all my decision. As much as I would like to be able to pick the right place to put these artifacts, no one was going to just sit there and let me figure it out for myself.

Brice tilted his head to the side and stared at me. "I'll tell you what. Why don't you leave two of the artifacts here with us and you can keep one for tonight? They'll be perfectly safe here. While I think you're being a bit paranoid, I don't want to discount your thoughts, especially considering that you got these artifacts in the first place."

I stared at him. It sounded like a generous offer, but I still didn't want to hand him any of the artifacts, let alone two.

Still, I realized that I wasn't in a position to make any demands. I was in Glyndwyr Brice's camp, after all.

"Alright," I said, pulling out the shield from the bag and the sword from a sheath on my belt. "You can take these, I guess. I'll just hold on to—"

"Yes, yes, I'm glad you finally decided to see reason," Glyndwyr Brice said. "They will be well taken care of. No need to worry about that."

I had to force myself to turn around and leave. Perhaps I was just being paranoid after everything that I had just gone through, but I had a really bad feeling that something wasn't quite right.

Rowan followed me outside, past the guards at the entrance and down the central path of the camp.

"Well, I'm sure you have nothing to worry about," Rowan said. "He seemed confident that he could contain the artifacts."

I stopped walking and turned to face him. "Really? Are you sure about that?" I asked, lowering my voice and glancing around to make sure no one was passing by.

"Because it really seemed to me like Glyndwyr Brice just wanted the artifacts for himself. Didn't you see the extravagant decorations everywhere and the fancy clothes and all of the elaborate setups in the rooms? He has taken all of the wealth that this camp has gotten and poured it into his own needs. Haven't you noticed how there aren't any supplies around here? Or new tents? You'd think that Brice could live with a few less outfits and buy some better living quarters for his soldiers."

Rowan frowned as he glanced back over his shoulder toward the tent. "Well, yes. I did notice some of that—"

"I'm sure he would have an amazing excuse. Maybe he'll say it's for our own good or we have to use them if we want any chance of winning this war. Does that sound at all possible? Because if it does, that's a serious problem. You know how dangerous those artifacts can be."

Rowan faltered slightly and frowned. "Well, I..." he hesitated. "I don't know if..." he again glanced back at the tent that we had just left. "You might be right, Joe," he finally admitted. "I was afraid I was overreacting, but did you see that compass hanging around his neck? Could that actually be the other artifact? If he's been literally wearing it for this long, I'm not so sure we can trust him at all."

I froze. "He has the compass around his neck?" I asked Rowan, slowly.

"Uh...well I wasn't sure if it was *the compass* or not. It might've been..." Rowan trailed off as he looked back toward the tent.

I stared at Rowan in shock. "You mean to tell me that he has been exposed to an artifact for a very long time, literally wearing it around his neck, and you just decided to tell me about it?!"

Rowan paused to glare at me. "I didn't know until just now, boy! Don't act like only you know about how dangerous these things are! I'm the one who told you about them in the first place."

I turned around and started walking toward the tent we had just left. "We have to get those artifacts back, now!" I said, motioning for Rowan to follow me.

"Wait, hold on just a minute." Rowan caught up to me and pulled me to a stop. "What exactly is your plan here, boy? Even if Glyndwyr Brice was going to use the artifacts for some evil purpose, which I still don't think is guaranteed, how exactly are we just going to go in there and take them away from him?"

I hesitated. He made a good point, but what other choice did I have? He knew as well as I did that the power of the artifacts was too easily corruptible. I had to act now if I wanted to save as many people as I could from the dangers of them.

"Look," I said to Rowan. "I still have the helm, right? How about we sneak back into the tent and see what's going on? That way, you'll know for sure that he's actually going to use them before we intervene, and we can easily get past the guards." Rowan nodded and followed me back toward the tent. Before we were in sight of the guards, I pulled out the helm and put it on. Again, I didn't notice any discernible difference in my appearance, but Rowan glanced around, obviously unable to see me.

"I'm right here," I said, patting his arm. "Hold my hand and you should be invisible as well."

Rowan looked somewhat doubtful, but he just took a deep breath and reached out to grab my hand and we set off for the front entrance. The guards were still in the same positions that they were in earlier, with a slight gap between them in which we might be able to squeeze through, though it would be close. We slowly approached them, careful not to make any unnecessary noise that could give us away.

"Ahem."

I froze. I looked up at the guard to my left who had just cleared his throat. My heart was beating so fast that for a moment I thought the guards might be able to hear it themselves. I took a deep breath. It was alright. They hadn't found me. I carefully continued moving through the small gap in between them. Just a little further. A little more.

There! I made it through. Now it was Rowan's turn. He slowly maneuvered through the gap, freezing for a moment as one of the guards leaned to the side slightly.

Panicked, I pulled his hand forward and we both tumbled forward into the tent, making a little bit of noise as we went. The guards turned to look, but we stayed right where we were on the ground and prayed that they wouldn't investigate any further. Luckily, having not seen anything in the tent, they decided to do just that. I let out a sigh of relief and then slowly got to my feet, helping Rowan as I went.

The trip back to the throne room was uneventful, though we were on edge the entire time. All it would take was one person to accidentally bump into us, and just like that, the whole thing would be over. That was just my sort of luck.

After a few long minutes, we made it to the throne room, which I was very glad to see still didn't have any guards at the entrance. We were free to just wander in and eavesdrop on Glyndwyr Brice.

"Yes, yes, I told you," I heard from inside the room. "We should be able to wrap this whole situation up tonight."

Rowan and I crept closer and closer to the throne until I could actually make out who was talking. Glyndwyr Brice was standing with his advisors at a nearby table, the sword and shield laid out on display. We carefully avoided the tables and chairs that were set out along the walkway to the throne, taking special care not to knock something over. One wrong move and it was over. My feet brushed against the thick rug that stretched along almost the full length of the room.

"Tonight?" one of the advisors asked. "That boy still has the fourth artifact. We need that if we can truly bring new rule to this continent. No one can have any power to go against us."

I held my breath. What had we stumbled into? A plan for taking over the entire continent? What happened to just getting their land back?

"My guards are all ready to strike," Brice said. "I have already sent word for them to retrieve the helm from that boy's tent. He has gotten too dangerous to be left alive at this point. A shame, really; he might have made a good soldier. I understand that the young prince is there as well, and honestly, that isn't someone that we want to risk rising to power and upsetting our new rule. He is still recovering from the events at the vault; perhaps it was a bit too much for him and he will pass away in his sleep tonight," he said with a smirk. "You never can be certain how serious injuries are. With any luck, tomorrow we will be well on our way to becoming the rulers of this land—with or without the help of these tiresome rebels!"

Glyndwyr Brice and his advisors roared with laughter and clapped each other on the back. I suppressed a shocked gulp. I knew that something wasn't right when I left the sword and shield with him, but I never imagined that he was so far gone that he was talking about a full invasion of the continent. Now, he had three artifacts in his possession.

How were we supposed to stop him?

We slowly walked closer to the group, trying to catch everything that they were saying. I was careful not to bump into anything in the room that might alert them to our presence, but unfortunately, that wouldn't end up being a factor because a few moments later, Rowan's foot caught on the rug beneath us, and he tumbled to the ground, releasing my hand in the process.

Everyone froze, before Glyndwyr Brice frowned at Rowan and shook his head. "Well, now," he said, his voice dripping with disdain as he slowly picked up the sword and shield laying on the table. "This is very disappointing."

23
Well Don't Just Stand There

Joe

Rowan slowly picked himself off of the ground and raised his staff as he backed away from Brice and his advisors. I stood next to him, trying to decide what to do. Should I take off the helmet and help him? Maybe try and stop this fight from even happening? It didn't look like we had a lot of advantages at the moment, considering that Brice had three artifacts and his advisors to help him, and Rowan and I were just two people. There was only so much that we could do.

"What exactly are you doing here?" Brice asked. "I don't believe that my guards let you inside, which leads me to believe that you snuck in. Sneaking inside a private area to observe military discussions sounds an awful lot like treason to me. And you know the punishment for treason."

Rowan glared at him. "It's about time that everyone finds out exactly what you are, Brice!" he growled. "You won't get away with anything this time."

Glyndwyr Brice just laughed. "Oh, really? Who will be there to prove what you say? They'll have to believe me, their faithful leader."

Brice approached him, moving casually in his direction as if he could take as much time as he needed. His advisors had all drawn weapons of their own. Two of them held swords and the third had a large axe. I had never seen them in action, but judging from their nice clothes and looks of confusion as they gripped their weapons, I got the feeling that they didn't really know what they were doing. At least I hoped so. I would take any extra help I could get.

Rowan shifted backward as he watched Brice, but I could see that he was slowly getting surrounded as they spoke, and I realized Rowan was about to be killed if I didn't step in. I ran around to Glyndwyr Brice and tackled him from behind, knocking him to the floor and throwing the sword and shield onto the ground near us. We both lay on the floor for a moment, dazed from the fall, before slowly rising to our feet. As soon as I could stand steadily, I dove for the closest artifact, which happened to be the shield. Brice went for the sword at the same time, so I managed to scoop up the shield and retreat before he even realized what happened.

"Ah, I see now how you got past my guards," Brice said, retreating towards his advisors and holding the sword out in front of him. "You had help from your invisible friend. Well, this ends now." He lifted his wrist up and shouted into a small device fixed there: "Guards, get to the throne room immediately! We have intruders."

I glanced behind me, my chest fluttering. How fast could the guards get here? A minute or two? We had to act now. I ran at Brice and his advisors, still invisible, and slashed my sword in the group. I saw one body fall, but before I could strike again, I was hit across the face with the end of a spear. Stunned, I stumbled backward, clutching my head. The remaining advisors and Brice were wildly swinging their weapons in front of them, hoping to stop me from using the invisibility to my advantage.

I quickly realized that we would have no hope of beating them before the guards got there if I didn't take the helm off. If I could bait them into thinking that they had the advantage, then we might be able to take them by surprise and overwhelm them. I quickly pulled off the helm, clutching it in my left hand, ready to put it back on at a moment's notice.

Brice smirked at me as I became invisible again. "Finally getting rid of your little toy?" he sneered at me. "About time you opted for the fair fight."

I almost laughed at the irony in that, but I was too angry. We had to win this fight, the future of the entire continent depended on it. If Glyndwyr Brice got all four artifacts, then truly nothing could stop him from taking anything that he wanted. I stepped back until I was standing next to Rowan, and I handed him the shield. "Here," I said. "You can probably do more damage with this."

We advanced slowly, weapons raised in front of us. Brice and his advisors held their positions, watching us get closer and closer. I wasn't sure what the plan was, but we had to act quickly before the guards got to the throne room. I charged at them, trying to get them to shift around and give Rowan an opening to attack, but they remained still, shields raised, waiting for reinforcements. I swung my sword at one of the advisors, but he blocked my attack and countered, pushing me back next to Rowan. Before we could try anything else, I heard shouts coming from the hallway getting closer and closer until several people burst through the doorway, heavily clad with armor and weaponry.

'Go, go, go!" one of them shouted, pointing in our direction. I counted six guards as they advanced toward us and took positions in a loose semi-circle around us, weapons drawn.

"Put your weapons down, now!" one of them shouted at us. "I will not ask again! Put them down now or we will be forced to attack."

I looked over at Rowan. He glared defiantly at the guards and didn't show any signs that he was about to set his weapons down. I nodded to him. There was no way that we could surrender now. We had to get those artifacts away from Glyndwyr Brice.

"Well?" the guard called out. "Which is it?"

We both remained silent, glancing around to make sure no one was trying to sneak up behind us. So far, no one had made any moves since they'd surrounded us, but I sensed that that was about to change. The main guard frowned and nodded to his fellow comrades. Slowly everyone started moving closer and closer. Rowan and I readied ourselves for the inevitable battle and watched the guards advance. We stood with our backs against one another, each defending one side of our small area. We weren't about to give it up without a fight.

A large explosion suddenly rocked the tent, almost throwing us to the ground.

The guards backed up, shouting to one another while three of them fell over from the shock waves. Rowan and I tried to attack in the confusion, but unfortunately most of the guards were still up, and they grabbed Rowan before he could recover.

"Stop right now or say goodbye to your friend!"

I looked up to see Glyndwyr Brice holding his sword up to Rowan's throat while two guards restrained him.

"Drop your weapon!" Brice yelled at me.

I opened my mouth to say something but closed it almost immediately when I realized that there was nothing that I could say to help the situation. Why would they listen to anything I said?

Glyndwyr Brice and the guards next to him stared at me, waiting for my decision, but I didn't know what to do. To lay down my weapons would mean assured defeat, and the artifacts would all go to Glyndwyr Brice. It would mean the conquest of the entire continent. I couldn't let that happen. But to refuse...well, that meant the end of Rowan.

"Alright, I surrender!" I called out, holding up my hands in the air.

"Drop your weapon!" he yelled again.

I hesitated for a moment, before setting down my sword and the helm on the ground. As much as I wanted to believe that I could take down Glyndwyr Brice all by myself, I realized that if I tried to do that, many innocent people, including Rowan, would die. I just couldn't be responsible for that.

"Excellent," Brice said. "About time you decided to make the right decision." He lowered the sword pointed at Rowan and smiled at me. "I'm so glad you didn't force me to do anything crazy. It really wouldn't have gone well for you, as I'm sure you have realized."

I glared at him, hoping he would just take the artifacts and be done with it; I really didn't want to listen to him gloat for another hour. Finally, he set his eyes on the helm at my feet, and cautiously walked forward. He reached down for it, hand outstretched. I vaguely considered kicking him, but what would've been the point? It would simply be a small delay and then he would have it. Not to mention Rowan and I would likely then be killed.

Suddenly, before Brice could grab the helm, I heard shouts coming from the entrance to the throne room and several people ran through the doorway, weapons drawn.

"Charge!" I heard someone yell, as these new participants rushed forward toward us. Among the people who had charged into the room, I saw Olwyn with her axes raised, Hezdek brandishing a small hammer that he, no doubt, used for making some small tool earlier, and right in front, leading the charge, was Matt.

Matt and the others quickly engaged the guards, killing several almost instantly. Glyndwyr Brice and the other guards and advisors pulled back and formed a loose defensive line farther down the room, leaving Rowan and me behind in the process. I quickly picked up the helm and my sword off the ground and helped Rowan to his feet. I stared at our new reinforcements in amazement.

"How-how did you know..." I stammered, glancing around at everyone, though mostly looking at Matt.

"I'll explain later!" Matt said, pointing at Glyndwyr Brice and his soldiers. "We still have some stuff to deal with at the moment."

Our small group paused for a moment, about twenty feet away from Glyndwyr Brice. We stared at each other, daring the other to make a move. I could see him growing visibly more and more upset as he realized that his grand plan had the potential to end right then and there.

Finally, he stepped forward and motioned for his soldiers to follow. "Let's end this," he said, staring at the helm in my hands. I readied myself along with my companions for the approaching conflict. We quickly formed a small line, those of us with shields in the front, and the rest of us standing close behind them, ready to leap into battle.

The guards looked hesitant to attack, but Glyndwyr Brice showed no sign of stopping, so they went on, eventually breaking into a run toward us. CLANG! The first guards crashed into us, but our shields managed to hold them back. We countered, pushing with our shields and forcing several of them to the ground.

I launched into battle with the nearest soldier. We struggled for a few moments, trading swings and blocking each other's attacks before I finally disarmed him and pushed him to the ground, knocking him unconscious. After that, I put on the helm. It was our biggest advantage in the battle, and I was sure Glyndwyr Brice would be using his artifacts.

Just then, I heard another loud crack and saw a blinding light, and sure enough, Glyndwyr Brice stood there, holding the shield in his hand, surrounded by soldiers who had been thrown to the ground. Before many of them could recover, he stabbed a few with his sword, killing them instantly. I knew we had to stop him soon, or else we would surely lose this battle, even with reinforcements.

While invisible, I started sneaking around the battle until I was on the opposite side. If I could just find an opening when Glyndwyr Brice was distracted, maybe I could tackle him and take those artifacts away from him for good. Even when he was distracted by killing my allies, his guards were still right next to him, fighting. The small battle was roaring just as intensely as any large-scale battlefield. Anyone could just swing a sword into seemingly open air at any moment and kill me. I had to be careful.

I took a deep breath, and carefully crept forward toward Brice. I crouched down slightly in hopes of distancing myself from anyone's swinging arms, but really all I could do was hope that I was out of range. My heart was pounding as I took one small step after the next, each one bringing me closer and closer to the enemy.

I could hear Glyndwyr Brice laughing as he swung his sword down again and again. I cringed thinking about the poor soldiers being killed, but I just clenched my teeth and kept moving forward. The only way to stop him was to get those artifacts far away, to a safe place.

I continued moving forward. Ten feet away…I could feel my heart threatening to burst out of my chest, but I just had to remind myself that no one else could see me. Five feet away…I began blocking out the sounds of battle around me and readying myself to attack. I was so focused on Glyndwyr Brice that the soldiers around me seemed to move in slow motion, and all I heard was a dull buzzing sound as the swords and axes clashed against one another. Three feet…two…he was right there. I could see him throw his head back and laugh again at the carnage he was inflicting upon my friends.

Suddenly, I jumped up and grabbed onto his back, my momentum sending both of us tumbling down to the ground. Our weapons, including the helm, loudly clattered down to the floor around us. My work wasn't done yet; I had to get to them first. The moment seemed to move in slow motion as the two of us struggled to recover from hitting the floor and started reaching for our fallen items. I reached out…almost there. Just a few more inches. Out of the corner of my eye I could see Brice crawling next to me, grasping for the artifacts that lay on the ground. He reached out toward the sword, just a few feet away from him. I strained toward it as well. Almost...there! I grabbed a hold of the hilt of the sword and swung it around toward Brice.

"Stop!" I yelled. "It's over. Stop moving!"

Brice showed no sign of stopping; he moved toward the shield, a mere half foot away from him.

"Stop!" I screamed.

I raised my sword. He left me with no choice. I closed my eyes and took a deep breath. THUNK!

My eyes flew open to see Brice lying motionless, face down on the ground, a large sword protruding from his back, and Matt standing over him.

"He-he was gonna get the shield," he stammered breathlessly. "I had to—"

"Y-yeah. I know, Matt," I said.

Blood poured out of the large slice in Brice's back, quickly consuming his flimsy silk shirt, staining it a dark scarlet. I stared at him for a few more seconds, almost daring him to spring back to life and keep fighting, but he stayed where he was.

His remaining guards had seen the entire scene, and the fighting began to fizzle out. Many of them almost immediately threw their weapons to the ground and held up their hands in surrender. With their leader dead, was there a point in continuing to fight for his cause? The battle ground to a halt, and almost all of the remaining guards surrendered. I took a deep breath and picked up the helm from where it had landed after I had jumped onto Brice.

My fingers poured over the cold black metal, tracing the simple indents along the seams absentmindedly. It was all over now. Maybe we could finally find some sort of peace in this world, now that two corrupt warlords, both representing completely opposite sides, were finally gone. This war that had involved so many people in the continent ended up not having a winner. Both sides would have used their power for evil. All we could do now was hope that we were smart enough not to do the same.

I felt a hand on my shoulder, and I turned to find Matt standing right next to me, a frown on his face.

"Joe..." he said, hesitating for a moment. "I don't know what to say. I should have listened to you and...Wyatt. I know how you felt about my father, but I'm just sorry that it took this long for me to realize that you were right."

"Matt," I said calmly, offering him a small smile as I stood up and enveloped him in a tight hug. "Don't worry. I knew that you would come around eventually. It's alright." I didn't have to tell him that I had had my doubts at one point. All that mattered was that he realized his mistakes now.

We both stood in silence for several long moments, watching the rebel soldiers round up the guards and clean up the room.

"Wait, how did you even know we were here?" I finally asked him. "And how did you convince the rebel soldiers to follow you?"

Matt finally cracked a small smile. "Well, that's a long story..."

I laughed. "I've got nowhere to be," I said, taking his arm and leading him off to the side of the battle. "Tell on."

24

It's About Time

Matt

I awoke to the sounds of cheering and loud conversation. For a moment, I laid on the ground, completely at ease, until the memories from earlier that night came rushing back to me. We had gone to the vault and…Wyatt was…dead. I fought with Father and the artifacts were…I looked around, suddenly realizing that I didn't have my shield with me for the first time since I had found it in Ordbridge, before all of this had started. I shook my head; I was glad to finally be rid of it. Those artifacts had caused so much pain to so many people. Something had to be done about them.

I was wrong about everything. Wyatt was right. Father had done so many horrible things and he didn't even care enough about his son to give him more than a passing glance after murdering him. I sat up, determined to find Joe and talk to him about what happened. I had barely considered that Wyatt was telling the truth this whole time until it was too late. It was time to pick a side.

I took a few wobbly steps forward before sitting down again. Perhaps I needed just a few more minutes of rest before I fully recovered from being knocked unconscious earlier.

I gave myself some more time, during which I reflected more on our journey. Now it was obvious how horrible Father had been. How had I not seen it before? Wyatt had even shown me the sacking of Entolas by the Sikrathian army and still I hadn't wavered. I sighed; all I could do now was try and show that I had changed.

I stood back up and walked out of the tent. I was greeted with a wave of noise coming from the center of camp.

I hesitated for a moment before lurching a few steps forward toward the noise.

"Woah, hold on just a minute," I heard from behind me. I turned to find Hezdek sitting on a small chair off to the side of the tent flap. "Where do you think you're going?"

I paused for a moment before taking a few steps closer to him. "Where's Joe?" I asked.

Hezdek raised an eyebrow and looked me over. "It sure doesn't look like you're alright to walk around. What's so pressing that it can't wait until tomorrow, anyway?"

I sighed. "I need to apologize for one thing," I muttered. "I should've realized what my father was turning into."

Hezdek stared at me for a few seconds before standing up and motioning for me to follow him. He led me toward the center of camp, where I had heard all the noise coming from.

"Alright, well, I'm glad to see you've finally come to your senses. Joe was pretty worried about you earlier; I'm sure he'll be very happy to see you. He and Rowan are meeting with Glyndwyr Brice to talk about what to do with the artifacts. I'll show you where."

I nodded. Hopefully, that meant that Joe would forgive me for dragging him along to the vault and all of the stupid stuff that I had done earlier. Hezdek and I began walking down the dirt path toward Glyndwyr Brice's tent, not bothering to make conversation. I was certainly too preoccupied to talk, and I could only assume that Hezdek felt the same, or at least understood what I was thinking. After no more than a minute, though, a group of Brice's personal guards rushed past us, without even a glance in our direction. Hezdek and I had to stumble to the side to avoid being crushed under their boots. As we watched, they ran down the path, before finally stopping in front of our tent.

"Go, go, go!"

The large group of soldiers suddenly barged inside my tent with their weapons drawn. I stopped in my tracks. What were they doing? Had they gotten the wrong tent? Hezdek finally noticed that I had stopped following him and turned to look at what had caught my attention.

"What are they…" he said, staring at the group of guards in confusion. They quickly realized that no one was in the tent, and they all stormed out, looking around the nearby tents and foliage. Hezdek and I glanced over at each other, eyebrows raised, and slowly backed away from the guards. Finally, one of them looked over in our direction and paused. He slowly took a few steps toward us to get a better look before spinning around and calling out to his companions.

"Hey! He's over here!" A dozen or so soldiers immediately started running over, weapons raised threateningly.

"Woah, woah!" I called out to them, holding my hands up in a calming motion.

"What's going on? Who are you looking for?"

One guard stepped away from the group and pointed directly at me. "Are you the prince?"

"Um…" I hesitated, looking at Hezdek again, who looked just as confused as I felt. "I suppose so—"

"Excellent," the lead guard said. "Then, on behalf of Glyndwyr Brice, I sentence you to death." Before I could respond, he swung his sword down toward me and I was almost too shocked to move out of the way, but at the last second, I jumped backward, avoiding his strike.

"Wait, what!?" I yelled. But there was no more arguing with them anymore. The rest of the guards advanced as well, swinging their weapons in my direction. I drew my sword (luckily I had remembered to fasten it to my belt before I left the tent) and deflected a few attacks. Hezdek raised his hammer and we prepared ourselves for another hard fight.

Hezdek and I slowly backed up, but the guards were quickly advancing toward us. We had to act soon or else we would be quickly overwhelmed. They raised their weapons threateningly, inching toward us. Before they'd surrounded us, I ducked under the outstretched hand of one of the guards and slashed at his feet, causing him to scream in pain and stumble to the side, into one of his companions, "Follow me!" I yelled at Hezdek, grabbing his arm and pulling him backward. The guards lurched forward but we ran just out of their reach.

We broke into a sprint down the winding path that led past the center of the camp. I heard their pounding footsteps closing in behind us as we made our escape. The guards shouted at us to stop, but there was absolutely no way that I was going to do that. I didn't want to look back in fear seeing them right behind us, but after a few moments of running, I stole a glance backward. Sure enough, the entire group of guards were no more than twenty feet behind us, still holding their weapons and glaring menacingly at us. Turning back around, I tried to coax a little more speed out of myself.

Hezdek and I continued to run down the path, each corner or sharp turn we encountered sending a wave of fear down my spine that the guards would close the small gap and catch us. I glanced back every so often, and each time they were no more than a few seconds behind us, just barely out of range. I began to realize that there was no way that we could outrun them. I'd already begun to tire, and I didn't sense any hesitation from the guards. We had to do something soon or they were going to catch us.

Hezdek was breathing hard next to me, no doubt this was the most he had run in years, and after a minute or so of running, he pointed off to the right of our path, past the tents.

"Everyone is gathered in the center of camp to celebrate. If we can get there, we might be able to get someone to help us. At the very least, they could probably stop them from killing us long enough to figure out why they're even after us in the first place."

I nodded and followed him as he left the path and ran straight for a group of tents set up to our right. I heard shouts from the guards, and they continued their pursuit, charging into the tents, now even closer than before because we had to slow down slightly to turn.

I tried to keep track of Hezdek as we ran through the clump of tents, but a heavy wind was starting to pick up, causing the sides of the tents to float up around me, obscuring the path. Everyone around me began to disappear in the confusion, until even the guards were lost in the maze of tents, still near but not directly behind me.

"Hezdek!?" I called out, still sprinting around the area, trying not to stop for even a second in case the guards appeared out of nowhere and attacked.

I heard the sound of footsteps behind me and I turned, hoping to see Hezdek appear from behind the tent flaps. I paused for a moment and listened. Nothing. All I heard was the faint sound of the party coming from somewhere to my right. I waited longer, not daring to move a muscle.

I waited for another few moments and listened to the wind billow around me, still waving the tent flaps all around. It was so loud that I was surprised that I had heard the footsteps earlier. Had I imagined them? Cautiously, I took a step forward, glancing around wildly for anyone sneaking up on me.

I took another step. And another. Still, no one was there. Maybe we'd finally lost them. My heart rate began to slow slightly, but I was still very much on edge. I had to find Hezdek.

"Ah, there you are!" I suddenly heard a gruff voice say from behind me.

"AHHH!" I screamed and leapt forward into a run, not daring to look behind me. I didn't have to look at whoever had said that to know it wasn't Hezdek. I ran as fast as I could, hoping that I was going in the right direction. Heavy footsteps sounded from behind me, getting louder and louder with each passing second. Just a little farther. A little more…

I could see light ahead! The center of camp was just around the corner. Almost there… THUMP! I ran through the last tent in my way and slammed right into a large wooden crate, knocking me to the ground. I heard my pursuer slow to a stop directly beside me.

"Finally!" he shouted. "No running for you anymore."

I frantically crawled backward, trying to put as much distance as possible between us, but he followed me with his sword raised above his head, preparing to strike. I had made it to the center of the camp and could see the celebrations a few hundred feet away. If I could just move a little further maybe someone would see what was happening. I held my sword in front of me hesitantly, but I knew from my position on the ground I wasn't likely to win this fight. I saw his sword start to move, and I heard a shout from behind the guard.

"NO!" A hammer slammed into his head, and he fell to the ground, unmoving. "Leave him alone!" Hezdek stood where the guard had been moments earlier. He brandished his hammer in front of him and was glaring at the man that he had just hit.

I scrambled to my feet and took a moment to catch my breath. We were standing on the edge of a large circular clearing where no tents were set up. Benches were scattered all around, as well as several stone buildings that I had seen a few rebels take food and supplies out of, and on one side was the kitchen area that we'd passed earlier. In the distance I could see the celebrations were still in full swing.

Hundreds of people eating, drinking, and chatting about their success at the vault. Several of them seemed to have noticed the commotion as Hezdek had hit the guard, and a few were running over to us, weapons at the ready.

But before any of them could reach us, the remaining guards appeared from behind the wall of billowing tent flaps, weapons raised and looks of rage on their faces.

I looked around frantically, but with all of the people here, we wouldn't be able to run very far without the guards catching up to us. I raised my sword again and glanced over at Hezdek, who looked back apprehensively.

The guards rushed forward and attacked; the ones closest to us immediately swinging their weapons at us, which Hezdek and I barely managed to deflect without our own weapons being ripped from our grasp. I realized that they were slowly shepherding us toward the stone wall of one of the storage sheds, where we would have nowhere to run. They were taking no chances that we would escape again.

At that point, I started to hear some shouts from the crowd: "What's going on? Who are these people?" No one moved to stop the guards, though.

"Hezdek, we have to break through!" I shouted, swinging my sword desperately toward the closest guard. The guard simply held up a shield and fully blocked my feeble attack before stepping to the side and slamming the hilt of his blade into my arm, throwing me to the ground and my sword out of my hand.

"AGHH!" I screamed, crawling backward as the guard swung his blade into the ground again and again, each time closer than the last to hitting me.

Just as I thought it was over for us, an axe flew toward the guard closest to me, embedding itself into his neck and throwing him to the ground. I stared at his body in shock for a moment before someone else appeared in his place, brandishing a second axe and scowling at the rest of her opponents. Olwyn had to come to save us yet again.

With a menacing battle cry, she dove into another guard, pummeling him with her weapon and leaving him on the ground before moving onto the next one within mere seconds. The guards seemed stunned by her sudden entrance, and it took a few moments for everyone to lurch back into motion.

I ducked under the first swing and jabbed with my own sword, at last able to bring one guard to the ground. With the death of the guards, the watching crowd grew too restless to stay still, and several people surged forward to restrain us, which they were not at all equipped to do. The guards continued to fight back against us, until eventually one of the onlookers was hit by a wide strike. The rebels pressed forward, until at last we were all overwhelmed by their numbers. They managed to take our weapons and hold us back from attacking each other any further.

I breathed a big sigh of relief. It wasn't a great situation, but at the very least I wasn't going to die at that very moment. There was still a chance to clear the entire thing up.

Olwyn held up her hands with some difficulty, as she was still being restrained. "We aren't your enemy! They are," she said, pointing toward the guards. The rebels slowly released us and the guards, but kept their weapons raised.

"You better explain what's going on here right now," one of them said. Olwyn bent down and grabbed one of the still-conscious guards off the ground, hauling him to his feet. "Did Brice order this!? Why did you try to hunt them down!?" she yelled at the closest guard as she pointed in our direction.

The guard looked pretty dazed. "Orders. Just…following…orders," he managed to mutter.

"Orders from who?"

The guard coughed and fell silent for a moment as he quailed under Olwyn's gaze before answering.

"Glyndwyr Brice! Glyndwyr Brice ordered us to kill the prince. He said he was a threat to our growing empire," he finally mumbled.

Olwyn dropped him in surprise and turned back to look at me as the crowd around us muttered to themselves: "Prince? The Prince of Sikrath is here? What's going on?"

The guard laughed to himself momentarily before lapsing back into a coughing fit. "Maybe you won't die now, Prince, but your friends are in there, handing over the artifacts as we speak. Soon, you'll have no power to stop us—" He stopped abruptly as Olwyn punched him across the face and knocked him out cold. He fell to the ground with the rest of his comrades.

"Hey! Enough!" The rebels surged forward again and restrained Olwyn. We all raised our hands in surrender and tried to look as non-threatening as possible. At least, that's what I did.

Hezdek frowned, obviously worried. "Joe and Rowan went to Glyndwyr Brice's tent to discuss the artifacts. If what that guard said is true and Brice means to use them to advance his rule…" he paused and glanced at the two of us, eyebrows raised, "We need to go help them right now."

"Hold on just a minute," the rebel who had spoken earlier said. "You better tell us what's going on right now or there'll be serious consequences!"

I took a deep breath. "Your leader is corrupt!" I shouted. "He means to use magical artifacts to completely enslave the continent, just as Sikrath tried to do to your people. He is the opposite of what you think he is. He doesn't stand for peace; he is exactly like who you've been fighting all these years!"

The crowd grew restless at these words and the main rebel stepped up next to me. "That's ridiculous. Why should we believe anything you have to say?"

Slowly, I reached into my pocket and drew out the enchanted amethyst gem. "I might be able to get you some proof," I said slowly, "from the very lips of your leader himself."

"Joe?" I called into the stone. "Can you hear me?"

There was complete silence amongst the crowd, as well as from the gem itself. Slowly, a low voice began to emit from it, barely audible at first, but slowly growing louder with each passing moment.

"My guard's...ready to strike," a recognizable voice said. "...retrieve the helm from...boy's tent. He is still recovering from the events at the vault; perhaps it was a bit too much for him and he will pass away in his sleep tonight," the voice had an obvious tone of amusement as it spoke. "You never can be certain how serious injuries are. With any luck, tomorrow we will be well on our way to becoming the rulers of this land. With or without the help of these tiresome rebels!"

The onlookers froze. It was unmistakable. Glyndwyr Brice didn't mean to help Kricoya or Sikrath; he was only looking out for himself.

The silence dragged on for a moment before it was instantly broken as everyone erupted into argument. Olwyn, Hezdek, and I waited, rather impatiently, for them to come to a decision, but it soon became clear that these rebels were so distraught about the thought of their glorious leader betraying them that they wouldn't be able to act, at least anytime soon.

After a few minutes of unbearable argument, one rebel stepped forward and leaned down to help pull us to our feet. He stared at me for a long moment before speaking.

"Maybe my companions don't see what needs to be done, but I certainly do. I'll get you to Brice's tent, and we might just be able to put an end to this madness once and for all."

We all nodded our agreement. "Who's with me?!" he shouted into the audience.

A small response welled up from the crowd, smaller than I would have hoped, but it was as good as we were going to get. Our small group quickly left the distressed chaos of the rebel crowd and immediately set out for the tent.

We made our way through the celebrations, pushing past several people and trying to move as quickly as possible without creating a panic. Eventually we made it out of the center area and onto one of the dirt paths that led all around the camp. We half-jogged-half-ran forward; we still didn't know for sure how much danger Rowan and Joe were in, and we didn't know if Glyndwyr Brice had even been alerted that we were onto him yet. If any measure of stealth could still be salvaged, we would have to try our best to keep it that way. Soon Brice's tent came into view, along with the two armed guards at the entrance. We paused for a moment about ten feet away from the doorway. The guards looked at one another wearily and held up their weapons.

"Woah, hold on," I said. "Can we go inside and just talk to Glyndwyr Brice? We just saw a soldier who told us some things that we would really like to confirm."

The soldiers looked even more distressed after my words, and they retreated several feet backward.

"Stand back! No entry to the palace will be permitted to violent rioters under direct orders from Glyndwyr Brice. We will use lethal force if needed to make sure that no one breaches these walls!" one of the guards said.

"You're holding our friends captive in there!"

"If you're friends with whoever is in there causing trouble, then you better get out of here before we finish up with them and come after you next!"

At this declaration we all drew our weapons. I eyed their armor and realized that we would have a very hard time getting through that doorway. We would need some sort of distraction or powerful weapon to get past those soldiers.

Suddenly, I remembered a piece of equipment that I possessed that I hadn't thought about since leaving Ordbridge.

"Hold on," I said to my companions. I reached into my bag, and after digging around for several seconds, pulled out the "rocket" that I had gotten from the soldiers the day we left Ordbridge. As soon as Olwyn saw it, she smiled. I grinned back at her and told the others to stand back; hopefully, I could remember how to use it. The guards were watching us apprehensively the entire time I was rooting around in my bag, but even as I pulled my arm back to throw this miniature bomb at them, they still didn't seem to know what was about to happen. Perhaps this would be their first introduction to one.

BOOM! The explosion rocked the ground and threw the guards backward. The stone below the tent was cracked and the entrance to the tent itself was torn to shreds. We were also covered with a light coating of rubble as the now loose stone and dirt flung toward us. We rushed forward, past the now motionless guards.

"Hurry, they know we're here now! Search everywhere!" Olwyn shouted to us. We ran down the hallway, glancing into every room that we passed on the way. I was almost surprised by how many rooms there were, but then I remembered just how much random stuff there was at the palace back home.

Finally, we started to hear voices nearby and what sounded like fighting. We rushed toward the sound, until we got to an open doorway. We all piled through, where we were met with the sight of Glyndwyr Brice and his guards facing off against Joe and Rowan, though it looked an awful lot like Joe and Rowan could use some help.

"Charge!" I yelled, leading the push forward to rescue them and finally put an end to all of this madness.

25
I Guess My Work Here Is Done

Matt

Joe and I sat next to each other in the throne room, taking a moment to look over the remains of our most recent battle. Glyndwyr Brice was dead. The king, my father, was dead. Who would step up to lead these two now leaderless nations? I was the heir to the Sikrathian Empire, but would the rebels willingly submit to yet another ruler? Perhaps all of us could go out and arrange something. They claimed that they were only looking for peace, right? Well, first we would have to convince them that their beloved leader was a fraud and that we had not just assassinated the best hope for their growing rebellion. Should be pretty easy.

I glanced over at Joe, who was staring at Glyndwyr Brice's body on the ground and the pile of artifacts now at his feet. I understood what he was thinking: had we killed one person under the artifacts' influence only to be taken over ourselves? I reached out to pat him on the back, but a small reflection blinded me for a moment; I looked over to see my once prized shield lying next to the other artifacts. I flinched. Even just looking at it was starting to give me a headache.

"Come on," I said, standing up quickly and offering a hand down to Joe. "We have to deal with those soldiers out there soon."

Joe looked up at me in surprise, as though he was startled that there was someone else in the room with him, before taking my hand and pulling himself up.

"Yeah, we definitely have some explaining to do, don't we?" He looked over at the remaining enemy soldiers, and then turned to me with a small smile. "They might be useful."

We strode over to the small group of prisoners, whose hands were bound as they sat on the ground next to Olwyn and Hezdek. Rowan and the soldiers we brought were dragging the bodies from the battle off to the side of the room.

"You," Joe said, pointing at one man in the small group who was dressed very differently to the others. He wore extremely expensive silk clothes and fine leather shoes that were not typically worn by a soldier. "You're one of Brice's advisors, aren't you? You helped him plan all of this."

The man looked up at us with disdain, giving no answer.

"Hey!" Olwyn said. "He asked you something." She moved her hand to rest over her axe and looked over at him, her message abundantly clear. The man sighed angrily.

"Fine," he said, glaring at Joe. "I suppose you could say that I helped him." He paused for a moment, growing visibly angrier and angrier. "You don't know what you've done! He was going to unite all of us into one strong kingdom, capable of defeating anyone that dared to oppose us! You have all ruined everything!" he wailed before again lapsing into silence.

Joe sighed. "Maybe you truly don't realize what those artifacts would have done to him, but believe me, any kingdom built using them is destined to fall into ruin. Now, come with us; you have some explaining to do to your people."

Joe hauled him up to his feet and walked him toward the exit. "Rowan, did you find anything that we could use to hold those artifacts for now?"

Rowan held up a large leather sack. "Yeah, I found this by the throne. It looks like it was designed to hold all of them at once."

Joe nodded. "Alright, can you go and get them, then?" He turned to the rest of us. "We should probably take the rest of the prisoners as well, right? We don't have enough people to split up, especially considering we might need backup later."

We all agreed, so after Rowan had safely stored the artifacts in the bag, we got the other prisoners to their feet and marched toward the exit. I walked up next to Joe, who held his sword at his side and closely watched the advisor.

"So, what exactly is your plan here?" I whispered to Joe. "How do you know that he'll tell the truth once we get to the rebels? Won't he just lie and say that we're making everything up?"

Joe looked over at me, eyebrows raised as though he thought the answer was obvious. "He talks about their plans being for our benefit," he whispered back to me, "but I would be shocked if he wasn't getting something good for himself in the process. If we make it clear that this is his only chance at getting out of this, I think he'll be more than willing to share what he knows, especially if we can guarantee his safety from the rebels."

I nodded. It made sense, or at the very least, was probably our best chance of convincing the rebels that their beloved leader was actually a power-hungry dictator. At least I hoped so.

He gave me a small smile. "I might also have another way of convincing him to listen if that doesn't work."

We all walked through the large palace-like tent until we made it to the entrance and came upon the bodies of the guards that we had killed. As we passed them, I couldn't help but feel sorry for them and their fate. How much of all of this had really been their fault? Were they simply following orders, or did they have a larger part in this whole plot? I suppose we would never know.

We marched past the entrance, towards the center of camp.

After a minute or two, Joe walked up next to the advisor. "So, let's get a few things clear before we get there, alright?" he asked him.

The man smirked back at him, and I got the feeling that he was not exactly open to hearing suggestions from Joe or anyone else.

"You might be thinking," Joe said quietly to him, leaning up right next to his ear, "That you can simply say that we assassinated Glyndwyr Brice and that the rebels should attack. Perhaps you even think that once we're dead, you can just slip into the now open role of general. Well, that's not going to work out too well for you. We have several witnesses here who heard and saw what Brice said, not to mention all the obvious corruption that was happening before we even got here. All these soldiers are low on food and clothes and equipment. Anyone will be able to see the truth once we tell them what happened, though I will admit that it will be easier if you help us. We're willing to offer you protection from everyone, and once this is all over, we can even see about getting rid of any punishment based on how helpful you are to us."

The man said nothing for a moment, his smirk slowly growing into an evil grin and then a full smile full of contempt. "Fool. No one knows you here. Do you honestly expect them to just abandon a leader who has given them so much hope for their futures? To ignore his advisors, begging for their help in killing his assassins? No. You will fail, and I will laugh as you try as hard as you can to stop our plan, as you call it. There is no stopping us. You have merely delayed the inevitable and it will soon be realized."

Joe frowned, although he didn't seem to be very upset by what the man had said. He reached into his bag and grabbed a leatherbound book.

"Well," Joe said, waving the book in front of him while trying to hold back a grin, "I didn't want to have to use this, but we found Glyndwyr Brice's personal diary back in the tent. He goes over your entire plan and says quite a few things about you having a large part in it. We don't really need your help with the rebels after all."

The man paled and opened his mouth to stammer out some explanation.

"But," Joe said, dragging out the word, "if you would be willing to tell your side of the story, how Glyndwyr Brice planned to control the entire continent and everyone who lives there, then just maybe, you may get a lighter punishment,"

For a moment, the man stared at Joe with a blank look before blinking several times and falling to his knees as he shook his head at Joe, begging for mercy. "Alright, alright! I'll tell my side of things, but I better get your protection and guarantee that I'll get a light sentence after this!"

Joe smiled at me before forcing a frown and looking back at the man. "Well, I suppose you can still have a shot at it," he said, pulling the man to his feet again. "Just as long as you don't make any more trouble for us."

He readily nodded his agreement and we continued on our way, the man walking slightly ahead of us. I looked over at Joe in confusion; I didn't remember any diary that Joe had found. And if he had, then why did we need the man in the first place? Joe glanced back at me, obviously pleased with himself, and leaned closer.

"You never can know the value of a good confusion spell until you get into a situation like this."

I stared at him in shock; I hadn't even noticed him casting anything—he must have been practicing. Soon, we made it to the outskirts of the center area of the camp, which was still packed with people. As we stepped into the crowd, most people paused whatever they were doing and turned to look at us. Gradually, the noise from the party died down, and as we made it into the center of the mob, everyone was staring at us with apprehensive looks. I glanced around at everyone, a bead of sweat trickling down my back. If the crowd turned on us, we'd be surrounded. We just had to hope that Joe's plan would work.

A small stage had been set up in the center of the area, probably for announcements or perhaps shows, which we all filed onto. For a moment, nobody moved, just stood in place, looking at each other in confusion.

We glanced at one another, daring someone to be the first to speak, before Joe finally stepped forward.

"Glyndwyr Brice is dead!" he shouted out to the crowd. Immediately there was uproar, with everyone shouting and talking over each other, demanding to know what was going on. Joe held up his hands for quiet and waited for everyone to calm down. It took several minutes before he could speak again.

"Your leader was not who he said he was. The great commander dedicated to helping his people. Perhaps he was at one point, but not anymore. He has been growing more and more corrupt with each passing second. Many of you might know that he had a magical artifact in his possession that had been passed down for generations. What you might not know, however, is that that artifact has been slowly poisoning his mind against his people, allies, and the greater good, forcing him to take more and more for himself."

The crowd began to grow restless. Sparse mutterings grew to full on conversations or even shouting matches as they tried to understand what was going on.

"Haven't you noticed the lack of supplies in the camp? The lack of new equipment, resources, and even food? Meanwhile, Brice's palace has grown more and more extravagant, showing no regard for a fair allocation of riches. Now, I realize this is tragic news, and many of you aren't inclined to just believe us, but we have someone here who knows a lot more about it than I do."

Joe stepped back and pushed the advisor out in front of the crowd before standing next to us again, looking exhausted from trying to reason with the mob. Throughout his whole speech, he looked more determined than I had ever seen him before. I could tell that he really wanted us to be able to make peace with the rebels and he was willing to work hard to get that.

The crowd had simmered down a little bit since the beginning of Joe's speech but they grew even more quiet as the advisor began to speak. He haltingly started to explain his side of the story, with some slightly threatening looks from Joe. Much to our surprise, the rebels didn't interrupt once while the advisor explained Brice's power-hungry motives. After he was done, silence hung over the crowd, while everyone seemed to process what had been said before they erupted into chaos again.

Finally, several people made their way through the mob and up onto the stage. They all wore uniforms, some cleaner than others, with looks of purpose on their faces. We shook hands and had a few quick introductions before one of them stepped forward and addressed the crowd.

"I realize that many of you are shocked by the earlier statement, as am I. However, it would be untrue to say that there were no signs of what was happening in the last few months. We all saw the corruption that these people speak of, but we dismissed it as our imagination, or blindly trusted our leader's judgment."

The rebels again grew quiet, perhaps finally able to understand what we were trying to accomplish. Maybe they just needed one of their own to tell them.

"Well, no matter what, he is now dead. Which means that we need a new leader, someone who can finally fight for the people of Kricoya. We need someone who can finally end this bloody war with Sikrath and give back to our people what they lost. I propose that we end this conflict right now with representatives from both sides meeting and trying to discuss peace after all these years of hostilities. Perhaps with new leadership we might finally accomplish something." He turned around and looked at us quizzically. "Are we in agreement?"

We all nodded enthusiastically, relieved that we weren't about to be killed, and also, to have a chance at giving peace to our empire. It was finally time to stop the war that my father started.

"We can manage those soldiers for you," one of them said, pointing to the enemy soldiers that had surrendered to us back in the battle. "If you'll just follow us, we can start our negotiations."

The officers led us off of the stage and past the large crowd, who had again grown restless and were talking loudly amongst themselves about the news. We followed them for a few minutes as we walked down one of the small, winding, dirt paths that went all over the camp, until we finally came to a large tent set up next to several normal-sized ones that were quite obviously being used by several soldiers.

The tent that we went to, though, was slightly different. For one thing, it was at least twice the size of its smaller counterpart, but also it was made out of a light blue material instead of the normal, bland white of the other tents.

The officers told us to wait for a moment and then they disappeared inside. We all stood there, letting the last few hours really sink in. The rebels who'd helped us earlier had stayed behind with the crowd, so it was just me, Joe, Olwyn, Hezdek, and Rowan standing outside the tent. I was ready to start the negotiations as soon as we could. The officers seemed very eager to resolve the conflict, and now that the two main aggressors were dead, I could very well see that happening. At the very least, I could confidently say that Sikrath was happy to end the war, considering that our little group was the entirety of the representatives from our county.

We waited for a few more minutes until the officers came back outside and motioned for us to follow them. They led us back into the tent where a small table and a circle of chairs had been set up in the center. The tent itself was very sparsely decorated with the light blue material acting as most of the color in the space. There was also a large bookcase up against the far wall from the entrance filled with dozens of books. I almost wanted to go straight over there and start looking through them, but the officers might have thought it was inappropriate, considering what we were trying to do. They took their seats on one side of the table, leaving us to go around and pick where we were each going to sit, which we managed to do with minimal argument.

"Alright," the officer who had spoken earlier to the crowd said. "I would like to start off this negotiation by saying that I don't know any of you or what you are looking for, but you did help us uncover a grave threat in Glyndwyr Brice, for which I thank you. That being said," he looked sternly around the table at us, "I have my peoples' best interests at heart, and I don't think that they are very comfortable with having you in our camp, given the fact that we are still technically at war with Sikrath. For that reason, and that we have a very unstable truce at the moment, I would really like to finish up with this discussion tonight, or tomorrow at the latest, and get the news out to my people. Preferably, that news will be one of peace, but make no mistake, I am more than willing to continue this war at any moment."

A silence fell over the table as we all looked around at each other, slightly unsure of whom should speak or what should be said. Finally, I realized that it most likely was down to me. I quickly cleared my throat.

"Well, great," I said. "We don't want war either, and we're more than happy to wrap this up as soon as possible."

The man nodded.

"So, uh," I said. "I guess we should start by asking what exactly you want."

He looked to his right and then his left at the other officers sitting next to him, as if trying to confirm his next statement, before nodding again.

"Well," he started. "My people want freedom from your oppressive government. For years Kricoya has been a relatively peaceful nation, but ever since the last war with Sikrath, we have lost almost everything. Our land was taken, our resources stolen, our people killed. Some thought that we might become a part of your empire and, though we had lost the right to self-govern, we would have representation and still be able to operate many things for ourselves. But that has, in no way, been what has happened. We have had to pay heavy taxes and give up many of our valuables, including our crops and natural resources. What we ask for is complete independence from the Kingdom of Sikrath and for your soldiers to never again roam across our lands."

I had expected something along the lines of independence or separation from the empire and I was not mistaken. Luckily, I had a bit of time to think about a solution.

I took a deep breath and prepared myself to enact my plan. I nervously tapped my fingers on the table, hoping that I wouldn't forget to say anything important. "I completely agree with you that things have not been going well over the last few years," I said. "Under my father's rule, Kricoya has steeply declined in many ways, and we would like to try and make up for that. I can't pretend that I was completely innocent through all of this; I lived in the palace in Ordbridge and got whatever I asked for, though I didn't know to what extent Kricoya was suffering due to my father's actions. Though, that doesn't excuse me from guilt, and now I would like to speak for all of Sikrath by giving you a formal apology for the atrocities that occurred in the last war."

I paused for a moment to see their reactions. All of them looked up with narrowed eyes, as if surprised and suspicious of my words.

"While I realize that most of your people might vote for independence, I have a counteroffer that I think will benefit all of us."

The officer's expressions shifted from one of suspicion to one of confusion.

"Look," I said, "all across this continent there are unique resources that are valuable to everyone and useful for so many things. If we are able to work together and share all of our materials, then we will be able to advance both of our ways of life incredibly quickly. Now, I realize that in the past, Sikrath has basically just taken all of those resources and let Kricoya's economy crumble and its people starve—but if we focus on sharing that wealth all over the continent instead of clumping it together in Ordbridge, then we'll be able to use all the land in Kricoya, as well as Sikrath, for more agricultural and infrastructural advances, instead of just letting it go to waste. We can help each other build up our societies and focus on a more peaceful way of life."

The officers still didn't look very convinced, which I understood. It sounded like a good plan, but how much of it would really happen?

"Of course, that doesn't resolve the issue of your independence," I said. "I propose that Kricoya become a formal state of Sikrath, meaning that they would get to vote and run for leadership positions and their say would be just as valuable as any other citizen of Sikrath. They would get the same rights, the same protection, the same respect as anyone else in the Empire. There would still be a king in Ordbridge, but Kricoya could keep a garrison to defend themselves and elect their own people to other positions, which would give them some security that we would keep our word. I think that we will be able to help each other so much more than if our nations split apart. Also, if we resolve this conflict peacefully and stay together, then I think that our people will have a much better chance of accepting each other and small conflicts between the two groups will decrease." I paused for a moment and glanced up at the representatives, unsure of what their reactions would be. "So, what do you say?"

I waited for their response with bated breath. If they refused the offer, then I really believed that there would continue to be some animosity between our two peoples for a long time. This would be our best chance at true peace. The officers exchanged looks for several moments before their spokesperson finally spoke.

"You will have to give us some time to discuss."

We all nodded in agreement, and they stood and walked out of the tent. The rest of us stayed in our chairs, looking around at one another. Olwyn smiled at me, something I didn't see too often. Everyone else congratulated me on coming up with such a solid plan, and they all said they agreed that if Sikrath and Kricoya were to separate, then our people would never get along.

After what felt like forever but must have only been a few minutes, the officers came back into the tent and sat down. Their expressions were hard to read, but they didn't look very hostile, which I took as a good sign.

"We have discussed your proposal," the main officer said, pausing for a moment to stare at me. "And we must say, it all sounds very nice. You have clearly thought this through at great length. If you can truly accomplish what you said, then it resolves many of our problems with your government. For now, we are willing to give you the benefit of the doubt, considering that your father is now dead and there will be new leadership."

I smiled. Surely this means that—

"However," he said. "There is one condition. I'm sure that my people will never be comfortable to continue to be ruled over by your royal family. They will see it as the same as before your father's death, and many people will not approve of our decision to remain with Sikrath."

I smiled again in relief; I thought for a moment they were backing out of the deal.

"Yes, you are absolutely right," I said. "I already thought that might be a problem, and I know the perfect replacement. After everything that my father did, I really wouldn't feel comfortable accepting the throne, anyway, but I know someone who will fight for the people, listen to everyone's problems, and is in no way used to being a royal. He'll be able to actually understand the people's issues." I smiled in Joe's direction and patted him on the shoulder. "Meet the new King of Sikrath."

26

Back to What I Know

Joe

I stared at Matt in shock. Did he just say the new King of Sikrath? I almost wanted to turn around and look for whoever he was talking about, because it clearly wasn't me.

"Wha-what?" I stammered. "What are you talking about, Matt?"

He just smiled at me. "Joe, you'll be great at it. Didn't you hear yourself talking to that crowd back there? You're a natural! You know what it's like to be an average person and I know you'll fight for the people's rights if you have the power to do something. I couldn't think of anyone more suited for the job."

I could barely absorb his words; I was still staring at him, flabbergasted. Could I really be king? I hadn't been taught anything about laws or ceremonies or whatnot. I would have no clue where to even begin!

Matt seemed to read my mind. "Don't worry; you'll have a ton of advisors that can help you figure things out. Honestly, I wouldn't know much more than you about how to run things. My father never included me in anything," he said with a slight edge to his voice.

He sighed. "Anyway, I think you'd be great. What do you say?"

I hesitated. Surely, this was against some law or something right? Would people really just go along with this? Again, Matt seemed to read my mind. "If you're thinking that people in Sikrath won't accept you, then don't worry. I'm the king's son! As the rightful heir to the throne, I can appoint whoever I choose to lead the kingdom."

I thought it over. As much as it didn't seem like a good idea, I suppose it would be kind of nice to go to the palace and not have to clean it for once. Not to mention that Ben's mother wouldn't be able to say anything about him dating a king! Slowly, a grin formed across my face.

"Alright," I said. "I'll do it!"

"Ahem."

We looked over at the officers again; I had almost forgotten about them.

"I don't mean to be critical," the main officer said, looking at me. "But I have no idea who you are or why you should be king."

"No worries," Matt said. "Joe here is the perfect person for the job." Matt began telling my whole life story to the officers. He rambled on and on and by the end of it, I was quite sure that they regretted even asking about me.

"Alright," the officer finally said. "I suppose we can accept that for now, but don't expect Kricoya to instantly lower our guard. If you are truly willing to do what you say you will for our people, then we may actually be able to come together as one nation."

"Excellent," Matt said. "Then I guess we have ourselves a deal."

The news was starting to sink in. I was about to become the King of Sikrath. I still could barely believe that after everything that I had lived through in Ordbridge—my family coming over from Esha, my father getting that low paying job as a janitor at the palace, and me joining him once I was old enough—I was about to be in control of all of it. It seemed like a dream to imagine walking into the palace and going up to sit on the throne. I could be with Ben, and no one could say I wasn't rich or powerful enough anymore!

Matt and the officers talked a little while longer to make sure that all of the details were worked out before one of them, who had been taking notes of our discussion, set his paper onto the table and gave me a pen to sign it. I looked over it and it seemed to just summarize everything that we had talked about. Hopefully, this document would mark the beginning of a great friendship between Sikrath and Kricoya—one that we could actually be proud of. I picked up the pen and signed before sliding the paper back to the officers who all signed it as well.

"Well," the officer said, looking around at us with, perhaps, a slightly warmer expression than he had earlier. "I suppose that about wraps things up. I'm very glad that we were able to finally come to an agreement between our two people, even if it did come at the cost of the death of our leadership. Now, will you folks be staying for a little while, or are you about ready to get back home?"

Matt hesitated for a moment before looking over at me, his eyebrows raised in question. Slowly, the others looked at me as well. I paused for a moment, not used to the attention, but after a moment of surprise and panic, I spoke.

"Well, we really should be leaving as soon as possible, but I imagine we could wait until morning. As much as we would love to stay for longer, we should be heading back to Ordbridge. We have quite a lot to do now."

The officer just smiled and nodded and led us outside. "Alright then. I assumed as much. I can offer you folks a wagon to help get you back to your camp in the morning if you wish. But either way, it was a pleasure meeting with you all."

We thanked him and assured him that he would be hearing more from us soon. After we stabilized everything in Sikrath, we would be sending aid to Kricoya to help with whatever project they wanted to tackle first, as promised.

And with that, we all headed back to our tents for the night. I could hardly believe everything that had happened today. It felt like I had just lived through a full week in just a few hours.

The walk through the camp felt very short and we all collapsed into our tents and promptly fell asleep as soon as we made it inside. Before we knew it, morning had come. We grabbed our stuff and got a quick breakfast, but we were all anxious to get back to Ordbridge and start working on everything, so we got in the wagon and headed out. I watched the tents slowly fade out of view as the wagon headed for the Sikrathian army camp. I couldn't help but wonder what the rebels would think of our deal. Most would be skeptical, and, no doubt, many would be angry that they wouldn't technically have their freedom, but I hoped that once they saw how different I was from Matt's father, they would have a change of heart.

Matt looked over at me. "I don't think we have anything to worry about back in Ordbridge. There'll be some push back from some of my father's old advisors, but the people will love you once they realize how everything is going to change."

We stopped briefly at the army camp to tell everyone about the new treaty.

"Meet your new King!" Matt declared to the assembled soldiers. I had never felt so nervous before as they all looked at me but as Matt talked more, they all listened and finally they began to cheer. For me. *I could get used to this*, I thought to myself as I waved back at everyone.

I was also pleasantly surprised to hear that the railway had been repaired during our little adventure. Apparently, Matt's father had ordered the repairs almost immediately after it had happened, as it was one of the most important overland trade routes in the empire. Dozens of workers were sent out as soon as possible and it was fixed within a few days. It certainly made things much easier for us to get home. All we had to do was travel an hour or so to the South and we would get to the nearest station.

The camp closely resembled the one that we had been at earlier before the rebels attacked, but much of it appeared to have been assembled very quickly, such as the cluttered trench line that was only about five feet deep. It wasn't too surprising because the army hadn't had a lot of time to rebuild after they were pushed back from their old camp.

After waiting a little while as most of the camp was packed up, we set out with a couple hundred soldiers and quite a lot of supplies. Hopefully, we wouldn't even need the camp at all anymore, but we still weren't sure that the deal would hold. We would have to be cautious, but I was still confident that it would work out.

As we walked, I couldn't help but feel like Olwyn was avoiding eye contact with us. Every time I would glance in her direction, she would turn away and stare off into the distance. Matt and I exchanged glances, unsure how to broach whatever conversation needed to be had. After several minutes of this, I had had quite enough.

"Olwyn! What's wrong?"

She looked over at me in surprise before quickly glancing down toward the ground and sighing. "Well, I suppose we should have talked earlier, after what happened in the vault. I-I stood by the king, against you the rebels, and...well, that just hasn't sat right with me ever since."

She looked up at us, sadness in her eyes. "Maybe you don't understand how the knight order works," she began. "But loyalty is stressed beyond all else. If you're not loyal, then you're nothing. That's what I learned growing up." She paused for a moment and frowned.

"So, when I worked for the king, I did my duty. Whatever he wanted done, I did it, without question. Who was I to examine his motives? But slowly, I began to see that the world isn't so black and white."

Olwyn was silent for a few seconds as she looked out into the distance. "I still believe in loyalty, but I've realized that loyalty doesn't have to mean obeying without question. You also need to be loyal to yourself, to your beliefs, to what you know to be right. And I didn't do that."

All four of us listened to her as she talked, our footsteps the only sound to fill the gaps in her speech.

"I told the king about you, Matthew. When you appeared after the train wreck, I wrote to tell him that you were with us, and he decided to come to the front lines because of that. If not for my note, so much of this wouldn't have happened. So many people would still be alive, including your brother."

Matt stared at her in shock before quickly rushing over and enveloping her in a hug. Olwyn froze for a moment, arms outstretched awkwardly in front of her, before slowly returning the sentiment.

"Olwyn, don't ever regret what you did. If what you said is true, then you just saved the entire Empire. With my father dead, we can finally have peace, even if…some people had to die to get it." He paused and stepped back. "I'm sure Wyatt wouldn't change anything that he did," he said quietly.

Olwyn nodded and smiled. I thought I caught a glimpse of a tear in her eye, but with a few quick blinks, it was gone.

"Hey, it's hard work doing the right thing, Olwyn," I said, nudging her arm slightly with a small grin on my face. "You'll get used to it."

Finally, we made it to the station and boarded the train. I felt happy to be going back to Ordbridge, but also sad to see the end of our journey. We'd all gone through so much together and I hoped that we would be able to stay close to one another once we were back.

We all took a seat in one of the cabins. A silence hung over the group as we realized that this was truly the end of our quest. Perhaps we should have been discussing a strategy for when we got to Ordbridge, but at that moment, all I wanted to do was spend a little more time with the people who had helped me so much throughout this journey. I looked over at Matt to see that he had a sad smile on his face.

I could tell he was thinking the same thing: we would never have made it even one day out of Ordbridge without the help of Olwyn, Rowan, and later Hezdek and Wyatt. For a while, I thought about a word to describe how I felt about these people who I had experienced so much with, and I was startled to realize that perhaps that word that I was searching for was "family."

It had been so long since I had anyone else to rely on or help me. Ever since my father died, leaving me alone in the world, I had learned to just accept what happened and move forward—but over time I grew distant towards those around me and resentful of those more fortunate. Now I could see what it was like to be one of those more fortunate people. It sure helps to have some good people by your side.

Eventually, the silence was broken, and we slipped back to our usual dynamic, with Matt staring out the window, endlessly entertained by every new plant or animal that we passed, Hezdek squabbling with Rowan about some tool that he had lost, Olwyn rolling her eyes and sighing, and me, sitting there enjoying the show. It felt nice to have this at least one more time, in case everything was about to change once we got to Ordbridge.

The trip took many, many hours, but it flew by compared to the amount of time we spent getting to the rebel camp from Ordbridge. Imagine if we had actually been able to take the train in the first place; the journey would, no doubt, have been quite different.

We finally pulled into the station that we had left so long ago. It didn't look very crowded, thankfully. I still had to prepare myself for the speech that I'd have to make later to the people. I tried to tell myself that it was just part of the job, but I was still sick with nerves. I hoped that would fade with time; some of it was, no doubt, from my disbelief that I, a mere servant, was now the leader of the most powerful empire in the known world.

A few people stood at the station, watching the train come in. At first, I assumed they were just waiting to board, but one man was staring intently at the train as it came in, and when I looked closer, it didn't look like he had any luggage. I squinted; we were still too far away to make out any features. We got closer and closer until finally I started to recognize him.

Ben!

I immediately rushed off the train and ran up to him with a pounding heart, enveloping him in a hug. He laughed and hugged me back.

"What are you doing here?" I asked after a moment. "How did you know we were coming back?"

He smiled at me. It had been so long since I had seen his smile that I had begun to forget what it looked like.

"Well, you know my mother has connections everywhere. One of the soldiers traveling with you sent word back here about some troops coming back to the capital along with the king's son, which I assumed meant you were coming as well." He paused and considered me. "You know, you seem different than before. Happier, maybe. Or more at ease. I was surprised you even hugged me with so many people around."

"Well, I suppose I am happier," I said. "I think that at this point, we need to stop hiding so much. Especially now that…" I hesitated for a moment, considering how to break the news.

"Yes?" he asked, eyebrows raised.

"Well, you see," I began. "Quite a bit happened while we were gone. I'll tell you all about it at some point, but I suppose I should just tell you the news now." I launched into the tale of going to the vault and having to get the helm and the death of the king, albeit a shortened version, as I didn't want to be standing there for hours. I also told him everything that happened with the rebels and how, thanks to Matt, I was going to become king.

He stared at me in shock for several long moments, opening and closing his mouth without saying a word. "You're actually going to be king?" he asked in disbelief. I nodded, amused, as I remembered my similar reaction to the news earlier.

Finally, he nodded and smiled again. "Well, this is great! Mother will surely approve of you now! I mean, you're going to literally be her king; what more could she possibly be hoping for?"

I smiled at him. He was right. Now that I was a noble like Ben, we wouldn't have to hide anymore. Just thinking about it was getting me even more excited for the coming weeks.

I swung an arm around Ben's shoulder. "So, what's been going on with you since I've been gone? Lots of adventure, no doubt."

Ben chuckled. "Well, if you call walking to breakfast in downtown Ordbridge an adventure, then I have quite the story for you." He took a deep breath, preparing to tell me about his glorious journey. "It all began on a midwinter's night. There was not soul in sight in any direction that—"

"Uh, excuse me," I interrupted. "When did this happen? It's early summer right now. Also, you said you were getting breakfast before and now it's in the middle of the night?" I smirked at him, trying not to laugh. "Do you usually have breakfast in the middle of the night?"

He sighed, pretending to be exasperated, but I could see the faint hints of a smile on his face. "I was taking a bit of 'creative license' one might call it. What's wrong with that? Anyway, where was I? Oh, yes! It was a dark midwinter's night..."

Matt

We were all anxious to get off the train and start working on everything, but I noticed that Joe ran off as soon as we stopped. I hurried off after him along with the others and saw he was rushing over to Ben Holverk. I smiled; we had work to do, but they should have some time together after so long spent apart.

The rest of us stood next to each other a little way away from them, discussing the future.

"So, are guys going to stick around for a while or just head out now?" I asked, looking over at Rowan, Hezdek, and Olwyn. "I imagine you already have some new scheme planned, Rowan?"

He smirked. "Well, perhaps, but it may surprise you to learn that I'm actually invested in how this turns out. I'm not leaving until I know for sure that it's going to work out. You can't get rid of me that easily."

"Oh, alright, great! And what about you, Hezdek? We were only originally going to take you to the nearest town, and now look how far you've come with us. I'm sure you could find plenty of business around Ordbridge if you wanted."

"Well," Hezdek grunted. "It pains me to admit, but I have to agree with the wizard. You can't get rid of us that easily; we're with you 'till the end."

I found myself blinking away a few tears as I smiled at them before turning hesitantly to look at Olwyn. She just sighed and rolled her eyes, but I could see her start to smile. "Well, I suppose since we've already come this far, it would be a shame to give up now. And I can't exactly leave the four of you to fend for yourselves. You'd all end up dead in about twenty minutes! So, yeah, we're with you."

"Well, if you guys insist," I said, grinning. "I suppose I could use some help. We should head to the palace and see what news everyone has heard about my father, and then we can move forward from there. Hopefully, Joe can make a speech about everything sometime today to make sure there's as little confusion as possible. But first," I hesitated, "there's one thing that we have to do."

I motioned for Rowan to pull out the bag containing the four artifacts that we had gotten from Glyndwyr Brice's tent. "I don't want to hold on to these even a second longer than we have to. Luckily, I have an idea of where we can keep these that might just work. Follow me."

I called out for Joe to follow us, and we paused for a moment as he said goodbye to Ben. They exchanged a few more words before Ben walked down the path that led into Ordbridge, waving back at us.

Joe walked over to us, still wearing a smile from his encounter with Ben. I was glad to see him so happy to be back home. He'd had a tough life working as a janitor in the palace. Perhaps now he'd find some joy in his life.

I led everyone down a path from the station to an area on the outskirts of Ordbridge. We walked for about ten minutes until we came to a small, wooded area. The trees stretched up at least twenty feet and formed a thick canopy above us. The light around us slowly faded with each step. There were a few houses near us, but for the most part, no one wanted the land, as it was primarily made up of rough marshland that was almost impossible to grow anything of value on. It was the perfect place for a secret hideout, which is exactly why my father built one there.

I led everyone through the shallow water and lush vegetation for several minutes until we came to the first and only sign of civilization in the wood: a small square building, made entirely of black metal. There was only one visible door and, I knew, only one key that could open it.

"My father built this years ago to store secret stuff or to hide in in case we were invaded. It's resistant to almost all forms of magic, so he hoped that it could be useful at some point. It sat here for years, unused, but my father always carried around a key to the door. And being the paranoid person he was, he didn't tell anyone else about this or make any copies of the key, which I suppose works out for us now."

I pulled out a small metal key from my pocket and held it up. "I, uh, found it on his body the morning after he...after he died," I said. "I just figured that I might as well take it and I didn't think about its usefulness until later."

I turned and looked over the box to find any openings or cracks in the metal, but I found none. It was completely airtight from what I could tell. "It would be the perfect place to hide those artifacts, so that no one will ever use them again. Only we know about their location, and once we lock them inside, I'm going to go melt down the key. If we had constant guards around it, then people would realize that something valuable was in here and maybe they would try to steal them. Maybe the guards would fall under their influence. The safest plan is to act as though there's nothing to see, so that no one will bother looking around here. Is everyone with me?"

I looked around at my friends, trying to judge their reactions. Did they agree with my plan or were we about to fight over control of the artifacts like all of their past owners?

Slowly, everyone nodded their heads and murmured their agreement. "It's a good plan," Joe said. "But I think that we need to tell everybody about the artifacts."

We all stared at him in shock before he continued. Tell everyone about the artifacts? What was he talking about?

"Look," he said. "If everyone knew that there were extremely dangerous magical artifacts out in the world and we taught them how to defend themselves if they were ever to encounter one of them, then that gives the whole kingdom a much bigger chance of never falling into another civil war between them. Instead of burying them, we need to tell people everything we know about them."

It sounded crazy at first. Telling people about these extremely dangerous and powerful artifacts? Surely, that would make it harder to hide them, right? But the more I thought about it, I realized that Joe was right. People needed to know about the dangers that they might face if these artifacts were ever to be found again. We didn't know that they'd be contained in the box forever. Perhaps the metal could counteract the shield's ability to build up enough energy to teleport, but we really had no idea. It was our duty to let them know what was out there.

"You're right," Olwyn said, frowning. "Everyone needs to know."

Hezdek and Rowan both murmured their agreement. Everyone had to be told.

"Alright, then," I said, "It's decided. We'll lock up the artifacts here and pass out information on them as soon as we can. It's the least we can do to keep people safe."

I cautiously walked to the door and inserted the key. At first, it was a little hard to turn, but after a moment, it lurched to the side and the door swung open. We all peered inside to see a very small room, lined with shelves on all sides. There was a small table in the center with two chairs but other than that, it was empty.

I walked inside and approached the shelf on the far wall before slowly opening the sack containing the artifacts and reaching inside. First came the helm, which I gently set down on the top shelf with a sigh. It would be incredible to be able to use these artifacts without fear of losing your mind, but sadly, it just wasn't possible.

Next came the compass. I lifted it out of the sack and looked over it briefly before setting it down next to the helm. I didn't want to take any chances by holding them for too long after what happened with the shield. It was best to just get this over with.

Next, I took out the sword and laid it down on the shelf below the other two. I had seen that sword so many times on my father's hip, but I never knew about its true power. It made me wonder what else I had missed in the past.

I took a deep breath and reached into the bag for the fourth and final time, pulling out my old shield. It looked so ordinary in my hands; I could almost believe that we'd grabbed the wrong shield. But I knew that we had the right one. There was no mistaking the engravings in the middle, which I now realized showed all of the shield's previous owners—brave leaders that used the shield, only to be betrayed by it later.

As I looked at the engravings, I noticed a new image was slowly coming to life on a previously empty stretch of metal. It showed a group of people running through a small doorway, weapons raised, as they charged down a long, open room, headfirst into a circle of enemies. The figure in front wielded a sword and seemed to be shouting something in excitement, with a look of determination on his face.

I realized with a jolt what the scene was: our charge into Glyndwyr Brice's tent to save Joe and Rowan. Why did the shield decide to show that to me now? Was it still trying to pull me in? Did it expect me to take it back and wield it again? I sighed. We really didn't know anything about how these artifacts worked, did we?

I felt a hand on my shoulder, and I turned to see Joe standing behind me. "Are you okay, Matt?" he asked, concern filling his face.

I smiled. "Yeah. Don't worry. I'm just fine."

I reached up and placed the shield right next to the sword and stepped back. I nodded once, and then before I could change my mind, I walked out of the room with Joe right behind me.

I paused to close the door, then made sure to test that it was really locked several times. Once I turned back to face the others, I suddenly felt a huge weight off my shoulders. I'd been so stressed the past few days as our journey came to an end and we were forced to step up and do what was best for our people. Now that the artifacts were under control, we could begin to worry about normal things, like introducing the country to their new king. You know, basic stuff.

    And so, finally, our small group stepped out of the marshes in high spirits, prepared to face the next thing, whatever it may be.

The End

About the Author

Jack Conway grew up in Portland, Oregon. He is currently attending the University of Oregon and is studying history. The Prince of Sikrath is his debut novel. He plans to continue writing fantasy as well as explore other genres, including graphic novels.

Made in United States
Troutdale, OR
12/05/2023